Katherine

a novel by
Lorin Hayes

ISBN-13: 978-1512156256
ISBN-10: 1512156256

For Frank and Harper

Prologue

Bricks.

Bricks scraping skin from bone, blood breathing down her back, bright red surging pain.

She sighed contentedly.

The other body pounded into her, against her, through her. Grinding her against the sweetest, hardest wall of bricks she'd ever had the great fortune to find.

And then it came, like a rising din, the piercing, electric murmur of voices. A ringing buzz of static that set her teeth on edge.

Focus on the bricks. The delicate flesh being shaved from her thin shoulder blades. The dazzling searing pain. But the terrible din of voices drowned out everything else.

The world began spinning—a swirling, dizzying display of popping lights and shrieking sound—and she was suddenly aware of the body pinning her to those lovely, lovely bricks.

It had gone utterly and completely still. Slack.

She began to have trouble taking air into her lungs, and she pushed at the mass of flesh now smothering her. It gave no resistance.

The man slid down the length of her body and crumpled in a heap on the ground, and that was when she registered all the blood.

Suddenly, a strange glow, coming from her own hand, caught her attention. There was a flash of light winking with each small movement of her wrist. At last, she realized what it was.

The blade of a knife, the light blinking from the bits of sharpened steel not thick with blood.

Very slowly, she breathed in as much of the heavy, humid night air as her lungs would hold, opened her mouth wide, and started screaming.

While she washed her hands in the blood

PART I

1

The full moon was virtually nonexistent behind the haze of night sky, a suffocating blanket trapping heat and moisture against the earth. The stagnant air felt oppressive, the simple act of breathing burdensome under the physical weight of the night.

It suited Ramon's mood.

As he marched out to the standard-issue sedan parked in his driveway, Ramon's anger blossomed into fury, and he let it percolate through his bloodstream.

It was his 30th anniversary, for Christ's sake. His goddamn 30th anniversary. All he requested was 48 undisturbed hours with his wife, a request he had made almost a year in advance. It wouldn't matter. Ramon would now hear about this from Consuelo for the rest of his natural born life, or hers anyway.

Grinding his teeth in irritation, Ramon unlocked the car door and lowered himself into the driver's seat. Beads of sweat immediately popped out along his hairline, and it felt like being sucked into an upholstered oven. Drops of moisture rolled down the back of his neck and into the hollow of his spine.

Pulling out of the driveway, Ramon began fidgeting with the air conditioning, even though it was clear from the shuddering dashboard: it was already giving him all it had.

"*Damn,*" Ramon muttered aloud, almost breaking off the plastic knob.

There was no doubt about it, a storm was coming, but this storm had been brewing for near on a week now, and Ramon wished that God would just get the hell on with it already.

For six miserable days, the skies over Austin had been swimming with waves of ever-rising, chart-topping temperatures. News of the heat, which wasn't particularly news as far as Ramon was concerned, seemed to be all anybody could talk about. Why people would waste their time talking about such things puzzled Ramon, mostly because he didn't see how there was a whole lot to discuss.

"It's mighty hot out." "By God, it sure is."

Ramon drove south on I-35, past the University of Texas football stadium and the pink granite dome of the State Capitol, and exited onto Cesar Chavez Boulevard.

A few miles east of the highway, he saw the first telltale signs of a fresh crime scene: lights flashing blue and red, police cruisers blocking traffic, uniformed officers stretching printed yellow tape between street signs.

Slowing, Ramon rolled down his car window and showed his badge to one of the officers. She directed Ramon to a parking lot behind a crumbling storefront.

Although much of East Austin had been gentrified in recent years, this area still retained its seedy origins. It was a dangerous section of the city, home to a variety of criminal elements. Ramon vaguely wondered where they'd all go when the inevitable march of community revitalization claimed this corner as well.

Ramon pulled into the lot and found the usual assortment of police vehicles. There were two ambulances parked toward the rear, the paramedics leaning against their rigs, drinking coffee. A sure sign somebody was already dead.

Climbing out of his car into the throbbing night heat, Ramon groaned. It was three o'clock in the morning, and it still felt like a goddamn greenhouse.

"Rain already, *por favor*," he muttered, removing a handkerchief from his breast pocket to wipe his forehead.

Ramon walked past the gathering crowd of onlookers, surprised to see all the manpower already on the scene.

When Ramon received the phone call summarily ending his anniversary weekend, he knew something major had happened. Judging from all the patrol cars and uniformed bodies lining the street, he had underestimated the situation.

I wonder who got himself killed, Ramon thought irritably.

Just then, a female voice shouted out to him.

"Lieutenant Hinojosa!"

Ramon turned to see a young blonde policewoman in a crisp blue uniform waving to him. Even at this hour, and in her markedly unflattering ensemble, Officer Tammy Lynn Geary looked every bit the small town Texas beauty queen she once was.

"Hope you didn't have other plans tonight," she said quietly, leading him behind the low, brick building that housed a biker bar known as Rey's.

In the back alley, they came upon a veritable flock of technicians supposedly going about the business of collecting evidence. In actuality, that many bodies milling about did not bode well for the actual retrieval and preservation of evidence, but this fact was clearly lost on somebody out to make an impression.

Again, Ramon Hinojosa wondered who got himself dead.

He tapped Officer Geary on the shoulder, stopping her mid-step.

"You want to fill me in on the basics?" he asked.

"One victim. Multiple stab wounds."

"Any suspects?"

"Yes, sir. She's already in custody."

Ramon noticed for the first time how flustered Geary seemed. He supposed it might just be her inexperience with dead bodies. Corpses did funny things to people.

Tammy Lynn Geary guided him over to a cluster of cops on the far side if the alley, at whose feet was a black plastic body bag. The officers immediately stepped back to give Ramon more room.

Bending over, he unzipped the bag to expose a head, the face frozen in the same mask of disbelief Ramon had seen dozens of times before. It was his experience that hardly any man sees his own death coming.

"I believe you know our friend here," Officer Geary stated.

Ramon nodded.

"Angel Ramirez," he added. "I thought he was still in Huntsville."

"Paroled last month."

"So much for sweet freedom."

Ramon could think of at least five people off the top of his head who wouldn't mind seeing Angel dead.

"This a gang thing?" he asked.

"No sir, doesn't look like it."

Crouching down lower, Ramon inspected the late Angel Ramirez. Ugly purple scratches lined his face and neck, and his swollen lips were caked with blood. Across Angel's throat were what appeared to be bite marks.

If Ramon didn't know better, he'd guess Angel went one-on-one with some wild animal, or a very angry cat.

Drawing the zipper down further, Ramon was mildly surprised to see Angel's jeans and black underwear down around his ankles.

"I take it he was like this when you found him," Ramon remarked.

"Yep," Tammy Lynn replied.

Ramon snapped on a pair of latex gloves and gently placed his hands under Angel's shoulder, turning the body onto its side. There looked to be five or more stab wounds concentrated between the shoulder blades, any number of which might have been fatal.

"What do we know about the angle of the wounds?" Ramon asked.

"Not much," Geary replied. "Pinter won't get to the body for a couple of hours."

"Pinter? I thought she was on vacation."

"Helicopter's been sent to pick her up."

Ramon arched an eyebrow in surprise.

There were plenty of assistant medical examiners around, but someone high up the food chain wanted Pinter.

Suddenly, a heavy metal door swung open from the brick wall, and yet another uniformed officer appeared.

"Shall we?" Geary said to Ramon, motioning to the entryway.

Standing, Ramon walked through the door into a narrow, dimly lit hallway.

Rey's was frequented mostly by bikers and their assorted hangers-on, and was somewhat notorious among Central Texas law enforcement agencies. The folks hanging out at Rey's were not the weekend motorcycle enthusiasts with matching jackets and day jobs. Rey's hosted a hardcore criminal element, which only made what Ramon found going on inside the bar all the more startling.

All around the room were the unmistakable signs of cooperation.

This was not Ramon's first time at Rey's asking about a dead body, and he'd always been greeted with cold glares and resolute silence. Tonight, Rey's clientele seemed to be falling over each other to talk to the cops. There were even some attempts at reenactment as they recounted the story.

"All right, Officer Geary," Ramon breathed, "what the hell is going on around here?"

Before she could respond, they were interrupted by a pinched, nasal voice.

"Hinojosa, there you are."

Detective Jared Hawthorne came up beside them, casually resting his hand on Ramon's shoulder. When Ramon tensed, Hawthorne quickly moved away.

"Did you see Angel?" Hawthorne asked, absently dismissing Tammy Lynn Geary with a wave of his hand. "That's one hell of a way to go."

Ramon nodded to Officer Geary and turned back to Jared Hawthorne.

"How about you bring me up to speed?"

"According to witnesses, she came in around midnight," Hawthorne told him.

"Who?"

"You don't know?"

Ramon shook his head.

"Well then, have I got a story for you," the younger man remarked with far more enthusiasm than was strictly necessary.

According to Hawthorne, the suspect walked into Rey's around quarter after midnight, already very inebriated, and her subsequent behavior was very provocative. After hitting on "damn near every dickhead in the place," the woman climbed onto one of tables and began to perform a striptease.

It was Angel Ramirez who stepped up to the plate.

"At approximately 1:15 this morning, everyone's favorite couple took the party out back," Hawthorne concluded, "and that is the last anyone ever saw of Angel . . . well, breathing anyway."

Ramon was having some difficulty processing the information. For one thing, Angel Ramirez was at least six and a half feet tall and 250 pounds.

"That had to be one hell of a big woman."

"Not if he had her up against the wall, giving it to her like that. Did you see his cock? It's a clear case of clitoris interruptus."

"It's *coitis* interruptus," Ramon corrected flatly.

"Whatever, it sure as hell caught Angel off his guard. We figure he had her lifted off the ground, against the wall. That puts her head a good foot above his."

"And you reckon she butchered him like a hog before he dropped her?"

"The poor bastard's weight must have held her up there. Once it was over, she slid down to the ground. It looked like she lost a whole shitload of skin off her back. Came right off on the bricks."

"Weapon?"

"Regular old steak knife. We sent it to the lab for testing."

"And the suspect? Where'd they find her?"

"Curled up in a ball, beside the body. Naked as you please, covered in blood. And screaming her damn head off."

"Where is she now?"

"Right this way, Lieutenant," Hawthorne said, extending an arm.

Ramon followed Jared Hawthorne out of Rey's and through the alley to another parking lot. It was located off a side street dark with shadows, and three patrol cars and a black Mercedes were parked in the rear.

"The suspect is still here? At the scene?" Ramon asked, confused. "Why?"

"Doctor's orders."

"Come again?"

"Said we had to wait until the drugs took effect."

"Who did? Wait, what drugs?"

"Because of her *fragile condition* and all," Hawthorne told him. "She's got enough dope in her system now to stop a horse."

Jared Hawthorne was an officious little prick under the best of circumstances, but Ramon was starting to feel like he was watching a foreign movie without subtitles.

"Would you mind repeating that?" Ramon commanded, stopping abruptly.

Before speaking, Hawthorne pulled a pack of cigarettes from the inside pocket of his suit jacket and shook one free, lighting it with a disposable lighter.

"She wouldn't stop that damn screaming," he explained, taking a long drag. "You wouldn't think there could be all that breath in one body. Put up one hell of a fight too, when the boys tried to take her. She didn't try to run or anything. Just tried to stab anyone who came near her with that damn knife."

"So you sedated her?"

"*We* didn't do anything to her," Hawthorne shot back, growing defensive. "We had strict orders not to touch her."

"Orders from whom?"

"Can't say for sure," Hawthorne replied coolly. "Someone high up the ladder, that's all I know."

Ramon took a deep breath.

"So, you're telling me you were *ordered* not to touch a raving and dangerous homicide suspect?"

"That's exactly what I'm telling you," Hawthorne answered. "Our job was to contain the situation and make sure she didn't hurt herself until her private doctor showed up. He's who gave her the shot."

Ramon stared at Hawthorne incredulously.

"Let me get this straight," he stated, carefully enunciating each word. "You waited around for a private physician, and then you let him sedate the suspect?"

"I did as I was told."

"Did you at least try to question the suspect?" Ramon pressed, aggravated.

Hawthorne laughed, a pitiless coughing sound.

"I don't think you get it, Lieutenant," he snorted. "There wasn't going to be any questioning that woman, not tonight anyway. She was out of her goddamn mind. A complete psycho who wouldn't stop that fucking screaming."

Suddenly, there was the sound of engines turning over, and Ramon saw the vehicles on the far side of the parking lot come to life. The cars began to move toward them slowly.

"Well, Lieutenant, looks like you won't be questioning her either," Hawthorne stated, crushing his half-smoked cigarette with one hand.

Ramon shielded his eyes from the oncoming headlights and grudgingly stepped aside. He watched as the patrol cars rolled by.

In the last car, a woman's face appeared in the back window, staring blankly. She was wrapped in a brown blanket, her vacant, unseeing eyes moving over Ramon as the car inched past. A nest of once-blonde hair, caked with dried blood, was matted to the woman's head, and her cheeks and neck were smeared with what now looked like motor oil.

Even with the heat, chills began to crawl across Ramon's flesh as his mind registered the image.

He knew that face. And in an instant, everything made sense.

"Dios mio," Ramon muttered.

2

Jackson Polke caught a fleeting glimpse of the alarm clock as it went crashing to the floor. The bright red numbers read 3:57.

"Son of a bitch," Jackson growled, picking his phone up off the floor.

Paige murmured, half-awake beside him.

"What?" he nearly shouted into the receiver.

"I'm sorry to bother you at this hour, Jackson," the voice on the other end of the line stated evenly. "This is Leland Bourke."

Jackson sat bolt upright, shaking the fog from his sleeping brain. "Yes, sir. Hello."

"I apologize for waking you."

"No, no problem, sir," Jackson replied groggily. "I'm sorry that I, uh. . .what can I do for you?"

"Well, if it's not too much trouble, I was hoping you could meet me at the police station."

"No, no trouble," Jackson assured him, fumbling for the light. "I can be there in about twenty minutes."

"That would be fine," Leland said. "I'll be expecting you."

"I'll see you soon."

"Oh, and Jackson," Bourke added before the line went dead, "thank you."

Jackson sat on the edge of the bed, stunned, until a grating, recorded voice asked if he would like to make a call.

"Where can you be in twenty minutes?" Paige asked without opening her eyes.

"You just go on back to sleep, darlin'," Jackson whispered, hanging up the phone.

Paige's eyelids fluttered open and she looked at her husband blearily.

"Where?" she repeated.

"Police station. That was Leland Bourke on the phone. That's all I know."

"The managing partner of your law firm?"

"That's right."

"Well, that's terribly dramatic," she mumbled, readjusting her pillows. "Can't wait to hear what it's all about."

Paige's eyes drifted closed again, and Jackson soon heard the soft sounds of snoring.

He threw on some clothes and grabbed his wallet from the nightstand.

A gust of heat escaped from the sauna-like interior when Jackson opened the door of his old Jeep. By the time he turned the key in the ignition and pulled away from the curb, sweat dampened Jackson's hair. He cranked the air conditioning, only to be hit in the face with an explosion of warm, stale air.

Jackson was under no illusions as to why Leland had summoned him, of all people, in the middle of the night. It wasn't that tough to figure out.

What Jackson could not figure out, however, was why the hell Leland Bourke was at the police station in the first place.

At the corner of 7th Street and I-35, Jackson parked in one of the many empty metered spaces. The glass and brick façade of the Austin Police Department loomed before him, the tinted windows like black bands wrapping the building.

Jackson followed a concrete sidewalk illuminated by powerful spotlights to a set of double doors. Smoothing down his dark blonde hair and buttoning the sleeves of his freshly pressed shirt, Jackson entered the lobby.

"I'm here at the request of Leland Bourke," Jackson told the duty officer at the desk.

A moment later, Jackson was escorted up to the third floor and deposited in a nondescript, windowless passageway. Leland Bourke emerged from a wooden door a few moments later.

"Thank you for coming," he said.

"Of course," Jackson replied.

"Coffee?"

"Please."

Jackson followed Leland around the corner to a vending machine of the sort they stopped making twenty years before.

"Tastes like crap, but it's caffeine," Leland noted.

Leland inserted a handful of coins into the coffee machine and watched silently as a tiny paper cup filled to the rim. Jackson noticed that Leland, who was always fastidious about his appearance, looked like he had also just rolled out of bed.

"Sugar?" he asked

"No, sir. Black is fine."

Leland handed Jackson a coffee cup and gestured to a worn wooden bench on the far side of the hall.

"We've got one hell of a mess here, Jackson," he said after they were both seated. "A goddamn nightmare is what it is, and it's only going to get worse. Things have spiraled entirely out of control, and now this has happened . . . but I'm getting ahead of myself."

Leland straightened his pant leg, and sniffed at his coffee.

"I was called here tonight, Jackson, by a very old friend of mine, as well as a longtime client of the firm. Do you know Josiah Mantooth?"

"I know of him, obviously," Jackson answered.

"Then you know he has a daughter."

"Yes, of course."

"This situation involves her," Leland sighed. "What I'm about to tell you is obviously in the strictest of confidence, although I don't know how private any of this will be tomorrow."

Leland then told Jackson about the astonishing events that transpired in an alley behind a bar called Rey's, and the death of a man named Angel Ramirez.

"She does have a long, well-documented history of mental illness," Leland concluded.

Jackson was too stunned to speak, so he simply nodded.

"This is a terrible, ugly business, and probably as sordid a scenario as a body could think up. Poor thing has been either hysterically incoherent or sedated ever since the incident. Her doctor says she's had a complete psychotic break from reality and is in a state of acute psychosis.

"Needless to say, we need to handle this as quietly and as delicately as possible."

"You want me to talk to Tommy Keane," Jackson stated, getting to the heart of the matter.

"Yes."

If it were any other district attorney, in any other city, Jackson would still be blissfully snoring next to his wife.

"I can open up communications, Leland," Jackson told him, "but I certainly can't promise anything."

"Any assistance you can offer would be greatly appreciated."

"I'll do what I can, but it might not be much."

"I understand," the older man said, rising to his feet. "Let me introduce you to the family."

Jackson followed Leland down the corridor to the door from which he'd earlier emerged. Jackson knew the police department was not ordinarily in the habit of providing conference space to the families of murder suspects, but this was no ordinary family, and this was certainly no ordinary murder suspect.

The woman under arrest and sitting in a jail cell far below their feet was Katherine Van Hoerne.

3

Leland loudly banged on the door before turning the knob, but failed to silence, or even momentarily disrupt, the furious shouting match going on inside the room.

"Don't you dare blame me . . ."

"If you'd only done like I told you, we wouldn't be here right now!"

"And *that* is what really pisses you off! That I didn't follow your orders!"

"What pisses me off is that you failed to protect my daughter!!"

"Let me tell you something, you miserable son of a bitch, I took care of Katherine, which is a hell of lot more than you can say."

"All I've ever done my whole life is protect Katherine!"

"I'm the one who's there for her! ME!"

"Gentlemen," Leland stated when simply clearing his throat had no effect.

"You call this taking care of her? Where the hell were you tonight?"

"Gentlemen!" Leland finally shouted, at last drawing their attention. "This is the person I was telling you about."

Silence descended on the cramped space as four pairs of eyes turned to study Jackson.

"This is Jackson Polke," Leland continued, "one of our associates."

Jackson stepped forward hesitantly, recognizing nearly every face in the room from newspaper and magazine photographs.

"Jackson, this is Josiah Mantooth," Leland announced.

"Sir," Jackson said, extending his hand.

Josiah Mantooth was of average height and weight, with a full head of steel gray hair and the fleshy jowls of a bloodhound. Jackson knew the lore, that Josiah had spent his teenage years in the rough West Texas oil fields, which left him with a misshapen nose from several breaks that never healed properly. He was one of the all-time great Texas wildcatters and parlayed his estimable fortune into an international conglomerate, Mantooth Industries. But no matter how far he climbed, his cragged, weathered mug would always reveal his roots.

Tonight Josiah wore a western cut tuxedo and black alligator boots polished to a sheen. Jackson vaguely remembered hearing something about a Houston fundraiser benefiting the Mantooth Children's Hospice.

Josiah eyed Jackson warily, deliberately, sizing him up from head to toe. After what seemed like a very long time, Josiah nodded stiffly.

"Any relation to *the* Jackson Beauregard Polke?" a female voice asked.

"Yes, ma'am. He was my great, great, great grandfather."

"Well then, you must be related to Clementine Polke."

"Yes, ma'am. She's my great aunt," Jackson replied.

Josiah's wife, Bobbie Dean Mantooth, smiled and said, "I feel better already."

She wore a scarlet sequined gown, slit low in front and high up the leg, and an astonishing collection of rubies and diamonds. Her hair was big and blond, her chest enhanced to the size of flotation devices.

Leland interrupted to introduce Jackson to Katherine's husband, Clay Van Hoerne.

"Senator," Jackson said, nodding to the dark haired man who had just been arguing with Josiah.

His handsome, sculpted features looked ravaged, and it was clear the man hadn't slept in days.

Clay Van Hoerne said nothing, just glared at Jackson coldly.

"Don't be rude, Clayton," Bobbie Dean scolded.

"You're not my mother, Bobbie Dean, so shut your face," Clay snapped.

"Watch it, boy!" Josiah snarled.

"Now, we're all extremely upset," Leland intervened calmly, stepping between the two men.

A slender, balding man stepped forward and approached Jackson. He was the only person in the room Jackson didn't recognize on sight.

"Hello, Mr. Polke," the man said quietly. "My name is Arthur Wiggins. I am the trustee of Mrs. Van Hoerne's estate."

"Mr. Wiggins," Jackson replied, accepting his handshake.

"Leland has spoken very highly of you," the older man told him. "We certainly appreciate your assistance."

"As I explained to Leland, I don't know how much assistance I can offer."

"I was given to believe that you and the district attorney were close," Josiah interjected sharply.

"Yes sir, we are," Jackson replied. "Tommy Keane has been like a father to me, ever since my own dad passed away."

"Then what's the problem?"

"No problem, sir. It's just that Tommy won't be influenced by me or anyone else."

Josiah turned his head and glared at Leland.

"I can open up communications with Tommy," Jackson went on. "If your daughter is ill, a trial won't do anyone any good. Tommy's not going to persecute a sick woman."

"How does that help us?" Clay Van Hoerne asked.

"If Mrs. Van Hoerne is mentally incompetent, the DA can facilitate a speedy determination and avoid a trial. But she'll have to be examined by the DA's experts, and the standard is high . . ."

"That won't be a problem," Josiah said softly, cutting him off.

"Again, this helps us *how*?" Clay's voice shot out, a distinct edge to the words.

"Proving a defendant incompetent is a long, drawn-out, very public process," Jackson answered. "In the meantime, Mrs. Van Hoerne remains incarcerated in the psychiatric ward of the Travis County Jail."

"And if Katherine doesn't go to trial, what happens to her?" Clay asked. "Do they just let her go?"

"No, of course not," Jackson replied. "She would be committed to a state hospital and her competency would be reviewed every few years."

Clay shook his head violently from side to side.

"Well, then, I'm sorry we've wasted your time Mr. Polke," Clay stated unceremoniously.

"Senator?" Jackson asked, confused.

"We won't be needing your assistance after all."

"What are you saying, Clay?" Bobbie Dean's voice cut across the room.

"What I'm saying is that we're going to fight this."

"Are you out of your goddamn mind?!" Josiah Mantooth bellowed. "We're going to throw ourselves on the mercy of Mr. Keane and the judge and whoever the hell else we can find, and get her into some place where she can't hurt herself or anyone else!"

"You mean get her committed," Clay shouted back.

"That is precisely what I mean!"

"Just like you always wanted. Imagine that!"

Bobbie Dean Mantooth was on her feet before Clay finished the sentence.

"How dare you," she cried. "Josiah has been a loving, supportive father to that poor girl."

"Supportive? He wants to lock up his only child!" Clay roared, his voice trembling. "To hide her away in some institution! To rip her away from her husband and child!"

"Josiah has never wanted anything but the best for Katherine!" Bobbie Dean countered adamantly. "For her to be safe and taken care of!"

"I took care of her!" Clay spat, tears forming in his eyes. "Me, not him, not you, not your lousy stinking doctors!"

"You did one hell of a job, boy," Josiah hollered. "Since she's facing the death penalty and all! You're the one who wouldn't listen when everyone—every goddamn specialist in the Northern Hemisphere—told you she needed twenty-four hour supervision!"

"Well, she's my wife, and I won't send her away!"

"Boy, I swear to God, if you make this any harder for Katherine than it has to be, I'll snap that scrawny neck of yours without thinkin' twice."

Leland Bourke slammed his palms against the wooden table dramatically.

"That's enough!" Leland shouted. "This isn't doing Katherine any good."

"I'll be the one to decide what's best for my wife," Clay announced hotly, veins throbbing in his neck. "And I say we get her the best lawyer we can find to fight this."

With that, Clay's voice finally broke and he turned his back to them.

Sighing, Leland took Jackson by the elbow and quickly led him out of the room.

4

Jackson awoke cocooned in a pile of sheets and assorted blankets, but his toes felt numb, like little frozen flesh cubes. He pulled his exposed feet back under the covers and tried to burrow even deeper into the layers of insulation.

He knew that outside his house, earth and air shuddered through a myopic prism of unrelenting, vibrating heat. Inside, however, they could be storing meat.

Paige kept the house ridiculously cold, and Jackson had learned not to complain.

He toyed with the idea of continuing his hibernation, but reluctantly pushed back the covers and got out of bed. Jackson pulled on jeans and an old sweatshirt, and padded down the hall to the kitchen.

He found the newspaper on the counter, still in its plastic sleeve, with a note from Paige telling him she'd gone to the grocery. Jackson started the coffee machine and unfolded the paper. Staring back at him from the front page of the *Austin American-Statesman* was Katherine Van Hoerne's smiling face.

The story would be national news by mid-morning, if it wasn't already. Everybody loved a scandal involving people like Katherine Van Hoerne.

With a cup of coffee in hand and iPad tucked under his arm, Jackson stepped out onto the back deck to warm up. It was like stepping into a steam room, and Jackson couldn't decide which was worse.

A quick search of "Katherine Van Hoerne" turned up almost half a million hits. Choosing articles at random, mostly from women's fashion magazines, Jackson began reading. He noted that most of the photographs were taken at charity functions.

Katherine was stunning—a tall willowy blonde with the regal bearing and icy stare of a supermodel. By all outward appearances, she seemed not to have a care in the world.

He found an archived article on the *Architectural Digest* website showing photos of the Van Hoerne's sprawling ranch in the Texas Hill Country. There was one of Katherine, Clay and their then 18-month old daughter, Charlotte, on a porch swing. In the background, horses grazed in the setting light.

There was an in-depth piece in *Texas Monthly* that appeared around the time of Clay's first campaign for state senator. The article detailed the Van Hoerne family's impressive political lineage, which included a governor, a secretary of state and other assorted state office holders, and spoke of Clay's bid for public office as a foregone conclusion.

Jackson's concentration was disrupted by the sound of his cell phone ringing.

"Hello?" he said, pulling the phone out of his jeans pocket.

"Jackson?"

"Yes."

"This is Leland Bourke."

5

Overhead, long tracks of harsh fluorescent light emitted an intermittent buzz as Ramon navigated the grim, gray corridors of the Travis County ME's office. The forbidding facility was located in the underbelly of a nondescript government building and more closely resembled an underground military bunker than a set of offices. On this Saturday evening, there were only a handful of attendants in scrubs and white coats going about the business of processing death.

After making his way to Examination Room A, Ramon took a deep breath and pushed open the swinging metal doors. He was immediately overwhelmed by the smell of formaldehyde, disinfectant and assorted gore.

Chief Medical Examiner Margo Pinter stood over a female cadaver, carefully removing what looked like a mutant umbilical cord from some B-grade science fiction flick, but was actually a lower intestine.

An involuntary groan escaped from Ramon.

"Ah, Hinojosa, good to see you still have the stomach for real police work," Dr. Pinter said with a grin.

"I know my own limitations," Ramon told her, which elicited a hearty laugh from Margo.

She carried the intestine over to a hanging scale and dropped it into the stainless steel bowl. After marking the weight on a clipboard and repeating it aloud for the benefit of a recording device suspended above the examination table, she gently placed the organ in a sealed glass jar.

"To what do I owe this pleasure, Lieutenant?" Margo asked, covering the hollowed-out corpse with a plastic sheet.

"Can't a guy just stop by to visit his favorite harbinger of death?"

"Flattery will get you everywhere."

Margo Pinter stripped off her bloody smock and latex gloves and tossed them into a canary yellow barrel marked "hazardous waste." She was a middle-aged woman of medium height with sharp, birdlike features, pale skin and a head of unruly, auburn hair. Her thin frame seemed almost skeletal under her pale blue scrubs, yet she gave the impression of a person with limitless physical strength.

"Actually," Ramon answered, "I heard that your vacation got cut short, and I wanted to extend my condolences."

"Just between you and me, I was kind of relieved to get called back," she confessed. "Don't get me wrong, I love my grandkids more than I love my own life, but five days trapped in the same house isn't what I'd call a vacation."

"You're preaching to the choir," Ramon smiled. "I swear, every hour of quality family time now takes a year off my life."

"So what can I do for you?" Pinter asked.

Ramon suggested they talk in Margo's office, mostly to get away from the ghastly fumes, but also to afford them more privacy. Understanding both motivations, Margo nodded and led him down the cement corridor to her large, windowless office.

"So, you're here about Ramirez?" she began, closing the door behind them.

"I'm that transparent?"

"Always."

"Fair enough. What have you got on our boy Angel?"

"Not too much."

"Why's that?"

"Mid- autopsy, I was told to cease and desist."

"Come again?"

"All I know is Angel Ramirez got killed and I was helicoptered back here for the autopsy ASAP. Then, just as I'm finishing up the preliminary examination, I get a call from the chief of police himself telling me to halt the exam."

"He asked you to stop the autopsy?" Ramon asked, taken aback.

"He *ordered* me to stop, in no uncertain terms."

"Did he give you any reason?"

"Just said the case was on hold pending further investigation, and there was no point in desecrating the body if we didn't have to."

"He was worried about desecrating Angel Ramirez?"

It was hard to imagine anyone on the police force being overly concerned with the sanctity of Angel Ramirez's earthly remains. For one thing, the body had already been pretty well desecrated by a knife, and for another, Ramirez had just finished a long stint in Huntsville for the aggravated rape of a 13 year-old girl.

"That's what the man said," Margo answered.

Ramon stared at the floor as he considered what he had just heard.

"Well, that's mighty peculiar," Ramon muttered thoughtfully.

"You got any ideas about what's going on here?" she asked him.

"I imagine it has something to do with the suspect we have in custody."

"Suspect?"

Ramon raised his eyebrows in surprise.

"I take it you haven't seen a newspaper," he noted dryly.

Margo shook her head.

"They arrested that senator's wife, Katherine Van Hoerne, for the murder."

"No kidding?" Pinter replied, leaning back in her chair. "Well, that's a hell of a thing."

"It still doesn't explain why they called off the autopsy."

"No, it does not."

Opening up the bottom drawer of her desk, Margo took out a bottle of scotch and two glasses.

"You still on duty?" she asked Ramon.

"Are you going to be cutting into Angel Ramirez?"

"Doesn't look like it."

"Then I guess I'm off duty," Ramon sighed, reaching for a glass.

6

Jackson turned onto the familiar tree-lined street a little after noon and immediately noticed the brand-new, cherry red pick-up truck parked in Tommy's circular gravel driveway. Parking behind the truck, Jackson retrieved a manila file folder and a six-pack of beer from the passenger seat, and walked around to the back of the house.

New Braunfels was fifty miles south of Austin, and Tommy had a place on the Comal River, a relatively quiet offshoot of the Guadalupe. The brick house was long and low, with terraced wooden decks led down to the water.

Descending the gently sloping lawn, Jackson saw Tommy Keane on the dock, holding a fishing rod in one hand and a can of Lone Star beer in the other.

"Anything biting?" Jackson called out, stepping onto the dock.

"The little bastards are just screwing with me," answered Tommy.

Propping the rod up against a sturdy metal chair, Tommy walked to the end of the dock and hugged Jackson tightly. At 63 years old, he was still a bull of a man, with a thick barrel chest and arms the size of tree trunks, and a hug from Tommy could knock the wind right out of a person.

"Fish or no fish, you're still driving back to Austin in one hell of a fine vehicle," Jackson said breathlessly when Tommy released him.

"You like that, do you?"

"That's a fine new toy you've got there."

"That's what my life is about these days, accumulating badass toys," Tommy replied, pointing to a new fishing boat moored to the dock. "What else am I going to spend my money on?"

The last of Tommy's wives, a legal secretary named Gerda, had left him six years before, accomplishing what none of the previous Mrs. Keanes had before: definitively ending Tommy's ongoing dance with the institution of matrimony. Without any children of his own or any close relations to speak of, Tommy had been enjoying his bachelorhood by blowing what remained of his money on whatever caught his passing fancy.

"Why don't you put those in the ice chest," Tommy instructed, reeling in his line.

Tucking the manila folder under his arm, Jackson lifted the lid on the oversized cooler and forced the beers deep into the ice. Taking out a cold Lone Star, Jackson popped open the can and took a long pull.

Tommy smiled at him. With his snow-white hair and a ruddy complexion, Tommy looked a little like a department store Santa Claus.

"You look more like your father every day," the older man said.

"Clementine says the same thing," Jackson remarked.

Jack Polke, the father in question, had been Tommy Keane's best friend starting in high school, and Jackson knew his father's absence still left a gaping hole in Tommy's heart. Because of that hole, and out of respect and love for his old friend, Tommy became like a surrogate father to Jack's only son.

"How is Clem?" Tommy asked.

"Same as always."

Tommy grinned and shook his head.

"She's one hell of a woman, your aunt."

"That she is," Jackson agreed.

Jackson had been sent to live with his great aunt Clementine at the age of nine, when his father's untimely death had left him an orphan. It was Clementine who had raised Jackson, often butting heads with Tommy Keane over his unsolicited child-rearing advice. In the end, however, Clementine and Tommy had forged a somewhat grudging but respectful partnership with respect to Jackson's upbringing, a partnership that in recent years had developed into something akin to friendship.

Tommy cast the line again and asked Jackson if he wanted to get his old rod from the house.

"No, I'm okay."

Although a soft breeze whistled through the trees, it was still uncomfortably warm. Jackson took a couple of ice cubes out of the cooler and held them to the back of his neck.

"So, are you going to tell me what you got there?" Tommy asked, gesturing to the folder tucked under Jackson's arm.

Without meeting Tommy's eyes, Jackson handed it over. He then emptied his can of beer, and reached into the ice chest for another.

"You better hand me one of those," Tommy told him, scanning the file's pages. "If this is what I think it is, you should have brought something stronger than beer."

"There's a bottle of tequila in the car."

Tommy grumbled but didn't say anything.

While Tommy Keane read through the documents, Jackson took off his shoes and sat on the end of the dock, dangling his feet in the warm water.

Several minutes later, Tommy closed the folder and rested his hands on top.

"I should kick Leland Bourke's ass," Tommy stated dully, his mouth a rigid line. "Dragging you into this shitstorm."

"He didn't drag me into anything . . ."

Tommy groaned loudly.

"Listen, I know I've gotten myself into some trouble in the past . . ." Jackson continued, but Tommy waved his hand.

"Oh please, you and Wes were kids. This is whole different can of bees."

"I don't think that's an expression."

"In any event, I find your involvement in this matter mighty troubling," Tommy told him pointedly. "Aren't you a might bit suspicious as to why they called you in?"

"I know exactly why," Jackson replied flatly. "You."

Tommy paused for a moment before speaking.

"And what, precisely, do they think you can do for them?"

"Not a hell of a lot, because that's what I told them," Jackson replied. "I told them I could open communications, nothing more."

"To what end?"

"If Mrs. Van Hoerne is as ill as they say she is, no one wants a trial."

Tommy didn't look appeased.

"You've got no business in this mess, Jackson. None at all."

"So, I take it you've been briefed on what happened Friday night," Jackson said, weighing each word carefully.

"The goddamn phone hasn't stopped ringing all weekend," Tommy told him irritably. "Josiah Mantooth and that son-in-law of his have everybody jumping through hoops."

"Except for you."

"Damn right."

"Which explains why they called me," Jackson said quietly.

Tommy turned to glare at Jackson.

"You here to offer me some kind of bribe, boy?" he demanded.

"I told them it would be a waste of time."

"Or maybe try to influence me because of our relationship?"

"Also a waste of time."

Tommy leaned back in his chair, satisfied, and sighed loudly.

"If this is about getting that woman out of jail faster, I don't care who she is, there's no goddamn express lane," Tommy told him.

"The family just wants to ensure Mrs. Van Hoerne gets the medical care and supervision she needs."

"They want her committed?"

"Yes," Jackson confirmed.

Tommy snorted and said, "That's for a court to decide. Not me, not you, and certainly not that asshole Leland Bourke."

"I'm aware of that," Jackson responded smoothly. "But if everyone can agree that Katherine Van Hoerne is legally insane, that she's not competent to stand trial, then the whole matter can be resolved quickly and with a minimum of publicity."

"And you're here to convince me that she's insane?"

"Absolutely not, simply to introduce the possibility."

"And this?" Tommy asked, holding up the file.

"I thought if you saw a summary of Mrs. Van Hoerne's medical history, you might be more inclined to consider the possibility."

"Well, according to this," Tommy said, waving the folder in the air, "your Mrs. Van Hoerne is one sick puppy."

"That seems to be the overwhelming consensus, yes," Jackson confirmed.

Tommy nodded thoughtfully and handed the file back to Jackson. Standing up, he shook out his legs and prepared to recast his fishing line.

"She'll have to be examined by my shrinks," Tommy said finally, his back to Jackson.

"Of course."

"And the charges would remain pending. I won't have her out on the streets free as a bird after a twelve month vacation."

"I understand."

"And just so we're clear, I'm not doing this as a favor to you or anybody else," Tommy stated curtly, turning to look Jackson in the eyes. "If Katherine Van Hoerne is mentally incompetent, the law is real straightforward on what happens."

"There can be no prosecution," Jackson added unnecessarily.

"That's right, and as an officer of the court, it's my job to assist in the determination of competency."

"I appreciate what you're saying."

"I mean it, Jackson," Tommy continued, deadly serious. "If I facilitate a quick resolution of the competency issue, it'll be because it's the right thing to do for all concerned, not because your asshole boss and his spoiled billionaire friend sent you here to work on me."

"There was no doubt in my mind," Jackson told him honestly.

"Just so there's no doubt in *their* minds," Tommy retorted.

"I'll make absolutely sure there isn't."

"All right, Jackson," Tommy sighed heavily, crushing his beer can against his leg. "I'll arrange for two doctors to evaluate her this week."

"And if the psychiatric assessments prove she's insane?" Jackson asked.

"Then my office will move to have Mrs. Van Hoerne committed to a psychiatric facility until such time as a team of doctors determines that she is competent to stand trial," Tommy replied in a professional monotone.

Jackson realized that he'd been holding his breath, and let it out slowly.

Just then, Tommy's reel spun wildly as something tried to make off with the lure. Tommy reeled in the line until it was taut, and hauled a squirming mass of fish onto the dock.

"Gotcha, you little bastard," Tommy grinned.

Then he gently removed the hook from the fish's mouth and tossed it back into the river. After wiping his hands off on his shorts, Tommy removed another brightly colored lure from his well-stocked tackle box.

"So, do you think she's crazy?" Tommy asked Jackson.

"Can't really say, I haven't met her. I can tell you, though, that nobody in that family has any doubt she's certifiable, and has been for a long time."

"Gotta wonder how they managed to keep it secret all these years," Tommy observed. "They're using you, Jackson. You know that, don't you?"

"Yes, sir. I know that."

"You be careful," Tommy warned cryptically.

"Of what?"

"Getting played by the big dogs."

"I'm a big boy now, Tommy," Jackson assured him.

"Fair enough," Tommy smiled. "Just watch yourself, son. These folks are way out of your league."

7

Ramon Hinojosa received the preliminary forensics report late Wednesday afternoon as promised. He was reviewing the information when Jared Hawthorne popped his well-coifed head around the corner.

"Conrad wants to see us," Hawthorne announced, tapping his fingers as if in a hurry.

Ramon followed Hawthorne down the hall to the office of their commander.

"Come in."

Nathan Conrad, all five feet, four inches of him, greeted them at the door, and shook Ramon's hand warmly. His trim, taut body was the result of a grueling weekly regimen of marathon training.

The office was spacious, with dark paneled walls lined with framed photographs of Conrad posing with important people. The shelves were overflowing with the medals and trophies Nathan Conrad had accumulated over the years from his running.

He asked about Ramon's family and then gestured for the men to sit down in a couple of upholstered chairs.

"It's getting late in the day, gentlemen, so I'll get right to the point," Conrad said, suddenly somber. "It's about the Angel Ramirez murder. I've gotten word that Katherine Van Hoerne will not be mounting a defense against the charges. Therefore, for the moment, the case is closed."

"Excuse me?" Ramon stammered. "What does that have to do with the investigation?"

"If the woman's guilty, there's nothing to investigate. Do you have any reason to believe she's *not* guilty?"

"No, but we've only just started to make inquiries. We don't even have an autopsy yet."

"We've got the initial autopsy results," Hawthorne noted. "And you have the forensics report."

"*Preliminary* reports . . ." Ramon interjected.

"Anything in the preliminary reports to suggest she didn't do it?" Conrad asked.

"Hell no," Hawthorne answered. "All of our witnesses put her at the scene, we've traced the murder weapon to a matching set of knives at her house, we've got her prints on the murder weapon, the wounds on both the suspect and the victim are consistent with our theory of the case . . ."

"Which is what, exactly?" Ramon demanded.

"That she stabbed him while he was doing her against the wall."

"That's a theory, Nathan," Ramon said calmly, trying to appeal to the Chief's better instincts. "Anyone could have been in that alley. We're talking about Rey's, here. Half of our so-called witnesses have gang affiliations. Any one of them could have taken out Ramirez."

"With a knife from the Van Hoerne's house? I don't think so . . ." Hawthorne countered.

"He's got a point, Ramon," Nathan Conrad remarked.

"I'm not saying he doesn't . . ."

"What are you saying?"

"That it's still the early stages of the investigation," Ramon replied, frustrated. "You know as well as I do that anything can happen from here."

"I appreciate what you're saying Ramon, I really do," Conrad told him, "but we just don't have the resources to waste on this."

"I hardly think it would be wasting resources," Ramon said, unable to keep the disbelief out of his voice.

"Well, the chief doesn't agree with you."

Nathan Conrad let his words hit home before continuing.

"The bottom line is that we don't have the manpower to investigate cases that aren't going to trial. Word is, this is one of those cases."

Ramon sank back into his chair.

"There's something wrong here, Nathan," he stated.

"Listen Ramon," Conrad said soothingly, "if there's any chance of a trial, or if anything comes up supporting a different theory of the crime, I'll be the first person to open this sucker back up. But until then, I can think of at least a dozen pending investigations that I need you on."

"I would like to go on the record as opposing this decision," Ramon informed him evenly.

"So noted," Conrad said, ending the conversation. "If that's all gentlemen, I have a dinner date with my youngest daughter."

Without another word, Ramon stood up and marched out of the office.

8

Tommy Keane put down the reports, pushed his reading glasses to the top of his head, and rubbed his eyes wearily. Glancing at his watch, he debated whether to go to bed and leave the matter until morning. Instead, he lifted a half-empty bottle of tequila from the cluttered end table beside him and refilled his glass, which was balanced on the well-worn arm of his brown suede chair.

Other than the light from his reading lamp, the room was awash in shadows. It was a markedly masculine room, with battered leather sofas and decorative dead animals. Dark wood shelves lined the walls, filled to capacity with books and legal texts, the overflow of reading materials littering the room.

Tommy pulled his tattered plaid robe tighter around his barrel chest, disrupting the pile of papers sitting in his lap. He hadn't expected the psychiatric evaluations back so soon, but both doctors finished their assessments in seemingly record time.

Returning the half-moon glasses to his nose, Tommy again turned his attention to the reports.

They had been prepared by two of his best, Dr. Dennis Wong and Dr. Leila Olyphant. It was not unheard of for Wong and Olyphant to reach radically different conclusions about a patient, but when it came to Katherine Van Hoerne, the psychiatrists appeared to be in complete agreement.

Acute schizophrenia with psychotic features.

According to the patient's medical history, Tommy read from Wong's report, *signs of schizophrenia first became apparent during her late teens. Since then, the disease has been controlled with a variety of drugs, most notably Thymetrazine, which has proved very effective in recent years. This explains the patient's ability to function normally.*

Flipping to Olyphant's evaluation, he read, *In all likelihood, the patient developed either an intolerance or some kind of immunity to the medication. As Thymetrazine is a relatively new drug, there is very little clinical evidence regarding long-term treatment. As a general matter, however, it is not uncommon for patients to develop adverse reactions to psychotropic drugs after extended use. In this case, the adverse reaction resulted in a psychotic episode.*

On the next page, Olyphant defined the episode as *a break with reality, during which time the patient was unable to differentiate between the reality of the world around her and the mechanisms of her own mind.* The psychiatrist went on to state that this particular psychosis included violent tendencies.

If it hadn't been so damn sad, Tommy would have laughed at the understatement.

While there was nothing in Katherine's medical history indicating a propensity for violence towards others, there was plenty to suggest a history of self-mutilation. There were countless trips to the emergency room for lacerations, contusions, broken bones and other injuries, all of which were self-inflicted.

Turning back to Wong's evaluation, Tommy reread the doctor's conclusions regarding Katherine's current mental condition.

At the present time, the patient remains in a psychotic state, the result of a total and complete split of the psyche, no doubt caused by the severe trauma in question.

Trauma. What a tactful euphemism.

The patient alternates between catatonia, hysteria and flagrant self-abuse . . . remains wholly unaware of her surroundings . . . neither cognitive of nor responsive to outside stimuli, including physical sensation and aural communication . . . For all intents and purposes, the person known as Katherine Van Hoerne has ceased to exist.

It struck Tommy that the so-called experts might think Mrs. Van Hoerne was more traumatized than Angel Ramirez, but they were both in complete agreement.

Only time will tell whether this psychotic state is permanent, both doctors concluded. *But in any event, the patient is not currently able to assist in her own defense and is mentally incompetent to stand trial.*

Enclosed with the reports were two Texas Certificates of Medical Examination for Mental Illness signed by Wong and

Olyphant, declaring Katherine Van Hoerne a person with mental illness meeting the criteria for court-ordered inpatient mental health services.

Tommy closed the file and swallowed the last of his tequila. Part of him had hoped for a different result, only so he could disentangle Jackson from the whole nasty business, but there it was in black and white.

Exhausted, Tommy hauled himself out of the chair and walked over to the telephone.

9

Jackson listened to the message for a third time, trying to decipher what he could from the tone of Tommy Keane's voice.

"It's me. The evaluations are back, and it looks like all the headshrinkers are in agreement. The charges will remain pending, but you can tell your new friends that I'll file the appropriate paperwork. Then you say adios. You got that? I don't care what they want you to do, you say no thanks and walk away."

Walking over to the lone window in his office, Jackson looked down on the streets of downtown Austin 25 floors below. A few blocks away, early morning joggers looped around Lady Bird Johnson Lake, its water streaked pink, orange and lavender, and the outline of St. Edward's University was visible at the top of the hill in the distance.

As Jackson watched Austin come to life below him, he thought of the pictures he'd seen of Katherine Van Hoerne. They were outdated images, Jackson had to remind himself. The woman who was Katherine Van Hoerne now spent her time rocking back and forth on her haunches or banging her head against the walls.

Both Leland Bourke and Josiah Mantooth stood when Jackson entered Leland's enormous office. Leland put a hand on Jackson's shoulder as he directed him to one of the high-backed, leather chairs facing his desk.

"Leland has just been filling me in on your meeting with Tommy Keane," Josiah told him. "I owe you a debt of gratitude. I've got to tell you, Jackson, I'm mighty impressed, and I am not a man easily impressed."

"I told you he would be an invaluable asset," Leland remarked, his head inclined towards Jackson.

"That you did, but I believe this young man exceeded even your expectations."

"I really didn't do anything," Jackson responded.

"What happens now?" Josiah asked.

"It's pretty straightforward, really. Tommy's office files a motion, Katherine's attorney responds with no objection, and the court enters a ruling. But keep in mind, they aren't dropping the charges against Mrs. Van Hoerne, which means that they'll remain pending during the entirety of her commitment. Make no mistake, if there ever comes a time when Mrs. Van Hoerne is deemed mentally competent, she may very well be facing a murder trial."

"I guess we'll cross that bridge if and when we come to it," Josiah replied quietly. "All we can do now is get Katherine the best possible care, and that's going to be in a hospital, not a goddamn prison psych ward."

Jackson nodded silently.

"I thought for sure Keane was going to fight us," Josiah continued. "I don't know what you did to convince him, but I'm grateful to you."

"Truly, I didn't do anything," Jackson repeated.

"Bullshit," Josiah barked. "If it weren't for you, I don't know where we'd be right now."

Josiah and Leland exchanged a look that Jackson couldn't decipher. Tommy's warning suddenly filled Jackson's brain.

"I would like you to represent Katherine at the hearing," Josiah told him.

"Me?" Jackson stammered. "Why?"

"You're already familiar with Katherine's case. And I believe you have proven that when it comes to my daughter, you will place her interests of my daughter above all other considerations."

Sighing heavily, Josiah rose from his chair and walked over to the bank of windows overlooking the hills west of Austin. He closed his eyes and tilted his head back slightly so that the incoming rays of sunlight struck him full on the face. It was several moments before he spoke.

"I'm under no delusions about what we're in for," Josiah said. "Every news outlet in the country is getting ready to feed on this like a pack of ravenous vultures. This tragedy—hell, my daughter's entire life—is about to be dissected and packaged for public consumption, and there's not a damn thing I can do about it . . ."

Josiah broke off, the deep lines around his mouth furrowed in a dark, dangerous scowl. He was not a man accustomed to facing a situation beyond his control, and the feeling of helplessness clearly infuriated him.

"Whoever represents Katherine is going to at the center of a feeding frenzy. I need someone I can trust. Leland can't do it, because it might create a conflict of interest with Mantooth Industries."

"Your daughter needs a seasoned criminal defense attorney . . ."

"You said it was straight forward from here out," Josiah pointed out. "Besides, I've been impressed from the beginning with how you've handled yourself. That was a hell of a scene at the police station, but you gave it to us straight, and that couldn't have been an easy thing."

Jackson knew this was a big opportunity for him, but he couldn't get Tommy's words out of his mind.

Just say adios. Just walk away and don't look back.

"This is my daughter's life we're talking about," Josiah added plaintively. "We need you. Katherine needs you."

The words had the desired effect. Again Jackson thought of the Katherine he'd seen in old photographs, and felt an inexplicable urge to protect her.

"I will represent your daughter to the best of my abilities, sir," Jackson told Josiah.

10

The proceedings had been closed to the public, and there were only a handful of people to rise when Judge Harold Boone entered the courtroom.

Katherine Van Hoerne had been deemed too ill to attend the hearing, so Jackson sat alone at the counsel table for the defense. Across the aisle from him, representing the State of Texas, was Melissa Smythe, an assistant district attorney assigned to the case by Tommy Keane.

"You may be seated," Judge Boone said. "Do the parties have anything to add before I render a decision?"

Jackson and ADA Smythe both replied, "No, your honor."

"Very well," the judge said, clearing his throat. "On this date, the court considered the issue of defendant's mental competency. Having reviewed the motion and the evidence presented, this court finds the defendant qualifies as mentally incompetent under Article 46.02 of the Texas Code of Criminal Procedure. Therefore, the court finds that Katherine Mantooth Van Hoerne is, as a matter of law, incompetent to stand trial for the crimes of which she is accused."

As Judge Boone banged his gavel, Jackson turned to give Josiah Mantooth and his wife Bobbie Dean and encouraging nod.

"The court hereby orders that Katherine Mantooth Van Hoerne be committed to a maximum security unit of a facility to be determined by the Texas Department of Mental Health until such time as Mrs. Van Hoerne has attained competency to stand trial. The court further orders that defendant's attorney of record, Jackson Polke, shall represent the defendant in all further proceedings in this matter unless and until he files with the court a Motion for Withdrawal or is otherwise removed from his appointment by the court."

With that, Judge Harold Boone raised his gavel one last time and stated, "Court is hereby adjourned."

Again, the bailiff shouted, "All rise!" as the judge retreated into his chambers.

Outside the courthouse, an army of reporters and television crews waited in the pouring rain for word on the fate of Katherine Van Hoerne. The weather had broken earlier that morning with a vengeance, and water was still falling from the heavens in historic proportions. The runoff was beginning to flood the street and sidewalk, and the grassy areas outside the courthouse had morphed into swampland, leaving the media horde milling about in ankle-high mud.

Working up his courage, Jackson surveyed the pandemonium outside. As he steeled himself for the onslaught, he felt a hand on his shoulder.

"I always said you were a criminal lawyer at heart," a familiar voice said.

Jackson turned to find Tommy Keane standing behind him. Their last conversation had turned into one hell of a fight, but the old man seemed to have forgiven him for taking Katherine's case.

"Where's Bourke? Primping for the cameras?" Tommy asked.

"I thought you weren't speaking to me," Jackson reminded him.

"I'm over it," Tommy replied with a shrug. "You're a big boy. You're entitled to make your own mistakes."

"Thanks, I guess. Is that an apology?"

"Hell no," Tommy grinned. "I still think you're a goddamn fool, but you stuck to your guns and did what you thought was right. And I'm proud of you."

"That means a lot to me."

"Yeah, yeah," Tommy replied dismissively. "Now go on, introduce yourself to the press."

Jackson took a deep breath, and with a parting glance to Tommy, walked out onto the courthouse steps.

PART II

FIVE YEARS LATER

1

She was lying in the corner of the room. Knees pulled in tight against her torso, back and buttocks wedged into the crook of intersecting walls, the woman squeezed herself into an ever more compact human ball. Her arms were immobilized, strapped across her chest and secured behind her shoulders in a twisted parody of an embrace. With her bare feet, she tried to wriggle ever deeper into the corner, as if by sheer force of will she could push herself through the solid barrier and disappear altogether.

All the while, keeping time with some ghastly internal metronome, she banged her head against the floor with all of her might.

Dr. Eleanor Dodds sat on the narrow bed, watching helplessly as her patient tried to bash her brains in. The protective padding prevented any damage, but the soft, rhythmic thud of skull against quilted fabric was still heartrending. Again, Ellie wondered what sort of messages traveled the neural pathways inside that mind.

The official diagnosis was schizophrenic catatonia with psychotic features. Self-mutilation was common enough among psychotics, but Ellie had never encountered a patient so intent on inflicting pain.

The patient would use whatever means were at her disposal to exact unspeakable punishment on herself, yet she rarely lashed out at the staff. Typically in cases such as this, the abuse was random and diffuse, with the patient attacking whomever she came in contact with. With this woman, however, the assaults were consistently directed against her own person.

Except for a two-way mirror affixed high on one of the walls, the stark white room was cushioned from floor to ceiling. The only pieces of furniture, a padded bed frame and a small table, were bolted to the ground, and the linens were fastened to the mattress with plastic belts.

Ellie had been assigned the case eight months before, soon after she joined the staff of the Dripping Springs Psychiatric Hospital. She was told the patient was beyond help, and Ellie had seen nothing during her brief tenure to indicate otherwise. With one glaring exception, Ellie had tried everything to reverse the psychosis, from experimental drug regimens to electroshock therapy, all to no avail. But Ellie was determined.

At first, her new colleagues seemed amused by Ellie's resolve, which they chalked up to the overzealous enthusiasm of a young doctor just out of residency. It was their esteemed collective judgment that further experimentation on this patient was futile, and that Ellie's only recourse was to make the woman as comfortable as possible and minimize the self-abuse with debilitating tranquilizers.

With each failed treatment, Ellie was forced to admit that they might be right.

Despite all of this this, Ellie refused to give up without exhausting every available medical alternative. She was determined to try one last protocol. It was the only option left. Unfortunately, it was also the only drug therapy strictly prohibited for use on this patient.

From the beginning, Ellie had wanted to try Thymetrazine. She knew there were dangers, especially in light of past events, but she believed it was their best chance of snapping the patient out of her psychotic state. The hospital administration, however, did not agree. Ellie was told, in no uncertain terms, that Thymetrazine was off limits.

It was a reasonable restriction, since it was the unanimous conclusion of the initial treating physicians that Thymetrazine somehow triggered the psychosis in the first place, but Ellie wasn't convinced.

Ellie had repeatedly appealed the prohibition, arguing that in light of the patient's condition, the potential benefits far outweighed the possible risks. After all, if the woman was beyond hope, how could it make matters worse?

The answer was simple enough: the medication might kill her.

Although Ellie believed this was highly unlikely, it couldn't be ruled out altogether, and there were plenty of psychiatrists on staff quick to point this out. The patient clearly had an adverse reaction to the drug, and since it was impossible to determine the exact nature of that reaction, reintroducing the medication into her system could prove fatal. No matter how improbable, the patient could conceivably experience heart failure, a stroke, or seizures, and this was a chance the hospital was not willing to take.

Ellie knew they were just covering their own asses. If the hospital authorized the treatment despite the documented dangers and the patient died, there would be serious hell to pay.

Even knowing all of this, Ellie remained undeterred. After the last of her appeals to the administration was rejected, she began writing letters to the Department of Mental Health, and even to the director himself, hoping to override the hospital's decision.

As expected, Ellie's employers were none too pleased with her attempts to go over their heads. She was aware of the whispering behind her back—that she had lost her professional objectivity to the detriment of her patient, that she was willing to risk the woman's life in order to make a name for herself. In the end, the director judiciously deferred to the determination of the hospital administrators, and Ellie's letter-writing efforts only served to make her something of a pariah with her colleagues.

Maybe I am losing objectivity, Ellie thought as she watched her patient thrash around on the floor.

Despite the straightjacket, the patient was now heaving her upper body off the ground and flinging herself against the wall, a vain attempt to injure herself against the protective padding.

Ellie felt a new swell of sympathy for the desperate, pathetic creature at her feet. Despite the steely armor of medical detachment she'd cultivated, this one had managed to get under Ellie's skin.

Shaking her head, Ellie reached into the breast pocket of her lab coat and extracted a folded envelope. Having already committed to memory the pertinent parts of the letter contained inside, Ellie simply stared at the envelope, mentally assessing the magnitude of its contents. With her index finger, she traced the engraved insignia of the Travis County District Court.

A sharp cracking sound drew Ellie's attention back to the woman writhing on the floor. With astonishing dexterity, the patient was convulsively whacking her skull against her own bony knees, at last accomplishing the desired effect. Rivulets of blood began to stream from her nose.

Ellie hurriedly shoved the envelope back into her pocket and reached for the stainless steel tray perched on the table beside her.

In an instant, she had the patient pinned to the floor, hypodermic needle in hand. Yanking off the protective cap with her teeth, Ellie plunged the needle into the patient's upper arm as the woman bucked and strained against her.

The effects of the Thorazine were almost instantaneous, torment immediately giving way to a drugged stupor, and Ellie rolled off her patient.

Standing up slowly, Ellie moved to the door and pressed a silent buzzer hidden within the folds of fabric, summoning nurses and orderlies.

With a heavy sigh, Dr. Eleanor Dodds pulled a handkerchief from her pocket and leaned over her semi-unconscious patient. As she had done countless times before, Ellie wiped the blood from Katherine Van Hoerne's face.

2

"It's after 9 o'clock, Mr. Polke."

Jackson rolled over onto his side, grumbled pitifully, and buried his face in a long, rather ugly pillow shaped like a trout.

"9:03, to be precise."

Accepting the inevitable, Jackson pushed himself up to a seated position on the couch, and tried to rub a kink out of his neck. Three hours of cramped, fitful sleep had left him sore and more tired he was before.

Jackson watched as his secretary, Loretta, moved around his desk, stacking mail and message slips in orderly piles and removing a ream of documents from his out-box.

"I'll bring you some coffee," she said quietly before leaving the office.

Yawning and stretching his knotted muscles, Jackson rose slowly to his feet.

God, I'm getting old, Jackson thought grimly as he waited for the blood to return to his cramped limbs.

His still youthful features were beginning to show the first signs of age, and his lean frame wasn't as easy to maintain as it once was. His dirty blonde hair was still thick, but there were clusters of gray strands at his temples. And now his joints were popping and creaking like rusty, unused hinges.

Jackson had never imagined feeling so old at thirty-four.

In a matter of weeks the 97 partners of Bourke & Donovan would convene to select the newest members, if any, of their esteemed ranks. Up for partner this year, Jackson had sacrificed the last 18 months of his life to billable hours and client development in the hope that single-minded commitment to firm profits would be rewarded.

On those mornings when Jackson woke up beside his trout pillow, Jackson reminded himself of the very bright light at the end of the tunnel, namely all of the cash, perks, and prestige that went along with being a B&D partner. It was this that Jackson focused on as he walked to his desk, as opposed to the pinched-nerve in his neck and the sharp tingling sensation shooting down his arm like an advancing army of fork prongs. His loosely knotted tie hung from his neck at an angle depressingly reminiscent of a hangman's noose.

Jackson used to joke with his co-workers that Paige's request for a divorce was almost a relief—one less thing to worry about.

Just as Jackson's computer came to life, Loretta stepped into the office holding a coffee mug bearing the bright green B&D logo.

"Leland Bourke called," she informed him. "Your tee time has been pushed back to eleven o'clock."

Jackson nodded his acknowledgement and reached for the coffee, but Loretta held it just out of reach.

"What is it, Loretta?" he asked.

"I was just wondering if you were going to return those messages," she said hesitantly. "That woman, well, she's been very persistent, and I'm not sure what else I should tell her."

"What woman?"

"That doctor lady."

"Who?"

"The one who's called here every day for the last week," Loretta explained patiently, pointing to the pile of pink slips on Jackson's desk. "She is really quite insistent. She would like to speak with you directly"

Jackson picked up the stack and shuffled through the messages. They were all from Dr. Eleanor Dodds, Katherine Van Hoerne's psychiatrist.

"And you told her that all medical matters involving Mrs. Van Hoerne are to be directed to the family?" Jackson pressed.

"Repeatedly. She told me, also repeatedly, that it is a matter of utmost urgency that she speaks with you personally. She is adamant."

"Please get this doctor on the phone," Jackson uttered, irritated.

Loretta nodded, placed the coffee on Jackson's desk, and backed out of the office. A moment later, a light on Jackson's phone blinked red.

"Dr. Dodds, this is Jackson Polke," he stated into the handset.

"Yes, Mr. Polke," a female voice replied. "Thank you for returning my calls."

"I understand that you've been harassing my secretary," he began tartly.

"Actually," the woman interrupted, "I was hoping to speak with you in person."

"Dr. Dodds, I really am very busy, and I believe my secretary has already explained you need to direct your inquiries to Mrs. Van Hoerne's family. In fact, I really shouldn't be talking to you at all . . ."

"But you're her lawyer."

"And as her lawyer, I am compelled to direct all inquiries regarding medical treatment to Mrs. Van Hoerne's family. It is not my place to discuss her treatment with you or anyone else."

Ellie Dodds suppressed her rising frustration and tried a different tact.

"I need your help, Mr. Polke," she said plaintively. "Katherine needs your help."

"Has Mrs. Van Hoerne's condition changed?"

"Unfortunately, no."

"Is there any chance she might be released?"

"Not at the present time."

"Then I don't how I can help you, Dr. Dodds," Jackson told her. "Unless this relates to Katherine's competence or the criminal charges still pending against her, this doesn't involve me."

"Not according to Judge Boone," Ellie said, a hint of anger creeping into her voice. "I have a court order clearly stating this does involve you."

"What order?"

The woman began reading to Jackson in a monotone.

"*In light of the petition by Mrs. Van Hoerne's treating physician, the Court hereby orders that the relevant determination of hospital administrators may be overridden, and alternative treatment options authorized, by consent of Mrs. Van Hoerne's immediate family OR HER ATTORNEY OF RECORD.*" Unless I'm mistaken, Mr. Polke, that's you."

Jackson was momentarily at a loss for words.

"Would you hold?" he said quickly.

"Of course."

Moments after barking over the intercom to Loretta, Jackson was reviewing the file. On the top was a document Jackson vaguely recalled crossing his desk some days earlier. An order issued by Judge Harold Boone.

After quickly scanning its contents, Jackson again picked up the telephone.

"Dr. Dodds, I apologize for that," he stated. "I have Judge Boone's order in front of me, and according to this, you've been very busy indeed."

"Meaning?"

"Let's see," Jackson drawled slowly, "it says here that after repeatedly appealing the decision of your superiors regarding Mrs. Van Hoerne's care—which, by the way, was medically sound and uniformly supported by your colleagues—you began a letter-writing campaign to overturn the decision. When that failed—again because none of your peers agree with you—you petitioned Judge Boone."

"So?"

"So, it says that your employers describe your conduct as 'borderline obsessive.'"

"They're entitled to their opinion."

"They certainly are," Jackson readily agreed. "They are also of the opinion that the alternative treatment you recommend is potentially life-threatening."

"The chances of that are miniscule," Ellie replied defensively.

"Says you."

"Mr. Polke," Ellie began, adopting a more deferential tone, "I believe that Katherine's psychosis could be alleviated, or even reversed altogether, by introducing a medication called Thymetrazine into her drug therapy. It is our only remaining option. If you would just give me a half-hour of your time, I can explain to you how the drug works and show you studies from around the country that support my recommendation."

"That won't be necessary," Jackson informed her curtly.

"Please, Mr. Polke, if you would just give me a chance . . ."

"I only have one question for you, Dr. Dodds," Jackson interrupted. "Have you spoken with Mrs. Van Hoerne's family regarding your treatment proposal?"

There was an extended pause while Ellie silently cursed herself for the way she'd handled this phone call.

"Have you?" Jackson repeated.

"Yes. I have spoken to both Katherine's husband and her father."

"And?"

"They declined to authorize the treatment, but . . ."

"But what?" Jackson answered with some satisfaction. "You aren't actually suggesting that I disregard the express wishes of the family, not to mention the determination of your own hospital, and authorize an experimental treatment that might very well kill my client?"

"Yes, Mr. Polke," Ellie said softly. "I guess I am."

"Well, then, I decline."

"I'm begging you Mr. Polke," Ellie pleaded, "you are Katherine's last hope."

"I'm sorry Dr. Dodds," Jackson told her, "but I'm certainly not going to circumvent the family's decision. Now, if you don't mind, I'm late for an appointment."

Ellie heard a click and the line went dead.

3

Jackson and Leland stood on the green waiting for Douglas Holland to extract his ball from yet another sand trap. Despite sporting thousands of dollars' worth of equipment, Holland was a genuinely terrible golfer. The first rule of golfing, as client development, was to let the potential client win, or at least come close, and Holland wasn't making it easy. Jackson would have to splice on the next two tees just to keep from humiliating the man.

It was a glorious early-autumn day, 85 degrees and a cloudless sky, without so much as a hint of a change in season. As guests of Leland Bourke, they were playing one of the Barton Creek Country Club courses, nestled in the scenic rolling hills and valleys west of downtown Austin.

Jackson cringed as Douglas Holland's ball flew out of the sand in the opposite direction of the green.

"Damn it!" Holland shouted. "How am I supposed to concentrate with all this damn noise?!"

In truth, the sound of construction was distant and not overly distracting, but no one was about to contradict the man.

After his high profile representation of Katherine Van Hoerne five years earlier, Jackson had become the go-to guy in Austin for very wealthy people who found themselves in very hot water. Thanks in large part to early referrals from Josiah Mantooth, Jackson quickly developed a thriving criminal law practice, the first B&D lawyer to do so, and he now had several younger associates working for him.

Douglas Holland, the founder and CEO of Holland Electronics, was under investigation by the IRS for tax fraud. Keith Yeager, Holland Electronics' general counsel, had arranged this golf outing with Leland Bourke and Jackson Polke.

While Douglas Holland considered his next shot, Keith Yeager, who had been passing the time talking on his cell phone, walked over to where Jackson and Leland stood.

"Maybe you two should go on ahead," he offered, gesturing over his shoulder to another foursome quickly working their way down the fairway. "I'll stay here with Doug."

"They'll wait," Leland assured him.

"It could be awhile," Keith said with a knowing grin. "It's all downhill after he gets it on the green."

From what Jackson had seen of Holland's putting skills, that was an understatement.

"Perhaps you're right," Leland agreed as Holland's ball suddenly sailed over their heads.

Leland and Jackson took one of the golf carts and drove along the meticulously manicured path toward the next tee.

"I think Holland's getting worse," Jackson said when they were out of earshot.

"If that's possible," Leland replied, laughing.

Leland hadn't aged a day in all the years Jackson had known him, like some freakish Dick Clark clone, and he was as polished and well-groomed as ever. Even his knit golf shirt, which bore the BCCC insignia on the breast, was starched and pressed.

"Has he said anything about B&D taking the case?"

"Not yet, but Yeager's really pushing for us. For you, actually."

Both men were quite aware that landing the Holland Electronics case would be quite a coup for Jackson. And it would go a long way toward impressing the B&D partners when it came time for the partnership vote.

"By the way, I've been meaning to ask you about Tommy Keane," Leland said gently, changing the subject. "How's he doing?"

"Not well," Jackson replied softly. "The cancer's metastasized into his liver."

"I'm sorry to hear that."

"Me too."

Cresting a sharp rise, Leland parked the golf cart under a tree beside the next tee. As they watched in the distance for Holland and

Yeager, Jackson recalled his telephone conversation earlier that morning.

"I spoke to a Dr. Eleanor Dodds today," Jackson remarked to Leland. "She's the psychiatrist treating Katherine Van Hoerne."

"What did she want?"

"She wanted me to authorize some kind of experimental drug regimen that's been vetoed by the hospital. It seems that Judge Boone issued an order stating that as the attorney of record, I could approve the treatment."

"Did you?"

"Of course not. I told her she needed to contact Mrs. Van Hoerne's family."

Leland nodded his approval.

"Apparently she's already been shot down by Josiah and Clay Van Hoerne, which is why she's been harassing me," Jackson explained.

"Harassing?"

"She's been calling constantly. Insisted on speaking with me personally."

"Is this becoming a problem?" Leland asked, his eyebrow arching.

"No, no problem. I handled it."

4

Jackson drove up to the Four Seasons Hotel a little after nine on Saturday night. He was late, having spent the better part of the evening sifting through the first batch of documents from Holland Electronics.

Jackson got out of his new silver sports car, handing the keys to one of the valets in exchange for a ticket stub. Buttoning up his tuxedo jacket, Jackson walked through the heavy double doors and into the tastefully opulent lobby of the Four Seasons.

Just past the reception desk, he descended an enormous marble staircase and presented his invitation to a remarkably perky young woman in a tight, shiny gown. Jackson headed straight for the nearest bartender and ordered a double scotch.

Hosted by the Daughters of the Republic of Texas, the annual Settlers Ball was the highlight of the Austin social season. Originally organized to salute Texas families whose ancestors populated the territory back before the Civil War, the guest list was now a who's who of the new Texas economy. As a direct descendant and namesake of the infamous General Jackson Beauregard Polke, a hero in the bloody battle against Mexico for Texas Independence, Jackson had been a regular at the Ball since he was 17.

Working his way through the crowd, stopping for the obligatory handshakes and air kisses, Jackson left the reception area and entered the ballroom. Round tables draped in white linen and decorated with autumnal flower arrangements were set up around the dance floor. Off to the side were long, rectangular tables laden with items up for bid in the silent auction.

Clearly, safety boxes all over town had been accessed as women reclaimed their most impressive jewelry. While the ladies were decked out in multi-hued finery, the only thing distinguishing one middle-aged white man from another, other than varying degrees of hair loss, was their choice of footwear. Keeping with the official dress code of

Texas Formal, the men sported a wide assortment of expensive cowboy boots, ranging from basic black snakeskin to colorful personalized designs.

After surveying the scene for a few minutes, Jackson found his great aunt Clementine holding court at one of the center tables. At 70 years old, she was still a "sparkplug of a gal," as Tommy Keane liked to call her, and a commanding presence in any room. She was a mainstay of Austin society, active in a multitude of civic and charitable organizations, and was currently serving as chairperson on several important boards, including that of the Daughters of the Republic of Texas.

Clementine Polke had outlived or outgrown four husbands over the years, but she always retained her maiden name, not out of any feminist bent, but because of her abiding pride in her family's history and heritage, such as they were.

With a glass of champagne in hand, Clementine was engrossed in an animated conversation with her friend Cissy Dawes, another preeminent society doyenne, and a throng of adoring, social-climbing minions. The younger women, eager to flatter and impress, hung on Clementine's every word as if she were revealing a new gospel.

Approaching the table, Jackson caught the tail end of the discussion.

"A woman must always, *always* have her own mad money," Cissy stated firmly, draining the last of her cocktail in one genteel gulp.

"Always," Clementine reiterated. "There are only two things that a woman needs in this world: her own money and her own bathroom."

The perfectly coiffed heads around the table bobbed up and down in agreement, obsequiously grateful for the wisdom imparted by the elders of the tribe.

"So true," Cissy concurred, signaling a waiter by holding up her empty glass and shaking the ice.

Jackson stood behind Clementine's chair and put his hands on her shoulders.

"There you are!" Clementine exclaimed, tilting her head for a kiss on the cheek. "You all know my nephew, Jackson."

"Of course!" the women chimed in unison.

Jackson greeted the ladies and sat down next to his great-aunt.

"You look wonderful," he told her.

She was wearing a black velvet gown and a long rope of pebble-sized pearls that looped around her frail neck several times. With her tiny boyish frame, square jaw, and prominent eyebrows, Clementine had always been more handsome than pretty, which seemed to suit her just fine.

"Thank you, dear. You look quite nice yourself," she replied, squeezing Jackson's hand. "So, which of these lovely young ladies is your date for the evening?"

"I was hoping you would do me that honor."

"I take that to mean you've arrived alone *again*," Clementine chided disapprovingly. "I swear, Jackson, if I didn't know any better, I'd think you were a homosexual."

"A what?" Jackson gasped, feigning shock.

"You heard me. A ho-mo-sexual," she drawled.

"Would you stop trying to fix me up if I were?"

"No, I would just have to find you a beard."

"A beard?" Jackson laughed. "Where the hell did you hear that term?"

"I watch television, thank you very much," Clementine retorted. "Besides, I do have gay friends, you know."

"Name one."

"My hairdresser, Merv."

"You are truly a woman of the world, Clem," Jackson responded, giving her another kiss on the cheek.

"I'm serious, Jackson," Clementine continued undeterred. "You need to get out there and start dating again. It's been over a year since the divorce was finalized."

"I'm aware of that."

"Well then?"

"Well what? You know how busy I've been."

Changing the subject, Clementine asked "Have you been to visit Tommy this week?"

"Not since Sunday," Jackson replied gravely.

"He looks like hell, Jackson."

"I know."

"I almost didn't recognize him, he's so thin."

After all their years of bickering over Jackson and just about everything else, Clementine and Tommy Keane had forged a remarkable bond, although neither would actually admit it. It was Clementine who often kept Tommy company during the long hospital stays, sometimes sitting at his bedside for hours.

"He might not tell you so, but he really appreciates your visits," Jackson said. "And so do I."

"Well, someone has to get the man a decent meal," Clementine grumbled, blushing slightly. "No wonder he's so skinny, what with that vile waste they try to pass off as food."

Despite the nurses' best attempts to stop her, Clementine routinely brought Tommy meals from his favorite restaurants. The staff also blamed Clementine for the bottles of tequila discovered in the patient's hospital room, but that was all Jackson.

"I need a refill," Jackson announced, kissing Clementine's hand before excusing himself.

"Have fun," Clementine instructed.

As Jackson moved crossed the room, he spotted Paige at the center of a tight cluster of people. Her hair hung loose around her shoulders, and a man Jackson didn't recognize held her elbow proprietarily. Jackson turned away quickly and stepped out of the ballroom.

While waiting in line at the bar, Jackson suddenly felt a slap on his back.

"To the newest generation of B&D partners," his co-worker, Billy Gaines, announced, holding up his glass of scotch.

"Isn't this a bit premature?" Jackson demurred.

"Who has time for modesty?" Billy shrugged, saluting Jackson with his drink.

Billy Gaines, who was also up for partner this year, had the rosy complexion and homogenous good looks of a college sophomore, but the hairline of a senior partner.

"Hey," Billy said, snapping his fingers as if remembering something. "Are you in for Slaughterfest?"

Slaughterfest was the annual hunting trip with the male B&D lawyers and the summer clerks who'd received permanent offers. It was ostensibly a recruiting function, which meant Bourke & Donovan footed the bill, but was in reality just an excuse to get sloppy drunk and kill things on someone else's dime. Billy was in charge of planning the event this year. He'd rented a ten-room lodge on a hunting lease in Lampasas and stocked it with enough booze and guns to outfit a significant guerilla army.

"Yeah, I'm in," Jackson answered. "But this time, we are quizzing those little bastards on what *is* and *is not* an endangered species. And if one of the clerks pukes again, *you're* cleaning it up."

"I told you to let that guy clean it up himself," Billy countered.

"Well, I might have, if he hadn't already passed out face-first on his fully loaded automatic weapon."

"You're a prince among men, Jackson."

"Spare me."

Suddenly, there was an earsplitting squeal, and Jackson watched a tiny, buxom blonde throw herself into Billy's arms.

"I've been looking everywhere for you!" she whined. "You left me, you bad boy!!"

"I've been trying to find you," Billy lied, kissing her heavily painted mouth. "Terri, I would like for you to meet a buddy of mine, Jackson Polke. Jackson, this is Terri."

"Oh my God!" Terri shrieked in an octave generally accessible only to dogs. "We just studied a General Jackson B. Polke in my Texas History Class! What a wild coincidence!"

"Wild!" Billy repeated, a huge smile splitting his handsome face.

"I have to use the little girls' room," she giggled. "Now you boys don't go anywhere!"

"We'll be right here," Billy assured her, pretending to catch her blown kiss.

"Cruising high schools again?" Jackson asked him, watching Terri slink away in a gown indistinguishable from lingerie.

"She's a senior at Southwest Texas University," Billy responded.

"Many months over the legal age limit, no doubt. Where'd you find her?"

"Remember that charity golf tournament I was in a couple weeks ago?"

Jackson nodded.

"She was one of the beer girls."

"Beer girl?"

"Yeah, you know, she drove the cart with the keg in it. Itty bitty uniform."

"Nice."

"Jealous?" Billy grinned.

"Shit," Jackson replied, without really answering.

Jackson felt someone tap his shoulder, and when he turned, he found Josiah Mantooth standing beside him at the bar.

"Josiah, I didn't see you there," Jackson said, taking Josiah's extended hand.

"Could I speak to you for a moment, Jackson?" Josiah asked.

"Of course."

With a perfunctory nod to Billy, Jackson followed Josiah through the crowd to a door leading out onto the terrace. From there, they walked down the limestone steps and across a sloping lawn to a bench overlooking Town Lake.

They sat down and Josiah pulled out two cigars.

"Will you join me?"

"Twist my arm," Jackson said, taking the illicit Cuban and drawing it across his nostrils.

Josiah clipped the ends and lit their cigars. Jackson noticed that time and gravity had impacted the flesh hanging from Josiah's face, making the resemblance to a bloodhound all the more pronounced.

"Leland tells me you've been getting calls from Dr. Dodds."

"I was," Jackson confirmed, a little surprised, "but she finally got the message."

"That's a woman who has trouble accepting the word 'no.'"

"I got that impression."

"Well, I wanted to thank you for bringing it to my attention."

"Of course," Jackson said, puffing hard on his cigar.

"I've talked to her superiors at the hospital. They tell me Eleanor Dodds has lost all objectivity when it comes to Katherine's case. She's a woman obsessed, and I'm quoting here. All she wants is to further her own career, and is more than happy to use my daughter as a guinea pig."

Smoke drifted over the lake, which looked like a giant pool of rippling mercury in the moonlight. A family of ducks swam in and out of the reeds at the edge of the water, and grackles congregated in the trees overhead.

"Is there any chance Dodds could be right?" Jackson asked.

"Not according to every other doctor on staff at the hospital."

"What about other hospitals?"

"Oh, Jackson," Josiah sighed wearily. "If I thought there was any chance, I'd give Katherine the damn injections myself."

"I know," Jackson said gently. "I was just hoping something could be done."

"You and me both."

The two men sat quietly, puffing on their cigars, lost in their own thoughts.

"What about Dr. Dodds?" Jackson asked eventually.

"She won't be bothering you anymore."

5

Jackson left his car at the Four Seasons and walked back to his new downtown, industrial-style loft. He considered taking a cab, but the almost-cool night air felt good against his skin.

As he approached his building, Jackson heard a woman's voice calling his name.

"Are you Jackson Polke?"

Looking around, he saw a tall, attractive woman glaring at him from the sidewalk.

"You are Jackson Polke, aren't you?"

"I am," he answered.

The woman walked over to Jackson, close enough he could smell her perfume, and stared him straight in the eyes.

"I just want to tell you in person that I think you are a miserable son of a bitch," she spat at him.

"What?" Jackson stammered.

"You heard me," the woman continued, poking the tip of her index finger into his chest. "You are a rotten, despicable excuse for a human being, and I don't know how you live with yourself."

With each word, another sharp poke to the sternum.

"I think there's been some mistake," Jackson said, stepping away from her jabbing finger.

In response, she shoved a crumpled piece of paper at Jackson—a printout of Jackson's photo and resume from the Bourke & Donovan website.

"What are you, some kind of stalker?" Jackson demanded, suddenly unnerved.

"Don't flatter yourself," the woman snorted.

"What the hell do you want?"

"What I *want* is to punch you right in the nose."

They were starting to get stares from curious onlookers.

"How about you lower your voice," Jackson suggested.

"Screw you!"

"Listen lady," Jackson retorted, trying to remain calm, "I don't know what this is about, but I suggest you get some professional help."

For some reason, this struck the woman as particularly funny, and she let out a loud, chortling laugh.

Jackson tried to move past her, but she wouldn't let him.

"Get the hell out of my way," he told her flatly.

"Or what?"

That was a good question, Jackson thought to himself. He wasn't afraid, exactly, just at a loss for how to handle the bizarre situation.

"Or I'll be forced to call the police," he announced, hoping the threat would carry some weight.

"You're going to call the cops?" she repeated in a mocking tone.

"Yes."

"And tell them what? That I called you some names? That I hurt your feelings?"

"That a seriously disturbed woman is loitering outside my building, making bodily threats."

"God, you are such a pussy."

"That's it," Jackson told her, finally losing his patience. He pulled out his cell phone and started to dial 911.

"You do that, call the cops," she taunted contemptuously. "Tell them I'm here harassing you, yet again. You won't have any trouble getting that restraining order now. Be sure they spell my name right. That's Dodds with two Ds. Well, three actually, if you count the first one."

Jackson stared at the woman, stunned.

"Eleanor Dodds?"

"Give the boy genius a medal."

The woman facing him was nothing at all like Jackson had imagined, to the extent he'd imagined Dr. Dodds at all. Somehow, his mental picture was of a homely, uptight schoolmarm or defrocked nun. In real life, Dr. Eleanor Dodds was young and beautiful, with legs up to her neck.

Jackson closed his cell phone and slipped it back into his jacket pocket.

"Aren't you going to call the police?" she demanded.

"I don't think that's necessary. I didn't realize it was you, Dr. Dodds."

"All the more reason to turn me in. That way, you'll have documented proof of my harassment."

"Why would I want that?"

"So you can get the restraining order."

"I don't know what you're talking about."

"Isn't that what you told him? That I was harassing you, that you feared for your safety?"

"Told who?"

"My boss!" Ellie snapped. "I hope you're satisfied. Thanks to your ridiculous accusations, I'm on suspended leave from the hospital pending a psych evaluation."

"Is this some kind of joke?" Jackson asked.

"Do I sound like I'm joking?"

"Well, you aren't making much sense."

"You know what, asshole, it's one thing for you to do this to me—hell, I can always find another job—but what I can't understand is how you could do this to Katherine. I'm the only one in that place who gives a damn about her. What do you think is going to happen to her when I'm gone? Do you even give a shit?"

"Dr. Dodds, I assure you . . ."

"I thought you were supposed to protect her! Isn't that your job, for God's sake? Or can't you be bothered?"

"Will you just shut the hell up for a minute?"

Jackson hadn't meant to shout at her, but it had the desired effect. Ellie blinked at him in stunned silence.

"Thank you," he said, getting control of himself. "Now, I don't know what's happened, but there has obviously been some kind of mix-up. I am not seeking a restraining order. And as for Katherine, her family and I only want what's best for her."

"Is that so?" Ellie scoffed. "Then why haven't any of her beloved family members come to visit her?"

"I'm sure they've been busy."

"For three years?"

"Did it ever occur to you it might be too painful for them to see Katherine like that?"

"Then why did they reject a treatment that could very well help her?"

"Oh, I don't know," Jackson responded sarcastically. "Maybe because your purported treatment might very well kill her?"

"But they never even looked at the medical evidence. Hell, they wouldn't even hear me out."

"Obviously, they spoke with other doctors at the hospital."

"Not that I know of."

"Then they must have consulted with their own experts."

"Who?"

"How the hell should I know?" Jackson responded irritably. "Why are we even debating this point? Your own colleagues think it's a crackpot idea."

"My *colleagues* are afraid of getting sued. What's Josiah Mantooth afraid of?"

"Losing his only child!"

"He's already lost her, Mr. Polke," Ellie pointed out. "My crackpot idea is the only thing that might bring her back."

"What are you suggesting?" he sighed.

"That Katherine's family is content to let her rot in that padded cell, without even lifting a finger to help her."

"That's ridiculous," Jackson told her.

"Is it? If it were my loved one, I sure as hell wouldn't just give up on her, not without thoroughly investigating the alternatives."

Suddenly, the fight seemed to leave Ellie Dodds' body. She looked defeated, almost diminished, as if her anger was the last thing holding her up, and without it, she was in danger of crumpling to the ground.

"I feel sorry for you," she told Jackson sadly. "You're just another empty suit."

With those words, Dr. Eleanor Dodds turned on her heels and walked away.

6

Tommy Keane was asleep when Jackson arrived at the hospital the following morning. There was a frightening array of tubes and machines hooked up to Tommy's frail body, and a thin blue catheter poked out of his skeletal, birdlike chest gruesomely. Permeating the air was a sickening sweet smell that clung to Jackson's nostrils, emitted by the ostensibly cheerful flower arrangements lining the room.

Before he knew it, Jackson was sitting beside Tommy's bed, his head in his hands, sobbing uncontrollably.

"Enough with the waterworks. I'm not dead yet."

Jackson lifted his head and fixed his swollen, red-rimmed eyes on Tommy Keane.

The cancer was eating Tommy from the inside out. Emaciated, Tommy's skin hung off his protruding bones like a deflated balloon. Only a few strands of white hair still covered his skull, and there was a noticeable gray pallor to his skin.

"What makes you think I'm crying over you, old man?" Jackson sniffed.

"Well, for one thing, you're getting me all wet."

"How are you feeling?"

"Like shit," Tommy rasped, propping himself up on the pillows.

Jackson leaned over and gently rearranged his pajama top to cover the catheter.

"So what have you brought me today?" Tommy asked.

Jackson reached over and retrieved a brown, paper sack from the bedside table. From inside he removed a box of chocolate pecan clusters.

"What, no tequila?"

"Turns out tequila and morphine don't mix."

"Says who?"

"The nurse who searched my bag before I came in here."

"Damn Gestapo," Tommy grumbled, popping a candy into his mouth. "They've started frisking your Aunt Clementine."

"That must be a sight."

"She gives as good as she gets, though," Tommy said, chuckling. "She slapped one of the orderlies the other day, for getting fresh. You should have seen the look on his face."

"She's a tough old bird."

"That she is."

"So, other than confiscating your stash, are they treating you all right in here?" Jackson asked.

"Oh, I suppose so."

"Well, you just give me the word, and I'll bust you out of this joint," Jackson told him, only half kidding.

"I'm due for some excitement," Tommy grinned. "So, you gonna tell me why you're here on a Sunday morning?"

"I always come on Sundays," Jackson pointed out.

"Not at the crack of dawn."

"It's not that early," Jackson said, glancing at his watch.

"For you, it's early. Why the hell aren't you in bed nursing a hangover after the Settlers' Ball?"

"Didn't you know? I'm the new poster boy for temperance."

"Out with it already," Tommy commanded.

"You've got enough going on."

"Jackson, I have a limited amount of time left. Don't test my patience."

"It has to do with Katherine Van Hoerne," Jackson began uneasily, before telling Tommy about recent events, starting with the phone call from Dr. Eleanor Dodds and ending with a blow-by-blow of the confrontation with Dodds the night before.

"I see you still have a way with the ladies," Tommy laughed when Jackson was done.

"It's not funny," Jackson retorted. "She could have had a gun or something."

"Sounds like you're lucky she didn't."

"That woman has some serious anger management issues."

"Is that what's bothering you, that she might decide to come back and clock you?" Tommy asked.

"No."

"Then what?"

"It's what she said."

"You mean about you being a despicable excuse for a human being?"

"Not that—although I didn't much appreciate it," Jackson replied. "It's that business about the restraining order."

"And you're sure you never gave Leland that impression?"

"I'm sure," Jackson confirmed. "I might have used the word harassment, but I certainly never said anything about fearing for my safety or getting a TRO."

"Perhaps Bourke and Josiah Mantooth just took the matter into their own hands," Tommy suggested. "You said yourself that Dr. Dodds has been pestering the family."

"But why drag me into it? Why not just nail her with that?"

Tommy mulled that over.

"It sounds to me like they don't want you talking to Dr. Dodds," he stated at last.

"But why? I already told the woman I wouldn't circumvent the family's wishes."

"That's a good question, Jackson."

"And another thing," Jackson continued, "according to Dr. Dodds, Josiah wouldn't even hear her out about the treatment. Wouldn't even look at the medical evidence. I can understand rejecting it once he heard all the facts, but Josiah didn't even look into it, just shot her down without hearing her side."

"You did say the drug was potentially dangerous."

"It is, but what have they got to lose? Obviously, the hospital won't approve it because they don't want to get hit with a massive lawsuit, but why not the family? If this really is the only chance Katherine has, why not give it a try?"

Tommy paused before speaking.

"Well, as a man lying on his deathbed," Tommy told him, "I can tell you that there isn't anything I wouldn't try."

The words snapped Jackson's attention back to the tubes running out of Tommy's chest and the perpetual hum of machines.

"Don't say that, Tommy," he whispered.

"Why not? It's true."

"Because I don't want to hear that shit."

"Okay, no more deathbed references."

"Damn straight," Jackson mumbled. "Don't make me kick your ass."

"You and what army?" Tommy shot back, smiling.

Then Tommy took Jackson's hand and squeezed it tightly. "You're a good man, Jackson. If this situation with Katherine Van Hoerne is bothering you so much, maybe you should check it out for yourself."

"Josiah wouldn't like it."

"Screw Josiah Mantooth," Tommy remarked. "He's the one who dragged you into his goddamn family drama in the first place."

"I know, but . . ."

"Just be careful," Tommy warned, cutting him off. "I've never trusted his motives where you're concerned, him or Leland Bourke. The whole damn mess stunk to high heaven."

"I'll be careful, Tommy."

"You better, because I might not be around to pull your ass out of a sling."

"Goddamn it, stop talking like that!" Jackson nearly shouted.

"Okay, okay," Tommy said, throwing his hands up in a gesture of surrender. "Want to watch some football?"

"Yes. Yes I do."

7

A few days later, despite his better judgment, Jackson was driving out to the Dripping Springs Psychiatric Hospital. Still wrestling with his decision, he contemplated turning back for the entire way.

Jackson had always prided himself on being a decisive, take-charge kind of guy, but the question of how to handle the Katherine Van Hoerne situation had turned him into a hesitant, wavering mound of gelatin. This going back and forth was driving Jackson to distraction, made only worse by the damn conversation he'd had with Richard Adams, the head of the hospital.

Jackson had contacted Dr. Adams first thing Monday morning to discuss Eleanor Dodds, and perhaps clear up any misunderstandings that might exist.

Dr. Adams explained that the hospital staff had been concerned about Dr. Dodds' behavior for some time, and when Josiah Mantooth lodged a complaint, he had no choice but to take action.

Josiah reported to Dr. Adams that Ellie Dodds was now harassing not only the patient's family but her lawyer as well, and that Mr. Polke was contemplating legal action, specifically a restraining order. It was this particular factor that resulted in Dr. Dodds' suspension.

Jackson quickly set the matter to rights, assuring Dr. Adams that while Ellie had been persistent and annoying, she had not been in any way threatening, and no legal action would be forthcoming.

The telephone conversation left an uneasy feeling in Jackson's gut. Why would Josiah mislead Dr. Adams? In all likelihood, he was probably just trying to get ammunition against the very stubborn, very determined Dr. Dodds. Still, it didn't feel right.

In the end, Jackson decided to check things out for himself.

The psychiatric hospital was located off of Route 290 on several wooded acres in the heart of Dripping Springs. The building itself was a plain, red brick structure five floors high with plenty of windows and white shutters, surrounded by a lush lawn, magnolia trees and dozens of blooming flower beds. It might have been mistaken for an apartment complex or a nursing home, if not for the iron bars on the windows and the burly guards patrolling the grounds.

Jackson showed his identification to a uniformed security guard and drove through the gate.

He was flipping through an issue of *Psychology Today* in an aggressively cheerful reception area when Eleanor Dodds appeared in front of him.

"Mr. Polke, this is certainly an unexpected surprise," Ellie said, her manner stiff but not unfriendly.

Her soft brown curls were pulled back in a severe bun, and she wore glasses with thick tortoise shell frames.

"I'm a little surprised to be here myself," Jackson admitted. "I take it your suspension has been lifted?"

Ellie nodded and said, "Thanks to you."

"Just cleared up a misunderstanding, that's all."

"I owe you an apology, Mr. Polke," Ellie told him soberly. "I had no right speaking to you like that."

"Don't worry about it."

"I don't usually lose my temper like that."

"Glad to hear it. You being a mental health professional and all."

Ellie Dodds didn't seem to find that terribly funny.

"Is that why you came all the way out here?" Ellie asked. "To check up on me?"

"Kind of," Jackson responded. "I was hoping to get a quick tutorial on Katherine's condition and this drug, and what exactly you hope to accomplish, Dr. Dodds."

"Come again?"

"Well, you're so sure this is the right course of treatment for Katherine, how about you try to convince me."

"What is this, some kind of cruel joke?" Ellie asked, unable to grasp the sudden turn of events.

"No joke," Jackson assured her. "Contrary to what you may think, I'm not a monster."

Ellie continued to stare at him, her eyes widening.

"Honest, I just want to verify for myself that Mrs. Van Hoerne is getting the proper care."

"Really?" Ellie whispered.

"Like you said, it's my job."

An hour later, Jackson knew more about psychotropic drugs in general, and Thymetrazine in particular, than he ever cared to. Most of the medical and scientific jargon went way over his head, but there was one thing he was certain of: Dr. Eleanor Dodds knew her shit.

Although clearly passionate about her work, Ellie was a scientist at heart, and it was as a scientist, detached and unbiased, that she presented her case. Her arguments were exhaustively researched, and while she was definitely intense, there was nothing in Ellie's words or demeanor to suggest that she had lost her professional objectivity.

Essentially, Dr. Dodds' position boiled down to this: once upon a time, Thymetrazine had been a wonder drug for Katherine, and there was every reason to hope it could be again. The Thymetrazine protocol had been suspended by uniform consensus at the time of Katherine's arrest. It remained the only course of treatment not tried since then, and it represented Katherine Van Hoerne's very last chance.

Jackson was on his second cup of coffee by the time Ellie finished her impromptu presentation. His head was reeling from the influx of caffeine and medical jargon, but he had absorbed at least most of what Dr. Dodds imparted, or the gist anyway.

"I certainly appreciate your conviction, Dr. Dodds," Jackson said when Ellie had finished, declining another coffee refill. "And thank you for taking the time to see me."

"Call me Ellie," she told him.

"Okay, Ellie," Jackson said quietly, trying to figure out how to break the news gently. "As much as I personally might choose another path, this is a matter for the family, and I have not heard anything this afternoon that is so undeniably compelling that I would override the express wishes of Josiah Mantooth."

"Compelling how?" Ellie asked evenly.

"Excuse me?"

"You need something compelling? That's what you said, right?"

"Uh, yes, but . . ."

"Fair enough," Ellie told him, standing up from the couch. "I want you to see something."

Jackson followed Ellie through the wide, vinyl-tiled corridors on the fourth floor of the Dripping Springs Psychiatric Hospital. There were several security checkpoints and a series of steel gates spaced every ten yards or so that Ellie accessed with a magnetic pass card. Even with the thick, concrete walls and metal barriers, Jackson could hear screaming.

More to block out the cacophony than anything, Jackson tried to make small talk with Ellie as they walked.

"So, do you live here in Dripping Springs?" Jackson asked her.

"I tried to for awhile," Ellie replied, seemingly unfazed by the ruckus, "but I'm not cut out for country living. Way too quiet, nothing to do. I got a place in Austin last year, and I'm much happier."

"You like Austin?"

"Yes, very much. You lived there long?"

"My whole life."

Midway down the last hall, Ellie stopped in front of a gray metal door. She flashed her card in front of a monitor and the door clicked open. Inside was a small room with a handful of chairs, and a metal desk in the corner. On the back wall was an enormous mirror that appeared strangely opalescent in the dim light.

Ellie sat down in one of the chairs and invited Jackson to do the same. When he was settled, Ellie pressed a button on a handheld remote device and the mirror disappeared in front of Jackson's eyes. Suddenly, he was looking through clear glass into a sterile, white hospital room, padded from floor to ceiling.

It took several moments for Jackson to register that the pathetic creature curled up in the fetal position on the narrow bed was Katherine Van Hoerne.

"W-what happened to her hair?" Jackson whispered, at a loss for anything else to say.

"She ate it," Ellie replied calmly.

Katherine's bald head was bruised and disfigured, like rotting fruit, and her face was a waxy lump of overlapping contusions, a veritable rainbow of purple, black, and greenish-yellow bruises. Her lips were split and swollen, and her nose puffed up to the size of a tennis ball.

Sensing his thoughts, Ellie explained, "There was another episode over the weekend, and the swelling hasn't gone down yet."

"Episode?"

"One of the new orderlies accidentally left a metal tray in the room. He came back a few minutes later, but by then she'd done that to herself."

"How?"

"She knocked the tray to the floor, then banged her head against it until she lost consciousness."

"Jesus," Jackson whispered.

Katherine looked wasted, cadaverous, her skin the color of chalk—nothing more than a pile of sharp, disjointed bones in a withered flesh bag.

Suddenly, Jackson was struck by the resemblance between Katherine and Tommy—withered limbs, lifeless pallor, hairless skulls—just battered, breathing carcasses waiting to die.

Stars began to explode in Jackson's peripheral vision and his mouth filled with saliva. For a moment, he thought he might be sick.

Jackson caught one last look of Katherine—staring vacantly at the two-way mirror, her glassy, unfocused eyes utterly blank—before he pushed his chair back with a crash and ran from the room.

Ellie found him several minutes later, his forehead pressed against the corridor wall and his eyes squeezed shut. Once Jackson had regained his composure, he turned slowly to face her.

"Do it," he said in a trembling voice.

"Come again?" Ellie asked.

"Do it," Jackson repeated more loudly. "Give her the goddamn drug!"

8

For Jackson, sleep was elusive that night.

In the harsh light of reality, far away from the hideous 4th floor of the psychiatric hospital, Jackson could hardly believe what he'd done. Authorizing the drug therapy without even informing Josiah and the family was a stupid, asinine impulse, and he regretted it more with every passing hour.

But then, when he did manage to momentarily nod off from sheer exhaustion, he was haunted by visions of the present-day Katherine Van Hoerne.

In his dreams, she was held captive in a giant birdcage of barbed wire, contentedly eating her own flesh. Katherine gnawed on the exposed bone of her forearm and the suddenly sensed Jackson's presence, lifting her head to him. Her eyeballs were missing, having been plucked from her head earlier, and black, gelatinous goo oozed from her hollow sockets.

"You did this to me!" she shrieked over and over in a wailing singsong, blood and sinew dripping from her rotted, toothless gums. That's when Jackson woke up with a start, a film of cold sweat covering his body.

Sometime during the early morning hours, Jackson was roused from his restless sleep by an insistent, relentless buzz. It took him several moments to recognize the sound. He looked at his watch, furiously kicked back the sheets and stumbled to the intercom.

"Who the hell is this?" Jackson demanded, fully expecting to hear the apologetic whining of some idiot neighbor who'd forgotten his keys.

"Josiah Mantooth."

Oh Christ, Jackson moaned, holding onto the wall for support.

Having no other immediate options, he buzzed Josiah up and then scrambled to throw on some jeans and a t-shirt. He was still buttoning his pants when he heard a thunderous knock on the door.

Jackson took a couple of deep breaths to clear his head and calm his nerves, and turned the doorknob.

"Josiah, what are you doing here?" he asked, trying to sound surprised and slightly indignant. "Do you know what time it is?"

Ignoring the question, Josiah pushed his way past Jackson into the apartment.

"I understand you've been trying to reach me," Josiah said evenly, making himself comfortable on a pale gray sofa.

"Yes, yes I have," Jackson answered, closing the door. "I was told you were in Houston on business."

"I'm back," Josiah informed him, pointing out the obvious. "What did you want to talk to me about?"

It was evident from Josiah's appearance on his doorstep at 3:30 in the morning, and the glacial expression on his hangdog face, that Josiah knew damn well what Jackson wanted to talk about.

In that instant, Jackson realized that he had underestimated Josiah's relationship with Richard Adams, and a chill rolled down his spine.

"Would you like something to drink?" Jackson asked, attempting to postpone the inevitable.

"No. I want to know why you went to see Katherine today."

"To see her for myself."

"Is that right?"

"That's right," Jackson replied calmly. "And you know what I found out? That she is dying in there, Josiah. And it is a slow, painful, horrific death."

"So you took it upon yourself to authorize an experimental drug treatment," Josiah said in a low, clipped tone, his words hanging in the air like a sour odor.

"Jesus, Josiah," Jackson sighed, exasperated, "it's hard to know what the right thing is anymore."

Josiah leaned forward, resting his elbows on his knees, and glared at Jackson.

"Then let me help you out, son," he said, his tone icy and even. "You're going to call that doctor friend of yours and tell her that you made a mistake. A serious mistake."

"I'm not sure I can do that," Jackson responded.

"You're not understanding me, boy," Josiah countered. "I'm not *asking* you, I'm telling you. You're going to call that Dodds woman and put a stop to this, now."

"Josiah, you should go see Katherine for yourself . . ."

"Who the hell do you think you are, telling me what I should and shouldn't do? You work for me, remember."

"Actually, I'm Katherine's lawyer," Jackson reminded him. "That means I represent her interests, not yours."

"You're not going to be anyone's goddamn lawyer if you don't watch it. You know what they say—mess with the bull, you get the horns."

"Are you threatening me?" Jackson asked incredulously.

"You do not want to screw with me, Mr. Polke," Josiah replied coolly.

"Or what?"

"Or I'll rip your goddamn head off and fuck your dead, dry skull."

Jackson was too stunned to respond.

"Close your trap, son," Josiah instructed, putting his empty glass on the coffee table. "It'll attract flies."

Josiah pushed himself up from the sofa and sauntered to the door. Before he left, he said, "You'll do the right thing, Jackson, and then it'll be like this conversation never happened."

When his cell phone rang ten minutes later, Jackson was still sitting in the same position, mouth still agape.

"Jackson, come quick," Clementine said when Jackson answered the phone. "It's Tommy."

9

"His body just isn't able to fight the infection," Dr. Fordham, the oncologist, told them soberly. "There's a chance he won't make it through the night, which is why we called you. We knew you'd want to be here."

"Can't you just give him an antibiotic?" Jackson asked miserably. "It's just a cold, for God's sake."

"Actually, the infection's spread to his lungs, which means we're now dealing with pneumonia."

"But you can treat that, right?"

"Normally, yes, but his white blood cells were all but wiped out during the last round of chemotherapy. With his immune system compromised, he's virtually defenseless against the spread of bacteria. We're giving him drugs to boost his counts, and we've got him on an aggressive antibiotic regimen. All we can do now is wait and see. And pray, of course."

"Pray?" Jackson snapped. "That's your brilliant recommendation—prayer?"

"That's uncalled for Jackson," Clementine reprimanded. "You'll have to excuse my nephew, Dr. Fordham. Obviously, this is very upsetting news."

"I understand," the doctor replied, bobbing his head in a gesture that struck Jackson as rehearsed.

"I think we should find another doctor," Jackson said as Dr. Fordham disappeared down the corridor, his white coat trailing behind.

"Don't be ridiculous, Jackson," Clementine retorted. "He's the best. Besides, there isn't a doctor on the planet who's going to tell you what you want to hear."

The hospital was even more depressing at night than it was during the day, which Jackson hadn't thought possible, and the hushed stillness and dusky shadows were downright creepy.

Jackson couldn't help but be reminded of his visit to the psychiatric hospital. His visit now seemed a lifetime ago, the events of the day a blur.

"Oh, darlin', you look awful," Clementine said, caressing his cheek tenderly. "Is there something else on your mind?"

"It's been a hell of a day, Clem," he said numbly. "That's all."

"You work too hard, Jackson," she chided.

"I'm fine. Really."

"Should we go in and see if he's awake?"

Jackson nodded, and the two of them put on the paper masks Dr. Fordham had given them earlier, looping the elastic bands around their ears.

Even with the mask, the smell was almost overpowering, a mixture of disinfectant, decay and desiccated flowers, and Jackson had to swallow hard to keep from gagging. Clementine didn't seem to notice as she took her regular seat at Tommy's bedside, and gingerly clasped his hand. Tommy's eyes fluttered open and he managed a weak smile, but it came across as more of a grimace.

"Did we wake you, darlin'?" Clementine whispered.

Tommy cleared his throat, a terrible hacking sound.

"A man can't very well sleep through his own death," he wheezed.

"I won't stand for any of that negative talk, Thomas Keane," Clementine scolded. "You're going to beat this bug, and I don't want hear any different."

Chuckling wetly, Tommy squeezed her hand.

Turning his head to Jackson, he said, "Your aunt here has been buying me all sorts of crazy new age books about the power of positive thinking."

"It can't hurt," Jackson said, pulling up a chair.

"Can I get you anything, darlin'?" Clementine asked. "Do you want something to drink?"

"I could sure use a beer," Tommy told her, only half joking.

"How about a root beer?"

"That sounds good, Clem," Tommy replied, a look of affection on his shriveled face.

"I'll go find one. Now, don't you boys go anywhere while I'm gone."

"Damn," Tommy teased. "There goes our getaway plan."

After she'd left the room, Tommy raised himself to a seated position and was immediately seized by a coughing fit that rumbled in his chest like a freight train. Jackson grabbed a cup of water from the bedside table and held the straw to Tommy's bloodless lips, and he managed a few sips.

"Should I call the nurse?" Jackson asked.

Tommy shook his head and wiped his mouth with a tissue.

"Hell no," he said. "The last thing I need is that old bat hovering over me."

"You sure?"

"I'm sure."

Jackson put the cup down and arranged Tommy's pillows to make him more comfortable.

"How's that?" he asked.

"Better."

"Is there anything else I can do?"

"You can stop fussing over me and tell me what happened with Katherine Van Hoerne."

"Nothing you need to concern yourself with," Jackson told him flatly.

"How about you let me be the judge of that."

"How about we talk about something else."

"Jackson, I'm the one dying here. I should at least be able to dictate the topic of conversation, seeing as how it might be my last and all."

Jackson desperately wanted to tell Tommy about the surreal events of the day. Ever since Jackson was a child, he'd relied on Tommy to make sense of the world and protect him from whatever was out there. Unfortunately, it was now Jackson's turn to be strong.

"Like I said, there's nothing to discuss," Jackson said more forcefully than he'd intended. "Now, can we please just drop it?"

Tommy searched Jackson's eyes and realized he wasn't going to budge.

"Have it your way," Tommy said finally. "But there's something I want you to know."

"What's that."

"A dying man does a lot of thinking, Jackson," Tommy sighed. "You end up reviewing your whole life like some kind of goddamn newsreel. Sometimes the good outweighs the bad and sometimes it doesn't, but it all comes down to one thing: a man's character. When push comes to shove, it's the only thing that really matters.

"You're a fine man, Jackson. You can trust that. When a situation arises, just follow your gut. Listen to your internal compass. At the end of the day, that's what counts."

"I understand," Jackson said, his voice hitching in his throat.

"I'm mighty grateful to have been a part of your life," Tommy whispered, fighting back his own tears. "Thank you for that."

"I'm going to miss you, you old goat."

"I love you too, son."

10

News that Eleanor Dodds had gotten permission for her audacious experiment spread through the hospital like wildfire, and a small crowd gathered in the observation room as Ellie inserted a needle in Katherine's IV. Ellie would have found all the sudden interest amusing if she weren't so damn nervous.

For all of her zealous campaigning for the Thymetrazine protocol, Ellie still didn't know what to expect. She had plenty of theories, but there was simply no way to predict how or when Katherine would respond to the treatment. For that reason alone, Ellie would have preferred not to have an audience, especially during the early stages, but there wasn't much she could do about it. The hospital staff would be watching her like hawks from here on out.

The first incremental doses of Thymetrazine were introduced into Katherine's system 48 hours before, and the initial results were positive. Within hours, the drug seemed to have a calming effect, lulling Katherine into a tranquil semi-conscious state and short-circuiting whatever impulse triggered her incessant self-mutilation.

To the casual observer, she appeared catatonic or even comatose, which was not necessarily an improvement, but Ellie saw the shift as promising and she steadily increased the dosage. To Ellie's disappointment, there had been no further results. Even with the higher concentration of Thymetrazine, there had been no visible change in Katherine's condition for over a day.

Her audience eventually dispersed, whispering among themselves.

Finally alone, Ellie leaned back in her chair and closed her eyes. She hadn't slept in days, refusing to leave Katherine for so much as a minute, and it was starting to make her irritable and slightly ill. The chair was extremely uncomfortable, but within moments, she was fast asleep.

Waking with a start, Ellie found a nurse standing over her.

"I'm sorry to bother you, Dr. Dodds," she said, "but I thought you might want to see this."

Bolting upright, Ellie rubbed her face and looked through the two-way glass. Katherine was still lying on her bed—but everything had changed.

Katherine's eyes were wide open.

Gone were the glassy, vacant, lifeless orbs that floated in her head like two dead fish. These eyes were clear, alert, focused.

Before Ellie could fully register this fact, Katherine pushed herself up on her elbows and looked around.

"Jesus, Mary and Joseph," the nurse gasped, crossing herself fervently before launching into a Hail Mary.

"Shhh," Ellie commanded, watching as Katherine examined her surroundings.

Katherine's eyes moved over and around the room purposefully, clearly assessing an unfamiliar environment. Katherine's face reflected a rapidly shifting emotional landscape, revealing, in turns, bewilderment, perplexity, apprehension and fear. Eventually, after she'd run the gamut of confusion and uncertainty, a dawning comprehension slowly spread across her once beautiful features.

She looked dazed and terribly confused, but Katherine Van Hoerne was clearly cognizant of a reality beyond the chambers of her own mind.

A flush of excitement coursed through Ellie's body and she moved closer to the viewing wall, practically pressing her nose against the glass.

Watching Katherine, Ellie could almost see the cogs and gears of her awakening brain, corroded and rusty from years of disuse, crank into action. It was like someone had suddenly flipped a switch, and the levers locked into place.

Katherine suddenly sat up and swung her legs over the side of the bed. She touched the floor with her toes hesitantly, as if testing water, and then put her full weight on her feet. Standing, Katherine quickly found her balance and began pacing the room.

"I'll be damned," Ellie muttered, almost breathless with anticipation.

The nurse reached out a hand to press the call button and summon additional staff, but Ellie stopped her.

Katherine seemed to be thinking—hard—and her pacing took on a frantic pace. Her lips moved soundlessly, reminding Ellie of a mathematician doing complex calculations in her head.

Ellie would have given almost anything to know what was going on inside her patient's skull at that moment.

As Katherine paced in a cramped circle, retracing her steps over and over, she seemed to become more and more agitated. And then she became, quite clearly and visibly, angry.

Abruptly, Katherine glared into the mirror accusingly, her eyes little more than smoldering slits. Ellie's flesh broke out in goose bumps.

In that instant, Katherine's rage boiled over and she flew into a violent screaming frenzy, tearing apart the bedding and trying to dislodge the metal frame. She picked up a metal chair inadvertently left in a corner sometime during her semi-comatose state, and hurled it at the mirror.

The chair bounced off the shatterproof glass, which seemed to only fuel Katherine's fury.

Ellie pressed the emergency call button and then, in a surprisingly calm voice, instructed the nurse to administer a mild dose of Thorazine to the patient. The woman nearly ran out of the observation room, shaking.

Ellie remained behind the mirror and watched as two huge orderlies rushed into the room, followed by two more. They eventually managed to get the chair away from Katherine and wrestle her to the floor. She struggled like a wounded animal—biting, scratching—exacting a significant amount of punishment in the process.

As soon as the orderlies had Katherine pinned down, the nurse barged into the room with a large syringe. Katherine saw it and began cursing at the top of her lungs.

Ellie observed all of this and her lips twitched into the beginnings of a smile.

11

Jackson stood outside Leland Bourke's office, trying to regulate his breathing.

His nerves were shot after way too many cups of bad coffee during his long hospital vigil. No longer able to avoid Leland Bourke's summons, this was the first time Jackson had left the hospital in two days.

Eleanor Dodds had phoned him only hours before with the news that Katherine was showing definite signs of improvement. Bolstered by this knowledge, Jackson rapped his knuckles against the wooden door and turned the handle.

"Jackson, it's good of you to come," Leland said, rising from his desk but not offering Jackson his hand. "Please, sit down."

"Thank you."

"How's Tommy?"

"Not great."

"I'm sorry to hear that," Leland told him, sliding into the chair behind his desk.

"I take it Josiah called you," Jackson began, getting directly to the point.

"What were you thinking, Jackson, interfering with Katherine's medical treatment like that? Josiah is understandably quite upset."

"I was thinking about the welfare of my client. I thought it was about time someone did."

"You are not the only person who cares about Katherine's welfare, Jackson," Leland told him, his tone reproachful.

"You should see her, Leland," Jackson told him. "She's unrecognizable—emaciated, bruised—like one of those skeletons freed from the concentration camps after World War II."

Leland lowered his chin and said, "I've been updated on Katherine's condition."

"Then you can understand why I authorized the treatment."

"No, actually, I can't," Leland corrected. "This is clearly a matter for the family, and the family alone, to address. You had no business inserting yourself into a private, complicated situation."

"So I should have just left her like that, to rot in that God-forsaken place?"

"Of course not," Leland snapped. "What you *should* have done is informed Josiah about the situation and let him handle it. Katherine is his daughter, for Christ's sake, not yours."

Jackson considered his next words carefully, aware that he was moving into dangerous territory.

"Perhaps Josiah isn't as concerned about Katherine's welfare as he would have us believe."

Leland's features hardened as he studied Jackson.

"Need I remind you," Leland replied in a silky voice, "that Josiah Mantooth is not only a very important client, but a close personal friend?"

Jackson met Leland's gaze head on and stated, "Maybe you don't know Josiah as well as you think you do."

The challenge hung in the air dramatically as the two men stared at each other hard, both refusing to blink.

At last Leland said, "Josiah intends to transfer Katherine to another facility, one where she can receive the proper attention. You can rest assured that from here on out, Katherine will be well cared for, which should allay any concerns you have about her welfare."

"What about the Thymetrazine?"

"What about it? That's an issue for the medical professionals and Katherine's family, not the lawyers."

For several seconds, Jackson deliberated. Leland was giving him an out—a way to extricate himself from the whole thing in good conscience—and it was an extremely attractive offer. Unfortunately, there were no guarantees that Katherine would be any better off than she was before.

"I'm sorry, Leland, but it's not that simple. According to Dr. Dodds, the Thymetrazine is working. I cannot sit idly by and watch a new batch of doctors terminate the drug protocol, a course of action I believe would greatly undermine my client's health and well-being."

"I suggest you take some time to reconsider," Leland told him, a distinct edge creeping into his tone.

"I don't need any more time," Jackson said with finality.

Leland placed his palms on the desk and leaned forward. Any semblance of a calm, cool demeanor evaporated.

"Who the hell do you think you are?" he hissed.

"I'll tell you who I am," Jackson replied in a monotone. "I am Mrs. Van Hoerne's attorney, and whatever plans Josiah has for Katherine will have to go through me."

Leland shook his head, as if gravely disappointed.

"Not for long," he responded, opening a desk drawer.

Leland extracted several documents and passed them over to Jackson. Leafing through them quickly, Jackson's hands began to shake.

He was holding three separate legal documents: an emergency motion to remove Jackson as Katherine's attorney; an official petition to the State Bar Disciplinary Committee for the immediate suspension of Jackson's law license and the initiation of disbarment proceedings; and a civil complaint against Jackson individually, charging him with gross legal malpractice and seeking unspecified damages in excess of ten million dollars. They were all signed, but none bore a stamp indicating it had been filed.

"You've got to be shitting me," Jackson whispered, the color draining from his face.

"Obviously, in light of these developments, I have no choice but to ask for your resignation from Bourke & Donovan."

"Obviously," Jackson repeated.

The tenor of Leland's voice changed almost imperceptibly as he said, "Of course, we can rip those documents up right here and now; it's entirely up to you."

The threat was so obvious, so *naked*, that Jackson actually blinked in surprise.

"Jesus, Leland, if I didn't know any better, I'd think you want to keep Katherine Van Hoerne crazy . . ."

"Watch yourself, son," Leland warned.

Clenching the documents in his fist, Jackson stood up and glowered down at his former boss.

"Go fuck yourself, Leland."

Jackson marched out of the office without another word. As he waited by the elevators, he felt his cell phone vibrate in his pocket. Clementine's name appeared on the digital display.

12

The empty bottle fell to the floor with a soft thud. Through Jackson's bleary tequila haze, the bottle split into two mirror images and then he watched the objects merge back into one.

Double vision. Under ordinary circumstances, a cause for concern, but today a reassuring measure of success.

Jackson was sitting in Tommy's favorite chair in the New Braunfels house, wrapped in his friend's ancient plaid robe. His goal was to get as much of the tequila into his system as he could before throwing up or passing out or both.

Hauling himself off the well-worn brown suede, Jackson stood up, swaying like a cornstalk in a stiff breeze. He staggered toward the bar, tripped on the rug and landed with a sickening crash on the floor, smacking his head against the coffee table on the way down.

"Shit," Jackson groaned, rubbing his forehead.

He might have stayed down for the count, were it not for the stacks of dusty books and magazines he saw on the coffee table, virtually all with old playing cards sticking out from between their pages. Tommy used cards to mark his place in things he planned to get back to.

Jackson fingered the cards gingerly and a wave of grief crashed against his ribcage.

Ignoring his throbbing skull, Jackson forced himself to get up and stumble to the liquor cabinet. He extracted another bottle of Heradura Reserve, twisted off the lid and swigged the amber liquid greedily, which created a lovely burning sensation as it went down.

Catching the shiny, black eye of a stuffed deer head mounted on the wall, Jackson raised his arm in a mock toast.

"To Tommy," he slurred.

Out of nowhere, a ringing sound echoed through the house. For several seconds, Jackson thought the deer had somehow figured out a way to respond.

"Go away," he shouted, when he finally realized it was the doorbell, but the ringing only became more insistent.

"Goddammit, go away!" he yelled, sinking back into the overstuffed chair.

He heard the front door creak open and a female voice calling into the house.

"Mr. Polke? Jackson, are you here?"

Eleanor Dodds moved into the room, navigating the darkened entryway with some trepidation, still unsure of whether she should be there at all. Ellie didn't want to intrude on Jackson's sorrow, especially since they weren't exactly friends, but her feelings of remorse and responsibility drove her on.

"Jackson? Are you here?"

All the curtains were drawn and it took a few moments for Ellie's eyes to grow accustomed to the shadowy gloom. When they did, she saw Jackson slumped down in a tattered chair, a bottle of booze resting precariously on his knee.

"Well, if it isn't Dr. Eleanor Dodds, headshrinker extraordinaire," he mumbled. "Whatever brings you all the way out to New Braunfels?"

She may have been the last person Jackson expected to see wander into Tommy's house, but in his present state of inebriation, nothing could really shock him.

"Your secretary told me that I could find you here," Ellie replied, bending over to switch on a brass lamp.

"*Former* secretary," Jackson corrected brusquely.

In the dim light, Jackson looked even worse. His blondish hair was sticking up in all directions, and there were ghoulish purple bags under his bloodshot eyes. He inexplicably wore a ratty robe over his jeans and white cotton undershirt, which gave him the appearance of a doddering old man. It was obvious he hadn't slept or bathed in some time.

"Your secretary said you've had a rough go of it," Ellie added gently.

"Ahh, Loretta, always looking out for me."

"She's worried about you. So am I."

"*Me? Moi?*" Jackson drawled thickly. "Why on earth would you be worried about lil' ol' me?"

"Well, for starters, you're obviously drunk."

"Ah, ah, ah," Jackson said, ticking his finger back and forth in admonishment. "I am not drunk, I am *shitfaced.* You'd know there was a difference if you were any kind of drinker."

"You got me there," Ellie replied, reaching to take the bottle away.

"Don't even think about it," Jackson growled, clasping the liquor to his chest, spilling some on Tommy's robe in the process.

Ellie sat on the arm of the battered leather sofa. Perched over Jackson, she watched him closely, concern and pity clouding her pretty features.

"Loretta, is it? She told me you left your job," Ellie said.

"Oh, *that*," Jackson chortled morosely. "Just the tip of the iceberg, *that.*"

"I'm sure things aren't as bad as they seem . . ."

"Did she tell you the rest?"

"Who?"

"My secretary."

"I understand that someone very close to you has passed away," Ellie replied softly, groping for the right words.

"His name was Tommy Keane," Jackson told her in a low, raspy voice. "This is his house. *Was* his house. It's mine now."

"Why don't you tell me about Tommy," Ellie suggested.

Jackson stared at her suspiciously.

"Are you trying to shrink me?"

"I just thought you might want to talk. That's all."

"Well, I don't!" Jackson thundered, rising unsteadily from his chair. "All I want is to be left alone."

"I don't think you should be alone right now."

"Who the hell asked you?!"

Jackson was now towering over Ellie, and she could smell the alcohol on his breath.

"I think you should leave," Jackson told her. "Now."

Ellie didn't much like the idea of leaving Jackson alone in this condition, especially with all the shotguns lining the walls.

"Aren't you going to offer me a drink?" she asked instead.

Jackson blinked at her dumbly.

"Where are my manners?" he finally answered, all other thoughts flying out of his nearly pickled brain. "You like tequila?"

"I like margaritas."

"Pussy drink."

"Do you have any white wine?"

"Screw that," Jackson spat. "In Tommy's house, by God, we drink tequila."

"Then tequila it is."

"Damn right."

Jackson stumbled to the bar and took a shot glass from the shelf.

Filling it to the rim, Jackson brought it over to Ellie. She took a tiny sip and tried not to grimace.

"Jesus, didn't you go to college?" Jackson demanded.

"I studied in college."

"Swallow it."

"All of it?" Ellie asked uncertainly.

"All of it."

"Right," she said, bracing herself. "Cheers."

Ellie brought the glass to her lips, tilted it back and choked the tequila down in one ferocious swallow. Coughing wildly, Ellie's face turned crimson.

"It gets easier," he told her.

"Oh yeah?" she wheezed.

"Trust me," he responded, refilling Ellie's glass despite her protests. "We're drinking to Tommy, and Tommy never had just one."

Ellie grunted and grudgingly emptied the second shot.

Nodding approvingly, Jackson slumped down next to Ellie on the couch

"He must have been quite a guy, this Tommy," Ellie said, once she could breathe again.

"The best," Jackson said sadly. "He would have liked you."

"Oh yeah?"

"Yeah. Of course, he'd be fixing to kick my ass right about now, but you he'd like."

"I doubt he'd want to kick your ass."

"Oh man, he would kick my ass from here to Sunday," Jackson told her grimly. "He warned me, you know. All those years ago, when I first got involved with Katherine's case, he warned me to stay the hell out of it. Did I listen? Nooooo. I was so sure I could handle it, handle Leland and Josiah and whoever else came along. What a goddamn joke."

Jackson looked so vulnerable, so lost, Ellie reached out and lightly touched his hand.

"I'm sure he was very proud of you," she soothed.

Jackson pulled his hand back and wiped at his eyes irritably.

"I'm just glad he's not around to see the mess I've made of my life."

"You don't mean that."

"The hell I don't."

"You can always find another job, Jackson," Ellie reassured him.

"Not without a goddamn law license, I can't."

"What does that mean?"

"Josiah's petitioning to have me disbarred."

"I don't understand."

"Which word did you not understand?" Jackson slurred. "Perhaps I can come up with a cinnamon."

"A *synonym*," Ellie corrected absently.

"A what?"

"What you meant to say was *synonym*."

"That's what I said."

"No, you said *cinnamon.*"

"Why the hell would I be talking about cinnamon?"

"You weren't, you just . . ." Ellie sighed. "Can Josiah really get you disbarred?"

"He's sure as hell gonna try."

"But why would he do that?" Ellie retorted, a little stunned. "Because you tried to help Katherine?"

"Pretty much."

"Well, you'll just have to explain to the judge or whoever that you were only looking out for Katherine's best interests and . . ."

"Josiah's suing me for malpractice, so might be hard to get a judge to listen," Jackson countered, taking a long swallow straight from the bottle.

"Malpractice?"

"Did I forget to mention that?"

"But you didn't do anything wrong!"

"Maybe we can sign you up for jury duty."

"This isn't right," Ellie said vehemently.

"Oh, it gets better. You especially, doctor, will appreciate this one," Jackson said, as if letting her in on some inside joke. "I'm not going to be Katherine's lawyer anymore."

"What?" Ellie whispered, finally grasping the full severity of the situation.

"Josiah's already filed an emergency motion to have me removed as Katherine's attorney."

"And then what?"

"And then Josiah Mantooth can do whatever the hell he goddamn pleases."

"What about Katherine's treatment?" Ellie demanded stubbornly. "She's finally making some real progress!"

"I think we both know the answer to that."

"What the hell?" Ellie cried, jumping to her feet. "He can't do this! We won't let him!"

"What do you propose we do? This is a man who, without a second thought, decimated my entire life in a matter of days, all because I had the audacity to disagree with him. And he considered me his *friend*."

"I don't care who he is, we can't let him get away with this!"

"Uh-huh."

"That's it? You're just going to roll over and play dead?"

"I wouldn't use that particular analogy, but yes, that is the idea."

"You're just going to let that son of a bitch walk all over you?!" Ellie shouted.

"Actually, I'm going to beg for mercy," Jackson told her, belching loudly. "If I'm a good boy and play nice, and get really lucky, he'll let me keep my law license. If I get super, duper lucky, he won't strip me of everything I own. Then, I can move far, far away and never, ever have to think about Josiah goddamn Mantooth again."

Ellie shook her head pointedly.

"No!"

"Maybe a beach somewhere," Jackson continued dreamily. "A little hut near the water, catching fish for my dinner, cooking over an open fire. . ."

"Okay Robinson Crusoe, you're just not thinking straight."

"I might enjoy getting back to basics."

"Goddammit, Jackson!" Ellie yelled. "You can't possibly kowtow to that horrible man!"

"Why not?"

"Because you just *can't*!"

"Just watch me, darlin'."

Ellie paused, before asking accusatorily, "What would your friend Tommy think of that?"

Jackson turned his head slowly and glared at her.

"Katherine still needs you," Ellie added plaintively. "Would Tommy approve of you just throwing her to the wolves? How proud do you think he'd be of that?"

"Screw you!"

"No, screw you!" she yelled back.

Jackson lurched off the couch and grabbed Ellie by the arm, swinging her around to face him. Her nose was inches from his, and she could feel his warm breath on her mouth. Ellie winced at the pressure on her arm, and Jackson immediately released his grip, dropping his hands to his sides.

"I'm sorry," he stammered, stepping backwards.

"No, I'm sorry," Ellie reassured him.

"Why the hell are you sorry?" Jackson asked, running his fingers through his thick hair.

"I'm the one who got you into this awful mess."

"I understood the consequences."

They stood there in silence for a few moments, not looking at each other.

At last Ellie asked, "Do you think I could have some more of that tequila?"

"Absolutely," Jackson replied, grabbing the bottle off the table where he'd left it. "What a fantastic idea."

Two hours later, Eleanor Dodds was as drunk as Jackson, and nearly as depressed.

She was sitting on the floor, leaning against the couch, studying a set of gleaming antlers branching from the beheaded remains of an enormous deer.

In her heavy, swirling head, the same thought circled around and around.

"There's something I just don't understand," she murmured thickly. "And it just won't get out of my mind."

Jackson was lying on the rug, his neck propped up by several throw pillows, the Heradura bottle resting on his belly.

"What's that?" he asked, unscrewing the lid and taking another swig.

"*Why?*"

"Why what?

"Why would he do it?"

"He who?"

"Him!"

"Josiah? Because he's a goddamn bastard."

"Yeah, but she's his daughter."

"Yes, she is."

"You'd think he'd be thanking you."

"You would."

"It's like he's scared or something. Like he's scared of Katherine, what she might say if she's ever able to say anything ever again."

"Perhaps he would rather his psychotic, homicidal daughter remain safe and secure in her nice padded surroundings."

"But it's like he's doing everything he can to keep her crazy," Ellie ruminated in a distant voice. "Not just institutionalized, but insane . . ."

Jackson tilted his head, focusing his blurry vision on Ellie's face. "Say that again."

"Huh?"

"What you just said, say it again," Jackson instructed in a suddenly serious tone of voice.

"Um, Josiah wants to keep Katherine insane?"

"*Not just institutionalized, but insane,*" he pressed, "like completely nutso, incoherent, can't even speak kind of crazy."

"Well, I can go through the clinical terms if you're interested . . ."

"Who the hell knows what's locked in Katherine's brain," Jackson went on. "Clay Van Hoerne said the son of a bitch always wanted her locked away . . ."

"What?"

"Yeah, it was quite a bone of contention. Clay refused to institutionalize Katherine, and Josiah couldn't make him."

"He's a United States Congressman now, Clay Van Hoerne, did you know that? Well, of course you did, he's your congressman, after all," Ellie slurred. "Did you vote for him? I didn't. Just couldn't."

Suddenly, Jackson sat bolt upright on the floor, his eyes wide and his mouth slightly agape.

"Holy shit!" he whispered.

"Holy shit what?"

"Holy shit, Angel Ramirez!"

"The man Katherine killed?"

"Jesus Christ, I can't believe I didn't think of this sooner. That goddamn son of a bitch!"

"Wait a minute, back up," Ellie said, losing track of the conversation. "I'm not following."

"Josiah got Leland to drag me into it from the start. Hell, he even got me to act as Katherine's attorney!"

"Why you?"

"Because of Tommy."

"*Your* Tommy?"

"*My* Tommy. He was the district attorney at the time."

"What about it?"

"It's complicated," Jackson said, "but suffice it to say that Josiah and Leland ensured that Katherine would never go to trial. At the time, I thought they were protecting her, but what if that wasn't it at all. What if they *wanted* Katherine to end up in the loony bin?"

"We don't like that term."

"Whatever. The point is, maybe this was Josiah's way of getting around Clay, to force Katherine into an institution."

"Wait a minute, are you suggesting Katherine was set up?" Ellie asked.

"Why not?"

"*Why not?*" Ellie echoed incredulously.

"I'm saying it's possible."

"That would mean someone else killed what's his name."

"Angel Ramirez."

"And set up Katherine to take the fall."

"Thus forcing her into an institution."

A heavy silence descended on the room as Jackson considered this, his head cocked to the side.

"Let's find out," he said after a moment.

"Huh?"

Jackson got to his feet and snatched up his cell phone.

"What are you doing?" Ellie asked.

"Calling the police."

"You're what?"

"You heard me."

"Are you nuts?"

"We don't like that term," Jackson responded, looking up the number for the Austin Police Department.

"What are you going to say?" Ellie demanded. "*Oh, hello officer, we were just trolling for conspiracy theories and I've got a good one . . .*"

"Seems to me, they should be coming up with some theories."

"Jackson, you're drunk—sorry, shitfaced—and you're being a jackass."

"Shhh, it's ringing."

"Hang up!"

"Hello, yes," Jackson said into the mouthpiece. "I'd like to speak to the detective who investigated the Angel Ramirez murder five years ago."

"What the hell, Jackson!" Ellie snapped.

"No, I'm not kidding," Jackson told the operator. "The name? Um, I'm not really sure. I think it was Hernandez, or Herrerra. Definitely Hispanic. Yes, I'll hold."

"You don't even know the man's name?" Ellie hissed.

"It was a long time ago."

"You think Josiah Mantooth is trouble now? Just wait until he gets wind of this."

"Just doing my civic duty."

"You're basically prank-calling the police."

"Am not."

"Are too. Civic duty, my ass."

"Be quiet," Jackson commanded.

"Don't mention me."

"Coward."

"Moron."

"Yes," Jackson said into the phone. "Hinojosa, that's it! Thanks."

"Oh, for God's sake," Ellie groaned.

"They're connecting me," he told her.

"You've gone off the deep end, Jackson."

"Is that your professional opinion?"

"Damn right."

A hundred miles away, Ramon Hinojosa was at his desk rubbing the bridge of his nose, his reading glasses propped up in his silvering hair. He was buried under a mountain of paperwork and due in front of a budget planning committee in less than an hour.

Ramon was again lamenting his decision to give up real police work for the bureaucratic hell that went along with being a commander, and cursing the cushy, paneled cage that was now his office. All in all, he was in a foul mood when the intercom on his telephone buzzed.

"Hinojosa," he said into the receiver, irritated by the disruption.

"Sorry to bother you Chief, but I have a caller on the line who wants to talk about the murder of one Angel Ramirez," the operator informed him. "I pulled it up on the computer and saw that you handled the case. Does the name ring any bells?"

Ramon knew very well who Angel Ramirez was.

"That was five years ago," Ramon said, surprised. "What's this about?"

"Don't know. You want to talk to this guy or what?"

Ramon hesitated.

"Put him through."

A moment later, Ramon spoke into the phone.

"Commander Hinojosa, how can I help you."

"Yes, hello," Jackson answered haltingly, his courage fading. "My name is Jackson Polke. I'm the attorney who represented Katherine Van Hoerne in the Angel Ramirez case."

"I know who you are, Mr. Polke," Ramon replied, unable to keep the surprise out of his voice. "What can I do for you?"

That's a good question, Jackson thought.

"Mr. Polke? You still there?"

"Yes, I'm here, I was just thinking."

"Thinking?"

"Yes, give me a moment."

"Perhaps you should have done your thinking before you placed the call," Ramon suggested impatiently.

"Right, yes, excellent point," Jackson faltered. "I'll phone back."

"Why don't you tell me what this is about, Mr. Polke," Ramon stated flatly.

"It's about Katherine."

"Yes."

"And the murder."

"Go on."

"It's just, well, you see, I've been doing some thinking, about what happened . . ."

"Spit it out, Mr. Polke."

"Do you think Katherine could have been framed?" Jackson stammered.

"Come again?"

"Do you think Katherine Van Hoerne might have been framed for the murder of Angel Ramirez?" Jackson repeated.

Ramon did not immediately respond.

"Why are you asking, Mr. Polke?"

"Because I think she might have been. Framed, I mean."

"Is that so?"

"Or not," Jackson back-pedaled. "Like I said, it was just a thought."

"Is this some kind of joke?"

"No, no joke. Well, maybe. Not a joke, exactly, but a guess. An educated guess, really."

The rambling and slurred speech were a dead giveaways.

"Are you drunk, Mr. Polke?"

"Well, yes, sort of," Jackson confessed.

"And you just thought you'd call up the cops for kicks, eh?"

"Not exactly. I was hoping to get some information."

"About what?"

"The possibility that Katherine might have been framed."

"You're asking *me* if Katherine Van Hoerne was framed?"

"I'm asking if it's *possible*."

"Well, anything's possible," Ramon snapped. "Do you have something you want to share with me?"

"Not really . . . well, maybe. I'm not sure."

"You're wasting my time, Polke," Ramon stated coolly, frustrated.

"I apologize about that."

"I'm hanging up now."

"Wait, please don't."

"Give me one good reason why I shouldn't."

"I was there."

"You were in the alley when Angel Ramirez was killed?"

"Oh, no, not there," Jackson said quickly. "I mean I was there for the decisions regarding Katherine's commitment. I know what happened."

"And?"

"And I think Josiah Mantooth wanted his daughter committed."

"So?"

"Doesn't that strike you as peculiar?"

"Not particularly," Ramon retorted. "My understanding was that y'all were desperate to avoid a trial."

"Precisely."

"Precisely what?"

"Josiah didn't want it to go to trial. He wanted Katherine institutionalized as soon as possible."

"Correct me if I'm wrong, but weren't you the one who maneuvered that?" Ramon asked, the details of the case swiftly coming back to him. "Weren't you buddies with the DA?"

"Yes," Jackson admitted.

"And what? Now you're plagued by regrets?"

"Something like that."

"The case is closed, Mr. Polke."

"Just hear me out," Jackson pleaded. "Please."

There was something about Jackson Polke's voice that kept Ramon on the line. Moreover, the mere mention of the Angel Ramirez struck an exposed nerve for him. The whole stinking mess still stuck in his craw five years later.

"You've got two minutes," Ramon stated.

"Okay, two minutes," Jackson repeated. "Right, where to begin . . ."

"One minute, 59 seconds, Mr. Polke."

"Um, so, here it is: Katherine has this doctor who's been pushing for a drug called Thymetrazine, but the hospital wouldn't let her use it on Katherine, so she petitioned the court. The court order said that the drug could be authorized by either me, as Katherine's attorney, or her family. The family said no way, and I said no way, but then I got really suspicious because Josiah used me to try to get Ellie fired, so I went to see Katherine myself and was blown away by her condition. To make a long story short, I authorized the use of Thymetrazine against Josiah Mantooth's wishes. Well, he turns around and gets *me* fired, and then slaps me with all sorts of legal bullshit, all to keep me away from Katherine, even though the drug is actually working. Are you following me?"

"I think so," Ramon said, although that wasn't strictly true.

"Mantooth doesn't *want* Katherine to get better, and he's doing everything in his power to make sure she doesn't. Josiah wants her locked up in an institution. That's what he's always wanted, but Katherine's husband wouldn't let him, and he finally got his chance when Angel Ramirez wound up dead. So, you see, she might not be guilty after all."

"That's quite a leap," Ramon muttered.

"Not really, not if you think about it," Jackson replied a little defensively. "It totally makes sense. Why else would Josiah go out of his way to destroy the very people trying to help his daughter?"

"Maybe he thinks you're a rotten lawyer and this Dodds woman is a rotten doctor."

"You aren't listening to me," Jackson barked. "He didn't even put up a fight when she was charged with murder. Because he *wanted* her committed."

"And none of this occurred to you at the time?"

"I thought Josiah was trying to protect her."

"Perhaps he was."

"I just want to know if it's possible Katherine didn't do it."

"Well, if you hadn't rushed her through the system five years ago, we might have been able to find that out," Ramon told him flatly.

"So you think it's possible?" Jackson asked hopefully.

"No, frankly. The evidence was incontrovertible. It was an open and shut case."

"I remember it looked pretty bad for Katherine, but what if she was just in the wrong place at the wrong time?"

"Not according to the evidence."

"And you're sure? Absolutely 100% sure that Katherine killed him?"

"Listen, Mr. Polke, I don't know what you did to piss off Josiah Mantooth, and I don't much care . . ."

"But what about the Thymetrazine?" Jackson interrupted. "Josiah is purposefully keeping Katherine insane!"

"Did it ever occur to you that he just wants to make sure his daughter doesn't end up in prison? Hell, it sounds to me like he's still protecting her."

"From her own doctor and attorney? Why?"

"You tell me."

"I don't have a clue!"

"Well, that's your problem, not mine."

"But aren't you even curious? Doesn't all this make you the tiniest bit suspicious?"

"You're grasping at straws, Mr. Polke. I have half a mind to arrest you for this stunt."

"On what grounds?!"

"Oh, I'm sure I can come up with something."

"Fine," Jackson sighed, defeated. "You do that. But just remember, it was you who dropped the ball."

With that, Jackson slammed down the phone.

"Well, you were right, I'm a jackass," Jackson said, turning to Ellie.

There was no answer.

Ellie was sleeping peacefully on the couch. Jackson pulled a heavy blanket from a wooden trunk and laid it over her prone figure.

Then, he went upstairs to pass out.

13

Ramon Hinojosa had every intention of going home after his budget committee meeting, which had gone on for an excruciating two hours. He deserved some quality time with his wife and his remote control, not necessarily in that order.

Instead, Ramon was turning his car around and driving back to the station.

This will only take a minute, he promised his wife, calling to let her know he'd be late.

Ramon hated to admit it, but he was bothered by Jackson Polke's phone call. He considered the man a drunken nuisance, but the discussion nagged at him, mostly because Jackson Polke had managed to stir up Ramon's own misgivings about the Ramirez investigation.

Ramon had such serious reservations about the handling of the inquiry five years before, Ramon wrote a letter of protest to the chief of police. It was the one and only instance during his entire career on the force that Ramon had taken such a drastic step.

Ramon wondered if there was any possible way Jackson Polke could know about that.

Back at the police station, Ramon went directly to the basement file room. Most of the pertinent information could be accessed via computer, but he was an old-fashioned cop who preferred the feel of paper and the sight of honest-to-God pen and ink. Towards the rear of the cavernous room was the metal cabinets housing closed files by year. Pulling open the appropriate drawer, Ramon began flipping through the faded brown folders.

He checked and double-checked, but the Angel Ramirez file was not there.

Ramon wasn't particularly surprised. It was hardly the first time an old file went missing. He headed back upstairs to his office and switched on the computer. Within seconds, the words "Ramirez, Angel" flashed on his screen.

Opening the file, Ramon began reading. His name appeared on the first page as the investigating officer, and Detective Jared Hawthorne was listed as second-in-command. After that, there was a brief description of the crime scene and a preliminary assessment of the facts.

And then nothing.

When Ramon tried access the rest of the file, there was nothing more to see.

"That can't be right," he muttered, convinced he'd screwed up somehow.

After nearly ten minutes of wrangling with his computer, Ramon determined there was no mistake. That was all there was on the Ramirez murder. The witness statements, background on the victim, notes from the investigating officers, initial autopsy report, preliminary forensics results—all missing. There was also no protestation letter from Lieutenant Hinojosa to the chief of police. Hell, there wasn't even so much as a reference to Katherine Van Hoerne, just "CASE CLOSED" in capital letters.

Ramon knew for a fact that the whole file had been input into the database. Under the pretense of budgetary cutbacks, but in actuality as punishment for his complaint to the chief, he'd been made to type in the damn information himself.

He picked up the phone and placed a call to systems support. The tech guy confirmed what Ramon suspected, that the rest of the file had been wiped off the system.

"Could it have been an accident?" Ramon asked.

"Heck, no. If there was a glitch, we would have lost all of it, not just parts."

"Who has access?"

"Anyone with a password."

"So, basically, anyone in the Department can delete a file whenever they damn well please?"

"Um, basically, yes."

"Can you trace it?"

"Um, no?"

"Well, that's just great," Ramon sighed. "Don't mention this conversation to anyone. Got it?"

"Of course, sir."

Ramon hung up the phone and turned off his computer. He sat there for a while, staring at the blank screen.

"What the hell did you stumble onto, Mr. Polke?" Ramon said aloud.

14

Jackson stood over the open grave, gazing at the gleaming white casket that would soon be covered with dirt.

The other mourners had already left for the wake at Clementine's house, but Jackson wasn't ready to leave.

Out of the corner of his eye, Jackson saw movement. He looked up to see Wes McCaffrey standing beside him.

Jackson nodded to Wes, acknowledging his presence, and Wes did the same.

"I figured I'd see you here," Jackson said quietly.

"I wanted to pay my respects. I've been waiting in the car for everyone else to clear out."

"You didn't have to do that."

About Jackson's height, with thick brown hair curling past his collar, cobalt blue eyes and handsome features that bordered on pretty, Wes hadn't changed one iota since high school.

"I can't believe the old bastard is really gone," Wes sighed. "I seriously used to think, when we were kids, that he was invincible, like some kind of freakin' superhero."

"Me too."

"We'd pull our stupid teenage bullshit and he'd charge in to save us, with that big barrel chest of his puffed up like a gorilla, larger than life. Remember when we set off the sprinklers during that pep rally?"

"Oh, man," Jackson said, grinning despite the ache in his chest.

"He actually got that prick of a principal to apologize to us."

"How about that time in Laredo?"

"Oh Christ, I thought we were going to wind up in some Mexican shithole jail for sure."

"We were lucky Tommy spoke Spanish," Jackson laughed.

"Remember how pissed he was? I thought he was going to have an aneurysm or something."

"You didn't have to drive home with him. He didn't say a goddamn word the whole ride, just sat there all red in the face, stewing."

"And he still took us fishing the next weekend," Wes said, shaking his head in wonderment. "He never could stay mad at you long."

"God, I'm going to miss him," Jackson told him.

The two men fell into silence, gazing into the grave, lost in their own memories of Tommy Keane.

After some time, Jackson cleared his throat and said, "Tommy would have appreciated you being here."

"Thanks for saying that."

"It's true. Everybody's going over to Clementine's for that tea and cookie bullshit. Want to come?"

"Oh, hell no," Wes smiled. "I'd be about as welcome as a priest in a whorehouse."

"It wouldn't be that bad."

"Who the hell are you kidding?" Wes retorted. "Listen, Jackson, I need to talk to you about something."

"That's funny."

"Funny?"

"Yeah, because there's something I wanted to discuss with you. I was hoping you'd show up today."

"Well, here I am."

Jackson hadn't seen or spoken to Wes McCaffrey in years, not since his friend's casual drug dealing had turned into a massive criminal enterprise that attracted the attention of state and federal authorities alike. A surveillance photograph of Jackson at one of Wes' parties eventually crossed Tommy's desk, and Jackson had kept his distance ever since.

"You first," Jackson said.

"You're not going to like it."

"In all honesty, my life can't get any worse," Jackson assured him.

"Someone's poking around, trying to dig up dirt on you. And they are going way, way back in time on this little fishing expedition. I'm working on figuring out who's behind it . . ."

"Don't bother," Jackson interrupted. "It's Josiah Mantooth."

"As in Mantooth Industries?"

"Yep."

Wes whistled.

"Damn, Jackson."

"And, just like Tommy warned me a lifetime ago, I'm way out of my league."

"Does this have anything to do with Mantooth's daughter? I remember reading somewhere that you represented her in that murder case."

"You always were smarter than you looked," Jackson joked glumly. "Let's just say that Josiah and I had a parting of the ways over what's best for Katherine."

"And now he's out for blood?"

"With both barrels."

"Good thing you're such a straight arrow."

"Let's not forget my myriad of teenage indiscretions."

"No one's going to care about that," Wes laughed. "Now, how about you tell me why Josiah Mantooth is trying to string you up by the balls?"

"Frankly, I don't have the faintest idea," Jackson admitted. "That's what I wanted to talk to you about."

"You didn't just want to catch up, for old times sake?" Wes said with a smile.

"Can I take this conversation to mean you're still in the information business?"

"I dabble."

"Good. I want you to find out everything you can about Josiah Mantooth. He's hiding something, and I need to know what it is."

Wes paused for a moment and studied Jackson's face.

"What are we talking about here?"

"I think you know the kind of shit I'm after."

"Something that will get him off your back, eh?"

"Yes."

Wes shook his head and said, "People like Josiah Mantooth are remarkably adept at covering their tracks."

"And you're remarkably adept at uncovering them."

Wes grinned widely.

"True, but I wouldn't get my hopes up."

"Will you at least try?" Jackson concluded. "I'll take whatever you can get your hands on, and that goes for the whole damn family."

"And then what?" Wes asked, taking a pint of Heradura Reserve out of his coat pocket. "You're hardly the extortionist type, Jackson."

"That son of a bitch is systematically destroying my life, not to mention screwing over his own daughter, who for the moment is still my client," Jackson snapped, his jaw clenched. "I would do anything, *anything*, to take him down first."

"You really think you're capable of that?"

"Hell yes."

Wes eyed him warily and shrugged his shoulders.

"I'll see what I can do," he said, tipping the bottle of tequila over Tommy's open grave. "For old times sake."

15

Ellie projected what she hoped was an air of cool, composed professionalism as she entered Katherine's room. Under the surface, she struggled to control her breathing and her insides were roiling and churning like they'd been dredged.

Katherine was sitting up in bed, watching Ellie closely.

The changes were already significant. Katherine's waxy, pallid complexion had a new hint of color, and keen interest replaced her vacant, expressionless stare. Katherine seemed aware her surroundings, and not only conscious of reality, but fully engaged.

She scrutinized Ellie with a mixture of curiosity and faint amusement.

Ellie crossed the room slowly, somewhat unnerved by the way Katherine's arresting blue eyes followed her every movement, and sat in a chair positioned at Katherine's bedside.

"Hello Katherine," she said in a soothing voice. "I'm Dr. Dodds."

The smirk on Katherine's face chilled Ellie to the bone.

"Hello Dr. Dodds," the woman replied sweetly. "I do so hate to disappoint you, but Katherine isn't here right now."

16

"All rise!"

Jackson stood, buttoned his suit jacket, and waited for the judge to ascend to the bench. Josiah Mantooth and his attorney, Delroy Duffy, were seated at the opposing table.

"The court is now in session, the Honorable Judge Harold R. Boone presiding," the bailiff announced, signaling to the handful of spectators to again take their seats.

Harold Boone was pushing 70, with wispy white hair and a face scored with crisscrossing lines, but he was still as sharp and commanding as ever. Clearing his throat, he slipped a pair of reading glasses onto his long nose and nodded to the courtroom deputy, who announced the case.

"Before the court is the emergency motion filed by Josiah Mantooth," Harold Boone stated in a monotone, "seeking the removal and replacement of Jackson Polke as Katherine Van Hoerne's attorney of record. Are the parties present?"

"Yes, sir," Delroy Duffy answered, rising to his feet.

Delroy Duffy was a small man with a penchant for expensive, western-cut suits and down-home southern expressions. His most remarkable physical feature was his thinning, grayish-brown hair, improbably brushed back from his temples in sweeping, feathered wings.

"Delroy Duffy for the kin and relations, your honor."

"Jackson Polke, your honor," Jackson announced.

The Judge removed his glasses and fixed his stare on Jackson.

"You sure about representing yourself?" he asked.

"Yes, your honor."

"You know what they say about a lawyer who represents himself, don't you, son?" the judge offered kindly.

"Yes, sir," Jackson replied. "He has a fool for a client."

"Do you fancy yourself a fool, Mr. Polke?"

"Not generally, your honor," Jackson told him plainly. "But I don't believe that applies here, since I am not representing my own interests, but the interests of my client, Mrs. Van Hoerne."

"Your honor," Delroy Duffy interrupted with a tone of disgust. "I must object."

"He's not testifying, Delroy," Harold Boone sighed. "There's nothing to object to."

"Still, I cannot in good conscience stand by while Mr. Polke misleads this Court," Duffy continued, gaining steam. "It would be a miscarriage of justice of the highest magnitude to allow him to characterize his relationship with Mrs. Van Hoerne in this manner."

"Spare me the theatrics."

"But your honor . . ."

"You'll get your chance, Mr. Duffy," Boone informed him curtly. "Until then, I suggest you zip it."

Before Duffy could get another word out, Harold Boone raised a thumb and index finger to his thin lips and made a zipping motion.

"Now, Mr. Polke," Judge Boone went on, "are you sure you wouldn't rather retain independent counsel?"

"Yes, your honor," Jackson confirmed. "I'm sure."

"Very well, then. Let it be noted in the record. Now, before I schedule the hearing, are there any preliminary matters that need to be addressed?"

"May I speak now, your honor?" Duffy asked obsequiously.

"Only if you have something pertinent to say," Boone warned.

"Well, your honor, it pains me," Delroy Duffy responded, "but we ask that you recuse yourself from the case."

Judge Boone remained perfectly calm, but his eyes narrowed to slits.

"On what grounds would you have me removed from the case?" he asked in an even tone.

"Well, your honor," Duffy started, "you and Tommy Keane were close friends. You were even a pallbearer at his funeral."

"So?" Boone demanded.

"Mr. Polke was also a pallbearer."

"So?"

"So, we are concerned that your relationship with Mr. Polke might, well, influence your impartiality in these proceedings."

"I've known you for 20 years, Delroy. You think that affects my impartiality?"

"Of course not, your honor. Your objectivity is beyond reproach."

"Evidently not," Boone countered.

"It's just that with Mr. Keane's recent death, a terrible loss for both you and Mr. Polke, you have an emotional bond . . ."

"I hardly think being on opposite sides of a casket makes us soul mates."

"I'm afraid my client isn't willing to take that chance, your honor, not when his the life of his beloved daughter is on the line."

"You got anything else to support this motion of yours?"

"Such as?"

"Oh, I don't know, Mr. Duffy, maybe some evidence," Boone suggested coolly.

"I believe the evidence already presented to the court is sufficient to sustain our motion," Delroy intoned.

Boone glowered at Josiah, but followed protocol.

"Do you have any response, Mr. Polke?"

"Absolutely, your honor," Jackson said, jumping up. "I strongly object to opposing counsel's request for recusal, as well as his contentions and insinuations. Barring the production of further *substantive* evidence, Mr. Duffy has failed to establish the Court's bias or prejudice in this matter, and therefore has failed to meet his burden for recusal. Moreover, in light of the Court's familiarity with and continued involvement in Mrs. Van Hoerne's case, it would be a great disservice to my client to bring in another judge at this juncture."

"I agree," Boone interrupted. "Request for recusal denied."

"But your honor . . ."

"You got a problem with that, Delroy, take it up on appeal."

"Yes, your honor," Duffy retreated.

"Anything else?"

"No, your honor."

"What about you, Mr. Polke? You got any preliminary matters?"

"Yes, your honor. I would ask that the Court grant an extension of time to allow the parties to prepare for the proceeding."

"Your honor," Duffy interrupted, "this is an *emergency* motion. The family is prepared to proceed at the Court's earliest convenience, preferably tomorrow."

"How much time do you need, Mr. Polke?" Judge Boone asked.

Jackson had intended to ask for a couple of days, but decided to take advantage of Boone's mood and Duffy's miscalculation. The longer he could postpone the hearing, the better his odds of finding something on Josiah he could use.

"Three weeks, your honor."

"Three weeks!" Duffy exploded. "Your honor, that's outrageous! A woman's life is at stake!"

"I'm aware of the stakes, Mr. Duffy," Boone said. "If Mrs. Van Hoerne could wait five years, her father can wait a few weeks."

"I strenuously object your honor!"

"Object all you want, Delroy. Mr. Polke, you've got your extension."

17

Ellie pushed the stop button on the digital voice recorder and stood up from her desk. Walking over to the window, she pulled back the drapes and stared through the bars at the starry night sky.

"Shit," she murmured.

Closing the drapes, Ellie returned to her desk and picked up the recorder, again listening as the childlike voice reverberated against the walls of her office.

"Cookies are all right, but do you have any marshmallows? They're my favorite. I like to squish them all up until they get real soft, and then gobble, gobble, gobble. My fingers get all sticky and gooey, but I don't mind. I just lick them all clean, like Otis."

"Who's Otis?" Ellie's recorded voice echoed.

"My puppy dog."

"Do you like puppy dogs?"

"Oh, yes!" the girl squealed, her faint lisp becoming more pronounced. "Sandy, that's Otis' mommy, she had lots of puppies. I got to play with them and feed them and help take care of them. When I'm a big girl, I'm going to take care of them all by myself."

"Did the puppies have names?"

"Of course, silly."

"Why is that silly?"

"They have to have names so you can call to them."

"Then you must have a name, for when people call to *you*."

There was no response.

"I have to call you something," Ellie persisted. "How about Fido? Or maybe Spot?"

"Those are dog names!" the child exclaimed, giggling. "I'm a girl!"

"So you are," Ellie acknowledged, "but all the little girls I know have names."

Again there was silence.

"It's a secret," the girl whispered at last.

"You can tell me," Ellie cajoled. "We're friends, right?"

"Yes."

"Friends have to be able to call each other by name, don't they?"

"I guess so."

"Well, you can call me Ellie. What should I call you?"

There was a pause, and then a hesitant, tremulous voice said "Penny."

"It's nice to meet you, Penny."

Then another voice boomed from the recorder.

"That is quite enough, Dr. Dodds. I won't have you upsetting the child."

"I didn't mean to upset her," Ellie's voice responded.

"I don't give two hoots what you *meant* to do," the voice scolded, the European accent unmistakable. "You're upsetting the poor thing and I won't have it. You understand me, Dr. Dodds?"

"Of course, Dr. March," Ellie told her, sounding duly chastised. "I apologize."

Ellie pressed stop and set the recorder down.

Spread out on the desk in front of her were the handwritten notes she'd taken over the last week, a rambling, incoherent mess of thoughts and ideas.

Taking out a fresh pad of paper and a ballpoint pen, Ellie wrote "DR. MARCH" at the top and circled it. Below that, she wrote "Older woman; deep baritone; European accent, possibly German or French." She then drew an arrow downward and noted, "Physicality: ramrod posture; pinched, dour expression; squinty eyes (believes she needs glasses?); shakes/palsy."

After drawing another arrow, Ellie inserted the words "Protector/Gatekeeper."

She ripped the page off the pad and set her pen on a clean sheet of paper.

"PENNY," she marked at the top, then jotted "Young girl, maybe six or seven; high-pitched voice; lisp; southern drawl."

Again she made an arrow and wrote "Physicality: hunched posture, chin held low; open, trusting expression; wide, innocent eyes; head tilts left; pouts; chews lower lip."

At the bottom of the page, Ellie scribbled "Needs Protection."

She tore out the sheet of paper and placed it beside the one titled "Dr. March."

Unfortunately, Ellie didn't know enough about the other personalities she'd encountered to add to the collection, so she pushed the pad of paper aside and again picked up the recorder.

Once her thoughts were organized, she pressed the record button and held the tiny microphone to her mouth.

"Date: December 2nd. Subject: Katherine Van Hoerne," she stated in a dispassionate tone. "Diagnosis: barring future evidence to the contrary, Dissociative Identity Disorder."

"Christ," Ellie muttered, turning off the recorder. "Multiple personalities. This is all we need."

18

Sitting in Ramon's office, Tammy Lynn Geary waited for him to return, her hands crossed deliberately in her lap so she wouldn't gnaw on her fingernails. She was wearing a navy blue suit and sensible shoes, and her blonde hair was pulled back into a severe bun. Tammy Lynn's looks might be assets in the outside world, but on the police force, they were a disadvantage she worked hard to overcome.

Just as Tammy Lynn was about to up and chomp down on a cuticle, the commander entered his office and sat down at the desk.

Ramon Hinojosa pulled at his necktie, another requirement of his new position he still wasn't used to, and undid the top button of his shirt. His thick mustache was flecked with gray and his skin lined, but he could still fit into the pants he wore a decade ago, something he was quite proud of.

"Don't look so frightened, Detective Geary," he told her, noticing the expression on Tammy Lynn's face. "You're not in any trouble."

Tammy Lynn exhaled.

"I wasn't sure," she admitted. "You were so mysterious on the phone."

"You didn't tell anyone, did you? About our meeting."

"No, sir."

"Good," Ramon answered. "I'm not ready for anyone else to get wind of this."

"Sir?"

"Especially that weasel Hawthorne," Ramon muttered under his breath.

Tammy Lynn allowed herself a thin smile.

"Don't repeat that," Ramon instructed.

"Never, sir."

If it had been up to Ramon, Hawthorne would have been transferred out of the homicide division the moment he was named commander. Unfortunately, Hawthorne was Nathan Conrad's obedient lapdog, and with Conrad the new chief of police, there was little Ramon could do to stop Hawthorne's ascent through the ranks.

"What I'm about to ask you is a bit unorthodox," Ramon began, selecting his words carefully. "It's a request, not an order, and you are free to decline. No hard feelings if you do; I just ask that, in any event, you keep this conversation to yourself."

"I understand," Tammy Lynn replied, her curiosity piqued.

"This relates to a murder investigation that was closed five years ago. As I recall, you were one of the first officers on the scene. You remember Angel Ramirez?"

"Yes, sir, I do."

"Well, certain information has come to light that leads me to question the integrity of the investigation."

"A cover-up?" Tammy Lynn asked, unable to keep the surprise out of her voice.

"I wouldn't go that far," Ramon told her.

"Are you saying Katherine Van Hoerne wasn't the killer?"

Ramon shook his head sharply and said, "No, in all likelihood, she killed him."

"I don't understand?"

"Let's just say that something stinks in Denmark."

"Sir?"

"Someone in this department purposefully deleted the Ramirez file from our computers and probably stole the original file out of the records room. I want to know who and why."

"Could the file have been misplaced?" Tammy Lynn suggested.

"Perhaps," Ramon said, "but that doesn't explain the computer business."

"But why?"

"That's what I need you to find out," Ramon explained. "It might be nothing, but my gut's telling me otherwise."

Tammy Lynn nodded, mindful that Chief Hinojosa's gut was notoriously on the mark.

"Have you contacted Internal Affairs?" she asked.

"Not yet, and I won't, not until I have something more to go on. In the meantime, I would like you to do some digging, on the QT. I'd poke around myself, but it would draw too much attention."

"But without the file, what do we have to go on?"

"Why don't you start with Mrs. Van Hoerne's family, specifically her father, Josiah Mantooth. I want to know if there's any history there, if he has any connections in the Department. Basically, Detective Geary, I'm asking you to fumble around in the dark without a flashlight."

"I can do that," she replied evenly.

19

"She *what?*" Jackson sputtered, spitting coffee into his lap.

"On top of everything else, Katherine appears to be suffering from multiple personality disorder," Ellie repeated flatly.

"You're shitting me, right?"

"Unfortunately, no."

They were sitting on the back patio of a coffee shop, protected from the drizzling rain by makeshift walls of clear plastic sheeting.

"Let me get this straight," Jackson stated, running his fingers through his hair in frustration. "The Thymetrazine worked, exactly as you hoped . . ."

"Better than I hoped," Ellie interjected.

"*Better* than you hoped," Jackson repeated, "but instead of bringing Katherine back, it just brought out a bunch of freaky alter-egos and a whole new batch of problems."

"That about sums it up," Ellie nodded.

"You've got to be fucking kidding me!!" Jackson hollered. "This has got to be some cosmic fucking joke!"

"My best guess," Ellie answered calmly, "is that Katherine suffers from both schizophrenia and MPD."

"Isn't that the same thing?"

"That's a common misperception. Think about it this way— schizophrenia is a psychotic disorder, which means that a person's brain, for lack of a better term, is wired wrong. MPD, on the other hand, is a neurosis usually triggered by extreme trauma. Schizophrenics are born with the disease; it's in their genetic make-up, while MPD is something certain people develop as a coping mechanism."

"And Katherine has both?"

"Evidently."

"Is that normal?"

Ellie tilted her head and looked at Jackson like he was the one who was crazy.

"Okay, bad choice of words," he modified. "Is that *typical?*"

"It's not unheard of."

"So it's rare, then?"

"Extremely," Ellie told him. "MPD itself is rare, despite what you see on television and in the movies. A lot of psychiatrists don't even believe MPD really exists."

"But you do?"

"Yes, but only in rare instances. Genuine, documented cases are few and far between. Nine times out of ten, it turns out the patient is faking it for his or her own purposes."

"What kind of purposes?"

"Typically, to avoid responsibility for certain actions."

"Like murder?"

Ellie nodded, sipping her tea.

"Death row is a veritable breeding ground for MPD claims," she added. "And people wonder why we doctors have such trouble agreeing on the disorder in the first place."

"Could Katherine be faking it?" Jackson asked.

Ellie didn't answer immediately, and then shrugged her shoulders.

"If she is, she's giving one hell of a performance," Ellie said at last.

"Then it's possible?"

"It's not entirely out of the realm of possibilities, but it seems highly unlikely."

"How come?"

"Well, first off because she has no reason to pretend."

"*Hello?*" Jackson said, as if Ellie wasn't paying attention to the conversation. "We're talking about a murderer, here."

"But that assumes Katherine even remembers the murder, which is a mighty big assumption, and that she has the requisite mental faculties to plot something that cunning. Frankly, after what she's been through these last years, I'd be surprised if she had the mental powers to peel a banana. Besides, why bother to fake it? She was certifiably insane at the time, regardless."

"Good point," Jackson acknowledged.

"Plus," Ellie went on, "Katherine would have to be one of the greatest actresses alive. I'm telling you, the symptoms she's exhibiting are right out of a med school textbook. Each personality that surfaces is totally unique, with its own voice, characteristics, physical traits, mannerisms. She'd have to be Meryl Streep to pull this off."

Ellie was quiet as a waiter in baggy shorts and a Butthole Surfers t-shirt refilled her glass from a pitcher.

"It actually makes sense," Jackson said softly after the waiter departed.

"What does?"

"Your MPD theory. It sure would explain Katherine's actions the night she ran into Angel Ramirez."

"You mean the stabbing?"

"Well, that too," Jackson said. "I was thinking more about how she ended up at Rey's to begin with. It's not exactly the sort of place you'd expect Katherine Van Hoerne to hang out. And then there's that whole stripping business."

"Excuse me?"

Jackson had almost forgotten that Ellie wasn't there five years earlier, and certain details were withheld from the press.

"When Katherine entered the bar—which is a real shithole, by the way—she was like a different person," Jackson explained.

"How so?" Ellie pressed.

"She was dressed very provocatively, drank heavily, flirted outrageously. By the end of the night, she got up on a table and started taking off her clothes, putting on a kind of show. After that, she went into the alley with Ramirez. You think that might have been one of Katherine's other personalities?"

"It's practically textbook," Ellie answered. "It's precisely the kind of out-of-character conduct that can prove up an alter."

"Isn't that fortunate," Jackson said sardonically.

"It is, actually."

It was now Jackson's turn to give Ellie the "you've got to be crazy" look.

"No, really," Ellie assured him. "This means that Katherine exhibited unmistakable signs of MPD before the psychotic dementia."

"So?"

"So, she was still functioning then—as Katherine—which means she was somehow able to control the alters, until that episode anyway."

"You've lost me."

"Just trust me on this," Ellie replied, ignoring the expression of utter skepticism on Jackson's face. "We now know that Katherine's in there. It's just a matter of bringing her out."

"Whatever you say," Jackson sighed. "I'll leave Katherine and her head to you. I've got enough to worry about."

Not for the first time, Ellie noticed just how sullen and dejected Jackson seemed. Physically, he looked better than he did during their last meeting in New Braunfels, but that wasn't saying much.

"How are you holding up?" she inquired gently.

"I'm hanging in there," he said without much conviction.

"What's happening with the hearing?"

"I got it pushed back three weeks. Any chance of Katherine testifying?"

Ellie nearly laughed, until she realized Jackson wasn't joking.

"Would that help?" she asked.

"If Katherine was well enough to testify, all of this would be a moot point."

"Um, I wouldn't hold your breath," Ellie stated seriously.

"No worries there."

"Do you have a plan? For the hearing, I mean?"

"Not yet."

"What about the other stuff?"

"Other stuff?"

"The malpractice suit and the disciplinary action."

"Ah, *that* stuff," he answered, as if just reminded of impending root canal surgery. "The malpractice suit is a civil case, so it will take a while for it to wind its way through the court's docket. As for the disciplinary complaint, the State Bar has postponed the proceedings until after the matter of Katherine's representation has been resolved."

"In other words," Ellie translated, "if the court decides you should be removed as Katherine's attorney . . ."

"The Disciplinary Committee will take it as evidence that I violated the Code of Professional Responsibility," Jackson finished for her. "And I lose my license."

"And then Josiah can use that as evidence in his malpractice case."

"You catch on quick."

Ellie reached across the table and touched Jackson's hand lightly. Surprised, Jackson managed an appreciative smile.

As they were leaving, Ellie remembered the other matter she'd wanted to discuss with Jackson.

"What do you know about Katherine's childhood?" she asked him.

"Not much, really," Jackson admitted, "mostly what I've read online. Why?"

"The more information I have, the easier it will be to deal with her alters," Ellie explained.

"Let me see what I can come up with."

20

Wes McCaffrey stood on his terrace high atop a limestone cliff overlooking Lake Travis. The storms of the last few days had finally broken and the sun shone brightly through the scattering clouds, but the lake remained a churning cauldron of mud and silt. Only a handful of speedboats skimmed across the surface of the brown water below.

In his hand, Wes held a large manila envelope, inside of which was a set of glossy 8x10 photographs. A knowing smile creasing his handsome face, Wes stared out at the water.

Of Wes McCaffrey's many profitable and varied side businesses, he enjoyed his sideline in information the most. Drugs paid the bills, but the information business—extortion, blackmail, bribery—gave Wes unique pleasure. Exposing frauds and hypocrites, especially those who had the audacity to hold themselves out as role models while condemning the human foibles of so-called lesser men, greatly appealed to Wes.

If Wes learned anything growing up under the iron fist of the Reverend John McCaffrey, it was that a man's public persona rarely reflected his true nature.

The fact that dabbling in the information business could also be highly lucrative was just icing on the cake.

Wes pulled the photographs from the envelope. They were slightly grainy, but there could be no doubt as to identity of the subject, and what he was doing.

"Well, Congressman, you've lost my vote," Wes muttered.

Wes' inquiries into Josiah Mantooth had yet to yield anything useful, but Katherine's husband, Clay Van Hoerne, had been a veritable goldmine. Whether this was because the black market for dirt on politicians was thriving, or because the Congressman's urges were insatiable and thus made him careless, Wes couldn't say. In all likelihood, it was a combination of both.

From the envelope, Wes removed a sheet of paper: a list of the Congressman's most important supporters over the years, and the dates and amounts of their campaign contributions. This was the real deal, including the actual faces behind various sham corporations and coalitions, not the bullshit figures reported to the federal government. It was an extensive list, comprised of some of the wealthiest and most respected names in Texas and much of the country, but there was one donor who left all the others in the dust. Far and away, the largest single contributor to Van Hoerne's campaign was none other than Josiah Mantooth.

Wes found this interesting. Also interesting were the copies of bank statements attached to the list, particularly the activity in the personal financial accounts of Clay's mother, Delia Van Hoerne.

Wes again marveled at the information that could be gathered if you simply knew where to look and how to ask—or if you employed the right hackers.

For years, Josiah Mantooth had been funneling money into three of Delia's private accounts. The amounts weren't huge, but they were consistent—a deposit every three months like clockwork, alternating between the accounts. Between the campaign support and the payments to Delia, Mantooth was being tremendously generous with the Van Hoerne family, and he didn't strike Wes as a man tremendously generous with anybody.

"So, why the hell is Josiah paying off Delia Van Hoerne?" Wes wondered aloud.

For a man with Wes' proclivities, the answer seemed obvious.

"Mmmm," he murmured into the gentle breeze coming off the lake. "What do you know that I don't, Delia?"

21

A few days after their lunch, Jackson drove into Ellie's apartment complex on a hilltop above Barton Springs. Ellie was standing in a patch of grass outside of her building holding a retractable leash, and attached to the leash was one of the biggest dogs Jackson had ever seen in his life.

Ellie waved when she saw Jackson pull up, and then quickly walked the dog back to her apartment. It was a monster of a dog vaguely resembling a wolf on growth hormones, with a luxurious coat of silver, gray, and charcoal fur. Ellie let the dog in the front door, and then ran over to the waiting car.

"Sorry about that," Ellie said, slightly out of breath.

"What in God's name is that beast?" Jackson demanded, only half joking.

Ellie laughed and answered, "Lola. She's a Malamute, but Lola's big even by malamute standards."

"Lola seems pretty big even by rhinoceros standards," Jackson pointed out, steering the car out of the parking lot.

"She's having a hard time adjusting to the heat down here in Texas, especially on our runs."

"You're a runner?"

"Yeah, cross-country team in high school, and I guess it stuck. I usually take Lola down to the greenbelt. That's the main reason I took my apartment, because it was close."

The stoplight turned green and Jackson turned onto on Lamar Boulevard.

"Where are we going, anyway?" Ellie asked.

All Ellie knew was that Jackson was taking her to meet a person who might be able to shed some light on Katherine Van Hoerne's childhood.

"My Aunt Clementine's house. She's been kind enough to invite one of the ladies from the DRT over for cocktails."

"DRT?"

"Daughters of the Republic of Texas. Clem was going to introduce me to this woman five years ago, so I could learn more about Katherine's background then, but things happened so fast—and frankly, at the time, there didn't seem much point. Plus, I got the distinct impression that Clem would rather not spend more time with Mrs. Tish Ambrose than is strictly necessary. I don't get the impression that my aunt much enjoys the woman's company."

"And this friend or whatever, she has information on Katherine?"

"According to Clem, Tish Ambrose was exceedingly close to the Mantooth family at one time."

"But not anymore?"

"Apparently, there was some sort of falling out. It seems that Tish does not approve of Bobbie Dean."

"Bobbie Dean?"

"Bobbie Dean Mantooth, Josiah's current wife."

"Ah. And that's why this Tish person is willing to talk to us," Ellie surmised.

"That's the plan, but we'll have to wait and see. Clem wasn't entirely sure if Mrs. Ambrose would cooperate, but it's worth a shot."

"Are you and your Aunt close?" Ellie asked.

"Clementine's my great-aunt, actually, but the term makes her feel old. And yes, we're very close. She raised me after my father died."

"How did your father die?"

"Officially, it was a heart attack, but the truth is he drank himself to death when I was nine."

"I'm sorry," Ellie said sincerely.

"Clem calls it the Polke family curse, alcoholism," Jackson told her. "She can trace it all the way back to our famous forbearer, General Jackson Beauregard Polke."

"Why does that name sound so familiar?"

"He was a famous Texas general during the war with Mexico, and later the Civil War. He was also a raging alcoholic, but they don't talk about that much in history class. One night, the good general went on a bender, stole a couple of horses from some neighbor who pissed him off, and wound up getting himself hanged. That's something else they usually delete from his biography."

"I bet."

"Don't mention any of that to Clementine, by the way."

"She doesn't know?"

"Oh, she knows, she just chooses not to acknowledge it. The general was one of the founding fathers of our great state, and Clem's devoted her life to preserving the Polke legacy. She does not take kindly to people who remind her of the more ignoble aspects of the family history."

"What about your mother?" Ellie asked, at last giving in to her curiosity about Jackson's personal life.

"She passed away when I was a baby," Jackson replied matter-of-factly. "That's about the time my father's recreational drinking turned into more of a professional endeavor."

"That must have been hard," Ellie remarked.

Jackson merely shrugged his shoulders.

"Clem took good care of me. Her and Tommy."

Jackson turned onto Niles Road and drove past the lush, manicured lawns and gated drives that lined the street. Slowing, he pulled into the driveway of a stately Georgian manor. He parked the car and turned off the ignition.

"Listen," he said quickly, "I've filled Clem in on everything, so we'll just follow her lead with Mrs. Ambrose. You ready?"

"I guess so."

They exited the car and walked up the front steps, and Jackson rang the bell. A short time later, a stooped, elderly woman wearing a starched blue uniform opened the front door.

"Hello Myra," Jackson greeted her, giving the woman an affectionate peck on the cheek. "You're looking well."

"Hmmph," Myra grunted. "I've got the sciatica, you know."

"I know," Jackson said with a compassionate nod.

"And the bunions."

"You mentioned that."

"Did I mention the hemorrhoids?"

"Myra, this is Ellie," Jackson announced.

Myra grunted again, this time in greeting.

"I'll let Miss Clementine know you're here," she told them, shuffling out of the foyer.

"Consider yourself lucky," Jackson whispered to Ellie. "Last time I had to hear all about her bladder control problems."

"There you are!"

A tiny woman burst into the entryway, her arms open wide. Clementine wore a pink cashmere sweater, a tasteful choker of freshwater pearls, and a cheerful smile. Jackson leaned down and gave Clementine a big hug before turning to Ellie, his arm still wrapped around the woman's diminutive waist.

"Ellie Dodds, I'd like for you to meet Clementine Polke," he said.

"My, aren't you a gorgeous creature," Clementine drawled, surveying Ellie from head to toe. "And so tall!"

"It's a pleasure to meet you Miss Polke," Ellie responded.

"The pleasure's all mine. Jackson speaks very highly of you, Dr. Dodds."

"Please, call me Ellie."

"And you may call me Clementine," she replied graciously. "Now, let's go into the library for a moment."

Clementine steered them past the winding staircase and down a long hallway, the walls of which were lined with old and clearly valuable portraits. Ellie presumed, correctly, that the faces staring down at her belonged to Jackson's ancestors.

"Creepy, ain't it?" Jackson said under his breath. "I call it the Gallery of Dead Polkes."

"You know I don't care for that expression, Jackson," Clementine chided him sharply. "I won't abide your disrespect."

"Sorry, Clem," Jackson replied with a wink to Ellie.

Clementine showed them into the library and closed the door behind them. The room was two-stories tall, lined from floor to ceiling with row after row of books, most of the bindings cracked and weathered with age. Scattered throughout the room were club chairs, brass reading lamps, and Plexiglas cases. The cases housed letters and historical documents that looked to be quite old. In the corners were bronze statues that Ellie recognized as the work of Frederick Remington.

"The Polke Family Archives," Jackson whispered in Ellie's ear so Clementine wouldn't hear, a derisive tone to his voice.

"All of this will go to a museum when I die," Clementine said proudly in response to the look of amazement on Ellie's face. "I can't very well trust Jackson with it."

"Too much responsibility for me," Jackson readily agreed. "Besides, who the hell would dust all this crap?"

"I'll never understand how you can be so flippant about your birthright, Jackson," Clementine snapped, the disappointment evident in her voice. "I would think you'd be more interested in the role your family played in the history of this great state."

"You'd think," Jackson said blandly, "but alas, no."

"I think it's absolutely fascinating," Ellie told Clementine truthfully.

"Where are your people from, Ellie?" the older woman inquired.

"Cleveland."

"Ah. Well, I'm sure it's lovely there," Clementine replied. "Now, I wanted a moment alone with y'all so we can talk, before we go in to meet my other guest."

"What can you tell us about her?" Jackson asked.

"Well, Tish Ambrose is not my personal cup of tea. However, she knows just about everything there is to know about Josiah and his family. The Mantooths and the Ambroses are all part of that horse and ranch set, you know. A very cliquey group. I never saw the appeal myself. Frankly, I find the whole subject of animal husbandry vulgar and painfully dull, but Tish lives and breathes that sort of thing."

"Did you tell Mrs. Ambrose that we were interested in information about Katherine's past?" Jackson asked.

"Certainly not," Clementine said. "She never would have come. Tish still feels a great deal of loyalty to the Mantooth family, particularly the late Gabrielle Mantooth."

"That was Katherine's mother, right?" Ellie interrupted.

"That's right," Clementine confirmed. "She and Tish were very dear friends, which is part of the reason Tish loathes Bobbie Dean so much. She finds the woman an affront to Gabrielle's memory."

"Forgive me, Clementine, but if Mrs. Ambrose won't speak about the Mantooths, why are we here?" Ellie questioned.

"I didn't say she *won't*, just that she wouldn't visit for the sole purpose of spilling the family's secrets. That would be an unspeakable betrayal. However, if the subject of Katherine happens to come up in conversation, that's another matter altogether."

"Does she know we're coming?" Jackson asked.

"I mentioned that you might stop by with a lady friend," Clementine replied nonchalantly, obviously enjoying the conspiracy.

"And she doesn't know what's going on between me and Josiah?"

"Tish has been in Argentina for the last several weeks on some pony shopping spree. Besides, I'm sure I would have heard about it if she did."

"How are you going to get her to talk?"

"It shouldn't be that difficult. Tish is a terrible gossip once she gets going. Besides, I know her weakness."

"What's that?"

"Jack."

"Who's Jack?" Ellie asked.

"Not who, *what*," Jackson corrected.

"Tish has a fondness for Jack Daniels and lemonade," Clementine explained. "If I'm not mistaken, Myra is serving her a second cocktail as we speak."

"We're planning to get the poor woman drunk?" Ellie asked, only marginally appalled.

"Of course not, darlin'," Clementine retorted with a gleam in her eye. "Like all good hostesses, I provide my guests with the refreshments of their choice. I can hardly be held accountable if my guests overindulge."

"Oh," Ellie said, not at all sure there was a difference.

"Y'all just leave Tish to me. And for heaven's sake, Jackson, try to pretend you're interested in ranching."

"Will do," Jackson promised.

With those instructions, Clementine led them back into the hallway. They crossed through several enormous, lavishly appointed rooms and made their way to a solarium at the back of the house. Enclosed almost entirely in glass, the room was decorated comfortably with white rattan furniture and overstuffed pillows in a variety of pretty floral prints. Through the glass, Ellie could see the pristine gardens and glorious rosebushes that were Clementine's pride and joy.

Sitting on a couch was a sturdy middle-aged woman with a long face and broad, flat nose. Her graying chestnut hair was styled in a short, no-nonsense bob, and she wore a denim shirt embroidered with daisies. The sleeves were rolled up, revealing skin like tanned leather from years of being in the sun.

"Where the hell have y'all been?" the woman demanded, trying to look put out.

"You'll have to forgive my rudeness, Tish," Clementine said sweetly, "but Jackson wanted to show his friend the archives. He has such pride in his heritage, you know."

"Trying to get in her pants, eh boy?" the woman cackled.

Before Ellie could rectify the misperception, Jackson was at her side, his arm draped possessively over her shoulder.

"There's nothing like a bill of sale circa 1846 to get the juices flowing," he responded. "No better aphrodisiac around."

Ellie was a little embarrassed, but went along with it.

"I'm just a sucker for all that historical stuff," she added.

"Not me," Tish Ambrose sniffed. "All the libraries and museums in Texas could burn to the ground for all I care. The only thing that affects my juices, so to speak, is acreage. Land is the only thing that amounts to a hill of beans in this world. That silly Scarlett O'Hara was a tramp, but she was right about that."

Clementine made the requisite introductions and then said, "I do hope Myra took good care of you Tish, while I was greeting my other guests."

In response, Tish Ambrose held up her glass, which was now mostly ice.

"She makes a mean cocktail, that Myra," Tish pronounced.

"Oh dear, it seems you need a refill," Clementine said apologetically, as if irritated Myra had been derelict in her duties.

"Well, maybe one more, just to be sociable."

As if on cue, Myra appeared with a silver tray loaded with drinks.

Before Ellie could decline, Jackson took a glass and forced it into her hands.

Once the drinks were served and they were all settled comfortably against the cushions, Jackson turned to Mrs. Ambrose and asked about her ranch.

"Four thousand acres of the finest land in Central Texas," Tish replied without a hint of modesty. "It's been in Walter's family for generations. You partial to the ranching business, Jackson?"

"Who wouldn't be?"

"It's a tough life, but a good one. We got ourselves some outstanding foals last spring. Wouldn't be surprised if we took all the cutting horse competitions in the Southwest in the coming years."

"Cutting horse competitions?" Ellie asked, trying to appear interested.

"That's when the horse and rider race against the clock to separate a single calf from a herd. We got us the best damn trainer in the state, not to mention the best livestock."

"Do you raise anything other than horses?" Ellie asked.

"Only about a zillion head of cattle," Tish chortled, as if Ellie had to be joking. "Finest Longhorns in Texas. Why we've got some bulls that . . ."

"Ellie here is a psychiatrist," Clementine interrupted, having already heard all she cared to about the Ambroses' prize bull semen. "She's on staff at the Dripping Springs Psychiatric Hospital."

"Isn't that nice," Tish said politely, itching to get back to the topic of steers. "Like I was saying . . ."

"As a matter of fact, Katherine Van Hoerne is one of her patients, isn't that right Ellie?"

"Yes, that's right," Ellie replied dutifully.

That got Tish's attention, and she turned to study Ellie more closely.

"That's quite a coincidence," Tish said slowly, her watery eyes now fixed intently on the younger woman.

"Coincidence?" Ellie asked innocently.

"I've known Katherine since she was running around in nappies. Her mama was a good friend of mine, God rest her soul."

"You don't say."

A look of concern flashed over Tish's features, and she said, "How is Katherine?"

"Not well, as I'm sure you're aware."

"She was always a beauty, that one, even when she was knee high. The spitting image of Gabrielle," Tish said distantly, raising her glass to her lips. "It's such a shame, what happened to that beautiful child."

"You mean the murder?" Jackson asked casually.

"No, I mean all of it."

"All of it?" Ellie prodded.

"Katherine had a dreadful time of it when she was a child," Tish explained. "Truth be told, it's no wonder she ended up the way she is."

"How so?"

"Between her mother's condition and everything else, it was bound to happen. They say it's in the blood, heredity and all that."

"What is?"

"Mental illness," Tish answered. "That can be handed down, mother to child. Isn't that right doctor?"

"In many instances, yes. Several recent studies have proven that diseases like schizophrenia can be passed through the genes," Ellie confirmed. "Are you saying that Katherine's mother had the same sort of problems?"

"Well, she didn't stab anybody, if that's what you mean, but Gabrielle was not what you would call *well*."

"How was she not well?"

Tish took another gulp of her cocktail and shook her head.

"Best to let the past stay in the past, I always say," she told them. "The dead should be allowed to take their secrets with them to the grave."

"Unless those secrets can help the living," Ellie observed with what she hoped sounded like professional detachment.

"I thought Katherine was beyond help?"

"I'm a doctor, Mrs. Ambrose," Ellie stated evenly. "I do not believe that anyone is beyond help."

"Is that what Josiah told you, Tish?" Clementine interjected. "That Katherine was beyond help?"

"Don't mention that man's name to me," Tish ordered. "I haven't spoken to Josiah Mantooth since the day he married that wretched Bobbie Dean woman, the gold-digging piece of trailer trash. That union is a disgrace, and Gabrielle is probably still turning over in her casket."

Tish's face had turned a peculiar shade of red, such was her disgust with Josiah Mantooth's choice of a second bride, and she drained the last of her drink. Myra appeared out of nowhere, pitcher in hand. Tish Ambrose did not refuse another refill.

"I never knew Gabrielle," Clementine remarked as if just making conversation. "Tell us about her."

"A real lady, that one," Tish said thickly, the effects of the alcohol finally starting to seep through. "But you can't be interested in a person who's been dead for twenty some odd years."

Jackson, Ellie, and Clementine all spoke at once, saying that they were, in fact, very interested.

Tish stared at them quizzically, but didn't seem to question their motives.

"Okay, then," she said, sinking deeper into the oversized pillows. "Gabrielle was from New Orleans, the Garden District. Very old family money and lots of it. A debutante and all that, and an incredible beauty to boot, just like Katherine. Blonde hair like spun gold, big blue eyes, a figure to die for. You get the idea. Married young, when she was still a teenager, but her first husband drowned in a boating accident. His name was Devereaux, and he left Gabrielle a widow and a single mother at the ripe old age of 25. I believe it was two or three years later that she met Josiah. He was just starting to make his fortune then, so he was prosperous, but not overly so. He was in New Orleans on business, something to do with transporting oil down the Mississippi, and he wound up at a gala in the Garden District. He took one look at Gabrielle and was done for. Chased after her for months before Gabrielle agreed to marry him and move to Texas with her daughter. Avery must have been about seven years old then."

"Avery?" Ellie asked.

Jackson glared at Ellie for interrupting the story, but Tish didn't notice.

"Gabrielle's daughter's name was Marie Avril, but Josiah thought it sounded too much like a Catholic saint, so he called her Avery. Once she was in Texas, the nickname stuck. Anyway, Gabrielle made a home here and had Katherine soon after. That's around the time I met her. Josiah had a ranch not far from ours, so we socialized quite a bit. Both Gabrielle and I were newlyweds with small children, isolated in the middle of nowhere, so we naturally became fast friends. There was a swimming hole on the Mantooth property, and we'd take the kids down there in the summer while our husbands were off working. We'd always bring a picnic basket and lemonade and while away the hours talking about everything and nothing. Looking back on it, I can't believe how young we were. It was idyllic, really, but that was before . . ."

Tish's voice trailed off and she absently swirled the ice cubes in her glass with her index finger.

"Before what?" Ellie pressed.

"Before . . . before she was lost to us."

"You mean before she died?"

"I'm afraid Gabrielle was lost to us long before then," Tish told Ellie sadly. "Oh, she had always had *spells*—days when she couldn't get out of bed, much less pull herself together for company. Melancholy, we called it, but I suppose today the proper term is depression. Of course, we didn't know about such things back then, and we certainly didn't discuss it. Josiah sent her to the best specialists, but they didn't seem able to do anything for her, so he ended up telling everybody that Gabrielle had a delicate constitution and tired easily. Really, what else could he say? "

"What happened to Gabrielle?" Clementine asked.

"The spells became more and more frequent, until she finally stopped getting out of bed altogether. She and Josiah had been married for about seven years at that point. To his credit, Josiah loved Gabrielle until the very end, but he couldn't save her. It broke his heart when she killed herself like that."

"Katherine's mother committed suicide?" Ellie and Jackson said, almost in unison.

"They called it an accident, but we knew better. Josiah had taken Gabrielle to live in Austin, so they could be closer to the doctors, not that any one of them could do a damn thing to help her. He bought a place not far from here, a rambling, three-story Victorian, as pretty a place as you're likely to find. It's not there anymore, of course. The fire destroyed it completely, and Josiah didn't have to heart to rebuild it, not that I can fault him for that."

"Gabrielle died in a fire?" Jackson asked, confused.

"Oh no, that was years later. Gabrielle jumped from the balcony off her bedroom window. Broke her neck, poor thing. Landed on the concrete patio, which I suppose was her intent. Poor Katherine witnessed the whole thing. And Avery, she's the one who found the body and ran into the house to get Josiah."

Tish's audience stared at her, dumbstruck.

"I never did understand how a mother could do that, in front of her own child, but I guess Gabrielle was too far gone by then to know any better," Tish continued. "Officially, it was pronounced a tragic accident, but I never believed that. It took Josiah a long time to recover. He withdrew from the world completely, and we didn't see him for a couple of years."

"How old was Katherine when her mother died?" Ellie asked.

"Six or seven, I suppose. Old enough to understand what happened, at any rate."

"You said there was a fire?" Jackson pressed.

"Oh God, the fire. I thought that would be the death of Josiah for sure, but he's a strong man. Had to be, for Katherine's sake. She was the only family he had left after Avery died."

"Are you saying Avery Devereaux died in the fire?"

"Avery *Mantooth*," Tish corrected. "Josiah adopted her after he and Gabrielle were married. He always treated that girl as if she were his own, which couldn't have been easy."

"Why not?"

"She was a strange child," Tish informed them, an odd expression on her face. "Very intelligent and well-mannered, mind you, but terribly quiet. Liked to be alone most of the time, never wanted to play with other children. Gabrielle said it was because

Avery was an old soul, the result of losing her real father at such a young age.

"The girl had her nose in a book every time I saw her. Not like my kids. I swear, if any of them read a book before high school, it is news to me. Anyway, Avery was just, well, different. The only person the child seemed truly comfortable with was that old nursemaid Gabrielle brought with her from New Orleans, and I swear that woman was some sort of voodoo witch."

"You mean like an actual voodoo priestess?" Ellie asked.

"I can't say for sure, but Gabrielle gave me that impression. All I know is that woman gave me the willies. Black as coal with golden eyes that bore right into you, like she was looking through to your soul or some such thing, always talking in that Creole jibberish. I was afraid she'd put a hex on me if I stared at her crosswise, but Gabrielle said that was silly. Not because the woman couldn't hex me if she wanted to, mind you, but because Gabrielle and I were friends. She trusted that woman implicitly. In fact, towards the end of her life, that old nursemaid was the only person Gabrielle would let near her.

"But I digress. You were asking about Avery. Like I said, a quiet, sullen girl. After Gabrielle died, Avery retreated into herself even more. Must have been about 14 then."

"Tell us about the fire."

"It was a few years later. No one's entirely sure how it started, but the house went up like a box of matchsticks, old as it was. Josiah barely managed to get himself and Katherine out of the blaze. He had third degree burns all over his arms from shielding the little girl. Avery wasn't so lucky. She didn't make it out. It was just a dreadful accident."

"And Katherine? What happened to her?"

"Well, she was never quite the same after that, as you can imagine. But she eventually took her rightful place in society. Josiah became consumed by work, to keep his mind off things in my opinion, and made mountains and mountains of money. Probably neglected Katherine terribly, but that's how those things go. And Katherine, she grew into a fine and beautiful lady, just like Gabrielle."

"In more ways than one," Jackson pointed out.

"It seems so," Tish agreed dully. "But if Katherine had spells like her mother's, she hid it well. Of course, they have medications now to deal with such things, so Katherine would have been far better off. In any event, Katherine seemed to be a normal teenager. Lots of parties and dances, although I don't know that she had many close friends. And she simply adored horses and being on the ranch. Became one hell of a horsewoman, in fact. I think that's what helped her get through the hard times, that and Clayton Van Hoerne."

"That's right," Jackson said, remembering the articles he'd read. "She and Clay met as teenagers."

"They met at Camp Longhorn the summer Katherine was 15. She was at the ranch, of course, and Clay was at the lake, but they met at one of those mixers. If I remember correctly, the lake kids were very standoffish, wouldn't have anything to do with the ranch kids. But then Clay saw Katherine across the room and that was that."

Jackson, Ellie, and Clementine waited on the edge of their seats for Tish to continue, but the woman had run out of steam.

"Well, you know the rest," Tish concluded dismissively. "Besides, that was about the time Bobbie Dean sunk her evil claws into Josiah, and Walter and I severed our ties to the Mantooths."

"Is Bobbie Dean really that bad?" Clementine asked, hoping to goad Tish into further revelations. "I mean, she's frightfully crass, but she hardly seems evil."

Tish didn't take the bait, just rolled her heavy-lidded eyes heavenward, as if only God could know the true extent of Bobbie Dean Mantooth's treachery.

"That vile woman could give the devil himself a run for his money," was all Tish would say on the subject before rising unsteadily to her feet and depositing her empty glass on the white wicker coffee table.

"I have to pee," Tish announced unceremoniously and weaved her way out of the room.

Jackson looked at Ellie and muttered, "Holy shit."

"Holy shit is right," Ellie replied, her hands trembling.

22

Ramon thanked the waitress as she placed a basket of tortilla chips, a bowl of salsa, and a large iced tea on the table.

"You want to order?" she asked him, taking a well-chewed pencil from her apron.

"I'm waiting for someone."

"Sure thing, hon," she answered, tucking the pencil back behind her ear.

He was seated at a red vinyl booth toward the back of a quiet, family-owned Mexican restaurant in his neighborhood. There was little chance of encountering anyone from the police department. Ramon dipped a chip into the salsa and popped it in his mouth. The salsa was extra hot, just the way he liked it.

By the time Tammy Lynn Geary arrived ten minutes later, he'd finished off the entire basket of chips.

Tammy Lynn spotted Ramon immediately and walked back to the table. She was wearing jeans and a casual shirt, and her tousled blonde hair hung loose, making her look about ten years younger than she did at the office.

"Sorry I'm late," she said, slipping into the booth and throwing an oversized handbag onto the vinyl cushion beside her. "Waiting long?"

"Not too long."

The waitress came over and Tammy Lynn ordered a Diet Coke.

"Did you find something?" Ramon asked.

"Oh boy, did I."

"By all means, don't keep me in suspense."

Tammy Lynn hauled the handbag onto her lap and pulled out a stack of papers held together with a binder clip. When the waitress returned with her soda, Tammy Lynn carefully shielded the documents from view with her arms. Once they were alone again, she passed the stack over to Ramon.

"As you can see, the Angel Ramirez murder was *not* the first tragedy to befall the Mantooth clan," she said, bringing the straw to her lips.

"What is all this?" Ramon asked, randomly leafing through the pages.

"Copies of police files. On the deaths of Gabrielle Devereaux Mantooth and Marie Avril Devereaux Mantooth."

"Who?"

"Josiah Mantooth's first wife and his oldest daughter, respectively."

"I thought Katherine was an only child?"

"She is now."

"I see," Ramon said.

"That is one screwed-up family," Tammy Lynn added.

Ramon set aside the papers and said, "How about you give me the condensed version."

"You sure? That makes for a very interesting read. A real page turner, as they say. I'd hate to spoil the ending for you."

"Just tell me what you know."

The waitress reappeared, asking if they were ready to order.

"You bet. I'm starving," Tammy Lynn replied. "What's good here?"

"Everything," Ramon answered. "The carne guisada is the best in town."

"I'll take that," Tammy Lynn told the waitress.

"Same," Ramon added.

The waitress nodded and shuffled off. Tammy Lynn leaned across the table and spoke in a low voice.

"Okay, here's what I've got. Katherine Van Hoerne's mother was one Gabrielle Devereaux Mantooth. She was a widow when Mantooth met her, and she had a daughter named Marie Avril, who went by Avery. Josiah adopted the kid after the wedding, and they had Katherine a year or two after that. In 1975, Gabrielle took a header off a third-floor balcony."

"Suicide?"

"Not according to the report. It was listed as an accidental fall. However, according to the handwritten notes describing the scene, the balcony she fell from had a wooden railing about waist high. Plus, they didn't find the body directly below the balcony, but several feet away."

"Then the angle of the trajectory wasn't consistent with a fall?"

"Not unless she took a running start. More likely, it was a swan dive off the railing."

"Was there any sort of mental profile in the report?"

"Nope, but it appears that Gabrielle was under a psychiatrist's care."

"How do you know?"

"The file notes show that a family physician was already on the scene when the cops arrived. I did some checking, and this physician was actually a shrink."

"So his wife's lying there dead, and the first person Josiah Mantooth calls is a psychiatrist?"

"There's no other way the doctor could get there before the patrol cars, not unless he was there when it happened. You want to know what I think?"

"I do."

"I think Josiah summoned the psychiatrist to deal with the children, and to give him time to get their stories straight."

"The kids were there when Gabrielle Mantooth offed herself?"

"Yep. Apparently, Katherine was in the room with her mother when she went off the balcony. She's the one who told the cops that Gabrielle lost her balance and fell."

"Jesus. How old was she?"

"Six."

"And the officers just took her word for it?"

"The older sister, Avery, confirmed it. She was playing outside in the yard at the time."

"And Avery just happened to witness the whole thing."

"That's what she said."

"Surely the investigating officers found that suspicious."

"I figure they were merely helping the family avoid a scandal. Mantooth was a powerful guy in this city, even then. Besides, with two eyewitnesses, it would have been a hell of a lot easier to chalk it up to an accident than trying to prove otherwise. Gabrielle Mantooth was dead either way."

"I suppose it wouldn't be the first time a suicide went down on the books as an accident," Ramon mused, "especially for people like the Mantooths. What about this Avery? You said there was a file on her death?"

"Yes sir, I did indeed, and that's when this all starts getting mighty interesting," Tammy Lynn replied cryptically.

Before she could continue, the waitress was standing beside the table, a tray of dishes in her hand.

"Avery Mantooth died in a fire two years later," Tammy Lynn went on after the plates were set down. "By the time they got to her, the body was burnt to a crisp. Made the ID with dental records."

"How did the fire start?"

"The official report says that Avery fell asleep with a lit cigarette, and the fire was fueled by an open bottle of nail polish remover."

"Let me guess. That doesn't ring true for you?"

"Yes and no. Based on the burn patterns, Avery's room was definitely ground zero, and they did find a glass bottle of nail polish remover in the debris. They also came across a bottle of vodka under what was left of the bed, which could explain how Avery slept through the whole thing."

"But?"

"But, the *entire* house was destroyed. It literally burned to the ground in less than two hours. That kind of damage, that fast, practically screams heavy-duty accelerant."

"Acetone?"

"From one little bottle of nail polish remover? Besides, even if that was the initial accelerant, how the hell did it get all over the house?"

"Was the house old?"

"Very. And, again according to the report, all of central Texas was in the midst of a serious drought at the time. The investigators concluded that these factors were responsible for the speed and ferocity of the fire."

"Seems reasonable," Ramon pointed out.

"They reached this conclusion in a matter of days. Not weeks, not months, but *days*. The investigation was wrapped up before the goddamn embers were even cold."

"And, again, you're not buying it?"

Tammy Lynn pushed at her food with her fork and seemed to consider the question.

"I might, if it weren't for the other thing."

"What other thing?"

Ramon noticed that the young detective now looked markedly uncomfortable, and she wore a strange expression that Ramon couldn't quite interpret. She speared several chunks of meat and shoved them into her mouth, chewing slowly and deliberately.

Tammy Lynn was stalling.

"Whatever we discuss here stays between us," Ramon assured her.

She nodded and put down her fork.

"Where were you in 1977?"

"Um, still pulling desk duty in San Antonio. Why?"

"Just checking."

"I'm not going to like this, am I?"

"Nope."

"Don't let that stop you."

"Do you know a Detective Ronald Stiles?" Tammy Lynn asked.

"Sure. Took early retirement a few years back. What's he got to do with this?"

"Back in 1975, Stiles and his partner were the investigating officers on the Gabrielle Mantooth case."

"And?"

"Two years later, in 1977, the two of them worked the fire."

"Nothing out of the ordinary there."

"At the express request of Josiah Mantooth."

Ramon could feel his insides tighten into a knot.

"How do you know?" he stated evenly.

"There's a transcript of the emergency call in the file. On the night of the fire, Josiah managed to get himself and Katherine out of the house and over to a neighbor's. He made the phone call from there, and specifically asked for Detective Stiles. His house is going up in flames, his oldest child trapped inside, and there he was trying to get in touch with Stiles."

"Did he?"

"No, Stiles was off duty at the time, so what does Josiah do? He asks to speak to Stiles' partner, who's not available either. Only then did Josiah Mantooth tell the operator about the fire and request assistance."

"So, someone else responded to the call?" Ramon observed.

"Yep, but Stiles and his partner showed up on the scene within the hour."

"Just in the neighborhood, I suppose."

"Or Mantooth had some home phone numbers."

Ramon noted that Tammy Lynn still hadn't spoken the partner's name out loud.

"How did Stiles end up in charge of the case?" he asked, frowning.

"Josiah Mantooth pulled some strings. Told the brass that Stiles was the only detective he trusted to handle the investigation. Mantooth being who he was, they were only too happy to comply. Public relations and all that."

Ramon took in a deep breath, and let it out slowly.

"Lay it out for me," he instructed.

"It's conjecture," Tammy Lynn demurred.

"I know, but I want to hear what you think."

She paused for only a moment.

"I think Stiles and his partner did Mantooth a favor with Gabrielle. Wrote it up as an accident even though all the signs pointed to suicide. Now maybe they did this out of the goodness of their hearts or maybe there was a little something in it for them, but either way, they got a big career boost out of it. If you check the records, you'll see that both men were promoted soon after Gabrielle's death—months, even years, before typically due."

Tammy Lynn drained the last of her Diet Coke and let her words sink in.

"Go on," Ramon instructed.

"Fast forward two years. Stiles and his partner are now senior and full-grade homicide detectives, respectively, in large part because of Josiah Mantooth's influence. Out of nowhere, Mantooth's got himself another problem. Now let's assume for the moment that the fire was just a terrible accident . . ."

"Which is a fair assumption," Ramon interjected.

"Even so, Mantooth still wants to avoid the stench of scandal associated with a long, drawn-out investigation. He needs a quick resolution, an immediate press release stating unequivocally that his daughter's death was the result of an accident. Who's he going to call? His old buddies on the force. They helped him out once before, it's reasonable to think they'd help him out again. And even if these decorated police officers aren't so inclined, he now has something to hold over their heads."

"Covering up the suicide," Ramon stated dully.

"Precisely. Plus, he's got bundles of dough to throw at the problem. There's nothing like a little cash to convert an unwilling ally. What does Stiles have to lose? The fire's an accident, so what difference does it make if the case is wrapped up in six days or six months? It's all the same to him. Hell, he could even justify it as a public service. He'd be saving the taxpayers' money and sparing police resources, after all."

"While lining his own pockets," Ramon observed dryly.

"Like I said, it's all conjecture. There's not a shred of proof," Tammy Lynn reminded him. "For all we know, Stiles and his partner did everything by the book."

"You're quite the optimist, aren't you?"

"Just trying to look on the bright side," Tammy Lynn responded, offering a weak smile. "I could very well be full of shit."

"Or not," Ramon sighed. "Either way, I can't just let this go."

"There's no reason anyone else has to know," Tammy Lynn offered. "It was a long time ago and, as my Granny Geary used to say, it's best to let sleeping dogs lie."

"Not my style," Ramon told her. "There's also the matter of the Ramirez file to consider."

"That might not have a thing to do with this."

"Or it might have everything to do with it," Ramon countered. "I need to find out what the hell's been going on in my department."

"I figured that'd be your position," Tammy Lynn told him, both relieved and deeply anxious. "You know what you're up against, right?"

"I do," Ramon answered flatly, casually swirling the dregs of his tea in the bottom of the glass. "Stiles' partner was none other than our esteemed chief of police, Nathan Conrad."

23

Arthur Wiggins was seated behind his desk, a view of the University of Texas campus stretching out behind him. With his long, slender body and prominent balding pate, he reminded Jackson of a better dressed Ichibod Crane.

"Thank you for meeting with me on such short notice, Mr. Wiggins," Jackson said.

"Certainly, Mr. Polke," the other man replied stiffly.

The office was typical of a banker, with muted tones and tastefully expensive furniture. The artwork on the walls was of the sort produced by the Audubon Society, depicting various birds in their natural habitats.

"What can I do for you today, Mr. Polke?" Arthur Wiggins prompted.

"I want to talk to you about Katherine Van Hoerne. As you may have heard, Josiah Mantooth is seeking my removal as Mrs. Van Hoerne's attorney."

"I did hear something to that effect," Wiggins answered, his expression inscrutable.

"Then you may also have heard about the circumstances surrounding Mrs. Van Hoerne's commitment, and her mental and physical condition."

"I've been briefed."

"By Josiah?"

"Among others."

"I assure you, Mr. Wiggins, my only concern here is Katherine's welfare."

Arthur Wiggins didn't reply, simply stared at Jackson with that unreadable gaze.

"I firmly believe that the choices I've made were in Katherine's best interest," Jackson continued, "and that removing me as her lawyer will only ensure that she'll never, ever crawl out of that miserable mental hellhole she's been relegated to for the last five years. Josiah seems willing to condemn Katherine to a life of continuing anguish, torment and neglect. I, sir, am not."

Jackson thought he saw a twitch of a smile at the corners of Wiggins' mouth.

"Josiah claims to be the one looking out for Katherine's best interests," the man countered.

"He's lying."

Wiggins seemed surprised by Jackson's candor, but not displeased. Jackson took that as a good sign.

"Now, I realize that by asking for your support, I'm putting you in a difficult position," Jackson continued, "what with Josiah being your client and all . . ."

"Josiah Mantooth is not a client," Wiggins informed him curtly.

"But, I thought you handle Katherine's estate?" Jackson asked, confused.

"I do."

"I'm sorry, but I don't understand."

"Katherine Van Hoerne's estate is just that: Katherine's. It is entirely independent of the Mantooth family's assets. She inherited a great deal of money from her mother and is quite wealthy separate and apart from Josiah."

"I see. I just assumed that you represented Josiah's interests as well."

"That was an incorrect assumption," Wiggins reiterated. "I do not now, nor have I ever, represented Josiah, Mantooth Industries, or the Mantooth Family Foundation in any matter, including the trust funds established for Katherine by her father. I deal only with the estate Katherine received from the Devereaux side of the family."

That struck Jackson as fairly peculiar. He had yet to come across a banker who wasn't bound and determined to get his hands on any and all business he could.

"May I ask why?" Jackson inquired respectfully.

"If you must know, it was a term of Gabrielle Mantooth's last will and testament that Katherine's trust remain wholly independent of Josiah's holdings and influence. Under no circumstance is Josiah permitted to have anything to do with the estate, no matter how tangential or removed the connection may be. As a result, I have scrupulously avoided any dealings with the Mantooths so as to avoid even the appearance of a conflict of interest in this regard."

It took Jackson a moment to grasp the implications of that statement.

"Are you saying that Gabrielle didn't trust Josiah?"

"I certainly cannot speak to Mrs. Mantooth's motivations."

"But she made absolutely certain that Josiah couldn't touch that money, meaning Katherine would never have to be dependent on him?"

"That is the effect of the provision, yes."

"Josiah is one hell of a shrewd businessman. Why wouldn't Gabrielle have trusted her husband with Katherine's estate?" Jackson muttered, more to himself than to Wiggins. "What was she afraid of?"

"Surely you don't expect me to answer that," Wiggins said flatly.

"No, no, I was just thinking out loud," Jackson replied, trying to absorb this new information. "So, I take it that this provision of Gabrielle's will would have also applied to her elder daughter, Avery, had she lived."

"Of course."

"I understand that Gabrielle Mantooth was not well. Mentally, I mean. Did Josiah ever try to use her illness to break the clause?"

Arthur Wiggins allowed himself a slow smile and said, "You've been doing your research, Mr. Polke."

"I have my resources."

"No, Josiah never tried to contest the will."

"But he must not have been too happy about it?"

Wiggins folded his hands on the desk and contemplated the question.

"I would say that he was embarrassed by it, and upset. Perhaps even a little heartbroken. He seemed truly devastated when I told him what Gabrielle had done. Not because he begrudged his daughters the money, mind you, but because of the insinuation. It implied that his wife had lost faith in him, and I think that was very, very hard on Josiah. That said, he never once, to my knowledge, attempted to undermine Gabrielle's intent."

"And when Avery died, the entirety of the Devereaux estate passed to Katherine."

"That is correct."

"What about now? With Katherine locked up in an asylum, what happens to the estate?"

"I'm not at all sure I should be discussing this with you, Mr. Polke."

"I'm still Katherine's attorney, for the moment anyway," Jackson reminded him. "Listen, Mr. Wiggins, I'm only trying to help her."

Arthur Wiggins eyed Jackson warily, taking measure of the young man sitting across from him.

"As it so happens, Gabrielle Mantooth's will specifically addressed this very situation," he said at last.

"You're kidding?"

"I rarely *kid*, Mr. Polke."

"But isn't that strange? Contemplating her own daughter's commitment sometime in the future?"

"It's not typical, but like you said, Gabrielle was well acquainted with mental illness. It is my understanding that there was a rather long history of insanity in her family, particularly among the women. When you view it from that perspective, such a provision is far more understandable."

"Tell me about the provision."

"Gabrielle's will states that if either of her daughters is ever rendered incapacitated for any reason—including mental defect—their portion of the estate passes directly to any offspring still living, under the stewardship of an independent third party."

"That would be you?"

"And my successors."

"Not Josiah or a husband?"

"It was Gabrielle's express wish that neither her spouse nor the spouses of her daughters ever have control of the Devereaux fortune. Katherine's husband is entitled to a sizeable allowance, so long as the marriage remains intact, but he is never permitted access to the principle or allowed to influence the decisions of the trust administrator."

Suddenly, a piece of puzzle fell into place for Jackson.

"That's why Clay Van Hoerne never divorced Katherine," Jackson uttered.

"Were Mr. Van Hoerne ever to dissolve his marriage to Katherine, he would forfeit any proceeds from her estate," Wiggins confirmed.

"But if Katherine remains incapacitated and married . . ."

"Then he continues to receive a quarterly stipend for the duration of his lifetime. Gabrielle's desire was that the allowance be used to raise the children of the marriage, but I have no control over what Mr. Van Hoerne chooses to spend this money on."

"Did Clay know about this? Before Katherine was put away?"

"He had to sign several documents before the wedding, verifying that he understood the terms of the trust."

"And what if Katherine was never declared incompetent?"

"Barring incapacity, the husband has zero claim to any part of the estate."

"And if she dies?"

"The estate passes according to the terms of Katherine's will."

"What does her will say?"

"That it all goes to Katherine's daughter, Charlotte."

"And Clay gets nothing?"

"A lump sum payment of a few million dollars, but nothing more."

"He's already up millions," Jackson mused.

"I doubt Mr. Van Hoerne sees it that way," Wiggins responded. "Clay was very much in love with Katherine. Quite devoted to her."

"Then what the hell has he been doing these last five years?" Jackson grumbled.

"Other than fulfilling his duties as a United States congressman and raising Charlotte as a single parent?" Wiggins said, an edge to his voice. "I see where you're going with this, Mr. Polke, but as you no doubt recall, it was Clay who fought to keep Katherine out of an institution. Besides, he has never shown more than a passing interest in the money. I believe he would gladly hand over every dime to have Katherine back the way she was. But surely this is not the purpose of your visit."

"No," Jackson replied, hesitating. "I came here today hoping that you would write a letter on my behalf to Judge Boone, indicating that you support my representation of Katherine."

"I'm afraid that's impossible," Wiggins answered evenly. "It is not my place to interfere."

"I would argue that it's your *duty* to interfere. It's your responsibility to ensure that Gabrielle's wishes are carried out, and it's abundantly clear that she never wanted Josiah to have absolute authority over Katherine's fate."

"You assume quite a lot, Mr. Polke."

"Am I wrong?"

"Yes, in my opinion, you are. The crux of Mrs. Mantooth's bequest was that a completely independent third party administer the estate. If I were to get involved in this, my impartiality would be called into question, and rightly so."

"But I'm talking about a woman's life here!" Jackson retorted. "You have to believe me when I tell you that Katherine's very existence is in peril."

"Please calm down, son," Wiggins instructed not unkindly. "I'm not insensitive to your plight. In all honesty, from what I've heard, you're the only person who's taken an active interest in Katherine's welfare for a very long time. You and that doctor. What's her name, Dodds?"

Jackson nodded numbly.

"Just between you, me, and these four walls, I sincerely hope you whip Josiah's hind-end in that hearing. What he's done to you is shameful, and his treatment of his daughter, well, it's even worse. However, anything I did to help you would only compromise my position as the trustee of Katherine's estate and put the entire trust in jeopardy."

"You know this isn't what Gabrielle would have wanted," Jackson pointed out feebly.

"You're right, it isn't," Wiggins admitted. "In fact, before her death, Gabrielle tried to find a way to prevent this exact scenario."

"How?"

"She wanted a provision in her will terminating Josiah's parental rights and mandating the appointment of a guardian for Katherine and Avery in the event they became unable to care for themselves."

"Is there such a provision?" Jackson asked hopefully.

"Alas, no."

"Why not?"

"You're an attorney, Mr. Polke. You must know that such a condition would be invalid as a matter of law. There was no way Gabrielle, from beyond the grave, could force Josiah to give up his parental rights, regardless of the circumstances. Trust me, she tried."

"All the more reason you and I should work together to stop Josiah."

"You don't seem to understand, son," Wiggins replied patiently. "The only thing Gabrielle could do to protect her daughters was to entrust the estate to an impartial trustee, a person who would never have any ties to Josiah Mantooth. Taking a public stand, either for or against Josiah, would undermine my perceived objectivity. You must see that my hands are tied."

"I suppose so," Jackson responded grudgingly, rising to leave. "Thank you for your time."

"There is *one* person who might be able to assist you," Wiggins said nonchalantly, driving Jackson back into his seat.

"I'm listening."

"Have you tried speaking to Katherine's husband?"

"Yes, but I haven't been able to reach him," Jackson said. "Frankly, I don't even know if there's any point."

"Clay Van Hoerne has as much of a legal right to decide Katherine's fate as Josiah, perhaps more. If you could convince him that you and Dr. Dodds might really be able to help Katherine, Clay may be willing to take up your cause."

"Unfortunately, I can't seem to get the man on the phone."

Wiggins nodded slightly and turned to his computer. A moment later, he was writing out an address and telephone number on a blank sheet of paper.

"Clay and Charlotte are in town this week," Wiggins said, handing Jackson the paper. "If you wouldn't mind, I'd rather Clay not know you got that information from me. You understand."

"Any suggestions on how to approach this?" Jackson asked.

"Just one suggestion, perhaps. Try to avoid the mother."

Jackson vaguely recalled a conversation with Ellie regarding her attempts to contact Clay about Katherine's care. Ellie had mentioned she couldn't get past the congressman's mother, Delia Van Hoerne.

"Thanks. I'll keep that in mind."

"And, Mr. Polke," Arthur Wiggins said, walking him to the office door. "I really do wish you the best of luck in your endeavors."

"Thanks."

24

"Sure ya ain't got no smokes?"

"I'm sure."

"What about one of them orderlies? I bet one of them boys has got a pack."

"This is a non-smoking building," Ellie informed her for the third time. "Even if they do, you are not permitted to smoke in here."

The woman leaned forward conspiratorially.

"Hows about you get us some cigs from one of them nice orderlies, and you and me, we go on out back and have ourselves a smoke."

"You know I can't do that, Lucille."

"Won't take more than a minute. Ain't nobody gonna be the wiser."

"It's against the rules."

"And you're a by-the-rules kind of gal, ain't ya Doc?"

It was said with a sneer, as if playing by other people's rules was a contemptible human failing.

"I take it you don't put much stock in that," Ellie countered.

"Me? Naw. Where's the fun in that? The only good thing about havin' rules is breaking 'em. Unless they're your own."

"Your own rules."

"Uh-huh."

"Like a personal code?"

"Yeah, I s'pose. *A personal code.* I sure do like your fancy talk, Doc."

"Tell me about your code, Lucille," Ellie prodded.

"Personal means it ain't nobody else's business," she retorted. "But, for you Doc, I'll make an exception, and let you in on one of my rules."

"What's that?"

"Never get caught anywhere without a pack of Camels."

The woman laughed, a low guttural sound devoid of mirth that rang hollow and false.

"Or alcohol, for that matter," she added. "You positive you ain't got some gin in that desk of yours, Doc? I sure wouldn't mind wetting my whistle."

"I'm positive."

"Let me guess: this is a non-drinking building as well?"

"Something like that."

"Well, there go two of my rules, shot to shit. Hows about men, Doc? You got any decent male specimens hidin' around here?"

"Do you like men, Lucille?"

"What's not to like? There's nothing better than the touch of throbbing manhood, don't you think? Or are you one them?"

"Them?"

"Lesbos. You like girls, Doc? Like the feel of titties, do you? Never could get a hankerin' for it myself, but to each his own. Or *her* own, as the case may be. Come on, Doc, you can tell little ol' me. I already *know* you ain't getting laid proper like."

"And how do you know that?"

"I can smell it on ya. There's no mistakin' the whiff of pent-up frustration. Maybe you ain't into the ladies; maybe you're just frigid. You frigid, Doc? That pussy of yours pinched up too tight to let anyone in, man or woman?"

They'd been down this road before, and Ellie was no longer surprised or angered. That was precisely what Lucille wanted, to bait her into a reaction, but Ellie had learned not to give her the satisfaction.

"If you're trying to get a rise out of me, Lucille, it won't work," she told her blandly.

"Just making conversation, Doc. That's all."

Ellie watched the woman closely. She was slouched down in the chair, her legs splayed apart suggestively, the hospital gown slipping down to expose one shoulder. Every movement, every gesture, every word, was designed to elicit shock, to keep others off balance. She exuded feral sexuality, wielded it like a blunt instrument, indiscriminately and unabashedly. It was a form of power for her, a power she relished and put to good use. Ellie had to switch out more than one orderly since Lucille first appeared.

Lucille was Ellie's least favorite of Katherine's personalities, and probably the one most likely candidate to wind up in an establishment like Rey's.

"Speaking of men," Ellie said casually, "where do you find them?"

"They find me, but I guess you wouldn't know about that."

"There must be places you frequent."

"*Frequent?*"

"Go to."

"I certainly ain't sittin' home at night, with my thumb up my ass, if that's your meaning."

"Do you spend time in bars?"

"I might."

"Ever been to a place called Rey's?"

Lucille let out a loud, mocking hoot.

"What would someone like you know about Rey's?"

"So, you're familiar with the place?"

"Maybe."

"Do you go there often?"

"Sometimes."

"Tell me about the last time you were there."

"How's that any concern of yours?"

"Let's just say I'm curious."

"Trying to pick up some pointers, Doc?"

"Perhaps."

"There ain't enough hours in the day for me to learn you what you'd need to know. You should just stick to libraries and loony bins, or wherever else you spend your time."

"You probably don't remember anyway," Ellie said, changing tactics. "That was a long time ago, and you're clearly not the woman you once were. Rusty when it comes to men, aren't you Lucille? No, I don't imagine you have any pointers for me, not anymore."

Lucille blinked at Ellie and then, abruptly, there was a shift in her demeanor.

She sat up straight, drew her knees together and the grin disappeared. Her mouth hardened into a flat, unyielding line, and every iota of sexy flirtatiousness vanished. She leaned forward and glared at Ellie.

"You must think you're awfully clever, Dr. Dodds," the woman said with no trace of Lucille's southern twang, her voice calm and controlled. "You don't give us much credit, do you?"

Ellie had seen this before, the sudden switch of Katherine's personalities, but she still found it unnerving.

"Really, Dr. Dodds, reverse psychology?" the woman taunted. "Isn't that a tad rudimentary, even for you? Surely you can come up with something more, well, impressive."

Lucille was gone. The voice was silky, seductive, without any of Lucille's crudeness.

Ellie didn't immediately recognize this alter.

"I'm sorry if I've disappointed you," Ellie said quietly, struggling to get her bearings. "Dr. March, is it?

"Nice try, but no."

The woman stared at the Ellie coldly, appraisingly, her features molded into a hard, cruel mask. She seemed to be examining Ellie, studying her, waiting for the next move.

"Katherine?" Ellie asked hesitantly, her voice uneven.

"Hardly."

"Then you have me at a disadvantage."

"Nothing new there."

"What I mean is that you know my name, but I don't know yours."

"You're very big on *names*, Eleanor," she said, easing back against the cushion of the chair, lounging almost cat-like. "Tell me, why is that?"

"I find it facilitates conversation."

"Didn't anyone ever tell you it's impolite to lie?"

"What makes you think I'm lying?"

"Well, you're either lying or you think I'm stupid. Which is it, Eleanor?"

"Neither."

"Come now, you can tell me about this obsession you have with names."

"I've already told you."

"Then you must think I'm stupid," the woman replied, a glint of malice in her eyes. "I believe I'm offended. No wonder you aren't very good at your job, Eleanor, insulting your patients the way you do."

"I certainly never intended to insult you."

"So, your insults are purely accidental? Just slips of the tongue, eh? Tsk, tsk, what would Freud say about that? Frankly, one does expect better from one's therapist."

Ellie realized that she was being manipulated, forced into a defensive posture, and she didn't like it.

"Why do you think I'm so interested in names?" Ellie asked, as if she were only marginally interested in the response. "If you ask me, you're the one who seems to have an obsession with the issue. I was merely trying to introduce myself."

The woman smiled, an icy, menacing expression that chilled Ellie to the bone.

"Excellent move, Eleanor, throwing it back on me. Sly, calculating, crafty—although I must say, not terribly subtle."

"I asked you a question," Ellie retorted sharply.

"So you did."

"Well?"

"Well what?"

"Didn't anyone ever tell you it's impolite to answer a question with a question?"

"Fair enough, Eleanor," the woman nodded. "I think you want names so you can jot them down in your blue spiral-bound notebook. A page for each name, circled at the top, an arrow for each personality trait. You're just trying to keep us straight, keep your thoughts and conclusions all in order. Otherwise, it might all seep right out of that pea brain of yours."

Ellie felt the words go through her like a bolt of electricity, leaving her mouth dry and her palms moist. The woman seemed pleased by Ellie's discomfort.

Before Ellie could formulate an appropriate response, there was a knock on the door and an orderly poked his head in the office.

"You about ready, Dr. Dodds," he asked, indicating it was time to take the patient back to her room.

"All ready," the woman who was not Katherine replied. "Tomorrow then, Dr. Dodds?"

Ellie nodded imperceptibly, and the orderly took the woman by the arm and led her away.

As soon as they were gone, Ellie raced to her desk and took a small key from beneath the blotter. Unlocking the bottom left drawer, Ellie yanked it open. Everything was in its rightful place—the notebooks, the digital recorder. When Ellie looked more closely at the lock, however, she could just make out faint scratch marks on the metal.

She took everything out of the drawer and piled it on her desk. Then she began to consider alternative hiding places.

25

Pulling over to the side of the road, the house in sight, Jackson took out his cell phone and dialed the number again.

"Is Delia there?" he asked.

"No, sir, she's out. May I take a message?" the feminine voice replied courteously, for the third time that day.

"That's okay. I'll call back."

Hanging up, Jackson took a deep breath.

Tommy used to say the trick to getting away with something sneaky is to just act like you own the place. Boldness was rewarded, the more audacious the better. Jackson intended to test that theory.

Easing the car back onto the street, Jackson turned down a long, looped drive, at the end of which sat a three-story Mediterranean villa roofed in terracotta shingles and laced with wrought iron. Behind the house, Jackson could just make out the glassy waters of Lake Austin.

Waving to the gardener as he drove by, Jackson pulled his car to the very front of the house.

Plan B was a half-rehearsed harebrained story about a fraternity reunion and being an old buddy and just stopping by to say hello. Plan C was the truth.

Plan A was straight up balls.

Leaving the windows open, Jackson stepped out of the car and straightened his tie. He again waved to the man on the lawn mower, who waved back, smiling broadly. Without missing a beat, not daring to look to his left or right, Jackson strode up the brick walkway to the massive, intricately-carved front door and reached for the brass doorknob.

Without hesitation, Jackson turned the knob, opened the door and let himself into the house without looking back.

This was Plan A.

He had one goal: find Clay Van Hoerne before getting thrown out or arrested or shot, or all three. All he needed was five minutes alone with the man.

Readying his fraternity buddy story if he was confronted by anyone, Jackson quickly stepped into the foyer and crossed into a cavernous great room. He darted into the first hallway he came across and was soon attempting to navigate the labyrinthine corridors, the house utterly silent.

Just as Jackson was about to give up, he heard a soft, distant whine.

He followed the sound to a murky and shuttered room in the back of the house. The whine soon revealed itself to be the tinny, canned sound of recorded voices. The room and its lone occupant were bathed in the dappled light of a television.

Jackson stared at the plasma screen in amazement. Staring back at him was the face of a young, beautiful Katherine Van Hoerne.

She was looking straight into the camera lens, her cornflower blue eyes bright. Lustrous honey blonde hair cascaded around her shoulders, and tucked behind her ear was a single daisy. Suddenly, Katherine began to laugh, and a tinkling, throaty sound filled the room like a song.

The video ended abruptly and the screen went dark. From the couch, Jackson heard ice clinking against glass.

It's now or never, Jackson thought.

"Congressman Van Hoerne? I tried knocking but no one answered," Jackson lied, tentatively stepping into the room. "I'm sorry to disturb you, but it really is important I speak with you."

Clayton Van Hoerne was slumped down on the cushions, a decanter of scotch in front of him on the table.

"Congressman?" Jackson repeated. "May I have a moment?"

Clay squinted up at him in the gloom.

"Polke, isn't it?"

"That's right, Jackson Polke."

The congressman's handsome face was a blotchy red, and tearstains marked his cheeks.

"It's been a long time," Clay remarked softly. "A very long time."

"Over five years."

"Five years," Clay sighed morosely. "Jesus Christ."

"You don't seem surprised to see me, Congressman," Jackson noted.

"Should I be?"

"I suppose not."

Clay Van Hoerne still exemplified the sort of well-bred, photogenic politician the American public so adored, all chiseled features that only improved with age. Even in his sweatpants and a tattered t-shirt, Clay still looked like he landed in Washington straight from central casting.

"Can I offer you a drink, Mr. Polke?" Clay asked, holding up his glass.

"It's Jackson. And no thank you, sir."

"You're not going to make a man drink alone, are you Jackson?" the congressman admonished, rising from the couch a retrieving a glass from the bar. "You'll have to forgive me. I'm in one of my maudlin moods, as my mother refers to them."

"I think that video would make anyone maudlin," Jackson observed.

"Ah, you saw that, did you?"

"I didn't want to interrupt."

"She was really something, wasn't she?" Clay said, handing Jackson a glass. "There's something about being back here, in this house. Every time, I end up torturing myself with those goddamn videos. It's like I can't help myself. Can't even step foot on the ranch anymore. Too many ghosts. My mother keeps after me to sell it, since it just goes unused and empty, but I can't bring myself to do it."

"I understand Katherine was very fond of horses," Jackson replied, at a loss for anything else to say.

"That's an understatement," Clay smiled feebly. "I think Katherine liked horses more than most people. God, you should have seen her ride, like she was one with the animal. Truly something to behold."

Jackson felt strange talking about Katherine as if she were already dead.

"You must miss her very much," Jackson said.

Clay eyed Jackson thoughtfully, but didn't respond. He then walked to the window, pulled back the heavy brocade curtain, and stared out at the lake, lost in his own thoughts. The silence was awkward, but Jackson waited patiently for Clay to return to the here and now.

After several minutes, the congressman turned away from the glass and cleared his throat.

"But you didn't come here to listen to me feeling sorry for myself," he announced, gesturing to the sofa. "Please, have a seat."

Jackson lowered himself onto the cushions, and mentally sorted through what he wanted to say. So far, the visit had not gone as expected, and Jackson needed to adjust his approach accordingly.

"It's obvious to me how much you miss your wife, Congressman," Jackson began, "and that you'd like to have her back home, with you and your daughter."

"Wanting and having are two very different things," Clay pointed out.

"But what if it's possible? What if there's a chance Katherine can recover?"

"There's not."

"I respectfully disagree, Congressman," Jackson countered. "Dr. Eleanor Dodds is making incredible progress with Katherine. I believe that if she remains under the expert care of Dr. Dodds, she might very well be able to come back to you."

"I hardly think Katherine's been under *expert care*," Clay snorted. "She's in worse shape now than when she entered that miserable place."

"Dr. Dodds believes in this new medication."

"I was told Eleanor Dodds is a borderline nutcase herself."

"Told by whom, Congressman? Josiah Mantooth?"

Clay hesitated before responding.

"Indirectly."

"So you haven't spoken to him personally?"

"Not for several years. He and I, well, we don't exactly get along, as you may remember. But he's Charlotte's grandfather, and despite my feelings, I won't stop him from being a part of her life. That said, it's best for all concerned that we don't speak, not directly. All communication goes through my mother."

"Your mother?"

"She's helping me raise Charlotte. Honestly, I don't know what either of us would do without her."

"Then it was Mrs. Van Hoerne who relayed the information about Katherine's situation? From Josiah?"

"Yes."

"And you just accepted his version of events? Excuse me for saying so, Congressman, but when did you start deferring to Josiah Mantooth when it comes to Katherine's welfare?"

"Around the time my wife started stabbing her lovers in back alleys," Clay answered coolly.

"I understand how you must feel . . ."

"You don't have a goddamn clue."

"That's true, I don't. But what I do know is that you still love your wife."

"Correction, I love the memory of my wife," Clay observed. "I don't even know what to tell my daughter—her mommy's not dead, but she's certainly not alive. How the hell do you explain that to a child?"

Jackson didn't respond.

"I know what you're thinking, that I abandoned my wife."

Jackson opened his mouth to disagree, but Clay held up a hand to stop him.

"In a way, it's true. Maybe I gave up too quickly, maybe I'm just weak, but I simply don't have the stomach for it. It was easier to let Josiah handle things. I may not like the man, but he loves his daughter and I trust him to do right by her."

"I believe your trust is misplaced, Congressman."

Clay looked at Jackson hard, his skepticism evident.

"I realize you and Josiah disagree about what's best for Katherine," Clay stated.

"It's more than a simple disagreement," Jackson retorted. "Josiah is systematically ensuring that Katherine remains institutionalized for the rest of her life. That's what he's always wanted, isn't it? Isn't that precisely what you fought against for most of your marriage?"

"I don't have any fight left in me," Clay admitted dully.

"Then let me do it—help me to fight."

"How?"

"By supporting me against Josiah at the upcoming hearing. You are Katherine's husband, and you have as much say in her legal representation as he does."

Clay's face softened for an instant, and he sounded almost hopeful.

"Do you really think this Dodds person, that she can make Katherine well?"

"I think she's the only chance Katherine's got."

At that moment, from somewhere inside the vast house, a female voice began calling out Clay's name. Gripped by a sinking sensation, Jackson realized who was home.

"Clayton? Honey, you back here?" the woman continued, getting closer.

"Please, Congressman, please," Jackson said in a rush, "help me to help Katherine by . . ."

The rest of Jackson's words trailed off as Delia Fahey Van Hoerne burst into the room. She was carrying several large shopping bags from Nieman Marcus.

"There you are! I've got some shirts for you to try on . . ." she said, stopping short when she caught sight of Jackson. "I didn't know you had company, Clayton."

"Mother, this is Jackson Polke," Clay told her as Jackson stood up from the couch.

"We've met, of course," Delia said, dropping the packages on a table and offering Jackson her hand. "It's nice to see you again, Mr. Polke."

"The pleasure's mine," Jackson replied.

Delia's lilting drawl and friendly smile were laced with gracious southern hospitality, but her eyes held all the warmth of stainless steel. They moved from Jackson to Clay like lasers, quickly assessing the situation. She was petite, even dainty, with a delicate bone structure and a helmet of expertly coiffed silver hair. Despite her diminutive stature, she had the bearing and ramrod posture of a military general.

"Why on earth are y'all sitting around in the dark?" she asked pleasantly, marching over to the windows and yanking back the curtains.

The room was soon awash in the harsh afternoon sunlight.

"There, that's better," she added cheerfully. "I hope I'm not interrupting anything."

Jackson got the distinct impression that Delia was only too happy to interrupt this unexpected scene.

"Oh my, y'all aren't drinking this early in the day, are you?" she admonished, her tone gently disapproving. "You know how I feel about that, Clayton. And Clayton, honey, what are you wearing? You go on upstairs and change those ratty clothes this instant."

"Jackson and I are in the middle of a conversation, Mother," Clay informed her tartly.

Ignoring the clear message, Delia said, "Surely, Mr. Polke, you don't mind if my son takes a moment to make himself more presentable, do you?"

"Um, well, no," Jackson answered obediently.

"There, you see? Now, Clayton, why don't put on one these nice shirts I just picked up for you," she said, pointing to the bags.

"As we have discussed many times before, Mother, I prefer to buy my own clothes," Clay responded sharply.

"Since when?"

"Since always."

"I was only trying to be helpful," she answered, seemingly stung by the rebuke. "All I ever do is try to be of use, with both you and Charlotte. I do what I can to make your life just a little easier."

"And I appreciate it," Clay said irritably, "but I'm perfectly capable of dressing myself."

Delia looked down her nose at Clay's holey t-shirt and worn sweatpants.

"I can see that," she sniffed sardonically. "I thought I threw those pants away."

"You did, but I fished them out of the garbage."

"Really, Clayton, those things are appalling. What happened to the new sweatpants I bought you last month?"

"I like these," Clay stated, sounding petulant.

"Fine, wear whatever you like," Delia said, taking on the calculated air of the wronged martyr. "Who cares what I think? I'm only you're mother. I might have brought you into this world, but *you* know best. God forbid I'd try to be of assistance."

Jackson quickly pronounced that he was just leaving anyway.

"So soon?" Delia remarked politely, the edge to her voice spilling over like acid.

"I'm afraid so," Jackson replied, suppressing the urge to run as fast as he could away from the woman.

"What a pity."

Jackson took out his wallet and handed Clay a business card.

"I'm no longer with the firm, but my cell phone number is on there. Please give me a call, once you've had a chance to consider what we discussed."

"I'll do that," Clay told him seriously. "You've given me a lot to think about, Jackson."

Delia Van Hoerne's eyes drilled into Jackson, but he avoided her glare.

"Thank you for taking the time to meet with me," Jackson responded, shaking Clay's hand. "Good day, Mrs. Van Hoerne."

"Good day, Mr. Polke."

Jackson turned and practically raced out of the house.

26

"What did she say exactly?"

"I told you what she said."

"Tell me again."

"Here, listen to it yourself," Jackson said, hitting a button on his cell phone and handing it to Ellie.

Ellie took the phone and listened to the message:

Hello, Mr. Polke, this Delia Van Hoerne. My son asked me to call you regarding the matter y'all discussed yesterday. He wanted to call you himself, but of course he's frightfully busy. There's no rest for a United States congressman, as I'm sure you can imagine. In any case, Clayton would like to express his deepest regrets but he won't be able to assist you with your legal troubles. We're both confident that you have Katherine's best interests at heart, but Josiah is her father, and Clayton feels obliged to give him the benefit of the doubt. Josiah loves his daughter very much, as we all do, and we trust in his decisions with respect to Katherine's welfare. I'm certain you can understand my son's position. Because of Clayton's hectic schedule, I would ask you to contact me directly if you have any further inquiries in this matter. Obviously that would be preferable to you letting yourself into my son's home uninvited. But, of course, we appreciate your concern for Katherine and wish you the best.

Click.

"Jesus, she sounds scary," Ellie muttered.

"You have no idea," Jackson told her, stirring the tomato sauce. "I'd say Delia keeps Clay's testicles in her hip pocket, and only lets him borrow the boys for special occasions."

They were in Jackson's loft, catching each other up on the events of the last few days. Jackson was fixing spaghetti, which was the extent of his culinary expertise, and Ellie was chopping vegetables for a salad. Lola had made herself comfortable on the couch, gnawing on a bone the size of a cricket bat.

"Do you think there's any chance he'll come around?" Ellie asked.

"Not with his mother crawling up his ass like a fungus. I'm telling you, I think Delia controls damn near every aspect of that poor man's life. I doubt she lets him out of her sight for more then ten minutes at a stretch."

"But you said he genuinely cares about Katherine?"

"I believe he does, but he's got his public image to think about. The last thing a politician needs is a messy court battle, and Josiah can throw a whole lot of shit Clay's way. Besides, how do you think the voters would react if they found out Clay washed his hands of Katherine years ago, and the only reason he hasn't divorced her is the hefty allowance he nets every year. I doubt it would play well in the heartland."

"Still, if he loves Katherine like you say, I'd expect him to stand up to Josiah."

"Josiah? Maybe. Standing up to both Josiah and Delia? No way in hell."

"Well, I guess we can cross Clay Van Hoerne off our list of potential witnesses," Ellie sighed, slicing a red onion. "What about Arthur Wiggins? You sure you can't get him to change his mind?"

"Not a chance."

"Even though he knows how Gabrielle Mantooth would feel about it?"

"Yep," Jackson said, dropping a mound of fresh pasta into the boiling water. "Just makes you want to choke the guy, doesn't it?"

"It makes me want to knock some sense into him with a tire iron."

"Careful, doctor, you're exhibiting some very hostile tendencies."

"I'd like to exhibit some hostile tendencies on Arthur Wiggins' head—and Clay Van Hoerne's, while I'm at it."

"I'd let you have a go at Delia. If there's anyone who deserves a good braining, it's her."

Jackson stirred the noodles with a fork, added a dash of olive oil and set the timer.

"What do you make of that business with Gabrielle's will?" he asked Ellie, who'd already heard Jackson's recap of the provisions. "What do you think was up with her and Josiah?"

"Wish I knew. It might help me understand Katherine better."

"Don't you mean Lucille?"

"Ugh, please don't remind me," Ellie groaned. "That one gives me a migraine."

"What about the others?"

"Harmless enough, especially the doctor and the little girl. Altogether, I've detected about five distinct personalities, but I'm putting my money on Lucille as the perp."

"The perp?"

"The killer."

"I got that," Jackson laughed.

"I watch a lot of *Law & Order* reruns," Ellie admitted.

"I see. So, you're thinking Lucille's our *perp*, eh? The *doer*?"

"Laugh all you want, but I'm telling you, it was Lucille in Rey's that night."

Jackson uncorked a wine bottle and filled two glasses.

"There might be six," Ellie added.

"Six what?"

"Six personalities."

"Oh yeah?"

"Someone came out the other day, an alter I didn't recognize. She's very smart, that one, and manipulative. Made me pretty uncomfortable, actually."

"Do you think she could be our *perp*?"

"Lucille's already admitted being familiar with Rey's, and the entire incident has her unique characteristics written all over it," Ellie answered. "I seriously doubt Katherine has more than one personality that fits the description."

Jackson poured the steaming pasta into a colander waiting in the sink, while Ellie removed a loaf of garlic bread from the oven, cutting it into hot, buttery pieces.

"It's been a long time since a man's cooked for me," Ellie told him, smiling.

"It's been a long time since I've cooked for myself, much less anyone else."

"Frozen dinners?"

"Take out, mostly. And cereal."

"Ah, the bachelor's staple."

They sat on barstools at the kitchen counter, Lola curled up at their feet.

"This is quite the domestic scene we've got going here," Jackson observed, lighting a couple of candles. "It's nice."

"To a home cooked meal," Ellie said, lifting her wine glass.

Just as Jackson was raising his own glass, his cell phone rang. Looking at the caller ID, Jackson excused himself apologetically.

"Have you found something?" Jackson asked into the phone.

"Yes and no," Wes McCaffrey replied.

"Meaning?"

"Yes, I've found something, but not on Mantooth."

"Who then?"

"Let's just say that the Congressman Van Hoerne has some tendencies of which his constituents are unaware."

"Kinky?" Jackson asked.

"Very."

"Excellent. Give me the details."

"Not just yet."

"I'm totally down with blackmail," Jackson told him. "I am so good with that."

"Let's call it leverage," Wes suggested.

"Whatever."

"In any case, I need to know more about Clay Van Hoerne. That's why I'm calling. Have you talked to him?"

"I have actually," Jackson responded. "Today in fact."

"What can you tell me about him?"

"Typical politician—smooth, polished—seems to care about his wife, but still has a public image to think about."

"Anything else?" Wes prodded. "Any other impressions?"

"Yeah, he's a total mama's boy. Embarrassingly so."

"Oh yeah? What's she like?"

"Cold, imperious, controlling. Think iron fist in a velvet glove. Frankly, she's actually kind of scary."

"So, you think Delia Van Hoerne runs the show?"

"Not a doubt in my mind."

"What about Mantooth? Is Clay in contact with him?"

"Not directly. They hate each other, haven't spoken in years. It's the mother who handles all communication with Josiah."

"What kind of communication?"

"Oh, you know, relating to the granddaughter and Katherine, I guess. Clay's relinquished all control over Katherine to Josiah, and has nothing more to do with either of them. Everything goes through Delia."

"Interesting," Wes murmured. "Very interesting."

"Why?"

"Just is."

And with that, the conversation was over.

27

Nancy Stiles led Ramon around back to her husband's workshop. Ron was leaning over a table saw, a pair of safety glasses propped on his bulbous nose, a cigarette dangling from his lips. The room was filled with swirling motes of sawdust and smoke.

The whir of the saw blade was deafening, so Nancy and Ramon waited patiently for Ron to notice them. When the drone of the machine finally died away, Ron looked up and pushed the large plastic goggles back onto his head. He smiled when he saw Ramon.

"What the hell brings you out here?" he asked warmly, stepping away from the workbench and stubbing his cigarette out in an overflowing ashtray. "It's been too long, Ramon, or should I call you Chief?"

"'Your Excellence' will be fine," Ramon responded, accepting Ron's firm handshake. "This is quite a set-up you got out here."

"You like it? Built it myself last year. Nancy got tired of having my shit all over the garage."

"Now, we can actually put the *cars* in the garage," Nancy remarked, giving Ron an affectionate peck on the cheek. "Ramon, are you sure I can't fix you a lemonade? I've just whipped up a pitcher, fresh-squeezed."

"No, Nancy, but thank you."

"I'll take some of that lemonade," Ron said, patting his wife's rear end.

"You can get your own damn lemonade," she retorted sweetly. "I'll leave y'all alone now. You just holler if you need anything, Ramon."

"What about me?" Ron called after her with a teasing grin. "What if I need something?"

"You know where the kitchen is," Nancy snorted before closing the door to the workshop.

Ron laughed and said, "She'll be back in 15 minutes with the pitcher. Just watch. Nancy takes real good care of me."

"How the hell you managed to land that fine woman is a mystery to me," Ramon told him.

"Don't I know it. She's the best damn thing that ever happened to me, so I hold on real tight."

Retirement appeared to agree with Ronald Stiles. Unlike some other former cops who had trouble adapting to life out of uniform, Ron was clearly thriving in his twilight years of leisure. He was a big man, almost six feet tall, with a slightly misshapen face, like that of a boxer who's taken one too many punches. He had a protruding belly, which strained against the buttons of his faded denim shirt, but otherwise, Ron looked fit and vibrant and altogether content.

"What are you working on?" Ramon asked, examining the wood on the expansive worktable.

"A rocking chair, for my youngest. She just gave me my third grandbaby, the first boy of the lot. They named the tyke after me, if you can believe it," Ron told him proudly.

"Congratulations."

"Thanks. How about you? How many grandkids you got now?"

"A baker's dozen."

"Whew," Ron whistled, taking out another Pall Mall from his breast pocket. "You got your hands full."

"We've been blessed," Ramon said, his tone and demeanor shifting. "Listen, Ron, there's something I need to discuss with you."

Ron lit a match, brought it to the tip of his cigarette, and inhaled deeply.

"I didn't think you came all the way out here to talk about offspring," he answered, blowing out a ring of smoke. "What can I do you for?"

"It's about Josiah Mantooth."

"There's a blast from the past," Ron mumbled, surprised.

"You remember him?"

"Sure, I do. Poor bastard lost his wife and kid in quick succession. What about him?"

"I need for you to tell me everything you remember about those incidents."

"You want to tell me why?" Ron asked casually, tapping his cigarette ashes into a pile of wood shavings.

"Just trying to get a handle on something," Ramon replied evenly, carefully avoiding the question. "You were the lead investigator on those cases."

Ron stared at him warily, but Ramon's expression was unreadable.

"You got the files, don't ya? Well, everything should be in there. I don't see what I can add to it."

"I'd like to hear your personal recollections."

"Hell, Ramon, I don't know that I got any. It was over 20 years ago, and my memory ain't what it once was."

"Just tell me about your relationship with Josiah Mantooth, Ron," Ramon pressed, an edge creeping into his voice.

"Who the hell said we had a relationship?" Ron countered, flicking away the butt of his cigarette. "I met Mantooth during the course of my investigations, that's all. There was no *relationship*."

"Then just tell me what you remember about the deaths of Gabrielle and Avery Mantooth. And don't tell me to review the files, because I've already done that."

"Then you know everything I do," Ron replied. "You want anything else, then you best tell me what you're after."

"What I'm *after*," Ramon told him flatly, "is the truth."

"Since when does a new commander have the free time to go second-guessing 20 year old investigations?" Ron asked, his eyes flashing. "Perhaps the chief of police would be interested in how you're using departmental resources."

It was a threat, and not a particularly subtle one.

"In fact," Ron went on, fishing in his pocket for another smoke, "why aren't you addressing your questions to Nathan Conrad? He was my partner, after all. Seems like you'd visit with him before coming all the way out here, interrupting my retirement."

"I came out here as a courtesy."

"Bullshit. You know what I think?"

"What's that?"

"I think you're trying to keep this from Nathan. I bet he doesn't have a goddamn notion of what you're up to. Why is that Ramon? Why would you deliberately keep the chief of police out of the loop?"

"I'm sure you'll bring him into the loop, Ron."

"I might just do that," Ron Stiles smirked, picking a piece of tobacco off his tongue.

"While you're at it, Ron, be sure to explain to Chief of Police Conrad how you're able to afford all these fancy tools," Ramon added pointedly. "And that matching set of BMWs for you and the missus you got parked in the driveway. Oh, and that speedboat. And all on a cop's pension."

"I got lucky at the racetrack," Ron grinned, unperturbed.

"Lucky enough to buy a condo in Maui, the one in your wife's name?"

"You've been a busy, busy bee, haven't you, Hinojosa?" Ron hissed, the rosy glow draining from his cheeks.

The two men glowered at each other. For an instant, Ramon wondered if Ron might try to bash in his skull with one of those shiny new hammers. It was a crazy thought, one he wouldn't have even entertained an hour ago, but Ramon balled his fists nevertheless.

Just then, Nancy Stiles walked into the workshop holding a pitcher of lemonade and two tall glasses. She stopped abruptly when she saw the anger blazing in her husband's eyes.

"I brought y'all something cool to drink," she stammered. "Maybe I should just come on back later."

"That's all right, honey," Ron told her. "Ramon was just leaving."

28

The woman sitting across from Ellie sipped from the paper cup genteelly, her pinky finger in the air as if drinking from the finest crystal. She sat tall and erect, with the posture and swan-like neck of a ballerina, and her legs were crossed demurely at the ankles, her knees locked together in an invisible vise. Her poise and bearing reminded Ellie of some turn-of-the-century aristocrat posing for a John Singer Sargent portrait.

Considering that she was wearing a flimsy hospital gown and drinking tap water from a paper cup, it might have been comical if not so pathetic.

"This is simply lovely, Dr. Dodds," the woman stated in a crisp yet somewhat hushed tone. "Thank you again."

"It's just water," Ellie replied.

"Regardless, it's quite refreshing."

"Do you want some more?"

"No, thank you," the woman replied, delicately setting the cup down on the table, careful to place it in the exact center of the cork coaster, "but I do appreciate your gracious generosity."

"You're welcome."

"Now, where were we?" the woman asked dreamily. "Ah, yes, Lucille. A frightful creature, is she not? I have no idea how she slipped in."

"Slipped in?"

"Perhaps I am not familiar with the appropriate terminology."

"Lucille is just another aspect of Katherine's psyche," Ellie explained. "As are you, Kitty."

"Lucille and I are nothing alike," Kitty laughed. "I should think you would know that by now."

"I agree, you are very different, but all of you are part of the same whole."

Like the rest of Katherine's alters, Kitty was fully aware of the others, but she seemed to hold most of them in disdain.

"I suppose Lucille serves a purpose, but God only knows what it is," Kitty sniffed. "Needless to say, I do not approve of her shenanigans."

"What shenanigans are those?"

"Forgive me, Dr. Dodds, but ladies do not discuss such things."

Above all else, Kitty was a *lady*. She was exacting about matters of manners and etiquette, and obsessed with propriety.

"But you recognize that each of you serves a purpose?" Ellie asked.

"Certainly. We protect Katherine, each in our own way."

"In what way do you protect Katherine?"

"Well, someone has to keep up appearances."

"Appearances?"

"There are certain standards that must be upheld. It is not easy to navigate the waters of polite society."

"And you help Katherine do that?"

"I do my best," Kitty replied modestly.

"What about the others? How do they help Katherine?"

"You would have to ask them that question."

"May I?"

"May you what?"

"Ask them."

"Is there someone in particular with whom you would like to confer?"

Ellie was surprised. Usually, the alters surfaced at random, abruptly taking over without any forewarning. This was the first time Ellie was offered the chance to summon one.

"I want to talk to Katherine," Ellie said.

"I'm afraid I cannot allow that."

"Why not?"

"Katherine is resting. The poor dear desperately needs to regain her strength."

"I would very much like to meet her."

"It is out of the question," Kitty stated with finality.

"Okay, then I want to talk to Lucille."

"Oh, Dr. Dodds, you cannot expect me to give way to *that* one," Kitty shuddered. "I refuse to have anything to do with that beastly woman."

"How about Penny?"

Kitty cocked her head to the side in consideration, and said, "I suppose that would be acceptable."

She closed her eyes, and Ellie watched as all aspects of Kitty's physicality changed. The regal bearing evaporated as her shoulders hunched and her knees fell apart, and her chin dropped towards her chest. A sweet little pout formed on her mouth, and she began chewing her lower lip. When the eyes fluttered opened again, they were wide, innocent, and trusting.

"Penny?" Ellie asked hesitantly.

"Yes," she replied in the high-pitched voice of a child.

"Do you remember me? I'm Dr. Dodds."

"Yes, I remember."

"I haven't seen you in awhile. What have you been doing?"

"Stuff."

"What kind of stuff?"

"Just stuff."

"You don't want to tell me?"

The girl raised her shoulders to her ears in an exaggerated shrug, and began to kick the bottom of her chair.

"That's okay, Penny," Ellie soothed. "We don't have to talk about anything you don't want to."

That seemed to put he child at ease. The kicking stopped, but she continued to nibble on her lip.

Ellie had a great many questions for Penny—they'd been building up ever since her conversation with Tish Ambrose—but she'd have to tread lightly.

"I have something for you," Ellie told her warmly.

"A present?" Penny squealed.

"Kind of."

Ellie stood up and walked over to her desk, and pulled a bag of marshmallows out of the top drawer.

"You said they were your favorite," Ellie said, opening the plastic wrapper.

The girl giggled with delight and snatched a marshmallow from Ellie's hand. She began to knead the white puff between her thumb and forefinger until it was the consistency of taffy.

"Aren't you going to have one?" Penny asked.

"Absolutely," Ellie said, reaching into the bag. "Penny, can I ask you something?"

"Uh-huh."

"It's about your mom."

The child frowned, creating two vertical ridges between her eyebrows, but she didn't put up any protest.

"Do you remember your mom?"

"Uh-huh."

"What was she like?"

"Pretty."

"What else?"

"She smelled nice. Like flowers."

"Do you get to see your mom?"

Penny twisted her head back and forth.

"Where's your mom now?"

"In Heaven."

"So, you understand that your mom's dead?"

"She's with the angels."

"That's right, Penny. She's with the angels," Ellie said, releasing her breath. "I want to ask you about what happened the night your mom went up to Heaven. Can you remember that far back?"

"It's not so long ago."

"It's not?"

"Nope."

Since learning Katherine was present when her mother died, Ellie wondered if Penny might not be the substitute incarnation of that young Katherine, if Penny could be the alter that retained the memories of that night.

"Can you tell me about the last time you saw your mom?" Ellie asked gently.

"I was sitting at her vanity table, where she got made up."

"What were you doing at the table?"

"Trying on her jewelry. She let me do that sometimes. I liked the rings best, but I had to be extra careful with those, cause they could slip off."

"Was your mom with you in the room?"

"Yes."

"What was she doing?"

Penny's head tilted sharply to the left in consternation.

"Stuff," she replied.

"What kind of stuff."

"Just stuff."

"Did she seem sad?"

Penny's brow furrowed.

"Penny, was your mom sad? Was she maybe crying?"

Her feet shot out, and Penny began to again kick the chair.

"Was there anyone else in the room with you?" Ellie pressed.

Penny suddenly sat upright, her spine rigid, and her face screwed up into a pinched, sour expression.

"That is quite sufficient, Dr. Dodds!" she snapped furiously, her eyes narrowing to a squint. "What is the matter with you, harassing an innocent child like that?"

"Dr. March, I presume," Ellie whispered, disappointed but not surprised.

"We ought never have let you near that child, the way you upset her!"

The voice was now a deep baritone, with a slight European accent.

"I apologize, Dr, March."

"I've heard that before, Dr. Dodds," Dr. March huffed. "What could possibly have possessed you?"

"I need information. Katherine is in trouble, serious trouble, and if I don't figure out a way to help her, well, you're all in danger."

"What are you trying to say, Dr. Dodds?" the woman asked gruffly, but not without interest.

"In a matter of days, a judge is going to decide Katherine's fate. It is very likely that I'll be replaced, and her new doctor will halt the current drug regimen."

"The Thymetrazine," Dr. March clarified.

"Precisely. Need I remind you what will happen to Katherine, to *you*, without the Thymetrazine?"

"No, you don't," the woman answered soberly.

"What's that like, Dr. March? The psychosis?" Ellie went on. "Is it just blackness, or do you get to experience some of the pain Katherine so relishes when she mutilates herself?"

A strange look flashed across Dr. March's face. The old lady mask slid right off in a rush of anger, the eyes glinted with rage. For a split second, Ellie thought she might be witnessing the emergence of another personality, but then, just as suddenly, the March façade fell back into place. Ellie was startled, but the moment was gone before she could wrap her brain around what had just transpired.

"That is unacceptable," Dr. March pronounced. "What do you need from us?"

"Excuse me?"

"What do you need from us, to ensure that doesn't happen?"

"Well, Katherine, for starters."

"Katherine?"

"Yes, Katherine herself. It would show the court that the treatments are working."

"Isn't there anything else?" Dr. March asked irritably.

"Not that I can think of. Can't you make Katherine come out?"

"Do you think we're hiding her from you?"

"Are you?"

"Certainly not," Dr. March retorted. "Did it ever occur to you that it's *your* fault Katherine hasn't shown herself? That it's due to a failing on your part?"

"Yes. It's occurred to me."

"Then let's reflect, Doctor. What can *you* do to bring about a change?"

"I've been trying . . ."

"Evidently not hard enough."

"How about you tell me what I can do?"

Dr. March sighed, as if trying to communicate with a remarkably stupid subordinate.

"Have you considered changing the dosage?"

"What?"

"Increasing the dosage of Thymetrazine. Surely you've given the matter some thought."

"Would that make a difference?"

"How should I know? You're Katherine's psychiatrist."

Ellie's mind was reeling. Worse still, she had the unmistakable feeling of being manipulated, toyed with somehow.

"I'm tired, Dr. Dodds," the woman informed her curtly. "I'd like to go back to my room now."

"Now?"

"Yes, now. If you could please call the orderly."

"But we're right in the middle of something . . ."

"Don't make me repeat myself, Dr. Dodds."

Ellie was about to argue—to beg if she had to—but instinctively understood further efforts would be futile. Frustrated, Ellie reached for the call button.

29

Ramon Hinojosa was scowling by the time he finished reading the newspaper article. Katherine Van Hoerne and Angel Ramirez were once again front-page news, irresistible fodder for the gossipmongers and media hordes, and Ramon was none too pleased.

Setting aside the paper, Ramon considered the ramifications of this legal pissing contest between Josiah Mantooth and Jackson Polke. He wasn't interested in the outcome of the hearing, only the extent to which this renewed interest in Mrs. Van Hoerne would affect his own investigation. Here he was trying to stay under the radar, and suddenly the whole damn case was back in the spotlight.

A waitress in a maroon uniform with the diner's name stitched over her ample chest came by to refill Ramon's coffee. Tammy Lynn Geary caught her before walked off.

"I'll take one of those, when you get a chance," she told the waitress with an appreciative smile, sliding into the booth.

"Sure thing, hon," the woman replied before shuffling away.

"You don't look too happy," Tammy Lynn remarked, noticing Ramon's frown.

By way of response, he slid the front page of the newspaper across the table.

"Ah," she nodded. "The hearing."

"Kind of hard to miss the screaming, banner headline," Ramon grumbled.

"What do you make of it?"

"Jackson Polke pissed off the wrong people."

"He claims that Josiah Mantooth is keeping Katherine crazy on purpose," Tammy Lynn noted. "You think that's possible?"

Ramon shrugged his shoulders.

"Doesn't have anything to do with us," he told her.

Tammy Lynn eyed him skeptically, but didn't disagree.

"So, I've got the proverbial good news and bad news," she announced, changing the subject. "Which do you want first?"

"I'll take the bad," Ramon answered. "It gives me something to look forward to."

"Okay, bad news first. I was able to track down the names of several witnesses to the Ramirez homicide, but so far, they're all either dead or MIA. I've got a few more leads, but I'm not holding out much hope. Moving on to the physical evidence, we are entirely shit out of luck."

"Why?"

"It's gone."

"What do you mean *gone?*"

"As in vanished into thin air," Tammy Lynn told him evenly. "Every shred of physical evidence from the Ramirez homicide is missing from the APD warehouse.

"It's got to be in that place somewhere," Ramon insisted.

"I spent the better part of yesterday on my hands and knees going through boxes, and I have the filthy clothes to prove it. The evidence from the Ramirez case—the knife, the bloody clothes, all of it—it's gone."

"Evidence doesn't just disappear," Ramon said, more to himself than to Tammy Lynn.

"Actually, according to the custodian of records, it happens all the time, especially after so many years. But I agree, it seems an unlikely coincidence in this instance. I think it's safe to assume that whoever made the file disappear, made the physical evidence disappear as well."

"What about a paper trail?" Ramon suggested. "Someone had to check the boxes out, right?"

"In theory, yes. In practice . . . well, that's a different matter."

Ramon became irate contemplating the convergence of treachery and incompetence.

"You ready for the good news?" Tammy Lynn asked.

"Will it improve my mood?"

"Won't make it any worse," she replied with a smile.

"All right, let's have it."

"As for the preliminary autopsy report, the ME's Office does keep its own set of records, which they've already faxed over to me. Also, you were right, Skip Lowell does keep personal records in certain cases, so I was also able to get my hands on a copy of the initial forensics report."

"I thought he might," Ramon said with a wry smile, recalling Skip's idea of writing a book about famous Austin murders after he retired.

"Skip Lowell also kept a copy of Katherine Van Hoerne's tox screen from the night she was arrested."

"I bet he did. Anything of interest?"

"Not that I can tell. Anyway, we now have photos of the knife and some other pieces of missing evidence, so that will be helpful. Not as good as the real deal, of course, but better than nothing. Oh, and speaking of photographs, get a load of this."

Tammy Lynn began rifling through her notes until she came to a section circled in orange marker.

"At the time of the Gabrielle Mantooth's death," she told Ramon, "the APD was farming out photography to outside contractors. The crime scene was shot by a guy named Mike Earley. As it turns out, Mr. Earley prides himself on saving the negative of every picture he's ever taken. I'm heading over to his studio in the morning, see if he caught anything useful on film."

"Not bad, Officer Geary," Ramon remarked, impressed. "Not bad at all."

30

The uniformed maid departed and Wes McCaffrey was left alone in Delia Van Hoerne's inner sanctum.

Throwing his leather attaché case on one of Delia's priceless antique chairs, Wes surveyed his surroundings.

The spacious study was decidedly feminine, awash in varying hues of rose and cream, with silk damask drapes and crystal vases brimming with freshly cut bouquets. Oil paintings of tranquil pastoral landscapes by noted French impressionists adorned the walls, and a single bronze statue—one of Degas' legendary dancers—was perched on a pedestal beside the window.

Wes did not wait long. Within minutes, Delia Van Hoerne breezed into the study in a cloud of expensive perfume.

"I'm so sorry to have kept you waiting, Mr. McCaffrey," Delia purred, clasping Wes' hand. "You must think me terribly rude."

"No, not at all, Mrs. Van Hoerne," he replied, squeezing the woman's bony, bejeweled fingers. "I was just admiring your paintings. That's a Courbet, if I'm not mistaken."

"Why, yes," Delia said with a delighted smile. "You have quite an eye."

"I just know what I like."

"Are you a collector?"

"Oh, I pick up items here and there."

Wes' dark hair was now cut short and parted neatly on the side, a small price to pay for authenticity, and he wore a three piece suit purchased the day before. By all outward appearances, Wes was every bit the proper businessman he purported to be.

"What line of work are you in, Mr. McCaffrey?" Delia asked him pleasantly.

Strictly speaking, as Wes was now face-to-face with the woman, he could drop the charade at any time, but he was enjoying himself.

"Import/export, sales, that sort of thing," Wes offered with a dismissive wave. "I've been lucky."

"I'm sure you're just being modest," Delia exclaimed, patting a rogue silver strand back into her immaculate helmet of hair.

"Modesty is not one of my vices, Mrs. Van Hoerne."

This had not been an easy meeting for Wes to arrange. He had tried the direct approach, but Delia Van Hoerne's personal staff rivaled that of NATO. After getting nowhere with untold numbers of secretaries, servants, and assorted underlings, Wes chanced an indirect approach.

Wes contacted one of Clay Van Hoerne's aides to inquire about making a sizable contribution to the Congressman's reelection campaign. During this conversation, Wes mentioned his interest in forming an independent political coalition to fund television and print media ads in line with the congressman's views—and attacking the congressman's opponent.

Within a matter of days, Wes received a phone call from Delia Fahey Van Hoerne inviting him to her home.

"I find it positively refreshing that you do not abide by false modesty, Mr. McCaffrey," Delia told him, lowering her diminutive, Chanel-clad frame into a seat behind a vintage writing desk. "False modesty is a tedious waste of time, as far as I'm concerned."

"In my experience, most, if not all, modesty is false."

"That is so true, except for my son, of course," she clarified with a flutter of pearly, manicured fingernails. "Now there is a man with a deep sense of humility."

"A rare quality for a politician," Wes observed wryly.

"I know it's hard to believe in the political climate today, but Clayton is the exception to the rule. He's interested only helping those in need and giving back to the community and the country he loves so much."

"We should put you in our television commercials," Wes said with a perfectly straight face. "Or would that be a conflict of interest, between the congressman's campaign and our organization?"

"What is the name of your group, by the way?" Delia asked.

"The Free and United Coalition, ma'am," Wes replied, beaming with feigned pride.

"I like it—very catchy."

"That's what we are, ma'am, a coalition of free individuals united for a common goal . . ."

"F – U – . . ." Delia began stringing together the acronym, but stopped suddenly, her mouth pursed in a tiny 'o'.

"Would you be interested in making an appearance in our television ads?" Wes ventured innocently. "Or would that be inappropriate?"

"Er, uh, yes, that would be inappropriate," Delia stammered, unsure whether to alert Mr. McCaffrey to the fact that his coalition had a most unfortunate moniker.

"Well, the last thing we want to do is compromise the congressman's integrity," Wes assured her with a winning smile.

Delia rested her hands on the desk and leaned forward, getting down to business.

"I understand that your organization is interested in purchasing air time to address issues near and dear to my son's heart, is that correct?"

"Something like that."

"You realize, of course, that Clayton cannot be *directly* involved."

"Of course."

"But I'm sure he'd be willing to offer input and ideas regarding, shall we say, strategy."

"We intend to push the congressman's agenda," Wes nodded.

"Might I suggest another goal as well?" Delia said delicately.

"Certainly."

"I believe it is important that the public be fully informed about the other candidate, *warts and all*. Don't you?"

"Are you reading my mind, Mrs. Van Hoerne?" Wes teased.

"Obviously, Clayton is loath to malign the character and good name of his opponent, but sometimes my son can be too darn nice for his own good. Politics is a messy business, and it's no place for the faint of heart."

"You do have a way with the clichés."

"Excuse me?"

"Nothing. Do go on."

"In any event, I can assure you that Clayton will remember your generous loyalty even after election day, Mr. McCaffrey. He's not one to forget who his true friends are."

Wes considered trying to extract favors, just for the hell of it—see how far he could push this—but decided it was time to focus his energies on the task at hand.

"Should we talk dollars?" Delia asked casually, as if any such discussion could ever be nonchalant.

"Actually, there's one other matter we need to address *first*."

"What's that, Mr. McCaffrey?"

"Your son's extracurricular activities. His *hobbies*, if you will."

"Such as?"

"Such as his fondness for leather," Wes answered cryptically, extracting a large manila envelope from his attaché case and passing it to Delia Van Hoerne.

Initially, Delia seemed confused, but removing the 8 x 10 glossies from the envelope, she flashed Wes a venomous glare.

"What the hell is this?" she demanded, her voice as cold and dangerous as an ice pick.

"The pictures more or less speak for themselves," Wes observed, loosening the know of his tie. "I must commend you, Delia—I can call you Delia, right? Your son is extremely photogenic. Not many men can pull off a dog collar with that kind of finesse . . ."

"What do you want?"

". . . especially with a baton crammed up his ass like that."

Delia slammed the photographs on the desk blotter, face down, and glowered at Wes with abject fury.

"If you don't mind my saying," Wes continued, bemused, "you don't seem all that surprised by your son's proclivities. Tell me, has he always had a penchant for whips and chains, or is this a recent development?"

Delia shoved the pictures back into the envelope and threw them at Wes.

"I guess you think this is funny," Delia hissed, her chin trembling with anger.

"Yes ma'am, actually I do," Wes told her honestly. "But hey, give me credit for coming to you first. In a way, you owe me."

"*Owe you?*" Delia barked incredulously. "You slither your way into my home under false pretenses, attempt to blackmail me and my only child—a public official, by the way, lest you forget—and I *owe you?*"

"I could have easily hawked these photos to the press, but I came to you first, out of respect."

"Spare me," Delia spat, pulling out a checkbook. "How much?"

"There you go, wanting to talk dollars again."

"I repeat, how much!"

"It pains me, Delia, it really does, that you would think this is about *money*," Wes sighed.

"Listen and listen good, you son-of-a-bitch," she responded in a low, dark tone. "This is a limited time offer—a limited time offer of a one-time-only payment. You got me?"

"Gosh, Delia, you sound like an old pro at this. Let me guess: others before me have come into possession of these priceless family heirlooms?"

"I don't have time for your games, Mr. McCaffrey. Either you give me a figure, or I'm ripping up this check and you don't get a dime. What's it going to be?"

"You can put your checkbook away, Mrs. Van Hoerne," Wes told her with all seriousness. "I don't want your money."

Delia was caught off guard, and eyed Wes even more suspiciously.

"What else could you want?" she uttered primly, drawing her suit jacket around her body.

"Don't worry, Mrs. Van Hoerne," Wes laughed. "Your virtue is safe."

"Well, I certainly didn't think . . ."

"For now, anyway," Wes added cheekily. "No, I need something else from you."

"Such as?"

"Information."

"What kind of information?"

"Information on Josiah Mantooth."

Delia blinked at him in surprise.

"Josiah? What about him?"

"That's what I want you to tell me," Wes told her.

"I don't understand."

"Come now, Mrs. Van Hoerne," he chided gently. "You know precisely what information I'm interested in."

"I haven't a clue," Delia insisted, slowly leaning back in her chair.

"The sooner you're straight with me, Delia, the sooner I'm out of your life," Wes countered, his gaze steely and determined.

"I don't know what you're talking about."

"I've already put most of the pieces together," he told her, bluffing. "I just need you to fill in the blanks."

"Pieces? What *pieces*?"

"Well, let's start with the money Josiah's funneled into Clay's campaign coffers. And then there's the way he's lining your pockets."

"Excuse me?"

"You know Delia, that generous check Josiah sends you every fiscal quarter."

"That money is for Charlotte," Delia retorted. "Josiah insists on contributing to her care and support, but of course Clayton refused, so Josiah puts the checks in my account. And as for his political donations, you aren't really questioning the man's right to exercise his constitutional rights, are you?"

"Got a ready explanation for everything, don't you Delia?"

"I don't need an explanation. It's the truth."

"Save it for the IRS, and whoever it is that oversees campaign finance irregularities."

That seemed to hit a nerve. Delia's jaw began to clench.

"You're starting to bore me, Mr. McCaffrey," Delia said, her voice belying her words.

Wes shrugged his shoulders, and readied himself for the next bluff.

"Josiah knows all about your son's sick, sexual perversions, Mrs. Van Hoerne," he stated coolly. "Why the hell did he never use it against him?"

This was the deciding moment, an audacious bit of bluffing based purely on conjecture. If Delia called bullshit—dared him to prove Josiah knew anything about Clay's S&M fetish—the game was likely over.

Wes paused, his expression impassive, waiting for Delia to put up a fight—or at least contradict such a bold assertion—but she didn't say a word. Not one word.

If it were poker, Wes would have said the woman blinked, and he took that as an admission.

"Not only did you manage to keep Josiah quiet, you even got him to fork over fistfuls of cash," Wes went on before Delia realized her mistake. "How the hell did you do it?"

Delia remained silent, but she dropped her hands into her lap and began to play with her rings absently: in poker-speak, a tell.

"The way I figure it, Josiah *did* try to use that information against Clay," Wes continued, "maybe he just wanted the bastard away from his daughter. Force Clay into a divorce, and lo and behold, Josiah regains control over Katherine, which is all the man ever *really* wanted. Please, Delia, correct me if I'm wrong here."

Again, no response.

"So, then tell me—how the hell did you turn the tables on him? What do you have on Mantooth?"

Still no response.

"Or should I refer this entire matter to the Internal Revenue Service?" Wes concluded.

Delia glared at the young man, weighing her options.

"I want the negatives," she said at last.

A familiar feeling of adrenaline and relief surged through Wes' body, and he nodded his agreement. It wasn't really much of a concession—he already had dozens of copies.

"And I never, *ever* want to see your miserable face again. Do I make myself clear?"

"You have my word as a gentleman."

"I do not find that amusing, Mr. McCaffrey," Delia sniffed.

She rose from her chair and crossed the room to the Courbet, which she pulled back to reveal a small titanium safe. From inside the safe, Delia produced a weathered, brown folder.

She returned to her desk and handed the folder to Wes. Inside, was a piece of paper on which was written a name, Monique Thibidault, and an address in Louisiana.

"I was merely fighting fire with fire," Delia stated. "Josiah was threatening my family. As you will find out, Mr. McCaffrey—if I ever have the great displeasure of laying eyes on you again—I will move heaven and earth to protect what's mine."

Wes did not doubt the woman's veracity for an instant.

"You're a much better poker player than I gave you credit for, Mrs. Van Hoerne," Wes told her with a hint of admiration.

31

The day before the court hearing was scheduled to begin, Ellie stood beside Katherine's bed staring at the syringe in her hand. Reaching into her lab coat, she withdrew a plastic cap and secured it over the needle. Then she dropped it onto a metal tray beside an empty glass vial.

Five hundred milligrams.

Katherine lay motionless on the bed, snoring ever so faintly. Retreating to the other side of the room, Ellie leaned back against the padded wall.

Five hundred milligrams. More than three times the previous dosage.

Ellie had never considered increasing the dosage so dramatically, but the seed had been planted in Ellie's brain by Katherine herself, or whatever personality Ellie confronted earlier in the week. Her encounter with Dr. March had solidified the idea, and the more Ellie thought about it, the more it made sense. A massive dose of Thymetrazine would shock Katherine's system, almost like rebooting a computer.

Ellie was mulling this over when an orderly peeked his head into the room.

"Dr. Dodds, your visitor is here."

Ellie nodded, and Jackson Polke walked into Katherine's room, the door closing behind him.

"Is something wrong?" Ellie asked.

"No, no, just wanted to see how Katherine's doing," Jackson assured her. "And you."

Ellie exhaled and went back to staring at Katherine's sleeping figure.

"What are you looking at?" Jackson whispered, afraid to disturb the silence.

"Katherine."

"Why?"

"Because."

"Has something happened?"

"Not yet."

"Not yet?"

"I'm waiting."

"For what?"

"Something to happen."

"Huh?"

"Shhh."

"Afraid I'll wake Katherine?" Jackson whispered.

"Highly unlikely."

"Is she sedated?"

"Not exactly."

"Then what?"

"She's resting."

"I can see that."

"Her body has shut down all non-vital functions in an effort to harness more energy."

"Why?"

"To metabolically process the higher levels of Thymetrazine in the blood stream."

"Um, okay," Jackson answered, making no attempt to hide his confusion. "Just tell me, is there any reason that I have to understand any of this scientific crap?"

"No."

"Good, because I'm too damn tired to think about it," Jackson said drowsily, stifling a yawn. "Do you mind if I just sit here and keep you company while you wait for whatever it is you're waiting for?"

"I'd like that," Ellie smiled.

Jackson lowered himself to the floor, resting his head against the wall's soft padding.

"Let me know if anything happens," he remarked before closing his eyelids.

Jackson woke with a start, barely conscious of the noise that yanked him out of a dream. It took Jackson several seconds to remember where he was, and why Ellie's head of soft, beautiful curls was cradled in his lap. She was asleep, using Jackson's knee as a pillow. He found himself staring at her, marveling at the delicate smoothness of her skin and the exquisite structure of her bones.

But then Jackson heard the noise again.

It was more distinct now—a breathless mewling sound—scarcely loud enough to be heard over Ellie's rhythmic breathing.

It was dark in the hospital room, save for a hazy glow from above the bed. Jackson squinted, until at last his eyes were able to delineate shapes.

The bed was empty.

Looking around, Jackson searched the shadowed corners of the room, and his gaze landed on a figure standing in front of the mirror affixed to the wall.

Katherine.

She was running her fingertips over the contours of her face, her mouth frozen open as she examined her reflection with horror.

The mewling sound that had been coming from Katherine morphed into quiet, unmistakable sobbing.

"Ellie, get up," he whispered, shaking her by the shoulder. "Ellie! Get up!"

Ellie turned onto her back and smiled up at Jackson.

"Hi there," she said, finally noticing that Jackson was pointing across the room frantically.

Sitting up, Ellie rubbed her eyes and stared into the gloom.

"How long has she been like that?" Ellie demanded in a whisper.

"She was like that when I woke up."

"Why didn't you wake me?"

"I just did."

Ellie crawled closer to Katherine and crouched in a squat. She motioned for Jackson to do the same.

"I don't want her to feel threatened," Ellie told him when he hesitated.

"What is she, a Doberman pinscher?"

"Shhh."

"Maybe I should let her sniff my hand."

"Will you please shut up?" Ellie commanded.

The sobbing was louder—still tight and constrained, but gaining in intensity. Katherine rocked back and forth on her heels, shaking her head despondently.

"Hello?" Ellie said carefully, standing. "It's me, Dr. Dodds."

"Oh God," Katherine began repeating over and over again, covering her face with the palms of her hands. "Oh God, what have I done?"

"I'm Dr. Dodds," Ellie said more loudly, inching closer. "Do you know me?"

"This can't be happening," the woman wailed, now openly weeping. "Oh God, this can't be happening."

"Katherine?" Ellie asked tentatively, stepping forward. "Is that you?"

The wailing instantly ceased.

"Are you Katherine?" Ellie coaxed. "Because if you are— Katherine, I mean—I'm awfully glad to meet you."

The woman dropped her hands and turned to Ellie, dazed, her eyelashes still heavy with tears.

"Yes," she said, choking back tears. "I'm Katherine."

32

Judge Harold Boone banged his gavel out of frustration and ordered his bailiff to search the corridors.

"And check in the basement," Boone added irritably. "Those damn snack machines are a nuisance. I knew they would be."

"Your honor," Delroy Duffy's voice rang out through the courtroom, "if Mr. Polke can't be bothered to appear on time, he doesn't deserve your leniency. He's thumbing his nose at the court, and those of us who manage to be punctual."

"Thank you for sharing your opinion, Mr. Duffy."

"I wouldn't be at all surprised if shame and wounded pride kept Mr. Polke from appearing here today. No, not surprised at all."

Harold Boone ignored the remark and opened a fresh package of lozenges.

"If I were you, Judge," Delroy added, "I would enter an order, *sua sponte*, granting the motion on the grounds that counsel failed to appear."

"Would you now?"

Suddenly, a crack echoed across the courtroom as Jackson banged open the thick, mahogany door.

"I apologize for being late, your honor," Jackson said breathlessly, his hair in disarray.

"Twenty minutes late, Mr. Polke," Boone replied sourly.

"It couldn't be helped, sir."

"Can we *please* get on with this?" Delroy demanded. "A woman's life hangs in the balance."

"Yes, let's get this show on the road . . ." Boone began.

"May it please the Court," Jackson interrupted. "There has been a development that I believe renders these proceedings moot as a matter of law."

"Moot?" Boone repeated, surprised.

"Moot.

"I have compelling evidence showing that the motion that is the subject of this hearing should be denied, and the matter dismissed immediately."

Delroy Duffy jumped up like he was coming off a starter's pistol, saying, "I vehemently object, your honor!"

"I have a video," Jackson went on, over Duffy's objections, "the contents of which render this hearing invalid as a matter of law."

"Objection on all sorts of grounds! Relevance, prejudice, authentication, constitutional issues . . ."

"Judge Boone," Jackson spoke more loudly, "you could view the tape in chambers, *in camera*, and decide if its contents support my argument. Then we could address Mr. Duffy's objections one by one, if necessary."

"Your honor, this is absurd!

"Pipe down, Duffy," Boone told him, contemplating this new development. "It seems like a mighty reasonable plan to me. Let's go look at your video."

Josiah Mantooth stood up, looking more furious than concerned, as he watched the trio leave the courtroom. Bobbie Dean came up behind him and rubbed his shoulders. He patted her hand gently, and they both returned to their seats. Expecting an extended delay, Bobbie Dean took out her cell phone, and Josiah unfolded a newspaper.

Before Bobbie Dean could access her emails, the bailiff entered the courtroom and called the court back into session.

It was a strange procession that followed: Delroy Duffy, wearing a bewildered, frazzled expression, like he'd been on the receiving end of a stun gun; Jackson Polke, boasting a genuine, honest-to-God smile; and Judge Harold Boone, who was shaking his balding head in sheer amazement.

"You live long enough, ladies and gentlemen, you see everything," Boone pronounced, retaking the bench. "There has been a truly astounding turn of events."

Jackson heard Josiah hiss, "What is he talking about?"

"I will leave to counsel the task of explaining these astonishing events to their respective clients. Frankly, I believe this is now a family matter, best discussed in private.

"Jesus Christ, Delroy, what is he talking about!" Josiah demanded, making no effort to keep his voice down.

Ignoring the outburst, Judge Boone continued.

"In light of recent developments that have just now come to the Court's attention, this proceeding has been rendered moot as a matter of law. Accordingly, the Court hereby finds that the motion filed by Josiah Mantooth in this matter is hereby dismissed without prejudice."

"Object, goddamn it!" Josiah shouted to his unresponsive lawyer. "Get off your ass and object! What the hell am I paying you for?"

"The Court further orders that, for the time being, Mr. Jackson Polke remain the attorney of record for the defendant," Boone added.

"Objection! I object!" Josiah sputtered. "I'm making a goddamn objection here, Harold!"

"The Court shall monitor this case for further developments and will convene a hearing in no more than six weeks to review any pending issues."

"You can't just ignore me, Harold! Damn it, I'm talking here!!"

"From now on, Katherine can make her own decisions," Judge Harold Boone announced to the courtroom. "This hearing is adjourned."

PART III

1

"What now?" Katherine asked, her voice little more than a choked whisper.

Ellie had just finished explaining to Katherine everything that had happened in the preceding five years, a painful experience for both doctor and patient.

Katherine's face was a stoic mask, but her clear blue eyes registered each horror and indignity clearly.

On the outside, of course, Katherine looked more or less the same, yet she seemed an entirely different person. More human, was how Ellie thought of it. The alters had all been one-dimensional caricatures, shallow facsimiles of real personalities. But Katherine was herself, a real person.

Ellie considered the question. *What happens now?*

"You concentrate on getting well," Ellie told her.

"Do people like me get well?"

"Yes, Katherine, people like you, people who suffer from a terrible, debilitating illness, can and do get well."

A single tear slid down Katherine's cheek, and she wiped at it roughly, as if annoyed by her own weakness.

"It'll be hard work, but now that we've got you on the right medications, it'll be a whole lot easier."

"And you'll stay on as my doctor?"

"If that's what you want."

Katherine took a deep breath and let it out in a long slow exhale.

"Will I go to jail? For killing that man."

"How about you let Mr. Polke worry about that, and you concentrate on getting well. For the foreseeable future, you'll be staying here."

Katherine nodded and took a fresh tissue from the box beside her.

"Do you think . . . I mean . . . can you really help me?" she said softly, the tears quickening.

"I'm sure gonna try," Ellie promised.

2

Ignoring the irate assistant stationed outside, Jackson stormed into Wendy Holcomb's office waving a sheet of paper.

"What the hell is this about?!" he nearly shouted.

The district attorney sighed and motioned for her assistant to leave, indicating the disruption was all right. Jackson noticed she didn't look particularly surprised to see him.

Wendy Holcomb was a stout, dour-looking woman who had been in office only a few years. She introduced Jackson to the man seated across from her, Commander Ramon Hinojosa.

He didn't seem surprised to see Jackson, either.

"We spoke on the phone," the man told him by way of greeting, eying Jackson pointedly. "You may not recall."

"Oh right," Jackson replied hesitantly, trying without much success to remember the specifics of that horrible night after Tommy's death.

"Mr. Polke," Wendy Holcomb said, drawing Jackson's attention. "Chief Hinojosa and I were just discussing Mrs. Van Hoerne's case . . ."

"I asked you a question—what the hell is this?" Jackson demanded loudly, again waving the piece of paper.

"I can only assume that's the letter from this office asking for an interview with Mrs. Van Hoerne," the DA replied smoothly.

"Why do you want to talk to my client?" Jackson shot back.

Jackson saw Holcomb and Hinojosa exchange a glance, their faces somber.

"We are reopening the investigation into the murder of Angel Ramirez," Ramon answered. "The Ramirez family deserves to know the truth of what happened that night. Obviously, we'll need to talk to Mrs. Van Hoerne now that she's . . . well, recovered. She remains the prime suspect."

An uncomfortable silence descended on the room. When Jackson spoke, his voice was low, harsh.

"Did you say *prime suspect*?"

"I did," Ramon responded evenly.

"Are you actually suggesting that you might try to prosecute my client for murder?" Jackson asked, stunned.

"If that's where the investigation takes us, then yes."

Jackson turned to stare at the DA, who simply nodded her head in agreement.

"You've got to be shitting me!" Jackson bellowed. "My client was legally insane at the time of the murder. What part of ape-shit crazy do you not understand?"

"Please lower your voice, Mr. Polke," Wendy Holcomb said calmly. "As a servant of the people, I am obliged to ensure that justice is served."

"Save that crap for the cameras!" Jackson fumed, reeling on Ramon. "And you! You don't give a damn about the truth, just getting your pound of flesh."

"That is quite enough, Mr. Polke," the district attorney told him. "The decision has been made. We will be proceeding with our investigation."

"Fine, have it your way!" Jackson stated hotly, making to leave. "But I'm warning you now, when we meet in court, I am going to kick your sorry ass from here to Sunday. And then, I'm going to slap both of you and both of your departments with the biggest goddamn lawsuit this state has ever seen—I'm going to bankrupt you and your spouses and maybe even your goddamn kids!"

With that, Jackson marched out of the district attorney's office, slamming the door shut behind him.

"The kid's got spunk, gotta give him that," Wendy Holcomb sighed after Jackson had left. "He might just blow this thing wide open for you."

"As long as he doesn't get in my way," Ramon answered brusquely. "God deliver me from well-intentioned, amateur sleuths."

"Well, I guess it's now official, for better or worse. This plan of yours is in effect."

"You got a better idea?" Ramon countered. "Trust me, I'm open to suggestions."

"I've already told you I don't."

"Then stop waffling. This trial will never see the inside of a courtroom."

3

"Could she really go to jail?"

"No," Jackson assured Ellie over the phone. "Katherine was insane. She's not responsible for her actions, and under the law that makes her innocent. That's all there is to it."

"Then why go through all this? Why waste everyone's time and energy with a trial?"

"Free publicity," Jackson answered. "Holcomb doesn't need a press secretary, she needs a Hollywood agent. And a case like this, with a defendant like Katherine Van Hoerne, could make her career. Hell, it could make her famous."

They should have been celebrating. After Boone had seen that tape of Katherine answering basic questions—establishing that she was oriented in the present, cognizant of her surroundings, aware of her situation—it took only seconds for him to rule in their favor.

And only minutes after that, Jackson received a hand-delivered letter from the district attorney requesting an interview with Katherine.

"How is she?" Jackson asked.

Ellie took a deep breath before responding.

"Hard to say," Ellie told him. "She's coherent, rational, but she has no memory of the last five years, including that night with Angel Ramirez. I had to tell her about that, about the murder and her own mental breakdown, and how she's lost this huge chunk of her life. It was pretty gut-wrenching."

"What happens now?"

"Intensive psychotherapy."

"We also have a defense to prepare," Jackson noted dully.

"I can't believe they would do this to her, after everything Katherine's already been through."

"And yet they are. I'm leaving for New Orleans tomorrow morning."

"New Orleans?"

"I got a tip from a friend of mine—the current whereabouts of Monique Thibidault, also known as Mama Tante. She was the Cajun nanny who worked for the Mantooths all through Katherine's childhood."

"You mean the woman Tish Ambrose told us about? The one who came with Gabrielle from New Orleans?"

"Precisely. Mama Tante now lives in a nursing home just outside the city. Unfortunately, according to the receptionist, she had a stroke a few years back that affected her speech, but I thought I'd go meet with her anyway."

"Want me to come along? Stroke victims often develop alternate means of communication," Ellie told him. "I have some experience."

"Sure. It's a one-day trip, coming back tomorrow night."

"Katherine will be busy with medical exams and cognitive testing, so that should be fine. When do we leave?"

4

Nathan Conrad and Jared Hawthorne appeared in Ramon's office the next morning.

"How have you been, Ramon?" Nathan asked, his tone neutral.

"Fine, and yourself?"

"Good, good," Nathan replied, taking a seat without being offered and motioning for Hawthorne to do the same. "I've been training for another marathon. You know how that is."

"No, not really," Ramon responded, rubbing the slight paunch of his midsection. "I never could understand the appeal."

"Running is my drug, Ramon, I admit it."

"I suppose there are worse vices out there."

"No doubt."

"So, what can I do for you gentlemen?" Ramon asked casually.

"I just thought the three of us should sit down, have a powwow of sorts," Nathan answered. "About the Katherine Van Hoerne case."

"You mean the Angel Ramirez case?" Ramon quietly corrected.

"Right. I spoke to the DA earlier. She informed me that the investigation into Mr. Ramirez's death has been reopened."

"The fact had come to my attention."

Nathan stated, "Since you and Lieutenant Hawthorne were the lead detectives on the case five years ago, I thought we should all get together and see where we are."

Jared smiled across the desk at Ramon and added, "I would have discussed this with you earlier, Chief, but you haven't been around much lately."

Ramon could have sworn the smarmy son of a bitch winked at him, but Hawthorne might have had dust in his eye, or a tic.

"So, Ramon, Jared—where are we?" Nathan inquired.

"I guess we need to go back to the old file," Ramon observed innocently. "Start there."

"You want me to get on that, Chief?" Hawthorne offered.

"Good idea, Jared," Nathan responded before Ramon could even open his mouth. "You're our point man on this. The commander has better things to do than legwork. Right, Ramon?"

"Right, Chief," Ramon agreed, managing to keep a straight face. "Hawthorne, you start reviewing the file, and get back to me."

"No problemo, Chief. I know how *busy* you've been."

"I want you to keep Hawthorne in the loop, Ramon," Nathan added with particular emphasis. "He needs to know everything you know."

"He's the point man," Ramon repeated.

Suddenly, the door to Ramon's office was thrown open and Tammy Lynn Geary burst in.

"Oh sorry, Chief," she stammered, backing out. "I didn't know you were busy."

"No, it's all right," Ramon assured her. "I believe we're done."

Tammy Lynn waited patiently while Conrad and Hawthorne stood up to leave. Walking out, Hawthorne leeringly appraised Tammy Lynn and then smirked at Ramon.

"What the hell is up with that guy?" Ramon asked after the door had closed. "He seems especially unctuous today."

"Oh that, he thinks we're having an affair," Tammy Lynn told him.

"He what?" Ramon croaked.

"He thinks we're sleeping together," she explained, seemingly unconcerned.

"You and me?"

"Yep."

"But . . . but, why?"

"Seems that Jared noticed us spending more time together, ducking out of the station at about the same time, that sort of thing. He put two and two together and, fortunately for us, came up with five. I haven't done much to quash his suspicions."

"Why not?"

"You'd rather he figure out the truth?"

"No, but . . ."

"The goal is to keep him off our backs, right?"

"I suppose so. But I would never want to do anything to compromise your reputation, Detective."

"Hey, at least it'll quiet all that speculation about me being a lesbian," Tammy Lynn shrugged. "Not that it matters."

Ramon dropped the matter somewhat grudgingly, and recounted for Tammy Lynn his meeting with Conrad and Hawthorne.

"So Hawthorne's off looking for the missing file," Tammy Lynn grinned broadly.

"After that, I'm going to send him to find the nonexistent evidence."

"That should keep him busy for a while. "

"Was there a reason you barged in earlier, Detective?" Ramon asked.

"Oh right!" Tammy Lynn exclaimed excitedly. "I saw the photographs. The ones Mike Earley took of the Gabrielle Mantooth crime scene. He's making copies for me now."

"And?"

"Not only is the position of the body inconsistent with a fall—which we already assumed—the trajectory indicated a near lateral propulsion."

"So Gabrielle Mantooth jumped to her death . . ."

"No."

"No?"

"Mrs. Mantooth was found on her back. The position of the body was not only inconsistent with a fall, it was inconsistent with a suicide. Unless, she decided to go out with an Olympic-caliber backwards dive, which seems highly unlikely."

Ramon mulled over the implications.

"Maybe the family moved the body," Ramon countered.

"Not according to the CSU team. They confirmed the body hadn't been moved."

"Could she have turned in mid-air, for God's sake? Hit a goddamn tree on the way down? Something like that?"

"No, sir."

Ramon sucked in his cheeks, as if recovering from something tart and sour.

"Then what you're telling me, Detective," he said with a sigh, "is that you believe Mrs. Mantooth was *pushed* off that balcony."

"Yes, sir," Tammy Lynn replied softly.

"You got anything other than the position of the body?"

"There wasn't scratch on Gabrielle's face—totally undamaged by the fall. There was, however, a large purple and black bruise on her left cheek, the shape and size of an open hand."

"You're sure?"

"Absolutely."

"Could Conrad and Stiles have missed it?"

"Not unless they were trying real hard."

"So, they weren't covering up a suicide at all. It was murder."

"Very possibly, yes."

"I want to see those pictures. I also want to see everything you've pulled together in the Ramirez case, including the forensics report."

"About that, Chief: a couple hours ago, Mrs. Van Hoerne's lawyer filed a request for copies of everything we have in the Angel Ramirez investigation. How do you want to handle it?"

Ramon leaned back, put his hands behind his head, and considered the question.

"Give it to him."

"All of it?"

"That's what the law says, right?"

5

After reciting the address for the cab driver, Jackson sat back on the worn leather seat and rolled down his window.

"Have you ever been here before?" Ellie asked, opening her own window.

"New Orleans? Oh sure, plenty of Fat Tuesdays."

"Fat Tuesdays?"

"Mardi Gras. How about you?"

"First time."

"Oh yeah? I'll have to take you down to the French Quarter for lunch. Show you around a bit."

"Will we have time?"

"I guess that depends on Mama Tante."

"What do you know about her condition?" Ellie asked. "Is she aphasic?"

"*A-what?*"

"Aphasic."

"All I know is what the lady on the phone told me—Mrs. Thibidault had a debilitating stroke that left her unable to talk."

"Did you instruct her to notify the staff of our arrival?"

"Um, I mentioned that I'd be flying into New Orleans today, and would visit Mrs. Thibidault. Is that the same thing?"

"Hopefully."

"Does it matter?"

"Not really. I was just hoping that we'd get to meet any staff members who have day-to-day contact with her."

"Why?"

"With aphasics, oftentimes there are one or two people on staff, usually nurses, who are more adept at communicating with the patient, because of their daily contact."

"Well, I'll let you take the lead."

"I told you having a doctor along might be useful," Ellie replied.

The cab crested a hill, and in the distance Jackson could see the Camellia Gables Assisted Living Center. Located in a meticulously restored manor house at the end of a long tree-lined drive, Camellia Gables sat atop the last few acres of what was once a sprawling cotton plantation. Although intended to be historically accurate, Jackson noted the building was outfitted with anachronistic modern conveniences, such as ramps and elevator-like devices, to accommodate the varying physical limitations of its residents.

After paying the driver, Jackson and Ellie climbed the exterior double staircase to the first floor veranda and pushed open the doors.

"Hello," the receptionist said brightly, wearing a button on her denim dress that read "Ask Me About Game Night!"

"Hello," Ellie responded.

"What can I do for you?" she asked cheerfully.

Jackson fought down the compulsion to ask about game night and instead told her, "We're here to see Monique Thibidault."

"Oh, Mama Tante," the receptionist replied, picking up a clipboard covered in cheerful stickers sporting such motivational messages as *Turn that frown upside down!* and *Inspire Others!*

"You're Jackson Polke?"

Jackson nodded.

"Then you're on my list," she exclaimed, checking off an item on her clipboard and pressing a buzzer on her desk.

"Excellent," Jackson remarked, tilting his head to read the letters on the side of her pen. "What does WWJD stand for?"

"What Would Jesus Do, silly," the woman replied, as if Jackson had crash-landed from another planet. "Are you not familiar with our Lord and Savior Jesus Christ?"

Just then, a pleasant looking nurse in a starched, white pantsuit arrived, introducing herself as Suzette.

"Do you work with Mrs. Thibidault closely?" Ellie asked Suzette as they followed her up a grand staircase to the second floor.

"I am the head nurse for in-patient care, so I get to spend time with all of our ailing residents," Suzette told them in a thick Louisiana drawl, "but I'm especially fond of Mama Tante. We all are."

"I understand that she's aphasic."

"Yes, poor thing, irreversible aphasia, from the stroke. Unable to speak, but her mind's still sharp as a tack. Mama Tante lets us know what she wants through blinking."

"When did she have the stroke?"

"Autumn of last year."

"Is that when she came to live here, at Camellia Gables?"

"Oh my, no, Mama Tante has lived with us for almost 20 years now, first in assisted living and now with 24-hour nursing care."

"That must be expensive," Jackson remarked, wondering how a retired nanny could afford a nursing home like Camellia Gables.

"The best always is, but Mama Tante doesn't have to worry about money."

"Is that so?"

"Well, yes," Suzette said hesitantly. "It's not a secret or anything."

"What isn't?"

"Mama Tante inherited a great deal of money from a benefactor."

"A former employer?"

"Perhaps."

"Gabrielle Mantooth, by any chance?" Jackson pressed.

"I have no idea, but it affords Mama Tante the ability to spend her twilight years in a wonderful environment. Not all of the elderly folks in this country are so fortunate."

"That's very true," Ellie agreed.

Nurse Suzette led them to a medium-sized room decorated comfortably in soothing mint green tones. Seated in a wheelchair, her left hand propped on an attached plastic tray, was Mama Tante.

Her body was shriveled and lifeless, a crocheted shawl draped over her drooping shoulders. The right side of the body hunched in on itself like an irregularly melted candle, and the weathered face was frozen in a gruesome, half-snarl expression. Most startling of all were the woman's yellow eyes, which studied her visitors with keen awareness.

"Mama Tante, this is Jackson and Eleanor," Suzette told her kindly. "They want to sit with you for a spell."

Other than the flutter of eyelashes, there was no movement from Mama Tante.

Ellie leaned down next to the wheelchair and said, "Is it one blink for yes and two for no?"

Mama Tante's wrinkled eyelids blinked once.

"Would you like to go out on the veranda?" Ellie asked.

Again, a single blink, but Suzette interceded.

"That's probably not wise. Mama Tante has a bit of a cold."

"That's fine," Ellie answered, sitting on the afghan-covered bed. "I think we'll be okay from here on out Suzette. You probably need to get back to your duties anyway."

"Perhaps I should stay . . ."

"Nonsense, Suzette," Jackson said, taking her by the arm. "You go on and get back to work. I think Dr. Dodds there has the hang of this blinking thing."

"But . . . I . . ."

"We sure appreciate your time and consideration," Jackson added before drawing open the door and practically shoving Nurse Suzette out. "If we need anything, I'll holler."

"Smooth, Jackson," Ellie mocked. "Very smooth."

"She's gone, isn't she?"

Ellie turned back to Mama Tante, smiled warmly, and said "Thank you for seeing us. My name is Dr. Ellie Dodds and I'm a psychiatrist. One of my patients is Katherine Mantooth Van Hoerne. This is Jackson Polke, Katherine's attorney. You were her nanny, right, when you worked for Gabrielle Mantooth?"

Mama Tante blinked one time. *Yes.*

"I understand that you were a trusted and loyal friend to Gabrielle."

Yes.

Ellie exhaled slowly and leaned closer to the woman.

"Katherine's in a great deal of trouble, Mama Tante. She's ill."

Yes.

"Mentally ill."

Yes.

"Gabrielle Mantooth was also ill, wasn't she Mama Tante?" Ellie asked.

Yes.

"She was ill for a long time, right? Often bedridden?"

Yes.

"And you took care of her, didn't you?"

Yes.

"Did you know Gabrielle for a long time?"

Yes.

"How long? Oh wait, scratch that. Was it more than ten years?"

Yes.

"More than 15?"

Yes.

"So, you knew Gabrielle's first husband?"

Yes.

"When he died, is that when you first noticed Gabrielle's depression?"

No.

"No? So you knew about it before then?"

Yes.

"Did it begin when she was an adolescent?"

Yes.

"It did?"

Yes.

Ellie glanced over at Jackson and said, "It's hereditary."

Because Ellie's head was turned, she missed Mama Tante's eyelids move, but Jackson caught it."

"She blinked once," Jackson told Ellie.

"Hereditary?" Ellie repeated.

Yes.

"Did you know Gabrielle's mother—Katherine's grandmother?"

Yes.

"Did she exhibit the same symptoms?"

Yes.

"Did it go back even farther?"

Yes.

"How would she know that?" Jackson interjected. "She can't be that old."

"People talk," Ellie ventured. "Right, Mama Tante?"

Yes.

"No offense," Jackson remarked dryly, "but maybe they should have stopped procreating."

"Oh for heaven's sake, these women didn't understand what was happening to them, and their husbands sure as hell didn't."

"Still," Jackson muttered.

"The disease would have affected each individual differently. On one end of the spectrum, there's a nagging bout of the blues. On the other end, behavior once mistaken for demonic possession."

"And right smack in the middle, you've got your garden variety psychopath," Jackson noted.

Returning her attention to Mama Tante, Ellie said, "Didn't Katherine have a half-sister, from Gabrielle's first marriage? Avery?"

Mama Tante stared at them coldly. Her eyelids never moved.

"What does that mean?" Jackson said to Ellie, who only shrugged.

"Mama Tante?" Ellie asked. "Did Avery show signs of the disease?"

The old woman raised her head but didn't blink.

"You do know that Avery is dead, don't you Mama Tante?" Ellie asked.

Yes.

"She died in a fire, not long after Gabrielle passed . . ."

Sighing, Jackson strode across the room and sat down on the bed beside Mama Tante.

"Mama Tante, do you remember Gabrielle's husband, Josiah Mantooth?" he asked her.

The yellow eyes narrowed, then blinked once.

Yes.

"Was he a son of a bitch back then, too?"

"Jackson!" Ellie scolded, but Mama Tante replied anyway.

Yes.

"So you didn't much care for the bastard, eh?"

No.

"Me neither."

"Jackson, may I talk to you out in the hallway," Ellie insisted, taking Jackson's arm.

"Mama Tante and I are having a discussion," he told her, pulling his elbow free. "Isn't that right, Mama Tante?"

Yes.

"We must be careful not to cause Mama Tante any undue stress, *remember?*" Ellie hissed.

"She wants to talk to me."

"Jackson, you're upsetting the poor lady!"

"Are you upset?"

No.

"See!" Jackson smiled. "Now, where were we, Mama Tante? Oh yes, Josiah."

Yes.

"Have you kept in touch, you and Josiah?"

No.

"Don't blame you. When did you stop working for the Mantooth family? Was it after Gabrielle died?"

Yes.

"But weren't you also Katherine's nanny?"

Yes.

"Didn't you want to stick around, for her sake?"

Yes.

"You did?"

Yes.

"Then why'd you leave? Did Josiah send you away?"

Yes.

"Do you know why?"

No.

"He didn't explain why he was dismissing you?"

No.

"We are aware that Gabrielle's death was not the accident it was purported to be," Jackson said, choosing his words carefully. "Gabrielle committed suicide, didn't she?"

No.

"You don't have to protect her anymore."

No.

"By being honest with us, you'll be helping Katherine," Ellie added.

No.

"No what? No you don't want to help Katherine?"

No.

"You do want to help Katherine?" Ellie struggled.

Yes.

"You do?"

Yes.

"But this won't help Katherine?"

"Mama Tante," Jackson said, cutting Ellie off. "Did Gabrielle commit suicide?"

No. No. No.

"I think we have our answer," Jackson reported to Ellie. "Gabrielle's death really was an accident."

No.

"No?" Ellie repeated.

No.

"Well, it was either a suicide or an accident . . ."

A sickening suspicion struck both Jackson and Ellie at once, and they talked over each other to ask the tired and frustrated Mama Tante the same question.

"Was she pushed?"

Yes!

"Holy shit!" Jackson shouted before getting control of himself.

"Holy shit," Ellie repeated in a whisper. "Do you know who did it Mama Tante?"

No.

"But you are positive it was deliberate?"

Yes.

"Were you there? In Gabrielle's bedroom?"

No.

"Was there an argument? Did you hear fighting?"

Yes.

"Could you identify the voices?"

No.

"Josiah!" Jackson spat. "Had to be!"

"We don't know that," Ellie cautioned.

"Come on Mama Tante," Jackson nearly begged, "tell me it was Josiah! Tell me you know 100% for sure it was that bastard!"

Mama Tante's eyes almost sparkled with amusement, but they blinked twice nonetheless.

"But it's possible, right?" Jackson pressed.

Yes.

"Aha! That's good enough for me!"

"The police probably won't find that persuasive."

"There's no statute of limitations on murder," Jackson pointed out.

Just then, Mama Tante's crab-like hand began to move.

"Did you see that?" Jackson asked Ellie, startled.

"What?"

"On the tray, attached to the wheelchair."

Ellie looked at Mama Tante's left hand, moving back and forth across the plastic. She noticed the fingers were curled as if holding a writing utensil.

Digging into her oversized tote bag, Ellie retrieved a pen and arranged it between Mama Tante's fingers. Then Ellie placed a small notepad on the plastic tray and held Mama Tante's hand over it.

It was a painfully slow process, and physically tortuous for the old woman. The left side of her body was literally shaking from the exertion, yet Mama Tante could only execute the faintest, most rudimentary of lines. Finally, she lifted the pen.

When she had finished, Ellie examined the paper.

"Are those supposed to be letters?" Jackson asked.

"Symbols maybe?" Ellie shrugged.

"Sanskrit? Hieroglyphics?"

"Don't joke, it has to mean something!"

"It's unintelligible!"

"Those lines clearly have some significance."

Jackson got down on his knees beside the old woman's chair, and his voice took on a pleading tone.

"Listen to me, Mama Tante, Josiah is making Katherine's life a living nightmare. Even now, he's trying to control her, control everyone around her. He would rather see her rot in a padded cell than live any kind of life."

Mama Tante's nostrils flared, and she shut her eyelids tight.

"We're running out of time and ideas, Mama Tante," he went on. "You are, literally, our last hope."

Tears seeped from beneath the old woman's eyelashes, and her withered arm banged the tray with a thud. Suddenly, out of nowhere, a cringe-inducing screech escaped her lips, crawling right up Jackson's spine.

Mama Tante's hand started to fly up and down, smacking hard against the plastic tray, while she wailed ever louder.

Mere seconds passed before Suzette appeared at the door.

"What is going on in here?" the nurse demanded, dashing to Mama Tante's side.

"We didn't mean to upset her," Ellie apologized, shoving the notepad into her purse.

"You need to leave. Now!" Suzette commanded, feeling for Mama Tante's pulse. "I told you Mama Tante was not well."

"But what you didn't tell us . . ." Ellie began before Jackson pulled her away.

"Of course, we understand," Jackson said, putting his arm around Ellie's shoulder and spinning her around.

"But . . ." Ellie protested feebly.

"We'll come back later," Jackson whispered, dragging her away as Mama Tante shrieked.

Jackson took Ellie to the French Quarter for lunch, and she barely spoke to him the entire meal.

"I had questions," she muttered over her eggs benedict, still sore that Jackson hustled her away from Nurse Suzette.

"I thought it best the nurse attend to her distressed patient," Jackson reiterated for the umpteenth time.

"I had one question for her," Ellie stated, holding up her index finger. "One."

"One question, my ass," Jackson snorted. "You were about to interrogate that woman."

"Well, Nurse Suzette has some explaining to do."

"Which she can do *after* she saves Mama Tante's life. Agreed?"

"Agreed," Ellie finally acquiesced.

Just as Jackson was finishing the watery dregs of his second cocktail, his cell phone rang. It was a brief conversation, and when Jackson hung up the phone, his fingers were shaking.

"We killed her," he said in dazed, hollow voice. "We killed Mama Tante."

Nurse Suzette was barely polite when Jackson and Ellie arrived at Camellia Gables later that afternoon.

"You needn't have wasted a trip back here," she told them sharply.

"How exactly did Mama Tante pass?" Ellie asked.

"Her heart finally gave out, poor creature," Suzette sighed sadly.

"I told you we killed her," Jackson hissed into Ellie's ear.

"Now, if you don't mind . . ." Suzette said, motioning toward the exit in a gesture of dismissal.

"Actually, Suzette, I have a few more questions . . ."

"I really do need to get back to work, Dr. Dodds. I'm sure you understand."

"Yes, of course," Ellie replied, sounding defeated. "We can show ourselves out."

Jackson and Ellie slowly retraced their steps back to the lobby. Just as they were about to leave the building, they were stopped by a shouting voice.

"Are you Mr. Polke?" a muscular flame-haired young man hollered, hurrying toward them from the elevator. "Mr. Polke?"

"Yes?"

"I was afraid I missed y'all," he told them breathlessly, dropping his knapsack onto the floor. "I told Suzette to come get me if you showed up, but she said you were in a rush."

"She did?"

"Shep Rowlins," he said by way of introduction. "I'm one of the physical therapists here at Camellia Gables."

"It's nice to meet you, Shep," Jackson replied. "This is Dr. Ellie Dodds."

"Good to know ya," he said, pumping her hand. "It's a hell of a thing about Mama Tante, isn't it? I miss the crotchety old mule already."

"Crotchety?" Jackson remarked. "I thought Mama Tante was beloved by the staff."

"Beloved? Mama Tante? Not likely," Shep laughed. "Don't get me wrong, 'cause I was genuinely fond of the biddy, but she was a royal pain in the ass."

"Forgive me, Shep, but you don't seem too shook up about her sudden death," Jackson observed.

"Mama Tante had the terminal stomach cancer, so it's not unexpected."

"I thought it was her heart?" Ellie interrupted.

"In the end, something has to go," Shep shrugged.

"Did you work closely with Mama Tante?"

"Hour-long therapy sessions, twice a day, five days a week."

"You communicated through blinking, right?"

"And a smattering of written symbols," Shep added.

"Oh," Ellie exclaimed, rifling through her purse for the notepad with Mama Tante's scribblings. "Can you decipher this?"

"Sure," he said. "That's me. Or the symbol for me."

"She was asking for you," Ellie told him. "Can anyone else decode her writing?"

"Nah, but most of the staff would know that symbol. Did you show it to Suzette?"

"No, I didn't," Ellie confessed, annoyed with herself.

"Wish I'd known about your visit ahead of time, so I could have arranged to be here."

"You weren't told?"

"Nope, not until this afternoon, when I saw Mama Tante."

"Hold up a minute there, Shep," Jackson said, staring at the physical therapist gravely. "You saw Mama Tante?"

"Yes."

"Was she breathing at the time?"

"Sure. Mama Tante asked me to unpack a keepsake box from her storage cabinet. She intended to give it to you, Mr. Polke."

"All that with the blinking?" Jackson marveled.

"I ran the errand for her, and when I returned to her room, Mama Tante had passed away, God rest her soul."

"Did you find the box?" Ellie asked, feeling a bit morbid.

Shep lifted his knapsack off the ground. Pulling back the flaps, he removed an antique linen letter box, yellowing with age and disuse.

"She wanted y'all to have this," Shep said, passing the box to Jackson. "Seems the right thing to do, it being kinda like Mama Tante's last wish and all."

6

Tammy Lynn was hunched over a stainless steel table conversing with a fingerprint specialist when Ramon entered the forensics lab. On the far side of the table, Skip Lowell rummaged through a bin of assorted knives.

"This is about right," Skip murmured, selecting a medium-sized steak knife and holding it up to the light.

"That's quite a trophy case you got there," Ramon observed with a smile.

"It comes in handy whenever some shit-for-brains, glorified locker room attendant can't keep track of his goddamn evidence," the head of forensics grumbled, setting aside the steak knife and returning the bin to its perch on a shelf.

"What are you doing?"

"Recreating the murder weapon used on Angel Ramirez, right down to the hair fibers, blood traces, and fingerprints."

"Based on your initial report?"

"And the photographs. Fortunately, I have always been a stickler for extensive photographic evidence."

"A reader just loves pictures, huh?" Ramon observed.

"Damn right," Skip nodded. "I'm going to write that book someday, you just watch."

"I look forward to it."

Ramon snapped on a pair of latex gloves and asked Skip for the weapon. Taking it delicately by the blade, Ramon examined the serrated edge.

"About the knife, Chief," Tammy Lynn began, "we've confirmed Mrs. Van Hoerne's prints on the handle . . ."

Tammy Lynn's voice tapered off as the door to the lab flew open and Jared Hawthorne walked through carrying a thick sheaf of papers under one arm.

"There you are, Chief," Jared said, stopping short when he saw the knife in Ramon's hand. "Is that the weapon that did Angel Ramirez?"

"No," Ramon replied truthfully. "What's up, Lieutenant?"

"I figured you'd want to see the file."

"What file?"

"The Ramirez file. There's nothing on the computer so I had to dust off the original file from records."

"You have the original Angel Ramirez file?" Ramon asked in a calm, quiet voice, catching Tammy's Lynn's startled gaze.

"Yeah," Jared replied, suddenly wary. "Why? You seem surprised?"

"Do I?" Ramon asked, his face utterly impassive.

7

"Hello, Katherine," Ellie said, walking into her patient's new accommodations. "How are you settling in?"

"Fine, Dr. Dodds."

In the few short hours Ellie had been away, Katherine had undergone something of a transformation. Her baby-fine hair had been trimmed into a hairstyle, and instead of the grim, hospital-issued gown and paper slippers, she wore a beige cashmere sweater and silk drawstring pants.

Katherine had been transferred to a new room and the change in surroundings was striking. The protective padding and heavy-duty restraints had been replaced with floral print wallpaper and Egyptian cotton sheets.

"Moving up in the world," Ellie smiled, walking to where Katherine sat on a sofa.

"Dr. Adams has been most generous," Katherine replied quietly. "I think he's afraid I'm going to sue him."

"He also found you something better to wear."

"Dr. Adams called my husband."

Ellie sat beside Katherine on the couch.

"Did you talk to Clay?" she asked gently.

Katherine shook her head, eyes downcast.

"That's okay," Ellie assured her. "You need to take things at your own pace."

"Clay saved my clothes," Katherine told her, clearly surprised.

"I guess he never gave up hope."

"He sent over a few things, including some recent pictures . . ."

Katherine's sky blue eyes misted over.

"Of Charlotte?" Ellie asked softly.

Katherine nodded, a single tear sliding down her cheek.

"That must be difficult, seeing those pictures. You remember Charlotte as a toddler."

"I didn't even recognize her," Katherine cried. "My own baby, and now she's all grown up."

"You've missed a great deal. Would you like to visit with Charlotte? See her in person?"

"No," Katherine said firmly. "Not yet."

"There's no hurry."

Ellie picked up Lola from home and drove to Jackson's apartment, where he had takeout waiting when they arrived.

"How's Katherine?" he asked, shoveling French fries into his mouth.

"As well as can be expected."

Jackson greeted Lola with a scratch behind her ears, and handed Ellie a grease-stained paper bag from the counter.

"You want a plate?" he asked, walking into the kitchen.

"Sure."

Once Ellie was settled and had started eating, Jackson retrieved the box they'd brought back from New Orleans and set it down in front of her.

It was covered in antique linen with pale blue piping and bits of frayed ribbon. When Jackson undid the clasp and lifted the hinged lid, Ellie could smell stale potpourri and mothballs.

"So, the keepsakes and mementoes we found in the box are just that," Jackson began, "and there wasn't any secret code or clues in the postcards either. I do think one of those photographs was of Gabrielle, but not 100% sure, but that's beside the point . . ."

"Please get to the point," Ellie commanded, her mouth full of food.

Without answering, Jackson ran his fingers along the fabric folds that lined the underside of the lid. When he pushed hard, there was an audible click, and the bottom of the lid popped open, like a yawning mouth.

Jackson removed an envelope from the secret compartment and placed it beside Ellie's plate.

Ellie put down a pickle, cleaned her fingers with a paper napkin and picked it up, noting that the blank envelope had never been sealed.

Lifting the flap, Ellie removed a single sheet of paper with shaking hands. The words were scrawled in a feminine hand, tearstains distorting the ink in spots.

Dear Arthur,

I am entrusting this letter to a loyal friend with the firm hope she never has cause to deliver it into your hands. If, however, you are reading this, please know that I write this declaration in sound mind. Please believe that. This testament is the truth. Unfortunately.

This concerns Avery. As we've discussed before, it is imperative that Josiah not have control over her finances should anything happen to me. What we have not discussed, and what I have told no other person until now, is why that is so important.

Josiah's affection for Avery has turned to obsession of the most depraved sort. She's told me before about his inappropriate advances. My own daughter—his adopted child—I can hardly stomach it. He denies it, but I know it is true.

She came to me this morning sobbing. He assaulted her. She barely got away. I saw the bruises. Enclosed are several photographs, should you ever need evidence.

Avery and I will confront Josiah together. Let him try to deny it then.

In any event, Avery has begged me not involve the authorities and I will respect her wishes. However, for her protection, I will leave this letter and the pictures with someone I trust.

I have asked that these items be delivered to you after my death if Josiah ever attempts to break the trust documents or otherwise make life difficult for Avery. Please use this information as you will.

Thank you, Arthur. I am most grateful to you.

Yours, Gabrielle M. V. H.

When Ellie finished reading, she lifted her eyes and for several moments stared at Jackson in stunned silence.

"Pictures?"

Jackson shook his head.

"Lost to time, I guess."

"Should we give this to the police?" Ellie asked.

"What for?"

"Jackson, this proves Josiah killed Gabrielle!"

"No, it doesn't."

"How can you say that?!" Ellie demanded.

"Listen, even if it explicitly accused him of her murder, it still doesn't matter in a court of law. "

"Why the hell not?"

"We can't prove Gabrielle wrote that letter. Or that she wasn't crazy when she wrote it," Jackson answered dully. "Shit, with Mama Tante dead, we can't even prove how we got it in the first place."

"Then, what the hell do we do now?"

8

Relaxing in his recliner with his feet propped up and a pillow behind his head, Ramon opened the weathered file folder stamped 'Ramirez, Angel – OFFICIAL' and began flipping through its pages. Toward the back he found a statement in his own handwriting: Ramon's written protest to the chief of police regarding the case.

Although Tammy Lynn had done a hell of a job recreating the file's contents, Ramon was glad to have the original. They now had witness statements, hand-written notes and various other irreplaceable reports.

They also had Jared Hawthorne by the balls.

It was just dumb luck that Hawthorne was an idiot of such monumental proportions. The man walked right up and handed over the stolen file. Ramon did some checking and learned that Hawthorne never even stepped foot in the records room, or attempted to access the file online. Why would he? He already knew it would be a waste of time.

"Lieutenant, my ass," he muttered, turning the page.

"You say something, mi amor?" Consuelo asked from her matching recliner, where she did her needlepoint under a brass, swan-necked lamp.

"Nothing dear," Ramon replied warmly. "Talking to myself again."

"Of course you are. Should I continue to respond periodically or ignore you?"

"I'll leave that to your discretion."

Ramon returned his attention to the file.

Jared Hawthorne had hung himself out to dry, and the dipshit didn't even know it yet. There was no harm in letting him dangle a little while longer, use him as bait for a bigger fish.

Ramon closed the Ramirez file and set it on his lap. Then he lifted another folder: Nathan Conrad's APD employment file.

For weeks, Ramon had been investigating Nathan's life but had found nothing remotely incriminating. Other than a relatively amicable divorce in the early nineties and a brief subsequent brush with personal bankruptcy, Nathan Conrad's life seemed utterly devoid of scandal. He was a doting dad, an exemplary police officer, and a respected member of the Austin community. Moreover, his financial records were in perfect order, right down to the last bank account, stock transaction, and real estate purchase. Whatever Josiah Mantooth used to buy off Nathan Conrad, it wasn't money.

That's when Ramon was struck by a realization: there was only ever one thing Nathan Conrad valued, and it was something you couldn't quantify so easily.

Ramon immediately contacted Wendy Holcomb, who managed to get her hands on a copy of Nathan's employment records, which Ramon now held in his hands.

Ramon opened the file and began reading.

Amid the countless awards and commendations were the standard forms issued whenever an officer received a promotion. Included on these forms were blank boxes designated "Citizen Outreach," and as always, a typed reference number appeared in the space. This indicated that the department had, within the last twelve months, received complimentary feedback from a public citizen regarding the officer's conduct, invariably in the form of written correspondence. Every single one of Nathan Conrad's promotion forms had such a reference number.

Ramon took a ballpoint pen out of his shirt pocket, and began jotting down the numbers in a notebook.

When he was finished, Ramon hauled himself out of his recliner, kissed his wife gently on the forehead, and went into the kitchen to make a phone call. After consulting his address book, he called Dr. Margo Pinter at her home in Galveston, where she now taught classes at the University of Texas Medical School.

"Yes?" she answered on the fourth ring.

"You up for exhuming a body, or have you gotten old and lazy in that ivory tower of yours?" Ramon stated into the phone.

"And hello to you too, Ramon," Margo laughed. "That's one hell of a greeting."

"Well, are you in or out?"

"Out," she replied without hesitation. "Decomposing corpses just aren't my thing anymore."

"Oh come on, you miss it."

"Not for a second."

"It's Angel Ramirez."

Margo paused for several seconds before speaking.

"I saw on the news you reopened the case."

"I want to dig up the body," Ramon told her. "I want you to perform the autopsy."

"I don't know, Ramon," Margo hesitated. "I've got midterms to grade, and we're watching the grandkids this weekend . . ."

"Margo, please, I'm calling in a favor here," Ramon interrupted, his tone somber. "I wouldn't ask if it weren't important. "

He heard Margo exhale loudly several times.

"Okay, but you're going to owe me, Hinojosa."

9

Lola rushed past Ellie on the trail and plunged into the creek bed, lapping up the chilly water thirstily.

When she'd had her fill, Lola hauled her soaking wet body onto the bank and shook herself vigorously. As usual, Ellie got caught in the spray and had to wipe a fine mist of brown water from her cheeks.

Lola was supposed to be on a leash, but it was a rule uniformly ignored, and Lola ran ahead of Ellie into the trees.

A wooded area in the heart of Austin, the Barton Creek Greenbelt boasted several swimming holes and miles of intersecting dirt paths for hiking and biking. The creek swelled and receded with the seasons, and today it ran deep and wide with accumulated rainfall, cutting off access to certain parts of the trail.

Ellie slowed as the muddy trail narrowed and split, the only available path veering up and away from the rushing water. Up ahead, Lola bounded over the stone outcropping like a goat, but Ellie scrambled up the steep, rocky terrain as she made her way across the wall of limestone.

Once the trail evened out and Ellie was able to resume her regular pace, she allowed her mind to wander. Predictably, her thoughts drifted to Katherine Van Hoerne.

Ellie had learned a great deal about her patient in a very short time. Katherine was surprisingly open and candid during their visits, determined to make her therapy productive. Although there was a great deal that she didn't remember, Katherine was able to shed some much needed light on the years leading up to her breakdown.

Drafting a sort of mental checklist, Ellie considered the pertinent information Katherine had revealed so far. First, there was the onset of symptoms. As was typical with schizophrenics, Katherine began to exhibit signs of the illness—blackouts, inexplicable loss of time, a strange voice in her head—during her late teens. In the early stages, these symptoms were relatively manageable and Katherine was able to keep her illness a secret. However, as the illness advanced, it became more and more difficult to hide her erratic behavior, especially the episodes of self-mutilation that occurred during her periodic blackouts. According to Katherine, the only reason she survived this dreadful period of her life was Clay Van Hoerne's unwavering love and support.

Katherine seemed amazed by Clay's loyalty, and overwhelmed by feelings of gratitude. The skeptic in Ellie wondered if Clay's apparent devotion had anything to do with Katherine's vast wealth, but she kept those suspicions to herself. In any event, Clay stood by Katherine during her darkest hours, protecting Katherine from herself and shielding her from the outside world when necessary. Perhaps more importantly, he forced Katherine to seek medical help and actively participated in her treatment.

This brought Ellie to the second item on her checklist, the matter of medication. After a decade of trial and error with numerous drugs and therapies, it was the Thymetrazine protocol that finally afforded Katherine some semblance of a life. Although it left her tired and frequently lethargic, the drug silenced the disembodied voice and put an end to the waking blackouts. She slept a lot, ten or more hours at a stretch, which seemed to do little to help her fatigue, and there were incidents of self-abuse during the night that Katherine had no recollection of. Otherwise, she was able to function normally during the day.

Ellie pressed Katherine about these nocturnal episodes, but Katherine could offer little insight, remembering only that she would occasionally wake to find bruises or cuts on her body that weren't there when she went to bed, like a sleepwalker who awakes in foreign surroundings. Clay tried to prevent the abuse, but there was only so much he could do since he had to sleep himself. Ellie asked if anyone else witnessed these occurrences, a servant perhaps, but Katherine explained that other than a nursemaid for Charlotte, who rarely ventured out of the child's room at night, there was no live-in staff.

For obvious reasons, the Van Hoernes wished to keep these episodes private.

Ellie was lost in her thoughts, lulled by the steady rhythm of her pounding feet. When two men approached her on the trail, she stepped to the side of the path, thinking they wanted to pass. Instead, the men halted abruptly and blocked her way.

"Excuse me," she said politely, trying to move around them.

The men shifted positions, one on either side of her. It was only then she noticed that both men were large and heavyset, and that they were eying her with intensity, their expressions serious.

Instantly, Ellie's flesh began to tingle in alarm as her nervous system reacted to a sensed threat.

"We don't want to hurt you, Dr. Dodds," the taller one said evenly.

"How do you know my name?" Ellie demanded, inching backwards.

"We only want to talk to you," he continued.

"Call my office."

"Don't make this harder on yourself than it has to be."

Everything seemed distinctly unreal, like she was dreaming. Ellie pulled out the pepper spray and aimed it at the man's head. He seemed unfazed.

"Put that away, Dr. Dodds. We're just here to deliver a message."

"What message?"

"Stop the Nancy Drew bullshit."

"Huh?"

"That's the message. Stop poking your nose in where it doesn't belong."

"Excuse me?"

"We know all about your little trip to New Orleans. This investigation of yours, it ends right now *or else.*"

At the realization that these goons weren't rapists, an odd feeling of relief washed over Ellie, and her anxiety gave way to rage.

"Or else what?" she snapped.

"Accidents are a fact of life, Dr. Dodds. I'd hate to see anything happen to that pretty face of yours, or worse."

"You came all the way down here just to threaten me?" she scoffed.

"Consider it a well-intentioned warning."

"Josiah Mantooth put you up to this, right? This is unconscionable, even for him!"

"Just stop the snooping, Dr. Dodds," the man went on, ignoring the question, "and you'll never see us again."

Just then, Lola, who had run on ahead for a swim, doubled back through the trees to find Ellie. She burst out of the undergrowth, her fur dripping wet, tail wagging. Making a beeline for Ellie's leg, Lola nearly knocked over the shorter of the thugs in her haste. Caught off guard, both men instinctively reached toward their waistbands.

"Oh God, don't hurt her!" Ellie screamed, panicking.

Sensing Ellie's fear, Lola turned to the would-be assailants, planting herself between them and Ellie protectively and emitted a low, menacing growl.

In response, the men leveled their guns at the enormous dog.

"Lola, no!" Ellie commanded sternly.

Sensing danger, Lola's basic impulses took over. Baring her teeth, hackles raised, Lola growled even louder.

"You better call that thing off, Dr. Dodds!" the shorter man instructed nervously, backing away slightly.

"Lola, no!" Ellie repeated, attempting to grab the dog's collar, but Lola was too quick. "Goddammit, Lola, NO!"

Fangs flashing, Lola began to advance on the two men. Even though they wielded guns, the men looked genuinely frightened of the shaggy beast, and as Lola drew closer, they readied their weapons. Before Ellie knew it, the situation spun entirely out of control.

Lola charged, ramming the smaller man in the gut and sending him flailing onto his back. Pouncing, Lola landed on his torso, pinning him under her weight, and locked her jaws around his neck, eliciting a bone-chilling shriek.

The second man jumped into the fray, savagely whacking Lola's skull with the butt of his revolver. The dog reeled on him, clawed his cheek, and then sunk her sharp fangs deep into his forearm.

A deafening retort pierced the air, and then another, and Lola dropped to the ground, bright red blood spreading across her beautiful silver coat.

"Oh Christ," the second man muttered, a wisp of smoke billowing from his gun barrel.

Dazed and strangely numb, Ellie fell to her knees and covered her mouth with trembling hands. She lifted her eyes and saw that the shooter looked as shocked as she felt.

They stared at each other for a moment, frozen, the queer silence broken by the piteous cries of the other man, who was writhing in the dirt and holding his neck, trying to staunch the flow of blood.

Jerked back into reality, Lola's assassin raised the gun again and aimed it at Ellie.

"I'm real sorry, doc," he said. "It wasn't supposed to go down like this."

Spurred by sheer survival instinct, Ellie rolled away from the grisly scene and lunged into the undergrowth, the crack of gunfire echoing in her ears. Springing to her feet, she raced down the hill, zigzagging through the trees.

Ellie didn't look back, but she could tell by the thunderous footfall and sound of breaking branches that the man was giving chase.

Her mind was suddenly, remarkably clear. Tearing through the woods, Ellie assessed her predicament with a cool and astonishing detachment. Her pursuer had a gun, true, but Ellie was thoroughly familiar with the twists and turns of the greenbelt, and accustomed to navigating its uneven terrain at high speeds. Moreover, she could run really far and really fast.

Mentally, she almost dared the bastard to keep up.

Bullets ricocheted off the surrounding tree trunks, sending chunks of bark flying, but Ellie paid no attention. She sprinted toward the creek bed, hurtling over a waist-high barbed wire fence erected to protect new vegetation, and raced toward another densely wooded area. Veering sharply, Ellie began running uphill, snaking back and forth in a switchback, making herself a more difficult target.

Up ahead, Ellie saw what she'd been racing towards, the green and white sign indicating one of the entrances to the greenbelt. Ellie was winded and her calves burned, but she redoubled her efforts.

Shots rang out and Ellie heard a bullet pinging off the metal sign. Darting straight up the embankment, Ellie ran full-throttle until she reached the small gravel parking lot at the top.

To her immense relief, she spotted a group of people bunched around an SUV, readying their mountain bikes for a ride.

"Help!" Ellie cried desperately, stumbling out of the woods, tree limbs scratching her face. "Help me!"

The group turned, and Ellie waved her arms, again pleading for help. From behind, Ellie heard her pursuer's feet crunching against the gravel.

Rushing forward, several spandex-clad bikers came to her aid. Seeing the cyclists, Ellie's assailant quickly retreated back into the woods.

"Holy shit, he's got a gun!" a young woman yelled, pointing at the departing figure. "He's got a goddamn gun!"

"I told you that was gunfire!" another exclaimed.

"Are you hurt, lady?" one of the rescuers asked Ellie, surveying her body for wounds. "Are you hit?"

Ellie shook her head, frantically trying to catch her breath.

"Please help!" she managed, wheezing.

"Don't you worry, lady. He's gone now."

"You don't understand," she stammered.

"You're safe."

A girl in a yellow jersey brought out a cell phone and dialed 911.

"No, please, we have to go after them!"

"Are you nuts? That dude's got a gun!"

"Oh God, please! You've got to help her!"

"Listen lady, the cops will be here any minute . . ."

"My dog's been shot!" Ellie screamed.

A guy in a neon orange racing jersey grabbed a first aid kit from his car and led the way as several people snapped on helmets and grabbed their bikes.

10

Jackson crashed through the double doors of the animal hospital and ran to the reception desk, slapping his palm down on the small, stainless steel bell.

"Jackson?"

He wheeled around and to find Ellie in a corner of the waiting room, a police officer hovering nearby. Her running tights and nylon jacket were torn, and there were ugly scratches all over her head, neck, and hands.

Hurrying over to her, Jackson took Ellie in his arms and whispered, "Thank God you're all right."

"They shot my baby," Ellie cried, her red-rimmed and swollen eyes swimming with tears. "She's in surgery."

"Shhh, it'll be okay," Jackson soothed.

Burying her face in Jackson's chest, Ellie's thin shoulders shook violently as she let herself succumb to the wracking sobs. Jackson held her tightly until the shaking subsided, his fingers laced through Ellie's soft curls.

Eventually, Ellie pulled away and looked up at Jackson's face.

He gently ran his finger over a long, nasty welt on her chin.

"Come on, let's sit down," he told her.

As Jackson was guiding Ellie to a chair, several uniformed police officers entered the waiting room, followed by Commander Ramon Hinojosa. Marching over to where they stood, Ramon glared at Jackson.

"They shot Lola," Jackson announced loudly.

"Lola?" Ramon asked, his eyebrow arching.

"The dog," Tammy Lynn explained.

"Ah."

"They shot at me too, you know, not just my dog," Ellie snapped.

"A sketch artist is on his way here," Tammy Lynn told her. "With your help, we'd like to have drawings of your assailants out on the wire within the hour."

"One of them is badly hurt," Ellie said. "You might want to start with the local emergency rooms, see if anyone came in with a canine bite to the neck."

"It's already being done."

"Good for Lola," Jackson observed.

"It sounds like Lola might have saved your life, Dr. Dodds," Tammy Lynn remarked.

"They weren't there to kill me, just scare me a little, but then things got out of hand."

"What did these men say *exactly*?" Ramon asked Ellie.

"Basically, that if I didn't stop snooping into Katherine Van Hoerne's past, I'd be sorry."

"They referred to Katherine Van Hoerne by name?"

"No, but they mentioned our trip to New Orleans. It wasn't hard to figure out."

"What trip to New Orleans?" Ramon asked, frowning.

"We flew there the other day to interview Katherine's old nanny," Jackson told him. "Obviously, Josiah Mantooth found out and got nervous."

"Let's not get ahead of ourselves, Dr. Dodds," Ramon sighed. "We don't have any proof that Mr. Mantooth was involved."

"Who the hell else would be behind this?" Ellie demanded.

Before the words left Ellie's mouth, a set of swinging metal doors banged open and a woman in blood-stained scrubs strode into the waiting room.

"Dr. Dodds?" the woman said.

"Yes," Ellie answered, squeezing Jackson's hand tightly.

"That's one resilient mutt you got there," the veterinarian smiled. "Lola's going to be fine. She won't be chasing squirrels any time soon, but she'll pull through."

"Really?" Ellie whispered.

"Really," the vet told her. "You've got your cyclist friends to thank. If they hadn't gotten Lola here as fast as they did, it would have been a different story."

"Can I see her?" Ellie asked.

"Give us just a minute to get her cleaned up and into post-op."

"Of course."

Turning to Jackson, Ellie grinned through her tears and threw her arms around his neck.

"Did you hear that?" she sighed into his ear.

"Yes, I did."

"She's going to make it."

"Yes, she is."

"All's well that ends well," Ramon proclaimed.

In a sudden fury, Ellie spun around and faced the commander.

"I hope you're not suggesting this is over," she spat.

"Of course not, I was simply . . ."

"Because this is far from over," Ellie hissed, cutting him off. "Don't give me that 'all's well that ends well' bullshit!"

"I'm sorry, Dr. Dodds, if I sounded glib," Ramon apologized.

"Well that's not fucking good enough!" Ellie shouted.

"What would you have me do?"

"Put Josiah Mantooth in a goddamn cell!"

"On what charge?"

"Two counts of attempted murder, to start with!"

"And at least one count of animal cruelty," Jackson added.

"You are just going to have to trust us for a little while longer . . ." Ramon told them, trying to sound reassuring.

"Why should I?" Ellie shot back. "As far as I can tell, you people have been sitting on your asses eating Krispy Kremes while Josiah Mantooth has literally gotten away with murder. And now he's going to get away with attempted murder!"

"What was that?" Ramon asked, cocking his head to study Ellie more closely.

"What was what?"

"What you just said. About a murder?"

"She meant it as a metaphor, ," Jackson interjected quickly.

"But Dr. Dodds said literally—that Mr. Josiah Mantooth *literally* got away with murder."

"It's an expression, Hinojosa."

"Tell me, Mr. Polke, did you two learn anything of interest on this expedition to New Orleans? Something you might like to share with the authorities?"

"I've tried sharing with the authorities, remember?" Jackson responded coolly. "As I recall, it was an exercise in futility."

"This is a criminal investigation. I'm not asking these questions to be polite."

"Why the hell should we tell you anything?" Ellie demanded.

Tammy Lynn stepped forward and in a low, calming voice said, "Because we want to see Josiah Mantooth pay for his crimes as much as you do."

"I seriously doubt that."

"Fair enough," Tammy Lynn replied. "*Almost* as much as you do. In any event, please believe that we intend to do everything in our power to see that Mr. Mantooth is brought to justice for any and all crimes he may have committed. You can help us do that by telling us what you may know."

It was now Jackson's turn to be suspicious.

"Huh," he said. "Tell me, Commander Hinojosa: did the APD learn anything of interest during the course of its investigation? Something you might like to share with Mrs. Van Hoerne's defense team? Huh?"

"Don't change the subject," Ramon instructed irritably.

"Do you need a refresher course on the rules regarding exculpatory evidence? As Mrs. Van Hoerne's attorney, I am entitled to review any evidence that might possibly exonerate my client."

"I am well aware of the rules, Counselor."

"If you're holding out on me, I'm going to haul your ass into court."

"And if you are holding out on me, Polke, I'm going to haul your ass down to jail and charge you with obstruction," Ramon countered, eyeing Jackson sharply. "You do not want to get in a pissing contest with me, son."

"We have nothing to say to you," Ellie informed them stiffly. "Nothing at all."

"Well then, you'll just have to listen, and listen good," Ramon retorted. "I don't know what kind of bullshit investigation y'all have been up to, but it ends here. You have clearly put yourselves and those around you in danger, and I for one don't want to be combing the hillsides searching for your missing corpses. Do you understand?"

Ellie prepared to argue, but Jackson put his arm over her shoulder and squeezed.

"I said *do you understand?*" Ramon repeated more loudly.

"Perfectly, Commander," Jackson replied for the both of them.

"This is a police matter now, and I don't need y'all mucking up my investigation."

"Of course."

"Not to mention getting yourselves killed."

"We understand," Jackson answered.

Ramon put his hands on his hips, chewed on his mustache, and glowered at Jackson.

"Do I look stupid to you, son?"

"No, sir."

"You think I don't know when a person's lying to me?"

"Um, yes, sir. Or is that a no sir?"

"You haven't heard a damn thing I've been saying. It's just going in one ear and out the other, isn't it?"

"No, sir."

"Goddamn it, Polke!"

"Shhh, keep your voice down!" a nurse ordered sternly, storming into the waiting area. "This is a hospital, for heaven's sakes!"

"Yes, ma'am," Ramon mumbled.

"Hmmph," the nurse grunted, and then turned to Ellie. "Lola's heavily sedated, Dr. Dodds, but you may see her if you like."

"Oh yes," Ellie replied, taking Jackson's hand.

"We aren't finished here," Ramon told them.

"Unless you plan on arresting us for something, we most certainly are," Jackson answered brusquely, his arm wrapped around Ellie protectively.

As the nurse led them through the stark white corridor, Ellie looked up at Jackson and said, "Are you really going to do nothing?"

"Hell no. You?"

"Hell no."

11

The following day, Ramon Hinojosa stood out in the driving rain, his thin overcoat soaked through like a soggy paper bag. He shivered as Angel Ramirez's remains were unearthed.

It was foul and ghoulish work under the best of circumstances, but the unexpected downpour only made it worse.

In the distance Ramon caught sight of a figure marching towards him, a burnt-orange, University of Texas umbrella shielding his head. Nathan Conrad.

He was shouting something Ramon couldn't make out in the pounding sleet, but Ramon could tell from the body language that Nathan was one unhappy police chief.

"What the hell do you think you're doing, Hinojosa?" Nathan Conrad roared, this time within earshot.

"Getting wet," Ramon replied evenly.

"Don't give me that shit! Who the hell authorized this?"

"I did."

"You ever hear of procedure, Ramon? Proper channels? This exhumation request sure as hell did not cross my desk!"

"Actually, I should say that Lupe Ramirez authorized it."

"Who?"

"Angel Ramirez's grandmother. Since she's a family member, I didn't need for you to sign off on the exhumation order, Chief."

"Jesus Christ, Ramon, I found out about this stunt from a pack of reporters!" Nathan bellowed. "They were demanding answers about an exhumation I knew nothing about! Didn't I order you to keep Hawthorne in the loop? This is a goddamn public relations nightmare!"

Through the unrelenting sheet of rain, Ramon watched Nathan Conrad work himself into a furious lather. His skin flushing scarlet, tiny veins popping out on his forehead, Nathan shouted to be heard over the storm.

Ramon no longer registered the words themselves, just the sanctimonious, indignant tone of Conrad's voice, which galled Ramon to no end. Impulsively, Ramon said exactly what was on his mind.

"Tough shit."

Nathan Conrad ceased his ranting and stared at Ramon, his beady eyes wide with disbelief.

"What did you say to me?" he asked.

"I said *tough shit*," Ramon repeated more loudly.

"Who the hell do you think you're talking to?"

"You, Nathan. I'm talking to you."

Puffing out his chest and rising up to his full five feet, four inches, Conrad tilted the umbrella backwards and said, "If you have a problem with me, Ramon, just say so."

"I've got a problem with you."

"Is that so?"

Ramon took a deep breath and said, "I know, Nathan."

"Know what?"

"I know what you and Stiles did."

Nathan Conrad's jaw muscle jumped, but he didn't seem all that surprised. By now, he had undoubtedly learned of Ramon's confrontation with Ron Stiles.

"I have no idea what you're referring to," he replied flatly.

"Come off it, Nathan. I know all about your arrangement with Mantooth."

"Arrangement?"

"Gabrielle Mantooth didn't fall off that balcony."

"Are you questioning the conclusions of two respected and highly decorated officers, Ramon?" Nathan sneered.

"I've seen the goddamn crime scene photos. That woman was pushed, and you and Ron Stiles covered it up."

"Now why would we do something like that?"

"Because Mantooth made it worth your while."

Nathan eyed Ramon with a fair degree of amusement.

"That's one hell of an accusation, Ramon," he said. "I sure as shit hope you've got something to back it up."

Ramon didn't reply at once, just glared at Nathan Conrad across the sheets of pelting rain.

"You covered up a murder, you son of a bitch."

Conrad smiled coldly.

"Prove it."

"I'll have your badge for this, Nathan," Ramon promised.

"Oh no, old friend. I shall have yours."

12

"I met Mama Tante," Ellie told her.

"My Mama Tante?" Katherine replied.

"Then you remember her?"

"Yes, but only vaguely. She left when I was still very young."

"Why did she leave?"

"I was told she returned to her family in Louisiana."

"Told by whom?"

"My father."

"Mama Tante didn't tell you herself?"

"No."

"But surely she said good-bye?"

"No," Katherine replied softly. "One morning I woke up and she was gone."

"That must have been difficult."

"She had a family of her own to care for," Katherine shrugged. "After Mother died, there was really no reason for her to stay."

"Did that make you sad?" Ellie asked gently.

"What?"

"That you weren't reason enough to stay?"

Katherine looked at Ellie as if stung, blinking back tears.

"I guess that is kind of sad, huh?" she whispered.

"Yes, it is," Ellie confirmed.

"I didn't think about it that way."

"How did you think about it?"

"That it would be selfish to be sad."

"Selfish? How?"

"Mama Tante wanted to be with her own kids, not somebody else's. It would be selfish to begrudge her that."

"Who said anything about begrudging her? This is about simply being sad."

"I had no right to be sad."

"Of course you did," Ellie responded. "Every living being has the inalienable right to be sad whenever they damn well feel like it."

"What was I going to do? Feel sorry for myself?" Katherine asked. "Wallow in self-pity."

"Why the hell not?"

"What?"

"With everything you've been through, I think you're entitled."

Katherine grinned weakly.

"How is Mama Tante?" she asked.

Ellie had debated whether or not to tell Katherine about Mama Tante's unfortunate passing, and decided it was best to be honest.

"She's dead," Ellie said.

"Dead? I thought you met her?"

"I did, but she passed away soon after we spoke. Mama Tante had been ill for some time.

"What did she say to you, before she died?" Katherine asked.

"She communicated through blinking, but was able to provide us with some helpful information."

"Such as?"

"Did you know there's a long history of mental illness on your mother's side of the family?"

"Not as such," Katherine said quietly. "My mother suffered from severe depression, but I know very little about the rest of her family. Most of them died before I was even born."

"What else do you remember about your mother, Katherine?"

"She was soft-spoken, sweet, incredibly beautiful. Everyone adored her, especially me, except of course when she had her spells.

"Tell me about these spells."

"She just wasn't herself," Katherine replied softly. "Whenever Mother wasn't feeling well, she'd take to her rooms until she was herself again. Only Mama Tante was permitted to enter."

"For how long?"

"It varied. Sometimes an afternoon, sometimes a month or more."

"And you never saw her during these episodes?"

"On occasion, I'd be taken into her bedroom for a kiss goodnight, but otherwise, no."

"Was your mother in the midst of a spell when she died?"

"I don't remember anything about that day, or my mother's death."

"Do you recall speaking to the police afterwards?"

"No."

"What about the fire that killed your sister? Do you remember the fire?"

"I know there was a fire and that Avery died, but no, I have no recollection of it."

Ellie paused for a moment before speaking.

"There may be a way to improve your memory."

"How?"

13

"I want you to start counting backwards from one hundred."

The curtains were drawn tightly shut in Ellie's office, and Katherine was lying on the couch, her head propped up by several pillows. Ellie was seated beside her in an armchair.

"100, 99, 98, 97 . . ."

Soon, there was a dreamy, detached quality to Katherine's voice, and the numbers came in increasingly random order. Katherine's breath was deep and even, and the counting slowed.

"26, 21, 17, 16 . . ."

"Thank you, Katherine," Ellie said, once certain her patient was under.

An eerie silence enveloped the office as the countdown was halted. When Ellie spoke, it was in a soft, soothing tone, drawing Katherine deeper and deeper into her subconscious.

"Katherine?"

"Yes."

"How do you feel?"

"Fine."

"Will you lift your arm for me?"

"Which one?"

"The left one."

Katherine raised her left forearm, her fingers dangling. Ellie told her to put it down, and Katherine dropped the arm to her side.

"Now, Katherine, I would like for you to look within yourself, and recognize the chambers of your own mind," Ellie began, her heart racing. "I want you to think of those chambers like rooms in a house, all branching off of a single hallway. Each room is sealed by a closed door. Can you see it with your mind's eye?"

"Yes," Katherine said dully.

"In your hand is a key that unlocks all of these doors. Once inside a room, you can leave any time you want simply by opening the door. You can then lock it again with your key. Do you understand what I'm telling you?"

"Yes."

"I'd like for you to open one door in particular, Katherine."

"Which one?"

"The one that leads to your mother's bedroom."

"I'm not to go in there."

"Your mother has given you permission."

"She isn't well."

"But she would like to see you."

"She would?"

"You may even play dress-up with her jewelry, if you'd like. You enjoy that, don't you?"

"Very much."

"Gabrielle has even given you a key, the one in the palm of your hand. Do you see it?"

"Yes."

"Use it to unlock the door to Gabrielle's bedroom."

"Mother isn't well," Katherine said hesitantly.

"That's why she wants you with her."

"Oh."

Ellie paused and asked, "Have you unlocked it?"

"Yes."

"Push the door open, Katherine, and step inside the room."

"I'm scared."

"You are perfectly safe. What do you see?"

"Mother's dressing table."

"What's on the table?"

"A big mirror."

"What else?

"Mother's perfume and cosmetics, and a wooden box that holds her jewelry."

"Is there a chair in front of the table?"

"A bench."

"Sit down, Katherine, and look in the mirror. Do you see yourself in the reflection?"

"Yes."

"The little girl in that mirror is six years old. Do you remember being six years old, Katherine?"

"Yes."

"Are you looking at the little girl in the mirror?"

"Yes."

"She is now the exact same age as you were when your mother passed away. It is now the very day she died. Do you remember that day?"

"Yes."

"You were in this bedroom."

"Yes."

"Playing at the dressing table, as you're doing right now."

"I was wearing Mother's jewelry."

"Is she angry?"

"Oh no, she laughs. She tells me to put on every last piece."

"And do you?"

"Yes, but I run out of fingers."

"Is your mother in the room with you now?"

"Oh yes," Katherine said, smiling. "She's feeling herself."

Katherine's expression quickly changed, and a worried line creased her brow.

"What's wrong Katherine?" Ellie asked.

"Mother, she's becoming very upset now."

"Upset about what?"

"I don't know."

"Is anyone there with you?"

"Avery. She's yelling."

"Can you hear what she's saying?"

"Yes, but I don't understand. They're both crying and shouting now, saying hateful things."

"What things?"

"Father's here. He must have heard them. All three of them, so angry. The door, it bangs shut, the pictures on the wall rattle."

"Katherine, who left the room?"

"Stop it. STOP IT!" Katherine shrieked, twisting her head violently from side to side. "Don't you hurt my mother!"

Katherine released a high-pitched scream, and then went abruptly, frighteningly silent. Suddenly, out of nowhere, Katherine lifted her hand and slapped herself hard across the cheek bone. And then again.

"Katherine!" Ellie stated authoritatively. "No."

Paying no heed, Katherine clawed her fingernails across the soft flesh of her arm, nearly drawing blood. She didn't make so much as a sound.

Ellie clapped her hands sharply three times, and immediately the mutilation ceased. Almost simultaneously, Katherine's eyelids fluttered open.

"Ouch," she whispered, rubbing her palm across the long, red welts marring her forearm.

"Can you explain to me what happened just now, Katherine?" Ellie asked, her voice hushed and unsteady.

Katherine simply shook her head and whispered, "No."

14

"Give it to me fast," Ramon ordered, barreling into his office and tossing his sodden raincoat in a rumpled heap on the floor. "I'm meeting with the district attorney in 15 minutes."

"I've autopsied the body," Margo Pinter told him, "and we've got a problem."

"Why am I not surprised?" Ramon sighed, gesturing for Margo and Tammy Lynn to be seated. Both women preferred to stand.

"I want you to take a look at these photographs and tell me what you see," Pinter stated, slapping a stack of photos onto the desk.

Doing as he was told, Ramon put on his reading glasses and examined the skeletal remains of Angel Ramirez's back.

"I count at least ten marks on the bones indicating stab wounds, presumably all from the same weapon, any number of which could presumably have been fatal."

"Not bad, Commander," Dr. Pinter commended.

"But I'm missing something?"

"Maybe this will help," Tammy Lynn said, setting a poster-sized diagram on top of the desk and pointing out the relevant markings. "This is Angel. These here are his stab wounds. And these arrows right there, they mark the angle and direction of the knife's thrust."

Ramon stood up and bent over at the waist to inspect the drawing more closely.

"What to do you see, Ramon?" Margo asked.

"The arrows, they're all pointing inwards and upwards," he replied numbly, falling back into his chair.

"Precisely! In and up!"

The former medical examiner grabbed Tammy Lynn by the elbow and turned her around, exposing her back to Ramon. She then retrieved a letter opener from his cluttered desktop and wielded it like a knife.

"Okay, based on the fingerprints, Katherine Van Hoerne was holding the steak knife like this," she said, gripping the weapon blade-side up, her thumb at the top of the handle as if readying for a fencing duel, or direct hand to hand combat. "And we are relatively certain that the suspect was facing the victim, like so."

Margo stepped in front of Tammy Lynn, who bent down so that Margo's head was above her own, and raised her arm to demonstrate.

"The only wounds the suspect could inflict from this angle would necessarily be downward, not upward," Margo explained, bringing her arm down in a sweeping motion.

"So, she wasn't up against the wall," Ramon said thoughtfully. "Where does that leave us? She attacked Angel from behind?"

"Not possible," Margo responded, circling Tammy Lynn until she was behind her. "The suspect was significantly shorter than the victim."

Tammy Lynn stood up to her full height, and Margo Pinter bent down to reflect the appropriate height differential. Again, she brandished the letter opener.

"In order to make those deep wounds between the shoulder blades, she would have needed to be *at least* four inches taller. The person who did this to Angel Ramirez was around six feet, six-one."

"Could she have been standing on something?" Ramon asked. "A crate or a box?"

"Nothing of the kind was recovered at the scene," Tammy Lynn told him.

"Could she have jumped up?"

"She would have needed a decent amount of traction to wield the knife with that force."

"But her fingerprints were on the murder weapon," Ramon pointed out.

"We know she had the steak knife in her possession when the initial officers arrived," Margo said. "She tried to fend them off with it, right? Isn't this how she would have gripped the knife during the struggle?"

Ramon looked at the knife handle in Margo Pinter's hand, and noted the positioning of her fingers.

"Exactly like that," he nodded.

"Well then, perhaps that's when Mrs. Van Hoerne's prints got on the knife."

"Which would mean that someone wiped the knife clean before Katherine picked it up," Tammy Lynn added. "It would explain the prints, and lack thereof."

"And you think this was someone other than Katherine Van Hoerne?"

"Why would she wipe off her fingerprints only to leave another set on the weapon?"

"Besides, under the conditions evidenced at the crime scene, it would be physically impossible for Katherine to have inflicted the wounds found on Angel Ramirez," Margo concluded.

Ramon frowned and eyed the doctor warily.

"You willing to testify to that under oath in a court of law, Dr. Pinter?"

"Yes," Margo told him. "I am."

"Great," Ramon grumbled, getting up from his desk and snatching his raincoat from off the floor. "That's great, just great. Which of you two geniuses wants to help me break the news to the district attorney that an innocent woman—and not just *any* innocent woman, mind you, but an innocent *Katherine Van Hoerne*—has been in a veritable hellhole for the last five years, wrongly accused of a crime she didn't commit? Mmm? Either of you?"

"You're on your own, Chief," Margo told him. "You have my report and the photographs, as well as the diagrams. Detective Geary here knows her stuff."

"Where are you going?" Ramon demanded.

"Far, far away from here."

"Coward."

"I am no longer employed by the Austin Police Department, remember? Therefore, I am under no obligation to stick around for the coming shitstorm."

"Disloyal coward!" Ramon shouted as Margo Pinter's departing form.

15

Without knocking, Nathan Conrad entered the interrogation room where Ramon Hinojosa and Wendy Holcomb waited for him, engrossed in hushed conversation, their heads tilted close together.

"Should I come back?" Nathan asked pleasantly.

"No, Chief," Holcomb told him, gesturing to a chair. "Have a seat."

"We would be much more comfortable in my office," Nathan responded, not moving, "but then we already discussed that, didn't we?"

"As I told you on the phone, Chief Hinojosa and I thought this would be more appropriate. Please close the door Nathan, and take a seat."

Nathan shut the door but chose to remain standing, his back against the one-way mirror that occupied nearly an entire wall.

"I've just gotten off the phone with the mayor," Nathan announced nonchalantly. "He sends his regards.

"Is that supposed to intimidate me, Nathan?" the district attorney asked.

"Merely stating a fact."

Ramon studied Conrad from across the room, impressed by the man's unerring composure. Their demand to meet him here, in a drab, austere interrogation room, left him seemingly unfazed.

"Before we begin," Holcomb went on, "I urge you to reconsider having an attorney present."

"That won't be necessary."

"Then I must insist you sign a waiver to that effect."

"Do you have a pen?"

Ramon looked at the wall clock over the door, noted the time, and said, "Chief Conrad, I have two questions for you."

"Only two, Ramon?" Nathan replied pleasantly.

"For the moment. First, were you aware that your former partner, Detective Ronald Stiles, accepted a series of cash payments from Mr. Josiah Mantooth beginning soon after the death of his wife, Gabrielle Mantooth?"

"No, and frankly, I challenge you to prove such an outlandish and blatantly slanderous claim in a court of law."

"Second, Chief," Ramon continued, "did you or did you not conspire with Lieutenant Jared Hawthorne to impede the investigation into Angel Ramirez's murder?"

"No, I did not," Nathan stated definitively, "and I resent your insinuation."

"All right then, Chief, that's all the questions I have for you," Ramon told him. "Ms. Holcomb?"

"I don't have anything to add," Wendy responded, shrugging her shoulders as if disappointed. "We'll be in touch."

"That's it? That's all you want to ask me?" Nathan snorted.

"That's all," Ramon nodded.

Nathan chuckled to himself, and stood up.

"I do hope you two got what you wanted out of this little stunt," he sighed, turning the door handle. "The next time we meet, I assure you, it will be under different circumstances."

Just as Nathan opened the door, Tammy Lynn Geary appeared from around the corner with a contingent of officers escorting Jared Hawthorne and Ron Stiles, both in handcuffs, down the corridor.

Ramon stepped past Nathan Conrad and into the hall, and nodded to Tammy Lynn.

"Where do you want them, Chief?" she asked.

"Three and four," he replied, referring to adjoining interrogation rooms down the hall.

As the group moved out of sight, Nathan Conrad turned on Ramon.

"What the hell do you think you're doing, Hinojosa?" he snarled, the color rushing to his cheeks. "I demand an explanation!"

"Not much to explain, really," Ramon countered. "They're under arrest."

"On what charges?"

"Take your pick. There's plenty."

Nathan grabbed Ramon by the arm and shoved him back into the interrogation room. He then slammed the door with such force, the mirror rattled in its casing.

"I want a goddamn explanation and I want it now!" he bellowed, the veins on his forehead popping.

Ramon leveled his glare at Nathan and said, "We traced the payments made to Stiles back to a shell corporation owned by a subsidiary of Mantooth Industries. It wasn't easy, mind you, but the forensic accountants eventually unraveled the money trail. They always do, especially with someone as greedy and stupid as Ron Stiles."

"What does that have to do with me? You've no doubt looked through my finances and know perfectly well I didn't take any payoff."

"Not with cash, no," Ramon conceded, "but with something you valued much more."

"What's that?"

"Your career."

Nathan's right eye began to twitch ever so slightly.

The reference numbers in Nathan Conrad's personnel file led Ramon to a storage box containing all of the recommendations, petitions, and other correspondence received by the police department over the years relating to Nathan Conrad's service on the force.

The people who supported Nathan's ascendancy through the ranks included a remarkable assortment of powerful people. Ramon contacted as many as he could, and discovered that the vast majority had either met Conrad through the Mantooths, or agreed to send their letters of recommendation at the urging of the Mantooths. Moreover, this "Citizen Outreach" seemed to reach a fevered crescendo every time Nathan was up for a promotion. There was also the matter of huge donations being made to the Police Widows and Orphans Fund in appreciation for and recognition of Nathan Conrad's estimable service to the community.

"Josiah Mantooth and his wife Bobbie Dean have been behind your rise to power all this time," Ramon stated. "Them and all their friends and acquaintances. The Mantooths' clout and connections got you where you are, Chief."

"As for Hawthorne," Ramon continued, "we confiscated his computer. You know, it's amazing what they can dig up on a hard drive. Turns out, it was your boy Jared who deleted the Ramirez file from the system."

"You are way out of line if you think Jared Hawthorne is anything less than an exemplary, upstanding police officer and an asset to your department . . ."

"IT'S OVER!" Ramon's voice boomed, instantly silencing Nathan Conrad. "It's over."

Nathan Conrad bit down hard, and glowered at Ramon.

"You know how this works, Chief," Wendy Holcomb said quietly. "He who squeals first gets the best deal. We've got those two morons dead to rights and they're going to jail, the only variable being for how long. Now I can't speak from experience, but I understand prison is particularly hard on a former law enforcement officer. Am I right about that, Ramon?"

"Stiles and Hawthorne are shitting in their pants right about now," Ramon observed. "Those boys are going to be scrambling to make a deal."

"So, Nathan, it all comes down to one thing—loyalty. How goddamn loyal are they when their necks are over the chopping block and the ax is raised?" Holcomb asked. "I repeat, he who squeals first gets the best deal."

His eyes narrowing to angry slits, Nathan Conrad scowled at his accusers. He then walked over to the table and pulled out a chair, the metal legs scraping across the floor with a sharp, grating sound.

"I want my lawyer," he announced icily, sitting down.

16

When Jackson arrived at the police station, he was taken to a large, windowless squad room on the second floor and deposited in a metal chair in a corner. A moment later, Ramon Hinojosa appeared beside him.

"Mr. Polke, thank you for coming . . ."

Wait," Jackson said, holding up his hand. "I don't know why you dragged me down here, Commander, but I have a few things I need to say to you, and I want you to pay very close attention, because I have had it up to my goddamn eyeballs with your passivity and inaction and, frankly, your flagrant dereliction of duty . . ."

"Mr. Polke . . ." Ramon tried to interject.

". . . My client has been the tragic victim of this department's laziness and ineptitude for long enough. Where is the justice for Katherine Van Hoerne, I ask you?"

"Mr. Polke, please," Ramon again attempted to interrupt, but Jackson was just getting started.

"Someone tried to kill Ellie Dodds yesterday, Commander," Jackson nearly shouted, drawing curious stares from around the room. "You know goddamn well that Josiah Mantooth was behind this. And what have you done? What are you going to do? Not a goddamn thing. You're probably spending more time and energy trying to send Katherine to jail than you are trying to find out who put the bullets in that poor dog. Dogs have certain legal rights, you know. I looked it up."

Ramon abandoned his attempts to get a word in edgewise, and waited for Jackson Polke to run out of steam.

"You and your department have shown a callous disregard for victims' rights, not to mention a bull-headed stubbornness that has compromised your investigatory powers . . ."

Jackson stopped to take a breath, and Ramon seized the opportunity.

"What would you like me to do?" he asked simply.

"I want you to arrest Josiah goddamn Mantooth, that's what!" Jackson thundered.

"Done," Ramon replied quietly.

"Hah."

"Done."

"I don't understand."

"You want Josiah Mantooth arrested, by God it's done."

"Are you mocking me, Commander?"

"Nope," Ramon assured him, pointing to the far side of the squad room.

Jackson stood and looked to the entryway, where he saw the hunched, shambling figure of a now aged Josiah Mantooth being led into the squad room by two uniformed officers.

"What the . . ." Jackson whispered, blinking hard.

"Is there anything else I can do for you today, Mr. Polke?"

"Um, huh?"

"Anyone else you'd like to have arrested?"

"Um, well . . ." Jackson mumbled. "Did I really see what I think I just saw, or am I seeing things?"

"Could you repeat that?"

"Probably not."

"You don't look so well," Ramon observed. "You want some water?"

Ramon motioned to a nearby officer, who filled a paper cup from the water cooler and brought it to Jackson. After Jackson had emptied the contents, Ramon cleared his throat and asked, "You all right?"

"Yes, thank you."

"Can you handle more good news?"

"More?"

"As you know, we've reopened the investigation into the death of Angel Ramirez. During the course of this investigation, we've uncovered evidence that, in all likelihood, clears your client."

"Excuse me?"

"Mrs. Van Hoerne might just be innocent."

"I'm sorry, did you say innocent?"

"We've also got a line on the goons who attacked Dr. Dodds," Ramon added, smiling thinly. "Do you drink coffee, Mr. Polke?"

"Yes."

"Come on, let's get the hell out of here."

17

Jackson and Ramon Hinojosa walked down the block to a pancake house and sat down in a vinyl booth towards the back. After ordering a pot of coffee and two mugs, Ramon began.

"It all started with that phone call," he told Jackson. "You were drunk, but the conversation touched a nerve. Tell me honestly, Polke—did you know about my letter to the chief of police?"

"What letter?"

"The letter I wrote five years ago, protesting the handling and closure of the Angel Ramirez investigation?"

"No," Jackson told him truthfully. "I didn't know anything about that."

"Then why call me?" Ramon asked.

"Weren't you the detective in charge of the case?"

"Simple as that?"

"It seemed the reasonable place to start."

"Damn," Ramon murmured. "And your suspicions about Mantooth? How did you know?"

"I didn't know shit," Jackson told him. "Not then, anyway. I was just suspicious, that's all."

"Well, because of your drunken ramblings, I went to reexamine the Ramirez file and discovered it missing."

Ramon proceeded to brief Jackson on both his unofficial and official investigations into the deaths of Gabrielle Mantooth and Angel Ramirez.

"When confronted, Nathan Conrad turned out to be more afraid of jail than of Josiah Mantooth," Ramon concluded, "and gave up everything in exchange for a plea bargain."

"He confessed?"

"As if his life depended on it—which, actually, it did. In any event, he finally admitted to covering up the Gabrielle Mantooth homicide."

Jackson paused for a full 20 seconds, his coffee mug frozen in mid-air.

"Did you say homicide?"

"Yes," Ramon nodded. "Photographic evidence proves that Gabrielle was pushed backwards off that balcony."

"I knew it," Jackson nearly shouted. "I knew he killed her!"

"How?"

"Well, I didn't *know* know, not for sure, but after talking to Mama Tante, I just knew in my gut that Josiah murdered his wife."

"Mama Tante was the nanny, right?" Ramon asked. "You were able to speak with her before she died?"

"How did you know she died?"

"What did Mama Tante tell you?"

"Not much, she was mute," Jackson answered. "Seriously, how'd you find out about that?"

"You mentioned a nanny in New Orleans, when we were at the animal hospital. What did the woman say, Polke?"

"She didn't *say* a damn thing. She blinked."

"She blinked?"

"One blink 'yes,' two blinks 'no.'"

"Okay then, what did the woman *blink*?"

"Mama Tante believed that Josiah murdered Gabrielle."

"Did she have any evidence?"

"No," Jackson admitted. "But she did give us a letter."

It was now Jackson's turn to tell Ramon all that he and Ellie had uncovered. Despite himself, Ramon was impressed with Jackson's amateur sleuthing skills.

"Well, at least we know how he got away with it," Jackson finished. "He bribed the cops."

"Listen, Jackson, about that nanny," Ramon said to him. "There's something you should be aware of. Monique Thibidault was murdered."

"Murdered? What the hell do you mean she was *murdered*?"

"She was poisoned by a nurse named Suzette Whitaker, who was trying to make it look like a heart attack," Ramon explained.

"Nurse Suzette?"

"Truth is, no one would have been any the wiser, if I hadn't requested an autopsy."

"Wait a minute, back up: you requested an autopsy?"

"After our conversation at the animal hospital, I tracked down this Mama Tante, and contacted Camellia Gables. A doctor informed me that Mama Tante had passed away just days before. For obvious reasons, I asked them to conduct an autopsy. That's when they discovered the concentration of drugs in her system."

"No shit," Jackson muttered.

"There's more," Ramon continued. "I asked New Orleans PD to pull the records on Suzette Whitaker's cell phone."

"Don't tell me . . ."

"Fifteen minutes after you and Dr. Dodds signed out of Camellia Gables, Nurse Whitaker was on the phone to Josiah Mantooth," Ramon confirmed. "Hours after that, Mama Tante was dead."

"No shit," Jackson repeated, reaching for the now empty coffee pot. Gesturing to the waitress, Jackson's thoughts returned to Katherine Van Hoerne.

"Were you serious earlier?" he asked Ramon. "When you said Katherine might be innocent?"

"Very serious. The evidence all but clears her of the Ramirez murder."

"How is that possible?" Jackson wondered out loud. "And why the hell didn't anyone figure it out before now?"

"Again, we have Nathan Conrad to thank for that," Ramon replied, recalling Conrad's lengthy confession. "He personally persuaded the chief of police at the time to close the Ramirez case ASAP—something about PR and whatnot—thus halting the investigation before it ever got started. Later, Nathan recruited a detective named Jared Hawthorne to make the files disappear, hoping to ensure the case would stay closed. That's why I had to convince the DA to pretend to pursue the charges against Mrs. Van Hoerne, so I could justify reopening the investigation."

"Hold on there," Jackson interrupted. "Are you telling me that prosecuting Katherine for the murder was just part of some scheme?"

"It enabled us to reopen the Ramirez case without having to go through Nathan Conrad."

"But the trial . . ."

"There was never going to be a trial. Of course, it never occurred to us that she might actually be innocent."

The waitress returned, and the two men sat quietly as she refilled their mugs.

"There may be one thing—or one *person*, rather—who can bust this whole sordid mess wide open," Jackson said after she'd left.

"Who's that?"

"Katherine Van Hoerne."

18

"No way, absolutely not."

"Damn it, Ellie, be reasonable!"

"Me? You're the one being unreasonable!"

"Have you heard a single word I've said?"

"Every word, and the answer is still no," Ellie informed Jackson flatly.

He gripped the phone in frustration and took a long, calming breath.

Sighing, Jackson paused and said into the phone, "Katherine Van Hoerne is a material witness to a murder—not a suicide, not an accident—a *murder*. Gabrielle was pushed off that balcony and the police can prove it. For God's sake, Katherine was there! She saw the whole thing. Jesus, no wonder she's so fucked up."

"I learned as much from Katherine herself today under hypnosis," Ellie answered.

"See! Katherine clearly needs to confront her demons."

"Those *demons* are precisely why I cannot allow Katherine to leave this hospital. She mutilated herself today, Jackson, she was so afraid of those demons. Katherine needs to remain in a safe, structured environment where she's comfortable and . . ."

Jackson hung his head wearily, rolled his eyes toward Ramon—who had just about lost his patience with this exchange—and said, "Did I mention we know for a fact that Gabrielle's murder was covered up by the police in exchange for cash and prizes? Josiah Mantooth bribed them. Did I mention that part already?"

"Tell her that the woman is *innocent*, for Christ's sake," Ramon hissed for the third time.

Putting his hand over the mouthpiece, Jackson whispered, "I can't tell her something like that over the phone."

"Why the hell not?"

"Because, it's *huge*—beyond huge—and Ellie deserves to hear it in person, that's the hell why not!"

"Give me that goddamn phone," Ramon growled, wrestling it out of Jackson's hand. "Dr. Dodds? This is Commander Ramon Hinojosa. Yes, that's right, we met at the animal hospital. How is the dog, by the way? Yes, of course, Lola. Good, good."

It was now Ramon's turn to roll his eyes at Jackson.

"Listen, Dr. Dodds, there is a patrol car currently en route to Dripping Springs to pick up Mrs. Van Hoerne. You can either ride along or stay at the hospital, that's entirely up to you, but Mrs. Van Hoerne will be delivered to police headquarters within the hour. Now before you start putting up a fuss, Dr. Dodds, you should know that we have uncovered evidence that clears Mrs. Van Hoerne of the Angel Ramirez murder, and therefore . . ."

There was a long pause.

"She didn't kill Ramirez, Dr. Dodds, someone else did, and if I am ever going to find out who that someone else is, I need Mrs. Van Hoerne to . . . Hello? Hello? Dr. Dodds, are you there?"

Turning to Jackson, Ramon said, "I think she dropped the phone."

Ellie and Katherine arrived downtown with their police escort 40 minutes later. Both Ramon and Jackson were stunned to see Katherine's remarkable improvement.

"I've explained to Katherine what we discussed earlier, on the telephone, all of it," Ellie told them, sitting beside Katherine in a chair facing Ramon's desk.

"Then you understand, Mrs. Van Hoerne," Ramon said, addressing Katherine directly, "that we believe you are innocent of the crimes for which you are accused, and we are dropping all charges against you, effective immediately."

"It hasn't really sunk in yet, I don't think," Katherine replied softly.

"That's to be expected, I imagine."

Ramon Hinojosa went through the details of his investigation with the two women, and what he had uncovered.

When he was finished, Ellie asked, "So, these dirty cops, did they plant evidence against Katherine?"

"No, nothing like that. Mrs. Van Hoerne was in the alley that night with Mr. Ramirez, and all of the preliminary evidence was damning," Ramon explained. "The knife she brought from home, likely for protection, was the murder weapon. Nathan Conrad merely agreed to facilitate a quick disposition of the case at Mantooth's request."

"Merely?" Ellie retorted.

"Nathan Conrad claims that he truly thought Katherine was guilty, and I tend to believe him. But you are correct, Dr. Dodds, it does not excuse his behavior," Ramon told her, turning to Katherine. "Because of Conrad's interference, it took us five years to prove your innocence. And for that, Mrs. Van Hoerne, I am deeply, deeply sorry."

Katherine nodded her acknowledgement, but remained silent.

"What the hell did happen to Angel Ramirez?" Ellie asked.

"Obviously, finding that out is our next priority. But five years is a long time for a case to go cold, and Angel Ramirez had plenty of enemies."

Ramon again turned his gaze to Katherine.

"You don't remember being there at all? At Rey's."

Katherine shook her head no.

"We believe that the actual perpetrator stabbed Angel, wiped the handle of the knife clean, and then returned it to Mrs. Van Hoerne's hand, which would explain why she was holding the knife when police arrived, and there was only one set of prints."

"And Josiah Mantooth simply took advantage of the situation," Jackson added, joining the conversation for the first time. "The son of a bitch always wanted Katherine committed, and when he finally saw an opportunity, he ran with it."

"It's likely Mr. Mantooth believed his daughter was guilty," Ramon pointed out, "but in any event, Mantooth manipulated the system to suit his own purposes. He wanted Katherine institutionalized regardless of the truth of the situation."

"But why?" Ellie questioned out loud. "Why was Josiah so bound and determined to lock Katherine away?"

"Because she saw him kill Gabrielle," Jackson blurted out. "Isn't that pretty obvious by now?"

"All we have at this time are theories," Ramon warned. "We may never know the whole truth."

Suddenly, a calm, cool voice interrupted the discussion.

"I can find out the truth," Katherine announced.

"How? Ramon asked.

"I can ask my father."

There were several moments of stunned silence in the room.

Ramon cleared his throat and said, "I can't promise he'll be receptive to that idea."

"Don't worry, Commander," Katherine assured him. "He'll see me."

19

Josiah Mantooth and Delroy Duffy sat side by side at the metal conference table, Ramon Hinojosa seated across from them. They were in yet another drab, windowless interrogation room, only this one was larger.

As Duffy and his client finished scanning the written transcript of Nathan Conrad's confession, Ramon observed them carefully. Duffy was his usual cocksure self, but Mantooth was a different story. He seemed nervous, unfocused, jittery.

Ramon had just finished outlining the charges against him when Josiah became so upset he had to reach for his heart medication.

Duffy concluded his examination of the document, removed his glasses, and rubbed the bridge of his nose.

"I'm going to need some time alone with my client," he told Ramon, his tone neutral.

"By all means," Ramon replied with a nod. "However, before we get to that, there's someone who would like a word with Mr. Mantooth."

"Who?"

"His daughter."

"Katherine's here?" Josiah responded, his voice suddenly animated.

"Out in the hallway," Ramon nodded.

"Hold up there, Commander," Delroy warned. "This is highly irregular."

"I am simply conveying the message that Katherine Van Hoerne would like to speak with her father."

"And Katherine, she's . . . *well?*" Josiah asked.

"Seems to be."

"I'm advising against this—"

"Shut up, Duffy," Josiah snapped. "I want to see her."

"As your lawyer—"

"I said shut up!"

The interrogation room was silent.

"Mrs. Van Hoerne has requested that I be present during this meeting," Ramon added, "as well as her doctor and her lawyer."

"That's fine."

"I presume you will also stay, Mr. Duffy?"

"You bet your ass," Delroy answered.

Ramon stood and pressed the button on an intercom stationed beside the door.

Within seconds, Katherine Van Hoerne, Eleanor Dodds, and Jackson Polke walked into the interrogation room and took their seats around the table.

Katherine sat across from Josiah and stared at her father without emotion.

Josiah's mouth began to tremble, his moist, beady eyes never leaving Katherine's face.

"You look well," he told her, his voice hushed.

It was true. Although still gaunt with shadows ringing her eyes, Katherine had reclaimed a glimmer of her former beauty.

"I wish I could return the compliment," she told him flatly.

Josiah pale, dry lips curled upwards as he shrugged his thin shoulders.

"I'm an old man now, Katherine, with an old man's heart."

"Did you do these things, Father?" Katherine asked without preamble.

Josiah sighed and looked away.

Without pause he answered, "Some."

"I must object," Delroy Duffy interjected. "My client has no intention of waiving his Fifth Amendment rights against self-incrimination—"

"Can it, Delroy," Josiah instructed. "I'm dying, for Christ's sake. What the hell can they do to me?"

"I cannot permit you . . ."

"I mean it, Duffy, either shut the hell up or get out. Your choice."

"Fine, Josiah," Delroy answered, pushing back from the table. "I won't sit here mute while you hang yourself. I hereby resign as your counsel."

"Resignation accepted."

Delroy Duffy stalked out of the room, and Josiah turned his attention back to Katherine.

"Yes, I've done some of these things," he repeated.

"Why?"

"Oh Katherine," he exhaled wearily, "you may find this hard to believe, but everything I did, I did for you."

"Surely you can manage something more original," she countered.

"I kept you safe, protected . . ."

"I'm not particularly interested in your excuses, Father," Katherine told him icily. "I'm looking for answers."

"You don't know what you're asking of me, Katherine. I've spent most of my adult life protecting you from all of this."

"And look how far that's gotten us. I lost five years of my life because of you."

"Katherine, I thought you killed that man. I was only trying to protect you, keep you out of prison."

"Perhaps, but because of your interference, I was locked away."

"I am so sorry . . ."

"You *owe me*, Father," Katherine asserted. "I want answers."

There was a long pause, the silence interrupted only by the slight wheezing sound coming from Josiah's chest.

"Oh Christ, Katherine, where do I even start?" he sighed wearily.

"Did you kill my mother?" she asked.

"What?" he snapped, surprised. "No! I didn't kill Gabrielle. I loved your mother."

"I remember you fighting," Katherine pressed.

"Yes, we fought, but I would never hurt Gabrielle."

"What about unintentionally?" Ramon Hinojosa interrupted. "The argument becomes heated, you and the missus struggle, somehow you end up on the balcony . . ."

"No!" Josiah shot back. "No, that's not how it happened."

"How did it happen?"

"I would sooner take my own life than hurt Gabrielle."

"Really?" Ramon countered. "Then who the hell left that palm print on the side of her face?"

"What are you talking about?"

"Your wife was struck repeatedly about the neck and head *before* she went over that railing."

"That's not possible," Josiah insisted. "You must be mistaken."

"No mistake."

"But I'd left Gabrielle not ten minutes before, and there were no bruises. Whatever injuries my wife sustained, they were caused by the fall."

"Did you examine the body, Mr. Mantooth?"

"No, not closely," Josiah admitted. "I just . . . well, I just couldn't . . . see her like that, I mean."

"What were you and Gabrielle fighting about?"

"My wife was mentally ill, Commander. We fought about a great many things."

"What kind of things?"

"Gabrielle suffered from paranoid delusions. Nothing I said, nothing I did, could get through to her."

"Paranoid delusions about you and your teenage daughter?" Ellie interjected.

"How can you possibly know that?" Josiah said, turning to Ellie.

"Gabrielle left a letter," she explained. "Avery told her mother what you did, what you'd been doing."

"You're lying," Josiah spat.

"Mama Tante gave it to us."

"Before you had the old gal murdered," Jackson added.

Josiah removed a porcelain pillbox from his breast pocket and swallowed two chalky white tablets.

"I can show you the letter if you'd like, Mr. Mantooth," Ellie continued. "If you don't believe me, that is."

"No, I believe you," he grimaced. "I thought it was Gabrielle's delusions, figments of her imagination, but it was Avery the whole time."

"You're going to blame Avery?"

"You don't understand."

"Make me understand."

"Gabrielle suffered from extreme paranoia. Every day, it was something new—someone poisoned her tea, or moved her things, or watched her as she slept. Eventually, Gabrielle stopped coming out of her room altogether. She was convinced that was the only way to remain safe. She barricaded herself in that goddamn bedroom like she was under quarantine."

"I get that, but . . ."

"Don't you see? If what you said about the letter is true, then it was Avery. Avery was the one filling Gabrielle's head with lies. She was the one fanning her mother's paranoia."

"Why?" Ellie asked. "Why would Avery do something like that if it wasn't true?"

There was a long silence before Josiah spoke.

"Because she wanted me," he said at last. "Avery seduced me soon after Gabrielle died."

"Ugh . . ." Jackson groaned.

"You have to believe me, Avery was the aggressor," Josiah told them. "It was what she wanted. Avery came to me at my lowest point, after Gabrielle died, and offered me comfort. She was there for me.

"I was heartbroken over Gabrielle. Watching her deteriorate like that, her sanity slipping away, day by day, week by week, it damn near killed me. Gabrielle warned me, before we got married, that there was this family thing, this disease. But even so, nothing can quite prepare you for the reality of it, or the terrible helplessness."

"So you pushed her off the balcony, to ease your burden?" Jackson shot back.

"I did not kill my wife!" Josiah exploded.

"Then who did?" Jackson shouted back.

"Katherine!"

A thunderous quiet descended on the room, and everyone turned to stare at Katherine. They watched as she rose from the table and began pacing around the room, her head tilted oddly to the side.

"I thought if Avery and I confronted Gabrielle together," Josiah continued, "explained to her this imagined affair was all in her head, I could make Gabrielle see reason. But I never got the chance."

"Because Gabrielle died?" Ramon asked.

"It was an accident. Katherine didn't mean to hurt Gabrielle, but there was a fight and they struggled, and somehow they ended up on the balcony . . ."

Suddenly, a low, controlled voice cut him off.

"Is that what she told you?" Katherine demanded coldly. "Is that what Avery told you happened?"

"She told me what happened, yes," Josiah replied.

"And you believed her?"

Josiah didn't respond for several seconds.

"I had no reason to doubt her," he said in a tremulous voice.

"She was a liar," Katherine stated, retaking her seat at the table.

Josiah's already colorless skin went a distressing shade of pewter.

"But . . . but Katherine, you were standing there when Avery told me," he stammered. "When I asked you if that's what happened, you nodded and said yes!"

"Avery threatened to kill me," Katherine answered. "Just like she killed my mother."

Ellie lunged from her chair and kneeled at Katherine's side.

"Do you remember?" Ellie asked, taking her hand.

"Yes, I remember."

Katherine's voice sounded strange, affectless, like she was reading from a teleprompter.

"All of this must have triggered. . ." Ellie began before Jackson stopped her mid-sentence.

"Is Josiah lying?" Jackson demanded of Katherine.

"My father did not kill my mother," she said.

"So, he's telling the truth?"

"He doesn't know the truth. He wasn't there."

"Tell us, then."

"He left us alone," Katherine went on accusatorily. "And that's when Mother and Avery turned on each other."

"Turned on each other?" Ellie echoed, hoarsely.

"Mother was figuring it out," Katherine explained in a distant voice. "She was finally seeing what Avery was doing, what she had always been doing.

"The lies. The manipulations. The terrible games. Mother was starting to understand."

"She didn't tell me," Josiah interjected. "I wouldn't have left you all alone . . ."

"That day, in Mother's bedroom, Avery tried to play the innocent, the victim. At first. But when she realized Mother wasn't buying it anymore, she dropped the façade. That's when Avery slapped Mother across the face. Hard."

Katherine hesitated, and Ellie squeezed her hand.

"Mother was screaming furiously," Katherine went on, "ordering Avery to pack her things and leave the house and never come back. They struggled, and Avery dragged Mother out onto the balcony.

"That was the last time I saw her."

By the time Katherine had finished, Josiah was crying.

"Jesus, Katherine, why didn't you tell me?" he asked miserably. "Why did you let me believe that you killed Gabrielle?"

Tears welled in Katherine's eyes, but she didn't answer.

"Why not?" Ellie pressed. "Why couldn't you tell your father?"

"She threatened me," Katherine whispered. "And she hurt me. Oh God, she hurt me terribly."

Katherine was suddenly overcome with deep, wracking sobs, and it took her some time to regain her composure. When she did, Katherine told them about growing up with Avery Mantooth as a big sister, and the picture that emerged was that of a classic sadist.

Avery loved pain—enduring it, inflicting it, watching others writhe in it—it was a singular, all-consuming passion. After Gabrielle's death, things escalated. With Gabrielle gone and Josiah barely functioning, Avery had absolute freedom to do whatever she pleased. Terrorizing Katherine became Avery's chief amusement.

Often, in the middle of the night, Katherine would wake to find Avery holding a pillow over her face, and she would hear that sweet, sickening whisper: *Tonight? Is this the night I finally get rid of you? Mmmmm, let me think . . . now or later . . . now or later . . . mmmm. Perhaps tomorrow would be better? Yes, I'll wait. Tomorrow then.*

"Oh God," Josiah Mantooth moaned, "I didn't know. I swear I didn't know."

"It only got worse after you started sleeping with her," Katherine replied.

"You knew?"

"Avery made sure of it. Said she could have me sent away any time she wanted, just like Mama Tante, and I would just disappear."

"I knew Avery had some issues," Josiah said, "but it never occurred to me . . ."

"What kind of issues?" Ellie asked him.

"Avery used to hurt herself, with razors, lighters, her own fingernails. Her whole life. Even when she was little, Avery would wrap string or thread around the tip of her index finger until it became a blackish-purple. As she grew older, well, she found other ways to hurt herself. And then there was. . ."

"Go on," Ellie pushed.

"The sex. She wanted me to hurt her," he answered. "At first, it seemed harmless. You know, leather, whips, that sort of thing. But then it intensified.

"Avery was utterly fascinated by physical pain. Feeling it, inflicting it, watching it be inflicted on others . . ."

"So, you were aware Avery was a sadist," Ellie cut him off, "yet it never occurred to you that she could pose a danger to your younger daughter?"

"I assumed it was a sexual thing," Josiah replied defensively.

"And the self-mutilation?"

"Like I said, Avery had issues, but there was never any sign she was harming Katherine."

"Evidently you weren't looking closely enough, Mr. Mantooth," Ellie stated with obvious disdain. "You should have protected Katherine."

"I did protect Katherine!" Josiah fumed. "You cannot fathom what I've been through trying to protect Katherine! Jesus Christ, I'm still protecting her!"

"From what?"

"From herself!"

"How?"

"By covering up what she's done!"

"We've already established Katherine didn't kill her mother, so that excuse is wearing pretty damn thin," Jackson nearly yelled.

"If it weren't for me, Katherine would have spent her entire adult life in prison."

"Read my lips, Mr. Mantooth," Ellie uttered. "Katherine didn't kill anybody."

"Who the hell do you think murdered Avery?" Josiah shot back.

Again, a blanket of silence fell over the room.

Jackson was beginning to feel like he was on one of those tilt-a-whirls at the amusement park.

"It's true," Katherine whispered. "I did it. I set her on fire."

"You what?" Ellie stammered.

Wiping her face of tears and breathing deeply, Katherine recounted the events of that night.

"I remember," she began, "Avery summoned me to her room. She wanted to play a game, the one where she threw lit matches at me. But Avery was too drunk to play, and she passed out. That's when I decided to play the game by myself."

In her telling, something in Katherine snapped that night. She grabbed a bottle of nail polish remover from Avery's bedside table, and poured it over her sister's face. Then she grabbed nearly a whole pack of matches.

Katherine seemed remarkably calm as she told them the story, like a disaster survivor too stunned to fully grasp what's happened.

"I killed her," Katherine concluded in a disbelieving tone.

From the other end of the interrogation room, Ramon Hinojosa cleared his throat.

"Maybe not," he stated.

"I don't understand."

"An accelerant more powerful than acetone was used that night," Ramon told her. "Likely more than one accelerant."

Katherine looked confused.

"How many, exactly Mr. Mantooth?" Ramon asked him casually. "What exactly did you use to create such a massive inferno?"

In a hushed voice, Josiah answered, "Vodka and lighter fluid."

"Wait, you . . . ?" Katherine whispered.

"I did what I had to," Josiah responded evenly.

"That's why you wanted to keep Katherine incapacitated," Ellie hissed at him. "So she wouldn't remember what you did to Avery! That you murdered her sister!"

"I only finished the job."

Overwhelmed by emotion, Katherine dropped her head into her hands and began to cry softly.

"I think we're finished here," Ellie announced, putting her arm around Katherine's shoulder.

"I agree," Ramon responded. "I have more than enough to begin the process."

Tammy Lynn Geary appeared at the door an instant later.

"Please show our prisoner to his cell," Ramon instructed, gesturing to Josiah.

As Tammy Lynn approached the old man, he held up a gnarled hand and said, "Just one more moment with my daughter, please."

"We have nothing else to say to one another," Katherine told him.

"I love you, Katherine! Everything I've done was only to protect you!"

"You keep telling yourself that," Katherine answered as her father was ushered out.

20

Drawing aside the curtain, Katherine stared out the window at a rolling white landscape. A light dusting of powdery snow covered Dripping Springs—the aftermath of an unseasonably cold winter storm that had just passed through—but the skies were clear and ice blue.

Katherine stepped away from the glass and let the fabric fall back into place.

"The snow is lovely," she said to Ellie, who was seated on the bed beside Katherine's open suitcase. "I'd almost forgotten about Christmas altogether."

"You have a lot to celebrate this year," Ellie smiled.

"Still, it all feels so strange," Katherine sighed, folding a black cashmere sweater and placing it in her bag. "It's hard to come to grips."

The telephone on the bedside table rang shrilly, and Ellie reached for it.

"Yes," she said into the mouthpiece. "That's fine. Send them in."

"Is that Clay?" Katherine whispered, looking pale and nervous.

"And Jackson," Ellie replied.

Katherine and her husband had been reconnecting during his visits to the hospital, but this would be quite a transition for both of them.

Taking a deep breath, Katherine placed the last of her belongings in the suitcase and closed the flap.

"Are you ready?" Clay asked his wife when he and Jackson entered the room.

Katherine and Clay were awkward around each other—stiff, formal—and there was no way of knowing what would happen with their marriage, but Ellie had hope the two of them might find a way back to each other.

"Thank you, Dr. Dodds," Clay said, clasping Ellie's hand. "Thank you for bringing Katherine back to us."

"You're welcome, Mr. Van Hoerne," Ellie replied.

"And thank you, Mr. Polke," Clay went on, facing Jackson. "We both owe you a debt of gratitude."

"How about I meet you at the car," Katherine suggested to Clay. "I'd like a minute."

"Of course," Clay nodded, picking up the suitcase. "I'll be out front."

After he was gone, Katherine turned to Jackson and Ellie, her eyes shining with emotion.

"It's my turn to thank you," she said, her voice tremulous, "but I don't know where to start. How can I possibly express the gratitude I feel? And how could I ever repay you?"

"Seeing you leave this hospital is really the only thanks we need," Ellie responded sincerely.

"It was nothing," Jackson muttered, grinning slightly.

Katherine grabbed his hands and squeezed them tightly.

"Thank you, Jackson, for fighting for me," she whispered.

"You're welcome," Jackson replied, squeezing back.

"And thank you, Dr. Dodds," Katherine said, wrapping her arms around Ellie. "Thank you for not giving up on me."

Before Ellie lost the battle with her own emotions, she gently pushed Katherine away and said, "Your husband and daughter are waiting for you."

Katherine nodded her understanding and exhaled slowly.

"Good-bye, Dr. Dodds."

"You're not getting rid of me that easily, Katherine," Ellie reminded her in a teasing tone. "I'll see you next week for our appointment."

"Right," Katherine smiled. "I'll see you then."

And with that, Katherine Mantooth Van Hoerne walked out of the hospital room without so much as a glance backwards.

Once she was gone, Jackson and Ellie collapsed onto the couch.

"Well, that's it," Jackson observed after several moments of silence.

"That's it," Ellie agreed numbly.

"What now?"

"For Katherine?"

"No," Jackson shook his head. "For us."

"Us?" Ellie asked, her lips curving into a shy smile. "Is there an us?"

"I guess that's something we should find out."

"And how do we do that?"

"We could go out to dinner."

"A date, eh?"

"Just like normal people."

Jackson turned, put his hands on either side of Ellie's face, and drew her close.

"You're not just toying with me, are you Doctor?" he asked with an earnestness he hadn't intended.

"No, I'm not toying with you."

"Because I think I could fall in love with you."

"You don't scare me, Polke," she replied softly.

"Good, because you scare the hell out me," Jackson answered, gathering Ellie in his arms and kissing her soundly.

EPILOGUE

EIGHT MONTHS LATER

The movers filed out of the house and down the stone steps to the driveway. Tossing the last of the heavy pads and blankets into the truck, the men slammed the rear cargo door shut and climbed into the cab. The driver rolled down his window to wave to Jackson as he backed the van onto the wide, tree-lined street.

From his new front porch, Jackson waved back.

Wes McCaffrey was sitting beside him in an old-fashioned rocking chair, a house-warming gift from Clementine, finishing his beer. When it was done, Wes stood up and stretched out his legs.

"I best let you get back to your boxes," Wes told Jackson, placing his empty bottle on a table. "So, you got a business card?"

Jackson reached into the pocket of his shorts and pulled out his wallet, extracting a small white rectangle from within.

"Polke & Associates," Wes read with a smile. "I like it."

"Well, I'm still working on the *& Associates* part, but I thought it had a nice ring to it."

Jackson went around to the back of the house where Lola was dozing in the warm sunshine.

The dog had made an amazing recovery. There was a smattering of scars on her chest from the bullet wounds, but the only lingering effect was a slight limp.

As he watched Lola roll over onto her back and paw the air, Jackson heard footsteps behind him and then felt the brush of lips against his neck. Spinning around, he pulled Ellie into his arms and kissed her, a slow, deep kiss that left Ellie a little breathless.

"Keep this up, and we'll never got those damn boxes unpacked," she teased, pulling away.

Jackson followed Ellie inside the house, where she went upstairs to unpack the home office while Jackson turned his attention to the kitchen.

An hour later, just as he was about to open the last box marked "DISHES," Jackson heard Ellie shouting from upstairs.

"What?" he exclaimed after flying up the staircase.

Ellie turned on him, her eyes flashing.

"What's wrong?"

"This," Ellie replied, shoving a piece of paper into his hands. "It fell out when I was unpacking your files. Why didn't you ever show this to me?"

Jackson quickly scanned the document.

"That is a lab report containing the results of Katherine's blood analysis on the night Angel Ramirez was murdered," Ellie explained, her tone sharp.

"Er, okay."

"Why didn't you tell me?" Ellie demanded.

"Because it never occurred to me?"

"Where did you get it?"

"What?"

"This lab report, where did you get it?" Ellie demanded.

The edge to her voice was starting to make Jackson nervous.

"It was part of the official police file—we got a copy in anticipation of Katherine's trial. Why?"

"I should have known about this," she told him, becoming more agitated by the second.

"If you say so."

"Jesus Christ, Jackson, did you even read it?" Ellie nearly shouted at him.

"Would you mind telling me what the hell is going on?"

"I can't believe we were all so stupid," Ellie muttered, smacking her forehead. "Idiots."

"Okay, now you're starting to freak me out," Jackson told her flatly.

"But don't you see?"

Ellie's laps around the room were beginning to make Jackson dizzy, so he grabbed her by the shoulders and forced her to gaze into his face.

"For the love of God," he stated firmly, "*what are you yammering about?*"

Taking a deep breath, Ellie got herself under control and said, "It's the tox screen."

"Right, the tox screen. What about it?"

"Look at it."

Jackson did as he was told and examined the information closely.

"Notice anything?" Ellie asked quietly.

"Her blood-alcohol ratio was through the roof?"

"Do you notice anything *missing?*"

"Sweetheart, I love you, but enough with the guessing games," Jackson told her, losing patience. "Spit it out."

"There's no mention of Thymetrazine."

Jackson stared at Ellie blankly and said "So?"

"On the night Angel Ramirez died, there was no trace of the drug in her system."

"Which is important *because?*"

"Because there should have been—in fact, considering the dosage Katherine was on at the time, there should have been a *significant* concentration of Thymetrazine in her blood. According to these lab results, there wasn't so much as a *trace*. Do you have any idea what happens to a person like Katherine if she goes off anti-psychotic medication cold-turkey?"

"She goes *psycho?*"

"It might very well have been Thymetrazine withdrawal that led to the psychotic break."

"Didn't the hospital do blood tests when she was admitted?" Jackson asked, still confused. "Didn't those tests show the same results?"

"Yes, of course, but by then she'd been in jail for days. The absence of the drug in her system was to be expected."

Jackson sighed and ran his fingers through his hair.

"All right, let's assume you're right and it was the medication screw-up that was behind Katherine losing her shit. Other than making sure it never happens again, why is this so damn important?"

"Because, according to Katherine, she was taking her meds," Ellie replied. "I need to understand what went wrong."

"I thought all of this was behind us," Jackson groaned.

"So did I."

Jackson paused before speaking.

"Okay, Dr. Do-Right. What the hell do you propose we do about this?"

"Talk to Katherine."

The wind whipped through Katherine's hair as her horse hurtled across the flat, grassy terrain. Her thigh muscles were burning and she panted from the exertion, but her face was glazed in a wide, contented smile. Digging in her heels and leaning forward in the saddle, Katherine's mind was numbed by the sound of thundering hooves.

When the stables became visible in the distance, Katherine released the animal's last burst of speed.

Katherine decelerated to a trot as she neared the fence, and veered toward the gate. After dismounting and handing the reigns over to a ranch hand, Katherine pulled a sugar cube from the pocket of her jeans for the horse.

Walking around the stables to the adjacent parking lot, Katherine climbed into a black Range Rover and followed a winding concrete drive up a hillside to the main house.

She was in the mudroom taking off her boots when her phone began to ring. Hoping it was Charlotte calling from her grandmother's house, Katherine answered on the first ring.

"Hello," she said into the receiver. "Oh, yes, hello Dr. Dodds. No, no, this isn't a bad time."

Clay Van Hoerne wiped his muddy cowboy boots on a porcupine-shaped scraper before walking into the house. Striding into the kitchen, he grabbed a longneck out of the refrigerator and picked up a stack of mail.

He was sorting through catalogues when Clay suddenly caught the echo of Katherine's voice, coming from the living room.

"Yes, I'm sure," he heard her say. "Absolutely certain. The first thing I did every morning was take my pills."

Clay moved quietly across the kitchen, closer to the entryway. He saw Katherine on the far side of the living room, staring out over the rolling countryside from the two-story picture window.

She was talking on the telephone, her back to Clay.

"I did, I *know* I did," she insisted. "Then I don't understand. How could the tox screen come back negative?"

Clay inched closer without making a sound.

"I'm telling you, Ellie, there has to be some mistake. Ask Clay, he'll tell you. I took my meds like clockwork . . ."

Before she could utter another word, Clay's long arms circled his wife's torso from behind, and he kissed her lightly on the cheek.

Katherine smiled up her husband and said into the mouthpiece, "I have to go now, but yes, that would be fine. We'll be expecting you."

She turned to Clay and wrapped her arms around his waist.

"Hi there."

"Hi yourself," Clay replied. "Who was that?"

"Ellie Dodds."

"Oh yeah?"

"She's driving out here this afternoon with Jackson Polke, to talk to me," Katherine said, pressing her cheek against Clay's chest. "They should be here in a couple of hours."

"Is that so?" he murmured.

"You don't mind, do you?"

"Why would I mind?"

Leaning back in the porcelain claw-footed tub, Katherine let the lavender-scented bubbles relax her limbs. It was some time before she reluctantly stepped out of the fragrant, steaming water and toweled off.

Wrapping a thick, white robe around her shoulders, Katherine drifted out of her bathroom and into the bedroom she shared with Clay.

To her surprise, Clay was sitting in the middle of their bed, his back against the silk upholstered headboard. He was still wearing his dirty jeans and faded work shirt, and his hands were folded between his knees. Oddly, he was wearing worn leather, work gloves.

At first, when she saw him waiting in the bed, Katherine thought he wanted her to join him, but the expression on Clay's face belied that idea. He was darkly serious.

"I am genuinely sorry, Katherine," Clay told her quietly, the tenor of his voice strangely hollow. "Truly I am."

"Why are you sorry?"

"If Ellie Dodds would just get on with her goddamn life," Clay answered. "I swear to God, that woman is like a hyena on a stripped carcass. Won't let go 'til she's licked every bone clean. It's only a matter of time before Dodds figures out who was screwing with your medication, and then before long, she'll put you back under hypnosis. And that, Katherine, is something I simply cannot allow."

"Clay, I don't understand . . ."

From between his legs, Clay pulled out a revolver, and pointed it at Katherine's midsection.

"I am genuinely sorry it has to be this way," he told her, "but there are things you still don't remember, and it has to stay that way."

"What don't I remember?" Katherine stammered, too stunned and bewildered to yet be afraid.

Suddenly, Clay jumped up from the bed and placed the barrel of the gun against Katherine's forehead.

"Sit down," he instructed, pointing to a small desk in the corner.

Katherine did as she was told, her brain and heart slow to process the reality of what was happening.

As she lowered herself into the armchair, Clay moved the mouth of the gun to Katherine's right temple. Sitting in front of Katherine was her laptop computer, open to a short document. Upon closer inspection, Katherine saw that it was a letter:

Dear Clay and Charlotte—I thought all of this was behind me, but now I know that it will never end. The questions never stop. My head never stops spinning. I will never be able to put it behind me. I am only polluting your lives. Please understand. I love you too much to bring all of this back into your life again. I know you'll be okay without me.

Katherine read the words several times before their meaning sunk in.

"No one will believe you," she turned to him, at last finding her voice. "You're mad to think you'll get away with it."

"No darlin', you're the one who's mad—certifiably insane, remember? Trust me, no one is gonna bat an eyelash when you go and off yourself."

"Ellie Dodds will," Katherine reminded him. "And she'll more than bat an eyelash."

"Yeah, well, we'll see what she's able to actually *prove.* Everybody else—the cops, the district attorney, anyone with half a brain who's read the newspapers in the last year—will have no problem believing Katherine Van Hoerne took her own life."

Clay closed one eye and aimed the weapon.

Only then did a true and genuine fear strike Katherine, and her mind and body registered the danger. Suddenly, she began to tremble violently and her eyes rolled into the back of her head.

For several moments, she remained like this, as if having a seizure. Then, the tremors stopped just as abruptly as they began, and Katherine went limp.

Clay's mouth went dry and his dick went hard as a bolt of excitement shivered down his spine. Not knowing whether to feel hopeful or nervous, Clay released his pressure on the trigger ever so slightly, and waited.

A minute later, Katherine's eyelids flew open and she fixed her stare on Clay. He noticed those cornflower blue irises held all the warmth of black ice.

"Avery?" he whispered. "Avery, is that you?"

"Did you miss me, lover?"

Her face was suddenly inches from Clay's, studying him with an inscrutable expression. He could feel her breath in his nostrils.

Slowly, she brought her lips to his. Taking his lower lip between her own, she sucked gently. Then she bit down, hard enough to break the skin.

"Oh Christ, Avery, is that really you?" Clay gasped.

"Yes, lover," she assured him. "It's me."

The woman everyone else called Katherine threaded her fingers through Clay's hair and yanked his head back roughly.

"And you have been a naughty, *naughty* boy."

Their bodies lay entwined on the floor, slick with sweat and other assorted fluids. Panting, Clay rolled onto his back and luxuriated in the pulsing, aching hum of his sated body.

"Damn, Avery," he groaned, "where the hell have you been?"

He turned to hold her, but Avery extricated herself from his limbs and slid away.

"Hey, where do you think you're going," he growled, reaching out for her arm. "You and me, Avery, we've got some catching up to do."

She shook off his touch and said, "Where are the cigarettes?"

"I quit," Clay told her, folding his arms behind his head.

"Where?" she repeated, her voice a seductive, husky purr.

"No, really, I quit. That shit can kill you."

There was a monetary pause.

"Have you ever known me to be a patient woman, precious?"

Clay Van Hoerne's lips curved into a broad smile.

"My closet, bottom drawer, behind the socks."

"That's a good boy," Avery nodded before walking over to the closet.

"You always did know me," he shouted to her.

"Better than you know yourself," she responded, emerging with a rumpled pack of Marlboros and a book of matches.

Clay felt himself growing hard again as he watched Avery stride naked across the room, lighting a cigarette. She was like a cat, all feline grace and bored detachment, the underlying feral threat always present.

Katherine never had this kind of effect on him. It was the same body, he knew that—the same long legs and supple curves—but somehow, Avery just wore it differently. She moved him in ways Katherine never could. She always had, from the very beginning. After that stupid dance, at Camp Longhorn, the night he met Katherine Mantooth.

The night he met Avery.

It was one his favorite memories. At the end of a long, lame night of slow dancing to Phil Collins, Clay offered to walk Katherine back to her cabin. He took one of his favorite detours, through the woods on the edge of camp, and led Katherine into a moonlit clearing beside Inks Lake. It was there that he pulled the girl into his arms, and crushed his lips against hers.

She was hesitant at first, but eventually Katherine returned his kisses, allowing Clay's tongue to explore the inside of her mouth. Taking this as a sign, Clay cupped her small breast, and began kneading it with his fingertips.

"No," she told him, pushing his hand away.

"Don't you like it?"

"It's not that . . ."

Clay silenced Katherine with a soft, lingering kiss, and soon he felt her body yielding. Clay slipped his hand beneath her shirt and under her white, cotton bra.

"Stop it," Katherine told him in a quavering voice.

He pushed her backwards, up against a tree trunk.

"I said stop it!" she stated more forcefully, shoving past him into the clearing. "I want you to take me back now."

"If that's what you want," he shrugged, walking over to her. "But that's not *really* what you want, is it?"

Grabbing Katherine by her thick hair, Clay pulled her to him and forced his tongue into her mouth. She jerked back and slapped him hard across the face.

"Lie to yourself all you want, bitch," Clay laughed, "but you aren't fooling anybody. You liked it, and *I know* you liked it."

Katherine turned, as if to walk away, but then a strange thing happened. She started shaking all over, and then her eyes rolled back until he could only see the whites. Then she dropped to ground like a sack of potatoes.

"Jesus H. Christ," Clay muttered, running over.

She was splayed out on her side, perfectly still except for her eyelids, which quivered uncontrollably. He tried to rouse her, but she was as limp and lifeless as a ragdoll.

For several moments, Clay watched her, fascinated.

Just as he was about to go get help, Katherine's eyes flew open.

"Jesus H. Christ!" he shouted. "Are you all right?"

She stared at Clay quizzically, appraisingly, and then rose slowly to her feet.

"Hello," she said, her voice inexplicably deeper, husky. "You must be Clay."

And with those words Clay met Avery and forged an unholy bond that had lasted a lifetime.

"Ashtray?" he heard the resurrected Avery ask, bringing him back to the present.

"Kitchen, maybe?"

"Not terribly prepared, are you lover?" she purred. "A good southern boy is always prepared, Clayton. Surely, if you remember nothing else from our time together, you remember that."

"Why don't you come back over here," Clay offered, patting the carpet suggestively, "and I'll show you what else I remember."

From that first auspicious beginning, Clay and Avery shared a mutual passion for pain. She tapped into his most secret fantasies, and her total lack of inhibition was irresistible. Clay simply could not get enough of her.

As for Avery, she was insatiable.

Clay understood it was a package deal. Katherine was the flip side of the same coin. He'd learned all about split personalities from television, but he didn't really give a shit. As long as Avery came to him at night and kept doing those things that set his skin on fire, he could put up with Katherine the rest of the time.

"We're expecting guests, Clayton, or didn't you remember?" Avery announced, stubbing her cigarette out in a ceramic candy dish.

"Oh shit, I almost forgot," Clay muttered, rubbing absently at the welts rising up on his neck. "What the hell are we going to tell them?"

"*We* won't be telling them anything, lover."

"Christ, Avery, go look in the mirror. Dodds is definitely gonna want an explanation."

Avery crossed to the dresser and gazed into the silver-plated glass. Her face was beginning to swell, and there were bruises along her jaw line and ringing her thin, swan-like neck.

"Perfect," she said to her reflection, sucking on her split lip.

"What's that?" Clay asked.

"Nothing, lover. You were saying?"

"What are we going to tell them?"

"Don't you worry, lover, I'll come up with something."

Clay rose from the bed and walked over to Avery, stroking her shoulders from behind.

"Damn, I missed you," he sighed, grazing her hairline with his lips. "I'm glad you came back to me."

"Are you?"

Clay took Avery's hand and placed it firmly between his legs.

"You have doubts?" he moaned, rubbing against her. "I only have one question."

"What's that?"

"What the hell took you so goddamn long?"

Clay tilted Avery's chin up, bringing her mouth towards him, and kissed her with bruising intensity.

"Your question seems awfully silly," Avery remarked when their lips parted. "After all, I have you to thank for my extended absence."

Clay examined Avery's face closely, and took an involuntary step backward.

"You did switch my pills, didn't you?" she asked, not unpleasantly. "What was I taking instead, by the way? Aspirin? Cold medicine? Certainly not anything good."

"Sugar tablets," Clay admitted quietly.

"Not rat poison?"

"I never wanted you dead," Clay told her, sounding hurt.

"No, just wounded," Avery replied blithely. "You wanted me *just a little* unhinged. That's why you tampered with my meds, because you wanted me weak, so you could control me. Make me dependent on you."

Clay didn't bother to deny it. He sat down on the bed, and stared at his feet.

"Unfortunately, lover," Avery continued in a low staccato, "you didn't know what the fuck you were messing with and got a whole lot more crazy than you bargained for."

"I am genuinely sorry about that," he told her plaintively. "I never meant for things to go so far."

"Oh, you didn't *mean to*," Avery responded. "Well then, I guess that's okay . . ."

Clay could hear the hitch in her voice, the raw anger just below the calm veneer, and it made him crave her all the more. He didn't have the sense to be afraid.

"I admit it, I made a mistake . . ."

"A *mistake?*" Avery repeated sharply.

"Fine, I screwed up, but Christ, Avery, you pissed me off!" he snapped, losing his composure. "I was so pissed off I couldn't think straight! All your lies, the running around, it was driving me insane."

It was the same old argument, the same tired accusations and demands, and Avery still had no patience for his theatrics.

"Oh yes, your ridiculous jealousy."

"I knew what you were up to, Avery!" Clay bellowed. "Doping my drinks so I'd pass out, sneaking out of the house, fucking other men—and don't even try to deny it, because I know better."

"Were you following me?" Avery asked, feigning surprise.

"You're damn right! I had to put a stop to your bullshit."

"Thus, the ingenious plan to switch my pills."

"You were out of control, Avery, breaking all of our rules . . ."

"Not our rules, lover, *yours*," Avery interrupted. "Your patently absurd rules."

"We needed boundaries, to protect ourselves. You agreed!"

"There was no harm in letting you believe that."

Clay exhaled deeply and raised his hands in a gesture of supplication.

"Okay, fine, I was jealous and went off the deep end. I freely admit it. I screwed up big time, and I'm sorry."

Despite his words, Clay didn't sound particularly conciliatory. But there was no mistaking the lust and desire darkening his eyes. He still hungered for her. Even now, after all the years and everything that had happened, Clay craved her like a junkie needing a fix.

"Am I forgiven?" he asked softly.

Avery stared at him with an inscrutable expression, her posture rigid.

When no response was forthcoming, Clay reached over and grabbed his jeans off the floor. Slowly, he extracted a thick leather belt from the belt-loops.

"Perhaps I should be punished," he said, rubbing his thumb over the heavy silver buckle. "Like you said, I've been a naughty, naughty boy."

Without meeting Avery's eyes, Clay extended his arm and silently offered her the belt. Several seconds later, Avery took it from his hands.

"It took me awhile to piece it all together," she told him flatly, smacking the leather against her palm. "In fact, the final piece didn't fall into place until just this very morning, when Katherine received that telephone call from Dr. Dodds. Funny, really, how helpful that woman can be at times. Just think, Clayton, if it weren't for her, I might never have put the whole thing together."

"Avery, come on, don't do this . . ."

"I woke up in an insane asylum, Clayton," she stated coldly. "With no memory of how I got there. Or how long I'd been there. A chunk of my life simply gone. Can you even conceive of that?"

Clay didn't answer.

"Again, we have to credit the tenacious Dr. Dodds," Avery went on. "Without her, I wouldn't have woken up at all. Tell me, lover, when Dodds contacted you initially, to approve the Thymetrazine, did you say no right away, or did you sleep on it first?"

"Avery . . ."

"No matter," she went on. "I did wake up, and that's the important thing. But you can imagine my despair, considering the drastic change in my circumstances. After a brief but savage tantrum, I gathered what remained of my wits and began formulating a plan."

"I was told you had multiple personalities," Clay said, a coldness creeping into his limbs. "Some little girl, and a German doctor . . ."

"And Lucille, don't forget Lucille," Avery smiled. "A gal straight out of a Kenny Rogers song, and particularly close to my heart."

"But why? Why make all that up?"

"To keep Dodds distracted, busy. Besides, I was terribly bored. I watched. I waited. When I was strong enough and ready to make my move, I roused Katherine and let her handle the rest. It's simply amazing the lengths people will go to on Katherine's behalf, to rescue and protect her poor lost soul."

There was something about Avery's tone that left Clay unsettled, and the chill he felt in his limbs was settling into his bones.

"Why are you telling me this?" he asked.

"Aren't you interested? In the results of your handiwork?"

"Avery, stop it, please . . ."

"You know what I remember most about waking up in that place?" Avery asked. "It was the sounds. These horrible, horrible sounds that haunted my brain morning and night. Can you guess what those sounds were, Clayton? The ones reverberating in my skull almost continuously? Hmmm? No guesses?"

Avery again smacked her palm with the leather belt, and approached Clay on the bed.

"It was the sound of that knife cutting into Angel Ramirez," she told him, her eyes flashing dangerously. "And the wet, sucking sound his flesh made every time you pulled the knife out again."

A powerful sense of foreboding rose up from Clay's groin like bile, and he found himself scanning the bedroom floor frantically.

Meanwhile, Avery walked over to a bedside table.

"Looking for this, lover?" she asked, holding up the revolver. "You really should learn to keep track of your firearms."

Avery gripped the weapon, and aimed it squarely at Clay's heart.

"You know what else I remember vividly from that night?" she asked him. "You wiping down that bloody steak knife, and forcing it into my fingers. And then you left me in that alley to take the blame."

Clay scrambled backwards onto the mattress, but Avery was instantly on top of him, pressing the gun to his nipple.

"Who better to take the fall, right?" she hissed. "Thanks to you, I was already psychotic."

Avery stroked the trigger, enjoying the look of sheer panic that washed over Clay's handsome face.

"I love you," he nearly shouted. "Jesus, Avery, you're the only person I've ever loved!"

"Is that why you tried to kill me earlier?"

Clay looked confused.

"Kill you? I could never . . ."

Avery crammed the muzzle of the gun into his chin.

"Newsflash, Clayton," she said, "you kill Katherine, you *necessarily* kill me."

"I thought you were already dead—or gone or whatever!" Clay shot back, his eyes pleading. "I've been waiting for you, Avery, to come back to me, but I lost hope. I didn't think I'd ever see you again!"

Avery cocked her head to the side and studied him intently, her face an unreadable mask.

"I love you, Avery, and damn it, you love me too," Clay persisted, his tone adamant. "We're connected. Deep down, in our very cores, we're connected to one another, like two halves of the same whole, and a connection like that doesn't just die."

Avery's laugh was loud and cruel.

"*You* made *me* possible."

Clay looked confused.

"I needed you to survive," Avery explained, "like my own personal Igor, there to facilitate my unnatural life."

"Bullshit," Clay shot back. "You and me, we need each other, and that'll never change, not as long as we live."

"That was always your problem," Avery sighed, dragging the barrel of the gun down to Clay's chest. "You always did overestimate your role in the equation."

Jackson drove through the open gates and down the long, winding road to the Van Hoerne ranch. Parking in the circular drive, he stepped out of the car and heard a loud, cracking retort pierce the air. Then another.

"Was that a gun shot?" Ellie gasped, but Jackson was already racing for the front porch.

He barged through the front door, Ellie on his heels.

"Katherine!" he shouted. "Katherine, can you hear me?"

They moved through the enormous house shouting her name.

"Shhh," Ellie whispered. "Listen."

The noise was faint, but undeniable—a muffled sound coming from the second floor.

Ellie and Jackson ran up the stairs, following the noise to an open bedroom door.

They moved slowly into the master suite. Draped across the bed was a naked and bloody Clay Van Hoerne, his eyes wide and staring.

"Katherine!" Ellie called out. "Katherine, where are you?"

The sound, which they now recognized as sobbing, became louder. Moments later, a hoarse voice cried out from the closet.

"I'm in here!"

Ellie ran into the walk-in closet and switched on the overhead light. She found a battered and bloody Katherine Van Hoerne curled up in the corner, a gun lying beside her.

"He . . . he was . . . going to kill me," she stammered, weeping hysterically. "I was . . . oh Christ, I couldn't stop him, but I had to . . ."

Dropping to her knees, Ellie took Katherine in her arms and pulled her close.

"He . . . Clay, he . . . raped me," Katherine sobbed, burrowing into Ellie's chest, "and he . . . he murdered Angel Ramirez . . . he didn't want me to remember . . ."

"He can't hurt you anymore," Ellie soothed, stroking Katherine's convulsing shoulders. "Clay can never hurt you again."

Some hours later Ramon Hinojosa stood before the fireplace in the Van Hoerne's great room, staring into its cold, empty mouth with a glazed expression. Tammy Lynn Geary walked over and stood beside him.

"The county sheriff was looking for you," she told Ramon quietly.

"He found me."

"And?"

"Mrs. Van Hoerne is shaken, badly beaten, lots of defensive wounds. Seems pretty clear she was raped. Sheriff says it's an open and shut case."

"And the Angel Ramirez case?" Tammy asked.

"Also open and shut. Clay admitted to his wife he knifed Ramirez out of jealousy."

"He almost got away with it," Tammy Lynn replied, shaking her head in disbelief.

"Justice has a way of extracting its own unique punishment," Ramon muttered under his breath. "Have you seen Mrs. Van Hoerne?"

"A few minutes ago. She was leaving with Dr. Dodds."

Ramon retreated from the fireplace and Tammy Lynn followed. They crossed to the foyer and out onto the wide front porch, momentarily blinded by the glare of headlights. They stood side by side watching an SUV drive up the circular driveway.

The car paused in front of the porch, and Ramon waved good-bye to Ellie Dodds and Jackson Polke.

"Where are they going?" Tammy Lynn asked him, waving as well.

"They're taking her home," Ramon replied. "Wherever the hell that is."

As the car moved slowly past, Ramon saw the battered face of Katherine Van Hoerne in the rear window. She was wrapped in a blanket, and her hair was dark and matted with dried blood. Her features, bruised and swollen, were barely recognizable.

Just before they drove off, for the briefest of moments, Ramon could have sworn he saw a smile cross her blood-crusted lips.

Made in the USA
Lexington, KY
09 November 2015